To Sheila

THE
FADING
SMILE

I hope you enjoy the book

Mike

THE FADING SMILE

MIKE BURKE

Matador
9 Priory Business Park,
Wistow Road, Kibworth Beauchamp,
Leicestershire. LE8 0RX
Tel: 0116 279 2299
Email: books@troubador.co.uk
Web: www.troubador.co.uk/matador
Twitter: @matadorbooks

ISBN 978 1788033 664

British Library Cataloguing in Publication Data.
A catalogue record for this book is available from the British Library.

Printed and bound by CPI Group (UK) Ltd, Croydon, CR0 4YY
Typeset in 11pt Aldine401 BT by Troubador Publishing Ltd, Leicester, UK

Matador is an imprint of Troubador Publishing Ltd

Acknowledgements

There are so many people to thank for their help and encouragement towards me in bringing *The Fading Smile* to publication.

Special thanks go to Marion for her thoughtful oversight and wisdom and to Cathy Hemsley, Chris Jones, Philip Ralli and Jacky for their feedback and comments.

I would like to dedicate this book to my children, Stephen and Emma and to their generation who might just have to inhabit, perhaps in part, the world of the *The Fading Smile*.

Prologue

Thomas Delaney lit another cigarette and inhaled deeply. The smoke stung the back of his throat, bringing some strange semblance of comfort. As he exhaled, a small smoke ring hung in the air, momentarily defying gravity and then gradually dissipating into the cold gloom of a January morning.

He reached for the starter in the dashboard in front of him. The darkness was punctured by flickering orange and blue iridescent light as numbers and symbols danced in a choreographed display in front of him. A split second later the re-assuring purr and groan of a growling highly tuned engine exploded into life.

'Where was Blue Admiral?' He was meant to have arrived half an hour ago. A nagging wave of self-doubt entered his mind. Why had he decided to share his quest with someone else when surely it was really a moment of personal destiny?

Delaney reached into his overcoat pocket. This was not the first time he had explored the ripped lining in the last hour. He had sought the reassuring presence of his mobile every few minutes, caressing its surfaces, thumbing its array of features and applications - checking its battery life and signal for signs that it was still compliant and roaming effectively. He waited for any message or call that might take his life in another direction. None came. None had been expected, yet still the possibility remained. He stubbed out his cigarette and replaced it with another.

Grey clouds choked the distant horizon obscuring the fading moonlight. No glorious bright new dawn greeted the start of a day so long anticipated. The suffocating gloom of the dreary weather reminded him of why he sought release and a step into the distant beyond. The cold, damp air clung to the inside of the cabin, suffocating his spirit and drawing his breath into the nicotine familiarity of his favourite brand.

The sullen purr of the car's V12 engine was interrupted by a distant low rumbling noise and soon the arc of headlights beamed around the misty vista of the unlit car park. Two penetrating beams pierced the rear-view mirror, accompanied by the crunch of tyres carving a trail through the gravel surface. A dark, hooded figure, barely visible through the struggling dawn light, loomed out of the blackness and started to grow in size as it approached his vehicle.

Delaney lowered his window.

"Torchmaster?" asked the figure.

"Blue Admiral?"

"Yep."

"Get in."

The dark figure slid into the passenger seat. The door closed with a reassuring thud. The figure lowered the hood of his coat to reveal his features in the flickering courtesy light of the car.

"Shit. You're a just a kid."

"Old enough to know what I'm doing," Blue Admiral insisted.

"You're still a child. Get out." Delaney reached across to open the car door. Blue Admiral resisted.

"Look. I've come too far to turn back now." He rolled up the sleeve of his jacket and opened the car door to reveal a distinctive tattoo framed in the light. Beneath the image were inscribed the letters 'WW2L4E.' They were freshly done and conveyed a reminder of rebellion and defiance.

The increasing weight of responsibility started to fall upon Delaney. He had prepared for this moment, he had made his stand, he had burnt his bridges and he was prepared to give himself totally to fulfil his destiny. Sharing those convictions online had given them a greater legitimacy. The response he had received merely strengthened his resolve, reminding him of the community who shared his sense of purpose. There were other soldiers out there willing to join him, to pay the ultimate price for a heroic cause, only he hadn't reckoned on the fragility and immaturity of this particular foot soldier that had rallied to his side. This was a high calling that each had to enter willingly and knowingly, not guided by the naïve impulses of youth.

"But you don't know what you're getting into and what it will cost you." Delaney insisted.

"People my age were flying bombers and commanding whole platoons in the last world war. I know the rules and I know what's at stake here." Blue Admiral replied.

"Yeh, but it's my rules. I get to say who joins me now that we're playing for real."

"I know what I'm getting into." Blue Admiral grabbed Delaney's arm to expose a matching tattoo, although more faded and worn than his own. "Look, we are united in our quest. That's all that matters."

"What matters is that it takes more than a tattoo to carry this through. You have too much to lose. Now get out." Once again Delaney reached across Blue Admiral to release the door mechanism, only for Blue Admiral to pull the door closed.

"Look, I know what you're up to. It's all about taking control and playing on another level right?"

"Wrong! It's no longer a game. This is about progressing to a level beyond that envisaged by any programmer. This is real. Real people, real lives, real outcomes. We're not pixels in a combat zone any longer."

"Yeh and I ain't no kid neither. Just because we met on the second level of plains of Tarpazium doesn't mean that I don't know how these things work. I know what's real and I know what's a game."

"But you've got your whole life ahead of you. I only shared this crazy plan with you because I thought you not only shared my vision but also my circumstances. I've got nothing to lose, you have."

"What I do, I do willingly, and this is something I want to do."

"But you can't. You don't know what it means."

"What the hell do YOU know about my life? Who gave YOU the right to say what I should and shouldn't get into? Have you any idea what I've left behind to get here?"

"Precisely. I have no right to draw you into this. So just go back to what you left behind. Make your peace there and get on with living. This isn't a day trip out in the country."

"I have my reasons. That's all you need to know. I want this just as much as you. Maybe even more."

An uneasy silence fell upon the two companions. Each sensing both the folly of their situation and their inability to escape its consequences. Like two addicts trying to convince the other to go on the wagon, they both had travelled too far only to go back at this point.

"Anyhow. I want to travel in style and this is one smart motor." Blue Admiral broke the silence, stroking the dashboard and looking around. "Classic Aston DB9 right?"

"Yeh." Delaney sighed, as if letting go of something. "Are you some kind of petrol head?"

"More a fuel cell racer, but I love old classic cars. You

don't see these sorts around much these days. What year is it?"

"2008."

"Wow. Classic car. Classic year. The year it all started to unravel, heh?"

"Kinda, financially I suppose. Anyhow what do you know about it? You were barely born then."

"No, but I read history. I meet people who remember those times."

"History? Suddenly I'm part of history." Delaney muttered as much to himself as to new companion.

The conversation faded as Delaney's attention began to focus upon the past, yet the past was not somewhere Delaney wanted to re-visit. It had already made too many claims upon him and shaped his present too profoundly. Now was not a time for retrospection, analysis or regret. He had done all those things. Now was a time to take control. To make a statement to defy history and not remain its victim. To explore the forbidden country.

"So, are we going to do this or not? This car is not designed to be driven in reverse." Blue Admiral's question summed up their choices perfectly.

"Yeh, let's do it."

Half an hour later the DB9 came to rest on the dew soaked grass of the South Downs.

"Look, Blue Admiral…"

"I know. You're going to tell me again that this is a one-way street. A moment of symbolic defiance and am I sure that I want to join you? Well, the answer is, yes. More than anything. I've longed for this moment. I don't want to be just a barcode or a pin number. I want to become a legend. I want to reach out and break the mould and there ain't no way I'm going to settle for anything less."

"Yes, but…"

"No, buts. I'm in. That's all you need to know. No-one is going to blame you for this. This is my decision. So, are we going to do this thing or not? Because if we aren't, then I can find another place, another way and another companion. There's plenty of options out there. I've bought my ticket already. It's just a case of when I choose to use it."

Delaney paused. The time for words was over. "OK. Let's do it."

Delaney's words hung in the morning air for a brief moment before he squeezed the handbrake, slipped the car into gear, revved the ancient V12 engine up to the top of its limiter and then launched it triumphantly forward over the edge of the cliff and into the ocean below.

Chapter 1

It's easy to lose something, to misplace your car keys,
leave your umbrella on a train or forget an important appointment.
But what if you've lost something that you didn't know you had in the
first place? Something you never fully recognised or valued, something
intangible and elusive, yet which feels so huge that it lies beyond
description and outside of conventional vocabulary. What if the only way
to understand what you had, was when you no longer possessed it; felt it;
recognised it, no longer stumbled upon it unexpectedly? What if it then
continues to cast a shadow over everything without ever coming fully into
view? You continue to see its vapour trail although the object has now
quietly slipped out of sight. The distant echo of departing footsteps down
a corridor after the door has been finally slammed shut. A fading smile,
hanging in the air where once a Cheshire cat stood.

– The Smiling Cat –

Leroy Finch scrolled down the familiar preface of *The Smiling Cat's* blog looking for new posts. Occasionally an interesting article would appear to cast some light upon the dislocation of everyday life, providing him with the indication that he was not alone. For most of the time it contained the usual collective ramblings of geeks, conspiracy theorists and eco-tree huggers, offering up their half-baked theories and invitations to come and join their like-minded groups. Nevertheless, he wanted to believe in *The Smiling Cat*. He craved the assurance that there were other like-minded people who shared his sense of grief, fellow travellers who mourned for what had departed or had been traded away in exchange for something inferior. If only there were some plausible explanation to account for the national mood of anxiety and loss, then he wouldn't feel so alone and out-of-step. But today *The Smiling Cat* wasn't offering up any such insights or even entertaining distractions. Disappointment oozed from every pixel.

Somewhere in the distance the distinctive rhythmic humming of a mechanized drone could be detected, hovering above the roof tops before swooping down and moving off in a high-pitched squeal of exaltation and renewed purpose. The long arm of the surveillance society ever present. Some poor soul was about to have their day ruined. Finch had learnt just to be grateful that it's wasn't him. It was the cost paid for constant vigilance against an ever-present threat.

After years of austerity, energy shortages and living with global warming, an age of anxiety was just another season to endure, another burden to be carried by those worn down by the process of constant adjustment to change. There were many theories to explain the nation's existential crisis, many other web addresses to explore and virtual communities to interact with, all concerned with explaining an age of anxiety to an interested observer. Yet plausible explanation and coherent social commentary are constrained by filtering all of life through 140 character messages and instant photo sharing. Leroy longed for a different perspective. He yearned for an insight that wasn't loaded with the weird values of some group of eccentrics. He longed for a clue to the nation's mood, some explanation that might satisfy his nagging curiosity, some narrative to explain the inexplicable. He just wanted to know why things were the same, but everything was different and why so few people seemed to have noticed or seemed to care?

He squinted in the bright morning sunlight and reluctantly folded up his computer tablet.

Above his head normality demanded his attention through the efforts of cheery digitally-animated posters flickering and gyrating to present endless possibilities designed to lure the compliant observer with offers of distant destinations, huge rewards and shiny new toys to play with. He recognised a number of the brands; others were less familiar, their strange and aspirational messages colliding with mesmeric, persuasive power. Marketing is a great leveller; you can't get more normal than that.

He swiped his wristband against the stainless steel pillar which marked the entrance to the Phoenix Light Rapid Transit system. There was no response. New re-branded name, same old London underground. He swiped again, this time the LRT's multi-functional barriers yielded in grateful acceptance for the remuneration offered and ushered him through. Elsewhere other travellers were rushing and striving to reach their destinations. Anxious to make appointments, to get ahead and to get on. They placed themselves strategically on the platform hoping to gain the smallest positional advantage when the carriage arrived. Chasing after time, as if time could ever be captured or outmaneuvered.

A tall, elegant businesswoman glided past on a mission to impress. An over-weight, middle-aged man in a crumpled suit struggled to keep up with her, their careers clearly on different trajectories. Elsewhere Chinese students huddled together against the bitter cold, hard-wired to their mobile phones, yet clearly excited and exchanging news. Around them a number of large African ladies, inappropriately dressed and encumbered with heavy trolley cases, struggled to progress their journey as they braced themselves against the wintry, morning air. Others passed by as if in a dream, locked into some private, digitally reproduced world, oblivious of their surroundings and sealed off from all external engagement.

A day just like any other, the fusion of the familiar with the strange, the ordinary with the extraordinary, the prevailing determination to feel secure whilst being troubled with doubt. All of life's contradictions extruded into a bubble of convention and familiar routine. However, bubbles have a habit of bursting and the containment vessel surrounding Leroy Finch's world was about to be pricked by the icy blast of forces far beyond his control.

The sequence of events that followed felt more like a series of images and experiences to him, rather than an exact chronology. He remembered important markers – the train arriving at the station – the doors opening – the crowd pressing in – making his way along the same sterile corridors he had traversed many times before on his daily commute. He even remembered some unusual details. A one-legged busker, presumably ex-military, playing at the bottom of the escalator. A pink taxi passing by in the street outside. An advertising van sweeping past with the details of the latest West End musical emblazoned on its side – a throwback to the days before advertising became digitalized and individually tailored to consumer spending patterns and key demographics.

He remembered passing the entrance to the Van Hegel building and the irritation he initially felt at the rudeness of a young woman in a hoodie who pushed him forcibly to one side just as a bow-wave of expelled air and bright light enveloped him and lifted him off his feet.

What followed was less distinctive. He didn't remember

the explosion itself, more its consequences. He could recall no sudden bang or any other loud noise, nor any fire or a visible blast, but rather an overwhelming release of energy and bright light. He did remember the young woman though. Her outline was the last thing he saw before passing into momentary unconsciousness, not that there was anything particularly remarkable about her other than her intentional move towards him. Had she pushed him aside before the explosion or afterwards, he really couldn't remember. Neither could he be sure whether she was entering or leaving the building. All he remembered was her purposeful intent; the reasons behind that intention remained a mystery.

As he lay on the ground, pebble dashed with glass fragments deposited from what had previously comprised the glazed entrance of the Van Hegel building, he felt helpless and remote, like an observer to an event happening to someone else. He felt no pain, just a numb sense of disorientation and unreality. Figures hovered over him. Light and shade fell across his face. Momentarily he wondered whether he had died and this was some new experience unfolding, but then he smelt the familiar odour of smoke and felt the trickle of something warm and sticky roll over his face. Concerned voices circulated around him, but no screams, no panic, just a strange stillness as if people were awaiting a prompt or cue to tell them what had happened and how to react, then more familiar sounds penetrated the stillness – sirens, screams, raised voices calling for help followed by the throb of surveillance drones hovering overhead.

Eventually he was helped to his feet by strange, faceless figures. He peered through the smoke and dust struggling to make out the features of people's faces, but grit and blood stung his eyes and soon he found himself being led into an ambulance as one of the walking wounded and all explanations were suspended as he became just another victim and casualty in the age of terror.

A week after the explosion and following his hospital discharge his story became one of quiet assimilation, stoically slipping back into well-worn routines as just another patient discharged from an impoverished public health institution, clutching a bagful of painkillers and a glossy information leaflet describing how to cope with accidents and trauma. His lacerated face held together with superglue and loss of the bottom part of his right ear comprised mere cosmetic details set alongside those who had lost limbs or suffered horrific burns as well as the unfortunate concierge who took the full force of the blast and lost his fight for life several days later. He must have been standing only feet away from Finch, yet he had no recollection of his presence or the terrible fate that had afflicted him.

Elsewhere the story lived on in endless public speculation and press interest. Why had the Van Hegel Corporation been targeted? Who was behind the attack and what did they hope to achieve? Why had the warning not been taken seriously and acted upon sooner? Why had the police not mobilised earlier and isolated the building in order to protect the public?

There was a time when Finch would have engaged professionally with such questions, seeking to provide analysis and commentary, but he was no longer a narrator, but rather a character within the unfolding story, another statistic in the war against terror. His story, just a walk on part; his injuries too minor to warrant broader consideration, his loss too inconsequential compared with the greater loss experienced by others.

The weeks ahead offered the predictable, cold certainties of commuting each day to meet the demands of a job he had come to loathe. Taking his place each day among the faceless crowds of strangers, determined to treat every day just like any other. Yet Finch knew that the axis had tilted, not just within him that day, but within the national consciousness that allowed such events to be become an accepted part of the everyday landscape. His compliance had been bought off some time ago. No longer was he driven by a quest to uncover an inconvenient truth. He had exchanged such pursuits for safer pastures and more tangible rewards. Like so many others, he had forgotten to be curious, his critical faculties suspended, set on one side, in return for acceptance that there really is no meaningful alternative explanation.

"Good to see you back, Finchie." Pete Johnson greeted him with a firm handshake as he entered the third floor office space of Qualcourt Investments, the financial services conglomerate that had been his place of employment for the last two and half years. "The return of the Finchmeister!" His boss appeared to want to elevate his reputation far above any reasonable assessment of his value to the company.

"It's good to be back, I guess." Finch virtually swallowed his words. "It's good to be anywhere at the moment, I suppose. Just grateful to be in the land of the living."

"Absolutely, the bastards. What are these people hoping to achieve? Violence never solves anything. I'd have them all shot if it was up to me." Johnson replied in a manner that suggested that he would have made a fairly determined attempt to carry out his threat. "Anyhow, enough politics. Come in, there's plenty of coffee on the go and once you're a bit more settled, we can have a few moments to de-brief and to catch up with developments here. It's been a busy few weeks while you've been away. You're going to have to hit the ground running, I'm afraid."

"No problem, Pete. I understand. Just give me a few minutes."

"Take as long as you need." Johnson replied over his shoulder as he turned on his heels to make a quick exit. He wasn't one for small talk and today he seemed to be chasing the clock pretty much like any other day.

Finch surveyed the scene. Corporate culture cast in its most sanitized form: all potted plants, water coolers and work stations. The only concession to individuality consisted of various company mission statements and motivational quotes dotted around the labyrinth of partitions into which employees were slotted. People floated past his work station, some stopped to welcome him back, others to sympathize, while still others sought to engage him in conversation, not knowing how to address the reason for his time off work and trying not to notice his scars and minor disfigurement. Others just passed by and nodded or exchanged knowing looks, as if re-integrating bomb-blast victims was a part of everyday life.

The rest of the day slipped by in something of a daze. He attended a couple of meetings, but had little idea what they were about and why he was there. He tried to re-engage with his previous workload and tell himself how important it was to present the company's corporate image in a way that corresponded to their new strategic step change programme. He wrote up his copy on the corporate events he had previously been working on with diminishing enthusiasm. It all felt somewhat empty of meaning.

The next few days passed slowly and uneventfully. Finch was aware of his boss's accommodation towards him, allowing him time to adjust to a work routine and come to terms with his status as one of the latest victims of terrorism. However, he sensed a growing distance between himself and those with whom he had previously worked so closely. They now resembled old friends that glimpse each other out of context, unable to decide whether to talk about their shared past or a common future.

Finch stared at his face in the bathroom mirror. He barely recognised the person looking back at him. It was a face without hope and devoid of joy. Gone was the twinkle in the eye, the boyish, cheeky smile of someone taking on the world with self-confidence and certainty. His visible scars were healing nicely, however, a feeling of dread gripped him, a sort of nervous anxiety that held him in its grasp, draining and diminishing him. Initially he had put this down to tiredness and his struggle to re-establish a work routine after his enforced period of absence, however, the feeling remained undimmed by the passage of time. It was creating a sense of distance and alienation between him and the world around. He suffered no vivid flashbacks or night terrors, but rather as a sense of detachment between what had previously seemed important and what currently occupied his wandering thoughts. The world felt stranger and more remote than ever. His senses of alienation heightened by an experience he could neither share nor fully explain to those around him. He felt like an outsider looking in on a game he neither fully understood, nor wanted to join in with.

Each day he would return to his empty flat and its unoccupied spaces, devoid of anything but the essential items of furniture and try to find security in his daily routines. However, gradually the working week turned into an obstacle to be overcome. The tightening in the pit of his stomach which greeted him at the start of each day grew more intense along with an awareness of a dark cloud overshadowing him. He was finding it increasingly difficult to find the energy to work the hours that his employer expected and found himself power-napping in business meetings and on the LRT to and from work. Some days travelling to work he would miss his station and arrive late without a convincing excuse. He sought refuge in the evenings and into the early hours visiting his favourite gaming sites, getting drawn into an alternative world of high stakes speculation and false identities, behind which he could construct a different kind of reality. He considered his struggles to be part of a private war he was waging with his internal demons, he assumed others to be unaware of his withdrawing, but he was wrong.

"Do you want to tell me what's bothering you, Finchie?" Johnson enquired at the end of a busy working week.

"What d'you mean?"

"Well, you've not been yourself, since you were in the... since the, umm... you know, since you returned to work" Johnson struggled to express himself eloquently at the best of times and this was certainly not one of those times.

"Well, you know, it's not easy, getting back into the groove – getting up to speed and that, but I'm getting there. Aren't I?"

"Not sure, Leroy. You know how it works here. We can't carry too many passengers. People are starting to notice."

"Notice. Notice what?"

"Your discomfort with the way things gets done around here. You know, deadlines slipping, details being overlooked. People will cut you a bit of slack initially, but they won't keep covering your backside forever."

"I wasn't aware I was being carried. Who's complained?"

"Oh no-one, no-one really. Well not in as many words, but the boys on the fourth floor are always after their pound of flesh. You know how it is. They're not known for their patience and understanding. Its dog eat dog around here. That's how we get to survive in this commercial environment. No-one gets to be carried for too long." Johnson cast Finch a knowing look. He was a fair boss, but a hard-nosed one. Finch wanted to defend himself or offer some kind of explanation, but somehow, the words just wouldn't come. Even the effort at self-justification felt tiresome and pointless. In truth, he knew that although his boss's assessment might be cruel, it was fair.

"Look, consider this a friendly warning, either get back in the harness and up to speed with everything that's going on here, or..."

"Or... or what?" Finch wasn't sure he wanted to hear the answer to his question.

"Or get yourself signed off for some more recovery time."

"But I am recovered. It was just minor injuries, they said."

"And a bump on the head." Johnson's expression suggested that a great deal more harm had been done by the explosion than merely the physical injuries that scarred his face. "Look Finchie, take some advice here. Get yourself sorted out one way or the other, before someone makes that decision for you." Johnson made eye contact as if encouraging him to read between the lines. The knowing look that passed between them held far greater significance than any long explanation.

Pete Johnson was not a bad man. In fact, there was much to commend about him as a boss. He may have lacked certain social skills, but he was honest, reliable and straight talking. He had been drilled in the art of managing the system, and remained a systems man right down to his Italian shoes. He lived and breathed by the book and found security in rules and procedures. If he had been a passenger on the Titanic they would have found him reading the instruction leaflet about finding your prescribed muster station, whilst others around would have been fighting to get into a lifeboat. He placed his trust in the certainty and shape of what surrounded him and believed that the system would always protect and always provide – an article of faith that even extended to the HR handbook and company disciplinary procedures.

Perhaps it was Pete's unflinching faith in that system, that caused Finch to have regard for his guidance, knowing that it was at least intended to help him to improve his performance and to head off any further action. Friendly words of advice often have more impact than formal warnings and Pete's intervention did at least partially succeed in galvanizing Finch to re-orientate his life once again around his work routine. Gradually his motivation started to rally again as he became more engaged and energized around his work and career.

He was still prone to lapses of concentration and feelings of tiredness, but at least he was able to deliver his copy on time and meet his important deadlines. He could climb the road to recovery. He could find the strength to function once again. He could cope.

Chapter 2

L ow wintry sunshine fell upon the LRT station bathing it in a milky, iridescent light. In the sky above a jet aircraft roared its frustration, awaiting a landing slot. Along the platform unenthusiastic commuters lined up in an orderly fashion, staring straight ahead as if transfixed by weary expectation. Someone sneezed, another cleared their throat, and a young mother folded up her baby's buggy demonstrating considerable dexterity as she held her child in her arms. Overhead a lady poured sparkling cereal into a sparkling bowl for a pair of sparkling children smiling through sparkling teeth as they ate their sparkling breakfast joined by their sparkling father about to leave for his sparkling new job. *'Put the sparkle back into the start of your day with multi-vitamin enriched Golden Crunchies'* the tag line read as another advert scrolled through the display screen. Beneath it, a simple message appeared. *'Next train 2 mins'*.

Finch was embarking on another late morning commute. He reached into his jacket pocket and unrolled his wafer thin computer tablet. Seconds later it fired up, offering warm and inviting welcome messages accompanied by an irritating jingle and an array of unsolicited branded images. The experience echoed along the platform as a chorus of fellow travellers followed a similar morning ritual. Each stared into their display screens, some with hand held devices, others with wrist bands or wafer thin tablets, transfixed by a myriad of digital possibilities. Plugged into the world, yet disconnected from each other.

Soon the Light Rapid Transit system carriage arrived, not too busy that morning, one of the advantages of a flexible, working day. Several empty seats presented themselves for immediate occupation. Finch didn't need a second invitation. As the carriage filled up, the normal hierarchy established itself among the passengers, with e-book and tablet users claiming the seats, whilst mobile operators stood in the aisles, plugged into their handsets and wristbands. Each surveyed the other with veiled contempt and superiority believing their brands and platforms offered the better on-line experience. Half way down the carriage a heated exchange took place between a black, pregnant woman hard-wired into her mobile who demanded a seat from a white businessman, feverishly investigating his tablet. He insisted that his need to work over-rode her need to rest and an uneasy standoff ensued. Two towering cultural edifices locked horns. Female verses male, black verses white, family verses work, mobile verses tablet, brand verses brand. All of life squeezed into a ridiculous stalemate of social etiquette. Eventually the businessman conceded, shamed into gallantry by the silent disapproving stares and audible tutting of his fellow commuters. Guilt can be such a civilizing force.

The free local news service opened up on Finch's tablet. The usual headlines, travel delays, product launches, road rage clashes between cyclists and motorists and the odd jumper on the line despite the newly installed suicide screens. He re-acquainted himself with an old familiar news blog but *The Smiling Cat* wasn't smiling this morning. The site was buzzing with outraged blogs calling down curses and threatening violence towards those behind the site whilst others tried to debate the justification for direct political action, claiming that when you are confronting evil. The words of Bonhoeffer were quoted:

> *'It's not sufficient just to bandage the wounds of the victims beneath the wheels of injustice. Sometimes you have to be prepared to drive a spoke into the wheel itself.'*

Other bloggers just heaped abuse on foreigners, liberals, environmentalists, anti-capitalists and anyone who they happened to disagree with. Finch quickly abandoned the site concluding he would never learn anything helpful from its contents. He located his bank's icon and entered the well-worn conventions and passwords; his fingers guided more by muscle memory than by any powers of recall. He checked for confirmation of his credit status following the activities of the previous night. It was as bad as he feared, but he had known worse. This was nothing that he couldn't handle. A quick diversion into his mailbox revealed messages waiting. He tapped the icon. The buffering seemed to take an eternity. His irritation and impatience grew. Seconds later, his mailbox burst into life as messages downloaded and distributed themselves balletically among various folders. A quick check revealed nothing urgent to deal with. Relieved, he closed down his in-box and opened up his e-book reader – a historical enquiry into the collapse of the Euro-zone and the emergence of neo-nationalism in Europe. It's always good to maintain a sharp political analysis of recent history, even if no-one is listening to your particular commentary anymore.

Fellow travellers shuffled on their feet, 'cappuccinos-to-go' were supped noisily, water bottles emptied and overhead adverts for public vaccination campaigns endlessly played on video loops, barely visible beneath the distinctive scrawl of '*WW2L4E*' (*Who Wants to Live for Ever?*). The work of subversive graffiti artists' intent of shocking and undermining public confidence in scientific progress. Finch had seen this graffiti elsewhere, usually on billboards or bus shelters, but didn't understand why there were people so determined to stand in the way of progress, particularly when it came to advancements in public health. '*WW2L4E*' was becoming an over-familiar tagline, emptied of much of its original shock value. It often featured on cheap tee-shirts as well as trending on social media, particularly in the popular '*My World*' chat rooms where social networking and gaming combined and people interacted through their virtual avatars to gain credits. Finch was regularly being invited to associate himself with the acronym through being invited to '*Like My World*' at WW2L4E posts by on-line associates and interest groups.

Elsewhere eye contact was avoided and no-one spoke. There was nothing to be said. Nothing else to challenge the mood of passive acquiescence.

"Are you a great lover of the arts Mr. Finch?" A smartly dressed man in a wide brimmed, felt hat and trench coat was addressing him from an adjacent seat. His voice penetrating Finch's consciousness as he dozed his way through a morning commute. He seemed to have emerged out of thin air, a strangely incongruous figure, a throwback to the past, like a character from a historical novel.

Finch reacted like any commuter; he straightened himself up, stared resolutely ahead and hoped he would go away. Then the icy blast of realism penetrated his private world. This stranger was addressing him by name. Was this someone he knew or just a member of the public with a long memory and good visual recognition skills.

"I'm sorry?" Finch offered a tentative response, as if it was his fault for not recognising his fellow traveller and greeting him accordingly. "Have we met?" He could be so middle class at times.

"No we haven't," the stranger re-assured him, "but we will. National Gallery. Noon tomorrow. Among the Impressionists. Don't be late." At that he rose to his feet.

"But who...?"

"Enough questions." The stranger dismissed his enquiry with a flick of his hat, adding, If you're still a man who looks for answers, then you'll be there tomorrow. "If you're no longer such a man, then I've made a mistake and you're not the man I'm looking for." The stranger turned his back as the train shuddered to a halt.

"But w.....?" Finch's question trailed off into the crowd as the stranger was swept up into the busying throng anxious to leave the carriage. He tried to track his exit, but the tidal wave of people just disorientated him. He thought he caught sight of his hat in the crowd, but then he was gone, absorbed into the anonymity of the multitude.

Bewildered by the experience. Finch questioned what had actually happened. Had he fallen asleep again whilst reading his worthy, yet rather dry historical retrospective and was now confusing his dreams with reality? Had a waking thought somehow been elevated to something that felt like a real encounter? Had that bump on his head, which Johnson had so helpfully reminded him about, disorientated him more than he had realised?

He sought refuge in familiar routines and returned to his mailbox, anxious to restore the equilibrium of his morning routine. However, there among his mail concerning design strategy, copy deadlines, corporate governance, gaming invoices and enquiries from desperate graduates asking about internships, sat a message about the Cresta Coffee National Gallery. He still could bring himself to use its new title, since the naming rights had been sold, but nevertheless, its name seemed to stand proud on the screen in 3D before him, even though he wasn't wearing 3D glasses to enhance his viewing experience that day. Why hadn't he noticed it earlier? He quickly tapped the icon and saw the message reveal itself.

To: Mr. Finch
From: An art lover

Just in case you are forgetful as well as lacking curiosity. National Gallery – tomorrow – noon – among the Impressionists.

The following day couldn't come quickly enough. Finch made an excuse to take an early lunch and then joined the crowds in the Cresta Coffee National Gallery, remembering to take an ancient smart phone in his pocket to record any conversation. Old journalistic habits die hard and besides, such methods could provide some hard evidence that he was not hallucinating and losing his mind.

After clearing security, Finch entered the Gallery and made for the chamber containing the Impressionists. He scanned the scene for signs of the stranger he had met on the Phoenix LRT. Various visitors circulated around the room, intersecting each other in untidy sequences. Some paused and starred, apparently transfixed, others slumped into chairs, ate yoghurt and sipped fruit juice rather too loudly for the required politeness.

"I'm so glad you made it, Mr. Finch." Once again he was surprised and caught off guard by the stranger approaching from behind. "I saw you arrive. I've been watching you for some time."

"Who are you? And how come you know my name?" Finch sounded incredulous, but if the truth was known, he felt increasingly vulnerable in the light of the power the stranger held over him. "Look, if you are some weird stalker or injured party from my former life, then I'm telling you right now, that you can't intimidate me that easily and I'm prepared to go to the authorities and get an injunction if I need to."

"Oh, Mr. Finch, you really couldn't be further from the truth." The stranger replied with a weary sigh. "Let me show you something."

With that the stranger walked over to the gallery wall on which was displayed Van Gogh's famous painting of his studio chair and invited Finch to join him. "What do you see here, Mr. Finch?"

Once again Finch was thrown off balance, whatever he had expected from such a meeting, an art appreciation lesson had fallen far outside of most of his scenarios. "Art has never really been my subject, but obviously the artist has painted a chair in an empty room, presumably the artist's studio."

"Very good. I see that your powers of observation have not entirely deserted you during your time in corporate marketing. But what else do you see?"

"Look, who are you and w…?"

"All in due time, Mr. Finch. All in due time. Just tell me what you see."

"I don't know." He didn't want to play the stranger's games, but found himself being drawn in. "A tiled floor. A door. Some vegetables in a box?"

"Doesn't it speak to you about anything?"

"Not really. It's just a load of brushstrokes."

"Of course, but step back and something wonderful emerges."

"Look, I don't know who you are? How you know all about me and why you brought me here to give me an art appreciation lesson."

"All will be explained, but first you must learn to look and to look again. Don't you see the onions in the corner, bursting into life. The connection between the solitude and emptiness of the room, the contrast between the yellow and the blue. You can see it in so many of his paintings, the 'Wheatfields' over there, the 'Sunflowers'. The vibrant yellows representing new life and joy, in contrast to the blue of his inner torment and depression. The inner and outer realities colliding. The presence of one suggesting the hiddenness of the other."

For a moment Finch was transfixed by the paintings, his expression glazed over in a moment of eternal significance, caught between the invitation to explore the inner world of the artist and his natural curiosity to make sense of his encounter with the stranger. An inexplicable stillness developed between the two of them. "So, what am I missing? What's been hidden in this picture then?" Finch asked, finding himself drawn into introspection.

"Nothing and everything. It's not for me to say. It's for the observer to discover."

"Wherever you look, things are the same, but everything is different." It was a mantra he was becoming increasingly familiar with, at least *The Smiling Cat* had shown him that. Suddenly the pieces fell into place. His browsing history had finally caught up with him.

The stranger cast him a knowing look, as if confirming something to himself. "Let's go somewhere quieter," He insisted before quickly surveying the room for some kind of invisible threat. "Then I'll explain what you need to know."

The stranger spoke with a sense of calm seductive authority. Despite all his questions Finch felt compelled to submit to his request. He led Finch downstairs, passing through a party of immaculately dressed school children all enthusiastically engaged with an educational project, and directed him towards the sanctuary of a basement coffee bar. Once there they settled into a quiet corner, the stranger took out a pipe and a pouch of tobacco.

"I trust that you are okay with tobacco?" The stranger enquired, in a manner that suggested that he was giving notice of his intention, rather than asking for permission. "People can still be a bit uptight about these things, but I think that it's wonderful that we're allowed to indulge ourselves again."

"Feel free, but some of us still prefer not to fill our bodies with poisonous fumes."

"You don't have faith in medical progress, Mr. Finch?"

"Let's just say, that I still need to be completely convinced when it comes to miracle cures."

The stranger looked thoughtful, yet inwardly re-assured, like someone who knew they were about to make a deal. He scooped out some of the contents of a leather tobacco pouch into his hand and proceeded to roll the tobacco between his fingers whilst tapping out a small, walnut pipe on a nearby ashtray, re-enacting some time honoured ritual with all the care of a master technician. He pressed tobacco into the pipe's bowl which immediately self-ignited producing volumes of bluey-grey smoke. As he wrapped himself up in a cloud of swirling smoke, he leaned back in his chair, put down his pipe and sighed deeply.

Finch decided to take the initiative. "So, I assume I am in the company of *The Smiling Cat*."

"Who?"

"The Cat. *The Smiling Cat*. The person behind the conspiracy theory news blog."

"I'm sorry to disappoint you."

"But, presumably you know all about *The Smiling Cat* and the community of followers?"

"Just a recruitment portal for various T-squads and group therapy for flat-earthers. I would never be so vulgar as to assume such an identity."

"But, I assumed…"

"Mr. Finch. You have many questions you want answering.

I understand that. I have taken you by surprise and no-one likes such surprises. But I have some questions for you as well."

"Such as?"

"Such as, what is the great investigative journalist Leroy Finch, the man who used to make politicians quake with fear, doing writing dreary copy about corporate finance for an in-house company magazine and concerning himself with conspiracy theorist news blogs?"

"If you really know that much about me, then I guess that you already know the answer to that question. Life changes. People change. Things move on."

"So why throw it all away?"

"What makes you think I threw it all away? It was the world around me that shifted."

"Some people have said that you just lost your mojo."

"That's total crap. I didn't lose it. The industry lost it. I was left high and dry by the tectonic changes that affected my profession, that's all."

"But we all have to live with change, Mr. Finch, and much of it isn't welcome."

"Back in the 90's we all believed that we could make a difference and have an impact, but not any longer."

"You did, make a difference. Do you think that I would have gone to all this trouble to find you if I didn't believe that you were good at your job? Besides, your recent browsing history suggests that your curiosity about political reality hasn't entirely deserted you."

It came as no surprise to Finch that the stranger knew about his browsing history. Open browsers were pretty much public property and besides he had nothing to hide or to be ashamed of. "My curiosity remains; it's my skill set that has departed."

"Oh come, come, Mr. Finch." The stranger replied as if dispatching an irritating wasp.

"Look around you," Finch insisted. "Ever since the *'Garden Party Bombings'* there's security at every public building, drones buzzing overhead, cameras on every corner. You don't need investigative journalism in a surveillance society. If information is our currency, then the market has been swamped and everyone is now an expert at acquiring it."

"Surveillance hasn't replaced well-crafted journalism; it's still a necessary tool." The stranger reassured him, while taking a long and thoughtful lung full of tobacco. "Sounds like an excuse, rather than a reason to me."

"Who gave you the right to judge me?" Finch was starting to become irritated by the tone of the stranger and feeling threatened by the direction of their conversation. "Look at you, with your hat and pipe, like some throwback to the '50's. What d'you know about the times we live in. Today it's all about greater public access to information. News is what happens on social media and video sharing sites. All journalists do these days is rummage through the twittersphere and pick out what appears new or important. *'Observe and Comment'* – that's what used to be posted in our newsroom – *'Observe and Comment'*, was our mission statement. We became voyeurs in the public acquisition of information. We no longer find out things any more than we make things in this country. We just provide the commentary; others source the news and provide the stories."

"So, you were the victim of technological advances?"

"I suppose you could say that. They just don't want old hacks like me anymore."

"And it had nothing to do with the considerable debts that you accrued at various on-line casinos and betting syndicates?"

"Look. I don't know who you are and why you think you know so much about me, but whoever you are, I will not be judged by you, or anyone else. You have no idea what really happened, all that debt was being managed perfectly well. It had nothing to do with my leaving." Finch stood up defiantly, knocking his chair away from beneath him and spilling what remained of his coffee. "So you can go and…"

"Please, please sit down Mr. Finch. We have so much to discuss and much of it will be to your very great advantage. I am not here to criticize you. I am here, because I believe in you, because I still think that you have what it takes. You still have the restless curiosity of someone who seeks after the truth." The stranger's words were surprisingly re-assuring, yet delivered in such an emotionally neutral manner, that they suggested much was still being held back.

Finch recovered his composure and returned to his seat as those in the café who had momentarily lifted their eyes from their frothy coffees to investigate the cause of the apparent disturbance resumed their private conversations.

"You see, Mr. Finch, good journalists are still needed. People who can ask the difficult questions and dig beneath the surface."

"Not anymore. Not people like me – not in the twenties anyhow."

"And yet, you still remain inherently inquisitive. That blogging site. *The Smiling Cat* and all that, why bother about such things unless you suspect that something is being hidden from you?" The stranger leant back in his chair and reached down into a leather case to bring out an ancient non-fabric tablet. His association with such ancient technology seemed entirely appropriate, as if he was cultivating a retro image that placed him firmly within a particular tribe. He fired it up to reveal a picture of a young woman, probably in her twenties, with long black hair, smiling and looking as though she had just stepped onto a red carpet. "Do you recognise this woman, Mr. Finch?"

"No, should I?" Finch cast a cursory glance in the direction of the screen. "I did serious political journalism, not celebrity intrigue."

"Look again. Look properly."

Finch reluctantly surveyed the picture for any sense of expectancy. "Uhh...still no. Sorry."

"You really have been out of the game for too long haven't you? She is Iona Dunwoody, heiress and daughter of Sir Reginald Dunwoody, probably one of the richest entrepreneurs in the country and owner of much of the technology that goes into all our information technology."

"I know of Sir Reginald Dunwoody, respectable pillar of the community. The 'go to' businessman in the current multi-platform news media. He's also into some fairly shady imports of coltan from Africa in order to supply those mobile gadgets we can't live without and he just happens to be a major donor and confidant of this current government."

"Good. I can see that you haven't entirely lost your journalistic instincts. Now let me show you another picture." The stranger tapped the screen of his tablet to reveal a grainy picture of a London street scene.

"So? You're showing me the streets where I walk every day."

"Be patient. Let me show you." The stranger tapped on a figure in the crowded street scene and then opened his fingers to expand the image. "This was taken by CCTV on the day of the explosion at Van Hegel's."

Finch straightened himself up, suddenly more engaged with the topic of conversation.

"Now, I see that I have your attention."

"Possibly, but what does this have to do with some rich heiress?"

"Let me show you." The stranger enlarged the image once more to reveal the outline of the woman in the hoodie who had pushed Finch aside that day. "Have a look at this." The stranger zoomed in on her face and then pasted the image of her face into a split screen alongside that of the heiress shown earlier. "Recognise her now?"

"She's the one who knocked me over. She might even have saved my life for all I know. But I never got to see her face properly."

"Pity." The stranger then zoomed in on the face of the woman in the hoodie and called up the portrait of Iona Dunwoody to set alongside. "Now d'you see the connection?"

"Yes, so what was she doing there that day?"

The stranger lent back in his chair and pointed his pipe at Finch in a slightly condescending manner of an old school master. "That's good, Mr. Finch. You are starting to think like a journalist again. We know that she was involved with those who planted the bomb that day. She'd already been seduced and gone native some time ago, but that isn't important. What really matters here, is finding her."

"Finding her and re-uniting her with her distraught family no doubt."

"No, I don't think that would be very likely at the moment, the way that things are between them."

"So, is this some sort of Stockholm syndrome or has Daddy's little girl really joined the revolution?"

"Possibly, we just want someone to find her and to ensure that she doesn't get into further trouble with these people."

"In other words, you want to me to find her before someone else does and the bad publicity starts to play out."

"I knew that you still had it in you, Mr. Finch. Let's just say that there are some very important and influential people that would like this matter to be dealt with quietly and privately."

"So why me and not the police?"

"Discretion my dear boy, discretion is needed. We can't have the police in their size twelve's wading in there can we? Especially when they start to get careless and chatty about the nature of their investigations. We wouldn't want any information leaking out into the public domain at the moment with this one. We need…what shall we say, a certain light touch and sensitivity here."

Finch leaned forward on his elbows, trying to take control of a situation he was constantly playing catch up with. "Let's cut the crap here. Why should I be so concerned about this posh socialite and her political beliefs, other than being personally grateful for her intervention? For all I know she's a fully paid up member of the T-squad and in up to her neck. What makes you think that I give a damn about any of this?"

"Oh, I think that you care, Mr. Finch. No-one with your back catalogue of investigations could get by if they didn't care."

"So, other than personal gratitude, what's in it for me? Why should I take the time and effort to find this woman?"

"Oh, we think that you will find it worth your while."

"And just who is the 'we' in this little equation? You still haven't told me your name or who you are working for."

"No I haven't, have I?" With that the stranger got up from the table. "I'm sure that you can join up the dots and complete the picture for yourself, Mr. Finch. In the meantime, you'll want some expenses no doubt." He slid a large, brown envelope across the table. "There's everything you need and more in there. Don't worry about getting in touch. I'll be keeping an eye on you and I'll make contact again."

"But what about my day job?"

"It's all been arranged. Don't worry yourself, Mr. Finch. It really has been a pleasure, and remember the Impressionists. The brushstrokes, the colours, the position of the subjects, the small details that point to a bigger story. Let the paintings guide you."

With that, the stranger once again turned his back, raised his hat in the manner only seen in old black and white movies and left the café without further explanation or ceremony.

Chapter 3

Catherine Stringer sat facing her inquisitor still trying to process the chain of events that had brought her to their meeting. Across the room Dr. Damien O'Brien uncrossed his legs and leaned into a high back leather chair interlocking his fingers in thoughtful silent preparation. He smiled a benign smile. Catherine cleared her throat, hoping he would take the initiative. O'Brien remained unmoved.

She gazed around the room, all glass and stainless steel, soft neon and back-lit wall units. It felt tranquil, yet anonymous and devoid of character, nothing to suggest its true function or purpose. A prison is still a prison if you don't want to be there, even if the chairs have won design awards.

"I don't know what you want me to say?" Catherine broke the fragile silence. Her words sounding child-like and pleading in the face of the stony silence of her host.

"It's not for me to say what I want. We are here to discover what you want, and to listen." O'Brien spoke softly, in a manner that suggested that he was well acquainted with such a question.

"Have you ever lost anything Mr. O'Brien?"

"It's Damien, and of course I have. We all have over the

years, but this is about you and not about me. Tell me about what you have lost."

"Ah, what have I lost?" Catherine allowed her own question to hang in the air as if she was examining it as an object of detached enquiry. She shuffled in her chair before composing herself, looked around the room for inspiration, poured herself a glass of water from a conveniently placed carafe and sat back, rotating the glass between her fingers. "Loss can be such a cruel thief." Finally, words came, as much with a sense of release as with any authority or insight. "It steals away familiar experiences and certainties, it changes perspectives and challenges received wisdom, it upsets the equilibrium that underpins our coping mechanisms. And yet," Catherine gathered herself in thoughtful reflection, "it can also open your eyes to what you have been missing. It can provide you with a whole new window onto the world."

"Whose loss are you speaking about, Catherine?"

"Well, our loss of course. The loss we all share." Mild irritation seeped into her response. The sort that a teacher reserves for the weariness of duty that requires an explanation to something that is clearly self-evident.

"Tell me about this loss." O'Brien briefly flicked an empathetic glance in Catherine's direction as he looked up from tapping purposefully on a small, fabric computer tablet.

Catherine sensed she was being manoeuvered into a vulnerable place from which she might disclose something that she had guarded for some time. "When you lose someone it's huge. The reality of that loss shouts in your face that your world has changed even though we know that the world for everyone else continues largely unaffected. You've hit an iceberg and you're holed beneath the waterline, but for everyone else life goes on, apparently unaffected. The sun comes up, the alarm clock goes off and routines remain. People just get on with stuff. Traffic rolls by the scene of the crash, unencumbered by the devastating blow that has been dealt to those involved."

"What you are describing is a very common experience for most people who are living with loss." O'Brien reassured Catherine, even though he suspected that she was running ahead of him. She seemed to be looking for permission to share her world with a stranger. "Please continue."

"Yes, but what happens when that order is reversed – when the bigger picture changes, but no-one notices. What if the shared experience of loss is so huge, that it affects and overwhelms everyone, totally transfiguring everything in its path? What if that loss transforms the landscape and yet everyone appears seemingly unaffected, not noticing important details that have changed? What if the whole country has suffered a loss that it doesn't quite understand?"

"But you understand such a loss?"

"I'm starting to." Catherine spoke slowly with quiet confidence, yet without arrogance or awareness of irony.

"I assume you are referring to the *'Garden Party Bombings'*?"

"Well, yes of course. Isn't that what I've been describing? The *'Garden Party Bombings'* cast a shadow over all our lives. We're constantly reminded how the world changed that day, but it also changed because of what followed…what was exchanged in the process."

"What do you think was exchanged?"

"I don't fully understand what we surrendered, but in return, we became more suspicious and fearful. We closed in on ourselves. We gave up on something precious in exchange for something inferior. You see that in everyone. The emptiness, the shallowness. People living hollowed out lives. It's like we're all avoiding speaking about something because it is just so huge and so personal. Like at a funeral, when people don't know what to say about the deceased and so they talk about the weather or the catering."

"But you're talking about an event that touched everyone's lives. But different people react differently."

"Yes, but the *'Garden Party Bombings'* robbed every one of their innocence and capacity to see the good in others. People can be incredibly resilient. It's a strong national trait to 'keep calm and carry on'. We learn to smile through gritted teeth. To accommodate a new reality, to treat the extraordinary as ordinary, but everything isn't normal."

"Are you talking about the national sense of loss or your own experience now?"

Catherine's eyes darted around the room, avoiding any direct contact with O'Brien. She sat on the edge of her seat intensely channelling her attention towards her inquisitor, yet in many ways remaining distant, like she was projecting an image or presenting a lecture to a group of disinterested students. "I don't recognise your distinction. It's both…and it's neither. The nation's loss and my loss connect and inter-relate. They are part of the same over-ridding narrative. They are one."

"But the nation's loss is about how other people feel. I want to understand what you feel?"

"I inhabit the loss of others in order to understand the nature of my own loss, because the nation's loss has brought about my own loss." Catherine announced triumphantly.

O'Brien stopped typing on his tablet, took off his glasses and sat back in his chair. He opened up his body shape to Catherine, like he was seeking to connect with her as a person, rather than as a client. He had heard many explanations to describe how people saw the world around them. He had learned how to inhabit the world of others, to share their pained and fractured perspectives with an emotional distance that prevented him from passing judgement or being crushed by their pain. Now he needed to call upon that resilience once again.

"Let's try to untangle a few things here." He paused in order to re-establish eye contact. "Tell me where you were on the day that the *'Garden Party Bombings'* took place."

"Me? I'm afraid I don't see why this is relevant." Catherine replied sternly, seeking to examine the source of O'Brien's question.

"Just humour me, this one time."

"Well, I was at home of course. I was in the garden. It was a lovely sunny day as I recall. It had been a joyous summer. Term had ended and we were having a faculty barbecue."

"So how did you hear the news?"

"I guess in the same way that most people did. Our handsets all responded at the same moment. A symphony of ring tones alerted us to a breaking news story. It created quite a stir as I remember."

"Yes, something similar happened to me." O'Brien revealed in an uncharacteristic moment of candour. He was not meant to reveal his own personal story, but in this case he couldn't help but think out loud. Catherine had hit upon a shared experience that he too felt the need to reconnect with. Everyone had their own story to tell about that day. He had heard countless narratives and had travelled with many other people as they recalled their emotional responses to those terrible events. The *'Garden Party Bombings'* had provided more than just a cash cow for the therapeutic and psychiatric community. It had become a defining moment in an understanding of shared national grief and post-traumatic stress and the subject of endless academic papers, lectures and popular self-help books.

It might have sounded ghoulish or in poor taste, but to Damien O'Brien the *'Garden Party Bombings'* was the best thing that had ever happened in his professional career. The trauma caused had released something hugely significant within the national psyche – a permission to be vulnerable, to speak about the experience of loss, hurt and disappointment that for so many had previously been buried or denied. The *'Garden Party Bombings'* had also marked his professional epiphany – a moment of authentication in the eyes of his non-professional friends, who subscribed to the curtain school of psychotherapy believing that most people should be able to pull themselves together when faced with any personal trauma. It was as if the bombings had taken the lid off the bottle for so many people and allowed their true feelings to be expressed. His career had blossomed and thrived as a result and therefore he felt sure that this event provided the key to unlocking the carefully prepared defenses and prosaic ramblings of his client.

"I guess, that many people learnt about what had happened in a similar way," Catherine suggested.

"So what happened next?"

"Well you can probably guess. We were all directed to live news feeds saying there had been an explosion at the Palace." Catherine's tone displayed her irritation at having to explain what she regarded as a blindingly obvious explanation to someone who clearly already knew what her answer would be.

"Can you remember what you did next?"

"It was one of those moments, like when the Twin Towers were hit. Everything just sort of freezes and goes into slow motion doesn't it?"

"Is that how you felt?"

"Well yes, it was surreal. I put on the TV and all the channels were taking the feed from the Palace. Smoke hanging over the building and a line of ambulances stretching up to gates."

"So when the whole story started to come out, how did it make you feel?"

"Shocked of course. We all were. I wouldn't describe myself as a royalist, but what happened to that young family and to the King was just ghastly, absolutely awful. Of course, they didn't tell us all the details at the time. They just said that there were some casualties among the Royal party at the reception. Then more news kept coming out…like a drip, drip of name after name. One devastating blow after another. Every snippet of information pored over in ever increasing detail by news commentators and experts. I guess they knew all along who had been killed, but wanted to soften the blow, sort of manage the nation's grief.

"And the other sad news?"

"The news about those footballers was almost lost in the ferment, but the images of those young men, the happy smiling faces we all remember, arriving at the palace carrying the World Cup and then the realisation that they too were among the casualties. It was hard to take it all in."

"So how did it make you feel at the time?"

"I was devastated, obviously. We all were."

"And afterwards?"

"You can't just shake off an event like that. It strikes at our very identity and humanity. Everyone was affected. You must have been as well?" Catherine paused in order to invite O'Brien to acknowledge his own emotional response. The offer was silently declined, as O'Brien refused to lift his gaze from his note taking or to express his own thoughts. Professional distance maintained, he finally looked up at Catherine to see her eyes burning into him, demanding confirmation and recognition. None came.

"Please continue," O'Brien replied calmly.

Catherine gathered herself and continued.

"The days of mourning seemed to go on forever. The carpets of flowers were everywhere. Little memorials springing up over every local football pitch. I've never experienced anything like that before. I guess none of us have."

"No…we haven't." O'Brien finally realised that a more active listening approach would perhaps elicit a more honest reflection from his client. The *Garden Party Bombings* were more than just the subject of academic enquiry, even for him. It was impossible not to recall those sad times without a lump in the throat. The collective national grief had been truly overwhelming. All that the nation held dear, decimated in one violent, meaningless explosion. No wonder it had created so much case work for him and his colleagues.

"Is that what you wanted to hear from me?" Catherine had transformed herself into the role of inquisitor.

"All I want," O'Brien replied, "is to help you. To understand how you feel. Nothing more, nothing less."

"Well, it was a horrible time for everyone. No-one would want to re-visit such a time again."

"I'm not asking you to re-visit it. I'm just trying to explore what emotions it stirred in you."

"What emotions do you think it stirred? I am a human being. *'If you prick us do we not bleed?'* Everyone who remembers that day remembers how upset they were. The nation's heart ripped out and for what? A group of fanatics protesting about… about some war hundreds of miles away and grievances going back generations – appalling events I accept, but a long time ago and far away."

"So what do you think changed as a result of those events?"

"Everything. Nothing feels the same any more. It was a watershed moment. We didn't just lose our innocence; we lost our capacity to celebrate, to rejoice in what we have, to believe in a nobler future. We even stopped singing 'Jerusalem' in public for goodness sake. We became suspicious of the outsider and sceptical about anything strange or unknown. We no longer recognised who we were, so we started to construct new identities for ourselves."

"You seemed to have reflected upon those events in quite an…" O'Brien paused, struggling to avoid any comments that would suggest categorization or judgment, "academic manner."

"Well, I am an academic." Catherine, cast O'Brien one of her characteristic, icy stares. "What d'you expect?"

"But art and design; not the social sciences."

"That comment displays your ignorance, rather than your insight." Catherine's waspish rebuke hit her intended target. O'Brien cast his eyes back down towards his notes suitably chastised. "Art and design transcends a number of disciplines. I'm not just some luvy, duvy art curator, who spends all her time servicing the weird and lavish tastes of nouveau riche Chinese and Russians. I'm interested in art that is useful, design that serves a purpose. The interplay between form and function. How design affects people's lives and brings them utility, as well as meaning. Connecting ideas with experience is what we do. So when I see something as transfiguring as the *'Garden Party Bombings'*, I recognise how ideas shape our world view and how the surrender of those ideas, leads to a whole new social experience – a new social context."

"And the academic interest. The correlation between the aftermath of a personal shock and a shared common experience. Is that what you have been trying to explain?"

"Oh good grief, no. That was only the beginning. What followed was much more significant. A much greater disaster."

"Can you explain what you mean?"

Catherine looked at O'Brien with a mixture of disgust and irritation. She suddenly realised where his line of questioning was heading. Why did no-one else see the connections that were so self-evident to her?

"You think that this…my being here today is some kind of after-shock following the main event. You're trying to cast a shift in public consciousness as some kind of psychological disturbance that I have suffered, aren't you?"

"What I think is not important. We are here to learn about what you think and how we might help you."

"Well, I can assure you, young man." The comment was

entirely inappropriate, Catherine was probably only a few years older than O'Brien, but she intended to display her seniority and what she regarded as her superior mental faculties in whatever way she could. "I am not re-living or channelling some decade old historical national trauma. What's important was not how people reacted or over-reacted to those terrible events, but rather what it affected in our national psyche – what changed as a result and how we all allowed that change to affect us as people."

"So what did change?"

"Well everything. Isn't that obvious? That's what I've been trying to explain to you my dear boy."

"Look, Mrs. Stringer." O'Brien's calmness was momentarily unsettled by Catherine's emphatic tone.

"I prefer Catherine, sometimes Miss Stringer or Doctor Stringer, but never Mrs."

"Catherine. We both know why we are here today. We are here because you were arrested outside the Department of Health and Science with a bucket of whitewash which you attempted to throw over the Secretary of State. Now, we could just pass you on through the courts to let the judicial process take due course. But those courts in their wisdom, think that you might be displaying some symptoms of trauma that might respond to…to…some kind of therapeutic intervention. So help me to help you a little."

Catherine sat back and crossed her arms in defensive mode. "But I really don't see how you could help me."

"Let's try. First of all, tell me about you son."

"My son?"

"Yes, Joshua. Tell me about Joshua."

Catherine appeared uneasy and reluctant. "He was just a lad…a lovely young man who was taken from me."

"Tell me about his birth, his childhood. What he was like growing up."

"I don't really see the relevance of this. Josh was just a normal child who had a very conventional upbringing."

"You brought him up on your own. Was there ever any contact with his father?"

"His Father! No, definitely not. I don't want to talk about that man. Josh and I managed just fine without him…without any man, thank you." Catherine recoiled as if stung by some distant memory that came from a place she preferred not to re-visit.

"Do you have any contact with Joshua's father?"

"No, I don't, and I said I don't want to talk about that man." Catherine looked pained and defensive.

"I see. But it couldn't have been easy bringing Joshua up on your own and combining your role as a mother with your career?"

"No, of course it wasn't." Catherine replied abruptly trying to close down the direction of their conversation. She folded her arms and sat back, like a sulking child refusing to oblige an insistent parent.

O'Brien looked exasperated, just when he thought that they might have been making progress, they seemed to have hit the buffers. "So tell me what your son meant to you?"

"Why everything of course. He meant everything. What mother would not focus her love upon her only child?"

"So how was that love expressed? How did you combine the demands of being a mother with those of the academic world?" O'Brien re-phrased his previous question in the hope that she would either not notice or be persuaded towards co-operation through his sheer persistence.

"Are you a father Mr. O'Brien?"

"Damien, call me Damien, and yes, I am."

"Then you will have some appreciation of the joy and responsibility of parenthood. You start off being guided through that painful and frightening process of giving birth until you emerge, exhausted, yet strangely elated on the other side. Then they place this tiny bundle of wrinkled and bloodied grey flesh in your arms and you see how the oxygen of life replenishes and animates this new life that you are presented with. No-one tells you to love that child and no-one tells you how to love. You just love them and where that love comes from is one of the great mysteries of life. That love appears but it never departs. It just changes and adapts, it grows and matures. Nothing can extinguish that sort of love and nothing ever will. I loved Josh then when he had never truly drunk from the cup of life, and…" Catherine, started to choke on her words, "I love him still, despite all that happened.

"You speak about him in the present tense. Why is that?"

"It's hard to switch off a mother's love, Mr. O'Brien. Despite all the pain he caused me and all the questions that remain about his death. You know careers come and go, relationships fall apart, but a parent's love endures, that sort of love endures."

"And the questions about his death. Have they been answered?"

"No, they haven't."

"So who do you blame for his death?"

"Partly the car driver they found at the bottom of the cliff with him, but I guess he was a victim, just like Josh." Catherine paused. "Initially I blamed myself. What parent wouldn't examine themselves in such circumstances? Was I too strict or too lenient? Was I there when he needed me? Did I stand too far away or too close to help him deal with his demons? No parent expects to bury their own child; you inevitably feel responsible in some way."

"Do you still blame yourself?"

"Partly, but I also see this bigger connection."

"You blame society?"

"Oh that would be too easy. Josh chose to take his own

life. The responsibility was his, yet what I seek to understand is why he felt that was the only way out."

"Who wants to live forever?" O'Brien muttered rhythmically, throwing out a familiar tag-line and looking for a reaction.

"Quite. But he was so young."

"You've seen the graffiti all over the public health campaigns?"

"Yes, you can't avoid it. But I'm not convinced that Josh was part of some anti-science or anti-capitalism protest movement. He hadn't given up; he was looking for a way forward, not a way out. He was just caught up in the zeitgeist."

"So you do feel that society was to blame. The mood music playing all around, drove him to take his life?"

"Perhaps, I don't really know. What I do know is that there must be something seriously wrong with a world in which the only way a young person can truly feel alive is by getting into a classic car and driving off the cliff at Beachy Head."

"But not everyone reacts the same way."

"No, but there are dozens of young people making the same gesture as Josh and no-one is asking why. Young people giving up or wanting an escape. What's more, the government is trying to suppress such stories. Why is that?"

"I don't know."

"Neither do I. But I'm certain that Josh became entangled in a pathway of cause and effect. The loss we all experienced, somehow affected him and because of that loss he did what he did. So I want to understand more about the impact of that shared loss."

"So it is all connected." O'Brien felt vindicated that his course of questioning had finally thrown up some insight.

"It is all connected. Josh didn't lose his life. He gave it away. What I want to know is, why." Catherine confirmed his observation with a degree of relief and self-justification.

"So, how short a distance is there between that connection and a bucket of whitewash in Whitehall?"

Catherine cast O'Brien a knowing sideways glance. "A lot shorter than you might think."

Chapter 4

Eighteen hundred feet above the surface of the Stryn Fjord, Eleanor Dupre waited for the wind speed to fall to a safe level.

There is a fine line to walk between the eager consumption of adrenalin and wanton recklessness, and Eleanor had successfully navigated that path on many occasions. Conquering the physical danger was all about exploring her personal limits and applying those parameters to the calculation of the risk. Not that she was someone to pass by an opportunity to explore those limits. Anyone who had successfully conquered the north face of the Eiger, Mount Blanc, K2 and Everest before her thirtieth birthday, was clearly not fazed by a physical challenge.

'Eleanor is a very determined girl'. Her various child-minders, teachers and tutors used to tell her parents, not that her parents needed reminding. Eleanor was never going to miss out on anything she saw others enjoying. Growing up alongside four older, high achieving brothers guaranteed that she was never going to be someone who would take a step back when faced with a challenge. On the contrary, new experiences enlarged her, shaped her, released her from the ordinary and

the everyday and allowed her to become someone who could define her own world and take centre stage within it.

Not that everyone understood or approved of the world she occupied. She had grown accustomed to those who counselled caution and restraint. Parents and well-meaning friends regularly questioned the attendant risks of her ambition. Yet the counsel of well-intentioned outsiders could never constrain her drive to overcome the limitations that others saw as defining her. Just because a genetic quirk had seen fit to bestow upon her one less foot than the requisite number generally thought to be required for an active lifestyle, didn't mean that she had to settle for the safe and undemanding path. She refused to let something as trivial as a prosthetic left foot prevent her from enjoying all the benefits of the outdoor pursuits enjoyed by her peers.

The headlong rush into activities offering danger and an adrenalin surge was more than a passing phase to Eleanor. This wasn't a lifestyle choice for her or a societal reaction to the security offered by the *'Great Advance.'* She had established her brands and chosen her tribe many years ago. Extreme sports were an expression of extreme living and sat comfortably alongside her former achievements, they represented a considered move and a natural progression from the mountain peaks that she had previously challenged and conquered.

Some of her friends had taken up base jumping many years before. It was only after she returned from her third Everest trip and turned thirty that she started to listen more seriously to their conversations and stories about their latest foray into danger seeking. She knew the risks. A university friend had been killed in a skydiving accident, yet that didn't worry her. Life was full of risks. You only had to speak with experienced climbers at Everest base camp to learn that or to have spent time in the death zone of those high altitude slopes to realise that the veil between life and death, triumphant success and ultimate failure, is very thinly spread.

She waited for calm. Spiralling gusts of wind whistled around the rocky outcrop on which she was perched. Her colleagues were eagerly waiting alongside, postponing the moment to commit until the windspeed had fallen. Eventually a growing stillness began to descend as a window for safe jumping formed around them. Excited voices were raised. High fives were exchanged. Motivational language spread among the group.

'Hey dude, let's do this thing.'

'Time to rock and roll.'

'Let's lock and load.'

'Totally awesome.'

'Go, man, go'.

She checked her equipment for the umpteenth time. She knew the routine well. She had packed a parachute dozens of times. She had faith in her equipment, her wing suit and her training. She adjusted her helmet, turned on her headcam, tightened her harness, braced her body in anticipation, turned downwind and launched herself off the precipice.

Immediately she felt the strong up-draughts from the valley below envelope and uphold her falling weight. Initially the up-draughts just slowed her descent, but then she was able to gain control as her wing suit inflated fully and she assumed the flight position. Soon she was flying with ever increasingly velocity. She could hear the whoops and yells of her colleagues around her. One of them came into view in front of her and even rolled over onto his back to show his skill and wanton abandon. She was travelling very fast now and skirting the rocky outcrops of the valley side. Pine trees passed just a few short metres away. She could even smell the heady fragrance of their sap and the pine needles as she sped past.

As she descended she was able to control her flight to bend and follow the contours of the valley. Cross winds started to check her descent, but it was nothing she couldn't handle. She adjusted her body position and slowed a little. Then a clutch of pine trees came into view, she tried to adjust her flight path to avoid them but a swirling down draught seemed to pin her into the valley side. She caught a branch full on her outstretched arm and immediately she knew she was in trouble. Spinning over onto her back, she engaged her parachute and felt it struggle to inflate behind her. Eventually the chute opened fully and began to slow her descent, but not quickly enough to avoid collision with another group of trees. She was slowing down, but also losing control. This was going to be a hard landing.

The impact when it came was sudden and brutal. She passed through several branches before turning over and falling incrementally through branch after branch. She heard the crack of her body impact against something hard and unyielding. At that point she lost consciousness and everything went black, yet strangely still.

Flashing lights and glimpses of blue sky appeared above her. She sensed movement and the presence of others. Her body ached with a numbing pain and then there was release and ease. A lightness of touch and pressure surrounded her. Gradually she became aware of voices and then images came into sight. She could just make out the outline of a crumpled body in a red wing suit. The body was surrounded by crouching figures and frantic downward movement was being applied to the chest of the figure. As the image came into sharper view an uneasy recognition gripped her. She was looking down on her own lifeless body.

She felt no pain, no fear and no sense of urgency to return. Everything felt strangely normal, despite the implausible sights that greeted her. It was as if all the components of her life were now in their right place and as they should be. She sensed growing warmth and the reassurance of something really, really good that was about to unfold, like a homecoming after a long journey. She knew that whatever awaited her would be good. A blanket of warm light embraced and supported her. An overwhelming sense of love and joy dispelled any fears or concerns she might have held. She sensed the desire to let go and surrender herself to what she was experiencing. A sense of completion lay before her, as if she was being beckoned to become who she truly was. She felt whole and empowered and totally safe.

Then a cold shaft of doubt gripped her. She wasn't ready. She felt torn before the homeward path that lay ahead and the familiar path that lay behind. Gradually a sense of heaviness surrounded her like gravity returning to exert its force upon her weightless body. Hands pushing her down, coldness, voices, movement and for the first time, penetrating pain. Her body was now her own to occupy. She was lying on a stretcher with someone leaning over her pressing rhythmically upon her chest. A face came into view. The force upon her chest ceased. The face smiled, a voice let out a gasp of relief. Activity ceased and tension evaporated, then everything went dark and still as she slipped once again into an uncertain unconsciousness.

"Eleanor, Eleanor. Can you hear me?"

"She's still not responding."

"She's doing fine. Just give her a bit more time."

"Eleanor, Eleanor. You are going to be OK."

Words started to cut their way through the wall of fog and confusion that filled Eleanor's mind. She felt warm and woozy. Her throat, sore and tender, yet gradually feelings of disorientation began to melt away. She sensed the closeness of others, the crisp coolness of starched hospital sheets and voices speaking in strange languages.

'Er du våkner opp min kjære? Hei Eleanor. Kan du høre meg?

No response.

"Hello Eleanor. Can you hear me?" A crystal clear Scandinavian ascent penetrated Eleanor's waking thoughts.

"Uh…what the…where am…?"

"Do not worry yourself. You are in safe hands."

Eleanor gradually began to fix her gaze on the outline of a figure dressed all in white leaning over her.

"Am I dead?"

"Oh no, for sure. You're not dead. Not unless we all are."

"Are you my guardian angel?"

"No, my dear. I am not an angel, just a nurse. You are in Helgeland Hospital…in Norway. You've been in an accident, but you are here safe with us now." The nurse in the all-white uniform straightened up and started to push buttons and write down numbers from an array of equipment that Eleanor was connected to. "The doctor will be on her way soon. She is not so good at English. But she is quite pleased with you. You are a very lucky lady…a very lucky lady indeed."

"What happened?"

"Don't you remember?"

"I remember; I remember something…something wonderful. Can I not go back?"

"Go back? Back to the mountain? No, I think that your… how you say…flying…jumping chute days are over for a while. They brought you here by helicopter. You were in pieces… literally pieces, we did not know about your foot. That gave the paramedic quite a shock I can tell you."

"Yeh, I bet it did. It's happened before."

"You have hurt yourself…you crash, like this before?"

"No, I mean the foot thing." No matter what was happening to her, it seemed that she could never completely escape 'the foot thing.'

"Oh yes, for sure."

"How long have I… been here…?" but Eleanor never heard the answer to her question. She was vaguely aware of the arrival of others, but a soft wooziness overcame her and sleep beckoned.

Chapter 5

Time can pass uneasily when you are incapacitated and marooned in a foreign country. People come and go, doctors visit, nurses attend, physios prod, twist and pull, care workers try to speak to you in their broken English, and through it all a surreal routine emerges, in which the patient becomes both a spectator and participant in their own recovery. Eleanor had spent so many years challenging and discovering the limits of her own physical endurance, strength and fearlessness, but now the isolation of her recovery provided her with the space to explore the relationship between her outer journey and her inner one.

As bones were reset, medication given and wounds dressed, her physical condition became less of a concern to her. There would have been a time when she would have grown impatient with the need to attend to her injuries. She would have seen such matters as obstacles that delayed her return to the sport and the active life she so cherished. Now, not even talk about changes in lifestyle or possible procedures to protect her damaged heart greatly concerned her. All she wanted were answers to the vision she had experienced. She wanted to know if she had just been dreaming or whether she had stumbled upon something of greater significance.

She felt like a stranger to herself, observing her life from the perspective of an outsider. It was as if her life were separated into two compartments, divided between the road towards her physical recovery and the journey towards her mental adjustment. Most of all, she felt alone, as if there was no-one who could accompany her on this journey of self-discovery, no-one who could help her to make sense of it all. Whenever possible, she would share her experience with the people who came into her life. Some were more responsive than others: a few seemed intrigued and even asked questions, yet others appeared embarrassed or knocked off balance by the direction of the conversation. From most there was just a blankness and emptiness that revealed itself when she tried to share her experiences, as if a great gulf in understanding separated them. She assumed this to be the result of cultural factors, the struggle to cast into words thoughts and feelings that people whose first language wasn't English could understand. It felt as if her entire experience had somehow been lost in translation.

After a couple of weeks spent recovering from the accident she was told she would soon be free to return home. However, before she could be discharged she was given an appointment to see a new doctor she hadn't previously met. The appointment took place at the far end of the hospital site, down a tree-lined pathway which led up to a bright angular, glazed building that looked as if its design had been lifted directly out of the Bauhaus architectural catalogue. The building was surrounded by beautifully landscaped gardens and gently cascading water features.

Eleanor hobbled over the highly polished black marble flooring of the entrance hall, struggling to persuade her healing limbs and her prosthetic foot to co-operate with each other. She had become very accomplished at adapting to new and challenging terrain over the years, yet the combination of sore ribs, a broken wrist and two badly bruised legs made the whole task of walking a more conscious and painful effort. As she gazed around the reception area, she noticed that the other patients didn't appear to be ill or injured like her. They wore their own clothes and appeared to wander around the building with little or no apparent purpose in mind.

She was shown into a white, marble-lined office decorated by various abstract oil paintings and prints. Inside sat a tall, fair-haired young man, sporting a ginger beard and an immaculately pressed collarless suit. He was examining a three-dimensional hologram image of the two lobes of a human brain which was rotating before his eyes above his desk. Beside him sat a half-smoked cigarette, yet he seemed preoccupied with the floating image and kept manipulating it so that it presented different features from different angles. Eventually he looked up to see Eleanor waiting patiently at the door; he took a drag on his cigarette and beckoned her in.

"Please sit. Your test results are in." He spoke perfect English, yet in a rather abrupt manner, still barely looking up or making eye contact.

"And?"

"And we need to talk about them before we can let you go home," he informed her.

"Is there a problem? Am I going to live?"

"Oh yes, your physical health is not giving us cause for concern. In fact, you are responding remarkably well, given what has happened to you. Your cardiologist has made a referral for some further tests when you return home. He is concerned that your condition is monitored and, if necessary, further intervention is made to stabilise any fluctuations resulting from the scar tissue on your heart."

"So, that's all good then?" Eleanor enquired, sensing that some important information was being held back.

"For sure, it is good. You have responded very well. There are, however, a few other indicators that are causing us some concern."

"Indicators? What indicators?"

"There are some anecdotal indicators arising from your accident that are inconsistent with an untroubled pathway towards full recovery."

"What do you mean by anecdotal indicators?"

"We are concerned by the persistence of the visual images that you witnessed during your acute myocardial infarction."

"My what?"

"Your accident caused the muscles of your heart to stop the flow of blood around your body and we are concerned that this might have starved your brain of the supply of oxygen in a way that caused some persistent delusional refracting to occur."

"I'm sorry, you've lost me."

"Your vision, your dream."

"Ah, yes."

"The stories you keep telling about what happened to you and your inability to recover from this waking, delusional state." For once, the young doctor expressed himself with an intensity verging on irritation, like a disapproving parent chastising a silly child. "We are concerned that this will impair your recovery and your assimilation back into everyday life in England."

"But I know what happened to me." Now it was Eleanor's turn to express her frustration. "I know what I saw and what I felt and it looked and felt to me as real as anything. As real as you and me, sat here, now. It wasn't a dream, it was real."

"But what you are describing is a classic neurological disorder brought about by trauma. It wasn't real. It was a trick of the mind."

Eleanor sat back in her chair. Her ribs were still hurting and her stump was especially sore that day. She knew all about

51

pain and the physical world of overcoming the limitations that life can place upon someone, yet she now felt as if she was being robbed of a wonderful gift, an experience that was truly beyond anything physical she had encountered before. She was being invited to deny something that had given her release and felt beyond the ordinary. It was like the times when people would caution her against tackling some new physical challenge, not realising the rush of adrenalin she would derive from throwing herself off a high building or learning to control her descent in a wing suit. Such experiences made her feel more alive than ever; they empowered and enlarged her in a way that most people would never understand. How could this young doctor ever see the world through her eyes? What did he know about pushing the envelope of your skills, strength and courage to the point at which it felt life enhancing? Had he ever experienced something beyond the ordinary, something transcendent that takes you outside of everyday experiences of a world in which you are defined and limited by the expectations of others?

"Look, let me explain." The young doctor moved forward in his seat and activated a hidden data projector built into a small tablet computer. At once the three-dimensional hologram he had been previously inspecting reappeared over his desk, rotating to reveal the dimensions of a human brain from every possible angle. "This is a profile of your cerebral cortex," the doctor explained.

"My brain?"

"Yes."

"But how? When?"

"We took a scan shortly after you were admitted to this unit. You are very fortunate, that we have such facilities here. Not every hospital in Norway has such advanced imaging systems, especially since the oil ran out and austerity was imposed upon our public finances."

"So what does it show?"

"Well, to be honest, very little. That is what is troubling me and my colleagues." He leaned over to pick up a pencil which he then proceeded to use as a pointer to describe the various parts of the rotating image of Eleanor's brain. "The brain is divided into two complementary hemispheres or halves. One controls the rational, empirical side of our nature and the other is used more for the intuitive and subjective parts of life."

"Like dreams and visions?"

"Possibly, but it's not that simple. They are complementary; both are needed in order for us to function normally. But for someone who has developed such a heightened sense of imaginative activity there are usually tracers or markers displayed to reveal such over-activity in that sphere."

"So you can tell if someone is having visions or going mad?"

"For sure. We wouldn't put it that bluntly, but everything is triggered by brain cellular activity. Everything can be rooted back to the brain, even visions and recurrent delusions."

"But you keep using the word "delusion". It's like you don't believe me or you want to take this experience away from me. But I know what I felt and it was real."

"For sure, it was real to you. But it was not real. It existed in your imagination but nowhere else."

"But how could I imagine something so extraordinary, something beyond my previous experience, something so unexpected, that felt so real?"

"Every experience has a physical or neurological pathology. Your joys, your sorrows, your memories, your ambitions, your imagination – they are all products of the interaction of nerve cells and their attendant molecules in the brain. This is all that there is."

"And that's supposed to make me feel better, is it?"

"Not better, but better informed."

"But what if you're wrong or just seeing a partial picture? What if we are all just waking from a dream? What if everything we see or feel isn't just a product of our brains, but really there is a greater reality out there – something that cannot be measured by our computers and our tests."

"Now I think you are being fanciful. Such matters are beyond medicine."

"But that doesn't make them less real or important."

"We deal with the world as we find it, the physical world. Everything beyond that is just a matter of speculation and imagination."

"Perhaps, but what if there were another way of seeing things? What if we are more than just a bunch of connected cells?"

"There is no other interpretive framework, only science and the tools of the physical universe. We are just machines – very complex, awe inspiring and wonderful machines – but machines nevertheless."

"But when I get to drive an expensive sports car, what I find exciting isn't the configuration of the cylinder head or the torque of the drive unit or even the sophistication of the engine management software. It's the feel of the thing, the smell of the leather, the feedback it gives going into every curve, the sense of power and control just balanced on a knife edge. It's all about the total experience: the brand, the colour, the status, the history of the make, its place within the panoply of motorsport and even the people you get to share such an experience with. Everything that goes into the package contributes towards my love of speed and accounts for why I want to drive fast. It's more than just engineering."

"But without the engine it is nothing. It's all just physical laws and how those laws feedback into human experience – a bit like your accident. Your love of speed brought you back to earth with a sudden, unexpected halt. Everything that followed was just your human reaction to that traumatic event."

"Isn't life all about those human reactions to such events?"

"Perhaps, but I am a doctor and I am concerned about your rehabilitation back into normal life. We have to live in the real world, the world we can measure and understand."

"But not everything that is real can be measured," Eleanor insisted. "Perhaps there are other ways of understanding life and who we are, other than through science?"

"Nevertheless, I have prepared this letter of referral for your doctor in England."

The young doctor slid an envelope across the desk towards Eleanor. She reluctantly picked it up and put it into the pocket of her dressing gown, not intending to ever open it or to speak of it again. It was clear that she was being lined up for special attention upon her return to England and she did not welcome what such attention would seek to rob her of. Whatever this young doctor thought or others felt, she knew that something special had happened to her on that mountainside. She hadn't expected it, neither had she made it up and no-one was going to rob her of what it had meant and how it had felt.

Following her return to the UK, Eleanor settled into a routine to continue her recovery at her parents' home just outside Maidstone. She tried to explain her experiences to them and other family members and also to friends who visited, but she received a similar reaction to the one she had encountered in Norway. It was as if they were still speaking different languages and occupying different worlds. No matter how much detail she entered into in order to describe what had happened, she struggled to find any common ground. It felt like trying to explain a three-dimensional concept using the language of only height and width. Those who listened to her story understood the words she used, but it was as if her words didn't connect with them or create any spark from which empathy or understanding could flow.

As the weeks passed, Eleanor found that she wanted to speak of her experiences less and less. She came to regard them as no less real, but rather personal and particular to her – something to be guarded and protected from cynical response or cool indifference. She gradually learned to take those experiences captive in her inner world. They become her most valued possession: her special memories, her private hopes and dreams. She began a personal diary just so she could capture the intensity and realism of her experience, not that words could ever convey accurately what she had felt and what had moved or changed within her as a result. All she knew was that the world now looked and felt different to her. No longer was it a playground to be conquered or challenged, but rather a place of mystery and new possibilities. She had pushed the envelope to its limits and discovered something strange, wonderful and unexpected lay beyond. She had realised that in all her adventures she remained a mystery to herself, and it was alright to recognise and affirm that mystery without needing to explain or justify it.

As she recovered from her injuries and started to establish familiar routines and relationships once again, she sensed a remoteness and distance between herself and those who had previously occupied an important place in her life. She no longer shared their values and priorities. She no longer fitted into any of their tribes. She was defining and occupying an exclusive tribe all of her own. She was living in exile – marooned in a world that no longer felt like home. Perhaps they thought she was mad or deluded or just given to weird fantasy. Perhaps she was. Why didn't they understand or at least help her to make sense of what had happened on that Norwegian mountainside?

Eleanor's growing sense of alienation from former friends

and colleagues created an awkwardness and tension that tended to set her apart from their concerns and preoccupations. Whilst for her friends everything remained unchanged, she had returned from Norway as a very different person. What hadn't changed, however, were her recreational needs. She still needed a place to unwind and a group of friends to belong to. So with great reluctance, following a particularly long session of physiotherapy, she tentatively agreed to join her old girlfriends in a high street wine bar as part of one of their regular girls' nights out.

Nicola had decided to join them that evening. Eleanor always had a soft spot for Nicola. She was not as self-aware as the others and as a result could be quite naïve and socially awkward, which often made her the butt of many "dumb blond" jokes. Perhaps that was why Eleanor warmed to her; she felt some kind of kindred spirit, as if they were both outsiders but in different ways. Being unfamiliar with the conventions of what post-accident topics of conversation were legitimate, Nicola wanted to know more about what had happened to her in Norway.

"So," Nicola announced, flicking away the ash from the end of her cigarette, "I hear that you have been flying with angels in Norway."

"How d'you know about that?" Eleanor asked.

"I've been reading your blog. It's caused quite a stir. Probably gone viral by now. Your celebrity star is rising again."

"It's not about that and I was not…" Eleanor paused to make inverted comma marks in the air, "…*flying with angels.*"

"But you're lucky to be alive, Ellie. Something as awful as that would upset anyone's equilibrium. I know it would mine."

"My equilibrium wasn't upset." Eleanor found herself in defensive mode, as if they thought her experiences were something she had invented just to invite attention upon herself. "I had a nasty accident. A very hard landing. I could have died on that mountain. I think that I am allowed to reflect a little upon that experience."

"Oh gosh, yes, rather. It must have been terrible. Don't get me wrong, max respect and big you up for all that extreme stuff you do. Total amaze and all that. But did you really like see yourself, lying there...from like...you know...another perspective?"

"Yeh...look, I'm not ashamed of what happened to me. It just happened. I didn't expect it and I had no preconceived ideas...it just happened. I'm not a national spokeswoman for such experiences or an expert or anything. All I can tell people is what I saw and how I felt."

"But don't you think that the shock of the accident could probably account for all that?" Gill decided to chip in at this point, as she put down her mobile for a momentary break from her compulsive texting. "You know, like one minute you're flying at a hundred miles an hour in that bat suit..."

"Wing suit."

"Yeh, whatever. Wing suit, and then you strike some tree and next thing you know like it's...totes hard shit, and you hit the ground but your mind is like still flying around and you're up in the air and that."

"Perhaps. I don't know. All I know is that I almost died... no, I'll say it. I actually died for a few moments on that mountain before they stabilised me. And during that time I became a spectator to my own struggle to survive...and...and I saw things... strange things...good things. Things I can't explain and that I didn't expect to encounter."

"Is that why you've gone over to all that 'Who Wants to Live For Ever' protest movement crap?" Nicola asked. "I see you're wearing the branding."

Eleanor smoothed her tee-shirt over her torso, displaying the 'WW24E' logo. Perhaps it had been a mistake to wear such divisive branding among the uninitiated. "Maybe. Maybe not. I just got sent a load of these in the post after I starting blogging about my experiences. It doesn't mean that I'm going to start spray painting The Shard with anti-capitalism graffiti."

Ironically Eleanor had considered doing something dramatic in order to get people to take her seriously. She had received a number of unsolicited messages from people claiming to be associated with the 'Who Wants to Live For Ever' protest movement, inviting her to join with them. One protester even enquired about using her skills and contacts in extreme sports to carry off some spectacular aerial stunt to suspend a banner between two skyscrapers in the City of London. However, she had no plans to join any protest movement; she was still processing her experiences and looking for meaning.

"No, I think it's really cool and that. Maybe the angels were like… those nurses you saw when you woke up in hospital." Nicola returned to her favourite subject of angels. "Like, loads of people believe in angels and that…they think that they look after them and help them and guide them. Perhaps you just caught a glimpse of those nurse uniforms and kinda made that connection?"

"Maybe I did. I don't know." Eleanor was now feeling once more that she had something to apologise for. "I don't remember saying anything about angels at the time. It was only the nurses who told me about that later after I came around. I thought I was dead not because I saw those nurses all in white, but because of what I had previously experienced."

"You must update your status then, Ellie," Christina urged her from behind a large glass of Pinot Grigio. "Angelic tribes are so of the moment. Got some really cool brands behind them as well."

"Look, I'm not looking for a new tribe to belong to. I'm not making a lifestyle branding choice here. This is serious.

This is what happened to me. Why don't any of you believe me or even respect my right to hold such views?"

"Oh no, Ellie, totes respect and all that," Christina insisted. "Just thought that you might want to turn this experience to your advantage. You know, update your status. Make it your brand. Chill out with people with similar experiences or interests."

"Look, I'm not searching for a new tribe to belong to or a new hobby to take up. Something happened to me on that Norwegian mountain, something amazing. Can you not understand that?"

"Oh yeh, sure must have been like really scary and unsettling, I guess."

"No, just the opposite in fact."

"What d'you mean?"

"Well, haven't you ever longed to push the envelope further and further in order to see what lies at the very edge?"

"Uh, not sure I'm with you, Ellie." Christina had one of her glazed over and vacant looks and took a big sip of Pinot Grigio as if to inoculate herself against the unfamiliar.

"Don't you ever just want to go further, longer, harder, higher, just to live more, to be out there, and to experience something new and enlarging?" Vacant looks surrounded her. "Don't you want to feel more alive, to go beyond the safe and the ordinary in order to experience new vistas?"

"You mean a bucket list?"

"No, it's not about a bucket list, it's about wanting... wanting something beyond, wanting more than all this." Eleanor pointed to everyone gathered in the wine bar.

"Sounds as though you need to go shopping, Ellie. I think a good dose of retail therapy is what you need," Christina suggested.

Eleanor realised she was getting nowhere. "I'm not taking any more of this. I don't care whether you believe me or not.

All I ask is that you respect my right to speak about the things that happened to me. If you can't do that, you can go and…you can…Oh, I don't know." At this point Eleanor suddenly stood up and stormed off, pushing aside furniture and stumbling over handbags. Nicola set off in pursuit, anxious to catch up. She eventually caught up with her in the street outside. "What gives with you?" she remonstrated breathlessly.

"What d'you mean? What gives with ME? I'm not the one calling into question my sanity."

"No, but you're also not helping yourself by being so…so defensive."

"Me? Being defensive? Look, you…"

"Ellie, just listen a moment, will you? I'm on your side. I believe that you had those experiences you say you had. Total respect for talking so openly about what happened to you. Lots of people wouldn't have been so brave."

"But you think I don't know the difference between a nurse and an angel. Just because I've got something missing at the end of my foot doesn't mean that I've got something missing upstairs as well."

"I know you haven't. Look, it's been ages since we last met and that…I know that life moves on and perhaps we live in different worlds these days, but I'm not unsympathetic. I want to know more."

"Yeh, so you can gloat some more and take the piss." Eleanor pushed Nicola out of the way and once again started to strive purposefully down the street with Nicola in her wake. Nicola set out after her again, catching her up and spinning her around on the spot.

"Look, Ellie can we stop doing this, especially in these high heels? It's killing me. I'm not taking the piss. We might not have seen much of each other recently, but we go back, don't we?"

"Yeh…sort of."

"So that has to mean something these days. Everything is changing all the time, but friends are forever, aren't they?"

"Look, what's your agenda here? Where's this leading?" Eleanor's irritation was starting to show.

"I don't have an agenda. Friends don't operate agendas; they just offer friendship." Nicola paused to regain her breath once again. Running down the street in high heels on top of a twenty a day habit presented something of a physical challenge to her. "Let's meet again. Just us. I'll pick you up at 10.00 tomorrow. What's the harm in that?"

Eleanor remained silent, still inwardly fuming at the reaction of her friends. Eventually, she regained her self-control. "None, I suppose," she grunted.

"So, see you tomorrow then, 10 am. You never know, it might be fun and besides there's something I want you to see."

The following day Nicola arrived promptly outside Eleanor's family home in a brand new fuel cell sports car. Life had obviously been kind to her since last time they met, but Eleanor was seldom impressed by ostentatious shows of wealth and success. However, she did enjoy the experience of being driven fast along country lanes, with the sun on her face and the wind streaming through her hair. The digitally produced grunt and roar of the fuel cell-powered car provided a convincing reminder of more innocent times when petrol-powered internal combustion engines propelled classic sport cars along such country lanes.

It was good to spend time with Nicola again. She was good fun. She also enjoyed tearing up other road users and humiliating the odd Neanderthal bloke in a battered hybrid family car. She and Nicola had once been very close but over the years their relationship had cooled and remoteness had developed between them, as with many of her old girlfriends. Extreme sports can repel the uninitiated. Such activities tend to attract highly motivated and solitary people who devote most of their energies to the challenge of the task rather than to developing deep and meaningful friendships. Socializing in the company of other climbers or base jumpers tends to involve testosterone-driven drinking competitions, wild storytelling and initiation rituals designed to prove that she was on a par with her male colleagues. She realised just how much she had missed the softer edges of female company and how she had neglected those whom she used to count among her friends.

"I'm sorry that I was a bit manic last night, Nicky."

Nicola looked across and smiled. She mouthed something, but it was snatched away by the wind and road noise. It didn't matter what was said. The sentiment was understood and friendship was again offered and received.

"It's just that after the accident everything has been a bit full on," Eleanor explained. "There's so much going on in my head at times, I just don't know how to process it all."

Nicola leaned across, "Are you starting to have doubts?" she shouted.

"Yes, absolutely. I'm starting to doubt everything."

Once again Nicola just looked across to her and smiled with a knowing yet reassuring expression.

They arrived in a large market town and parked in the grounds of a rather well presented boarding school. "My old hunting ground," Nicola explained. "The Principal lets me park here whenever I'm in town. He and Daddy go back a long way."

After passing through a stone archway, encrusted with flint, they turned left and saw a huge gothic sandstone structure emerge before them. "Oh, an assembly building. I saw plenty of those in Norway. I haven't been inside one for ages though." Eleanor felt like an excited schoolgirl, taken on a trip out to see a historical monument.

"You'll probably notice some changes these days," Nicola said in a knowing manner.

Having entered the large wooden doors Eleanor took a few moments to get accustomed to the light. The first thing she noticed was the glass screen onto which various moving digital displays were projected. She could also make out a list of entrance prices.

"Don't worry, I'll get these. I get a discount anyway. Annual membership brings all sorts of add-ons." Nicola remarked, before swiping her mobile phone over one of the stainless steel pillars that marked the entrance route. "I don't suppose you had to pay last time you visited one of these places."

Eleanor couldn't remember. Entrance fees were the least of her concerns as she struggled to orientate herself to the sights that greeted her. "So long ago – can't remember. It felt different then. Not sure why."

Once inside, they were able to push their way past groups of Chinese tourists with their attendant, highly animated guides, barking out commentary in a manner that sounded like drill instruction to a group of conscripts.

"You get more tourists than locals these days," Nicola explained, "especially from the Far East. Apparently, it all means something different out there and they can't get enough of it."

Eleanor nodded in a knowing manner, but in reality she was fairly clueless about the sights that greeted her and what they might mean to all those visiting. It did feel magical though, like one of those fairy castles that her mother used to describe to her when she was reading a bedtime story. It also felt safe and secure, something she had not encountered since her experience in Norway. "I like it," Eleanor remarked, "I don't know why, but I just like it here."

Nicola smiled approvingly. "I thought that you might. Come and have a look at this over here." She led Eleanor past crowds of people hooked into headsets, transfixed by multilingual commentaries and interactive icons popping up on their mobiles, capturing their attention as they followed the GPS pathways around the building. They weaved through the hubbub of chatter and hissing headsets that formed under the high vaulted ceiling and found their way into a small side room where there were chairs and cushions laid out in front of brightly coloured, stained glass windows. There were small tea lights flickering in the breeze and the smell of aromatic oils and burning incense. "I love this place, it's so peaceful."

"Yes, amazing, beautiful, especially on a day like today." Eleanor's attention was drawn to the pictures etched in the stained glass. "So, what's their story?"

"Not quite sure. You probably need to join one of the tours to find out. I'm not very good on the history, but I know that it's very old. Apparently, there has been a building on this site since the fourth century or something."

"Who are these people?" Eleanor was curious about the robed figures depicted in the windows.

"I think that they must have been the people who founded the Assembly Building, although it would have been a bit different in those days, I guess."

"And these people with the circles behind their heads?"

"Well, that's what I wanted to show you. They're angels. There are angels everywhere in here. It's all about angels. So I guess that they must have had an experience a bit like yours. Maybe they saw angels or thought that they met angels and the angels sort of helped them and guided them and looked after them."

"And this fit-looking bloke in the middle? Who's he and what that plus sign fixed behind him?"

"I don't know all the stories, but I gather that he was the sort of top angel bloke. The kinda main man, messenger and guide. He keeps appearing with the addition symbol because he can add something special to those he guides and speaks to. Positivity and all that."

"Oh, I see. I'm familiar with the plus sign. You see a lot those around. I thought they were just motivational statements about being positive. But I didn't know what the fit bloke had to do with it all." Eleanor hesitated; she felt strangely out of touch with such matters. Like a little girl who had entered adult life, only to discover that an important part of her social education had been overlooked but no-one had felt the need to tell her.

"There's a special symbolic meaning and symmetry built into the design of this place. All about positivity, I think. You know glass half-full, rather than half-empty, be the change you want to see, and all that stuff. You can even buy special positivity symbols over there." Nicola pointed towards the far side of the building. "Some have the man angel on the front and some are just on their own. But they all mean the same thing. My guardian angel is over here. Let me show you."

Nicola shuffled out of the side room and then skipped over to the other side of the building, weaving in and out of various groups of visitors. Overhead piped music could be heard and the melodic tones of Robbie Williams' 'Angels' repeated endlessly on pan pipes. "Look, here she is," Nicola called out loudly and excitedly, motioning for Eleanor to join her. "St Cecilia, guardian angel of all musicians. She can guide and inspire people musically."

"I didn't know you still played."

"Oh yes, I still tinkle the keyboard a bit. Perhaps your angel is a mountain guide or flying angel. There are lots of those here as well. Whatever interests you, whoever you are, they'll have a guardian angel just right for you."

"Oh, I see, but as I keep explaining, I didn't actually see any angels or meet an angel. It was just when I was coming out of sedation that I mistook the nurse for an angel." Eleanor felt the need to explain herself once again, but realised it was futile. Nicola was on a quest and was clearly enjoying herself.

"Yeh, I know. It's just that I thought that we might be onto something here. I thought that this would ring a few bells for you. Oh, that reminds me, they've got *'It's a Wonderful Life'* as an app for your mobile and *'A Matter of Life and Death'*, *'City of Angels'*, *'Dogma'*, *'Constantine'* – all the classics, and there's loads of stuff to buy and download. You can even go and search online for your guardian angel and then sync all your brands with it. There are dozens of angel tribes that you can join or just update on your status."

"Sounds fun." Eleanor added ironically.

"Yes, it is," Nicola replied enthusiastically. Irony was clearly wasted on her. She was really keen to show Eleanor the in-house megastore for all the merchandising. She explained that Eleanor could purchase an angel figurine customised just for her. "Everyone can have a guardian angel. If you don't already have one that's looking after you, they'll find you one. They're not that expensive really, considering what you get."

Nicola's voice trailed off into the distance as she sought some future Winterval gifts for her family. Eleanor tried to look interested as she browsed the angelic themed china figurines, paintings, wind charms, jewellery and designer clothes, but in truth her attention had wandered and her enthusiasm had long since departed. She longed to return to what she had experienced on the mountainside. The authenticity of that experience contrasted sharply with the tenor of what surrounded her in the Assembly Building. She didn't want to appear rude or ungrateful, but she had no desire to explore the world of angels any further. Her initial sense of wonder had collapsed under a barrage of merchandising. The magic had quickly evaporated once she realised what the building was dedicated towards promoting. Not even a very pleasant tea room, restaurant and interactive visitor centre could retain her interest.

Eleanor tarried as much out of politeness and regard for

Nicola's enthusiasm than because of any continuing sense of real interest. She was unsettled by the lack of stillness, the buzz of raised voices and the annoying throb of piped music. It resembled more a shopping mall than a place of peace or reflection. Yet underneath the veneer of conspicuous consumption she sensed that some deeper, more profound purpose must have originally been served by the building. Why else would people have built it to such a scale and with such beauty so long ago? Surely not just to promote relics and trinkets and Winterval gifts.

There must be a different narrative to explain its pictures, symbols and purpose.

Chapter 6

There is never a good way to learn that your services are no longer required, but when he discovered a letter on his desk following his meeting at the Cresta Coffee National Gallery, Finch knew instantly what to expect. The letter gave the impression that the redundancy had been planned for some time and claimed that the move was part of a new strategic initiative to *'refocus the core activities of the company around new corporate values in a highly competitive financial market.'* Finch wasn't convinced; he knew that this was personal. Phrases like *'functional redundancy'* and *'downsizing the in-house marketing team'* couldn't disguise the convenient timing and nature of his redundancy notice. He knew that the company had marked his card some time ago and was anxious to offload him as soon as possible.

Johnson denied that it had anything to do with his enforced absence and struggle to reintegrate into the pace of corporate life, but everyone in the office knew that the company wanted to see him go. Johnson explained that brand identity built brand loyalty, and brand loyalty built market share. He simply hadn't been providing the kind of copy needed in order to establish the new, energetic culture of brand identity that the company required. It was nothing personal; simply a business decision.

As far as Finch was concerned this was constructive dismissal, but Johnson was having none of it. A short and acrimonious exchange passed between them in which various insults and expletives were exchanged. Finch couldn't believe that he was being kicked in the teeth when he was down and by people on the fourth floor who were younger, less experienced and probably less able than him. Most of all he hated being pushed around; the victim of other people's decisions.

Whatever was said in the heat of the moment and whatever the company motives were, Finch knew that beneath his anger and burning resentment lay a small flicker of relief. He didn't really belong in corporate marketing. The stranger at the gallery was correct in that regard. However, no-one likes to be pushed, even when they were considering how they might jump. So, after their respective parentage had been questioned, Finch and Johnson finally agreed to part on reasonably amicable terms and even managed to exchange a formal, departing handshake. The generous redundancy package offered by the company would be helpful and it seemed best to accept it without further acrimony, even though Finch could barely restrain his desire to punch Johnson on the nose as a final gesture, for no other reason than it was something he had always wanted to do.

The journey home that night felt like a trek into the unknown. Familiar sights and sounds faded into the background as the prospect of an uncertain future loomed in front of him like a giant, black edifice, obscuring the light and dominating all his thoughts. The explosion had robbed him of more than a small part of his right earlobe. He felt as if all his reference points had been torn up. The security of regular work had evaporated before his eyes and now all that stood between him and the widening abyss of growing debts was the surreal encounter with an art-loving stranger and the prospect of investigating some shadowy political intrigue. Wherever he looked, uncertainty and insecurity presented themselves on every side.

Finch dragged himself up the stairs to his first floor apartment. He located his favourite, much travelled sofa and acquainted himself with a microwave Indian takeaway and a six-pack of cheap lager. The apartment felt even more empty than usual. Furniture and fittings were kept to a minimum; lavish excess had departed in a series of transactions to local cash converters and eBay, the result of a messy separation and the need to liquidise his assets. Now only a few essential items remained. The old sofa, an ancient iPod docking system, numerous gaming consoles, a home cinema set-up, a few DVD box sets gathering dust and a number of treasured books, mostly history and politics that remained unsold on eBay along with some framed photos recalling happier times.

His career might have hit a dead end but at least the events of earlier that day provided him with some sense of purpose He located the envelope the stranger had given him and emptied its contents onto his faded sofa. Various files, photographs and an old-fashioned memory stick lay before him. The photos were versions of the grainy CCTV shots he had been shown earlier, along with a few publicity photos of Iona Dunwoody at various corporate hospitality events. A number of the photos must have been taken more recently as they depicted Iona from unusual angles and clearly from long distances revealing her looking unkempt, angry and sullen. He recognised these as surveillance photos, although not very good ones; certainly not the sort that the paparazzi would offer any respectable news organisation when seeking to unmask scandal or corruption.

The hardcopy files revealed some interesting background information about the Dunwoody business empire, but disclosed little that wasn't already in the public domain. Other files seemed to be concerned with various pharmaceutical and bio-genetic companies, but only provided outline information. They were more like calling cards and invitations to investigate, rather than any hard evidence of criminal or unethical business practice. Apart from these corporate briefing files, there were a few reports that looked like they had been cut and pasted from official or security services investigations. They appeared to have been heavily redacted and had all departmental references removed or blanked out, along with various names and reference numbers. However, he could still recognise their source as one not usually accessible to the public or even the most inquisitive investigative journalist. It resembled information that had been disclosed by an office junior or intern rather than a professional. It was sloppy and badly executed, yet nevertheless remained intriguing. Finch knew how to read between the lines of such botched attempts to hide important references. This was obviously a controlled leak, albeit a rather clumsy one.

Outside police sirens wailed, accompanied by the distinctive throb of a security drone hovering somewhere nearby. Why had he been singled out for such a cloak and dagger assignment when there were security contractors arrayed with the latest technology and manpower who could do a much more effective job?

He thought about the comment the stranger had made about 'keeping an eye' on him. Did that mean he was already under surveillance? He looked out of his second floor window onto the night street scene below. Everything appeared normal. There was a white van parked opposite, but he was sure that it had been there for some time. He wasn't used to the idea of being the object of enquiry. It made him feel uneasy and not a little guilty, as if he had something to hide rather than something to discover. He was much more at ease with the dark arts of investigative journalism, occupying the role of the hunter in pursuit of the truth, rather than the hunted.

He quickly located the memory stick which had been part of the package and found an old laptop to load up the external drive onto his data cloud. When he finally hooked up the interface between the two different forms of technology, he discovered a pathway leading to his own current account details. He was amazed to find a total of over £150,000 had been recently deposited. One entry was from his employer and clearly formed part of the redundancy deal that he had previously learnt about. The timing of such a payment merely confirmed his suspicions that such an arrangement had been planned for some time. However, there was also a considerable sum in addition to this payment from an unknown source that had been paid by direct cash transfer on the previous day, presumably connected with his meeting with the stranger in the gallery. However, no other details were provided and, despite his best efforts, it proved impossible to confirm who had made the payment.

The following week was spent trying to come to terms with what had taken place on that one eventful day. The nights were the most difficult. He had never slept well, the legacy of too many nightshifts and long working days. His time in hospital had probably provided the best night's sleep he had enjoyed for years. Each night he wrestled with disturbing thoughts. He would often check the street outside to see if there was anything unusual about the scene. The white van had gone, but there was a hybrid street car that he didn't recognise. He noted the registration number. It would form part of a traffic log, to discover whether there was any pattern to the street parking. He knew that most surveillance was now remote and electronic, but the possibility of something more physical and locally based remained.

The evenings were also the time when he was tempted

to log on to his favourite gaming sites, just to check who was playing in Sydney, Tokyo and Hong Kong and to see whether his old gaming pals were in the mood for some serious head-to-head action. The more time he had available, the greater the compulsion to indulge his curiosity and feed his habits. Most nights there was some interesting action going on that he knew he could take advantage of; it was just a matter of prioritising his time online and using the little credit still available to him in the most effective manner. He fantasised about the easy money he could make. He knew he could come out on top. He had been stung in the past, but he had learnt from that experience and now he knew his limits and, most importantly, he knew to quit while he was still ahead. If only he wasn't shut out from so many sites. If only there were more sites willing to cut him some slack and extend him just a little more credit, then he could become a serious player again. Perhaps his luck was about to change? His recently acquired cash injection could help to set up a number of new accounts, along with a new in-play identity to get him back into the game again. This time the outcome would be different. From now on he would be in control.

During the next few days he decided to use his newly acquired income to launch himself back online with the gaming community again. The games energised him once again and provided a welcome distraction from any negative thoughts about the future. He even tried to contact a few colleagues from the office to talk about his sudden departure and to make some sort of attempt to sign off in a more positive manner. The reactions he received were universally polite, yet guarded, marked by coolness and an unwillingness to discuss anything beyond what was strictly necessary. He took the hint and decided to back off.

As his evenings filled up with time spent in various online gaming rooms, so his days were increasingly devoted to exploring the new project the stranger had commissioned. He tried to get in touch with some former hacks he had known during his reporting days, but many of them had similarly moved on to new challenges and new careers. Two had actually died, yet from the one or two he managed to contact who remained in post it was apparent that they had moved on in other ways and now operated a very different methodology for gathering information and researching topics. Several former colleagues refused to talk to him altogether: emails bounced back or else he was constantly redirected to voicemail servers, even though he suspected that they were available to take his call. Whatever he tried, he came up against a wall of indifference. In an act of desperation, he decided to access the old journalistic archives. It had been years since he had ploughed through these ancient databases. He had normally delegated such routine duties to junior reporters or interns. However, this time his clumsy attempts to reacquaint himself with the archive ended in failure after he discovered that all his access codes were now invalid and his security protocols obsolete.

The enormity of the task facing him slowly began to dawn. Why had he been singled out when he no longer had access to the tools of the trade and the personal contacts on which his former reputation as a reporter had been built? Why had he been asked to take on this challenge when the social media commentators and the security services had taken over such operations? It just didn't make any sense. Former glories or reputation no longer opened doors for him. He would have to pursue this assignment on his own, acting more as a private individual than a freelance professional.

It was at times like this that he really missed Hannah. The six years since she had left the matrimonial home had been marked by loneliness and regret. Memories of the things that had been said still haunted him. He blamed himself for what had happened. He knew that forces beyond his control had shaped those events that had led to their marriage imploding. If only he could have cherished Hannah more and given her the attention she deserved, rather than using her as his emotional punch bag to take out all his frustration. He realised that he had become toxic to her. He had cocooned himself within a private world she could never enter. The humiliation she endured when going shopping only to be refused payment on their credit card, the threatening letters, the visits of the bailiffs, the unsavoury company he kept, the promises he broke, the secrecy and the lies. No husband should ever place such a burden on the person they have vowed to love and cherish.

He had promised Hannah that moving out of frontline journalism offered him a chance to start all over again. It would provide a new way of working, new colleagues and new routines along with a place where he could avoid the poisonous relationships and work patterns that had led into his dark, private world. His new career, despite its creative limitations, had indeed provided him with the space to gain more self-control. Although a new work environment had initially removed the need to self-medicate as a way of dealing with work pressures, the change had come too late for Hannah. She had been worn down by the inability to make plans and to build the secure family home she had always wanted. He suspected that she had cheated on him. There were many signs, if he had cared to notice them. He wouldn't have blamed her if she had. He had become dead to her emotionally and sexually, as closed off to her personally as was his line of credit. The only person surprised when she finally left was Finch himself. Everyone else who knew them realised that their marriage had been over for some time. Her leaving was an act of self-preservation, merely acknowledging the distance that had grown between them.

Finch had convinced himself that life without Hannah was just a provisional arrangement until he could sort out his finances and start to get ahead again. She would return one day, or so he hoped. But six years had passed and her unwillingness to show up, after learning of his injuries in the bomb blast suggested that her absence was now a permanent fixture. Even so, her leaving still ate away at him. His sense of isolation was compounded by the loose ends and uncertainties that he struggled to reconcile in his personal life. Being out of work would have been easier to bear with Hannah at his side, but now, with no-one to de-brief with at the end of each day, negative feelings and fears grew more intense within him.

Finch checked out the scene in the street below his flat. There was a strange car parked halfway down again. He logged the number and cross-referenced it with previous entries. Different number, so no pattern. He decided it would be a good time to take out the rubbish and fill the recycling box. He wandered up the street, rubbish bag in hand, checking out the suspicious car for any mysterious passengers. There were none and suddenly he realised just how ridiculous he would appear to his neighbours wandering up and down the street at midnight, wearing a dressing gown and flip-flops and carrying a rubbish bag full of empty lager bottles.

Each night Finch would scrutinise the street scene outside his flat. The art-loving stranger's comments about keeping an eye on him were starting to get under his skin. He continued to note down car and van registration numbers and cross-reference them for signs that someone was installed nearby, listening in or logging his movements. One time he thought he had found a suspicious vehicle but it turned out to a local plumber who was doing some cash in hand work out of hours for a neighbour of his. He even took delivery of an electronic surveillance scrubber that he had seen advertised online. The package took the form of a flat black disc which was intended to be located next to his Wi-Fi router in order to scramble all out-going digital traffic, along with a detection device that looked like a cheese grater and was meant to reveal any active electronic penetration. Having struggled to install the scrambling device, he completed a thorough sweep of his flat for any surveillance devices. Nothing registered on the cheese grater, yet despite a negative result he remained highly suspicious that his movements and communications were being monitored.

His isolation would have been easier to bear if he could have called upon the support of a greater number of friends. Cultivating meaningful friendships had never been his priority and now he was paying the price. He realised that many of those he considered friends were really work colleagues whose friendship he had previously cultivated in the interests of the assignments he had pursued. Outside of those colleagues, the virtual community that passed for real friends didn't provide an effective support network and he longed for the phone to ring or the inbox to fill up with expressions of emotional reassurance or for someone to offer him a friendly 'hello'. It therefore came as something of a surprise one evening when Greg turned up at his door seeking a bed for the night.

"Finchie! Good to see you, my old pal!" Greg had obviously been drinking and the persistent ringing of his doorbell at 1.30am presented an unwelcome calling card.

"Greg? Look, it's a bit difficult at the moment. Can you come back some other time?" Finch knew that Greg was not someone who would take a hint or respond to subtlety, especially at such an hour and in such a state. "This really isn't a good time for me."

Greg looked genuinely hurt and seemed to crumple in front of him. Like most drunks, he could be quite manipulative, but seeing him wither on his doorstep genuinely moved Finch. When the tears started to flow, Greg's cause became irresistible.

"Look, Finchie. I'm at the end of my tether here…I don't know where else I can go…She's kicked me out and I've got no-one else to turn to." Greg was slumped on the floor in a foetal position, sobbing gently.

"I'm sorry to hear that, Greg, but this has happened before. I'm sure you can patch things up."

"I can't. I can't." Greg was sounding even more pathetic and childlike. "You don't understand."

"Look, you better come in. You'll disturb the neighbours sat out here." Finch's resistance finally melted away as he ushered Greg into a spare bedroom.

After a noisy and disturbed night, which involved regular visits to the bathroom to throw up, Greg emerged sullen and grey from the spare room.

"You look like shit." Finch's candour was not entirely inaccurate.

"Thanks, pal. I know." Greg wearily grabbed a beaker and filled it with orange juice straight from the fridge. It hadn't taken long for him to make himself at home.

"Good to see that you remember where everything is." Finch made no effort to disguise any sense of irony. This was not the first time he had entertained Greg in such circumstances.

"It's amazing how memories can be so resilient." Greg shaded his face against the bright morning sunlight piercing the kitchen window. He surveyed the sparse landscape of the apartment. "I see you're still going in for the minimalist look."

"Yeh. You know how it is."

Greg knew all right. There was no need to speak further on the subject. "Look, I really appreciate all this. I know I'm a pain in the arse, but I really will be on my way just as soon as I get a few things sorted out."

"Is there any point in asking what happened?"

"You know, the usual stuff. She takes me back; everything

is fine again and then I start to spend too much time at work. I keep staying late and hanging out with WPC's half my age. Things happen. We get it together, but it means nothing. She gets suspicious. Things are said. I deny it and then the next thing I know my clothes are on the front lawn when I return home."

"Greg, have you heard of something called a 'learning curve'?"

"A what?"

"A learning curve. It maps the experiences of normal people and how they respond to those experiences over time. It shows that people take on board information received and adapt their behaviour accordingly."

"And your point is…?"

"My point is…what are you doing with your life? You've been to this same place many times before. Can't you see how you are screwing things up over and over again?"

"Well, now that you put it that way, I see what you mean. But it really isn't as simple as you think. I know it seems like the old pattern keeps recurring, but it really wasn't like that this time."

"You made it sound like it was."

"Sure. I know. Look, it's early, I'm hung over and I've got nowhere to live and no clean underwear. I'm just giving you the highlights – the full witness statement will take a bit longer if you're interested."

"Oh, spare me the details, Greg." Finch really didn't have the time or the sympathy to deal with Greg. He might be a former school friend, but he had played upon his patience and loyalty far too often to be spared a verbal lashing when one was required. "If you were to present yourself before a judge with your history, you would be treated as a repeat offender."

"A bit harsh?"

"Well, someone has to take you by the hand and lead you down 'Reality Street' every now and then."

"OK, so you're such a grounded person, living such a perfect life then?"

That comment hurt. There really was nowhere to hide when it came to him and Greg.

"No, not necessarily. I never claim to be. But you're like a dog returning to its own vomit. You're stuck in a loop, and unless I'm very much mistaken, you are the one who presented himself on my doorstep in the middle of the night and who is now drinking my freshly squeezed orange juice, taking a shower in my bathroom and wearing MY BATH ROBE! So, I think I do have the right to occupy the slightly higher moral ground on this occasion."

"OK, OK. I get it. Don't worry, I won't be here long."

"That's not the point, Greg. It really isn't the point. It's just that…Oh, I don't know."

It was hard to maintain a sense of exasperation with Greg; they were both cut from the same cloth. Listening to his story was a bit like holding a mirror up against his own life. They had both screwed up, only in different ways. Greg could be infuriating, but he was also given to childlike enthusiasm, generosity and could be good fun. You could knock him down with a comment or a gesture and he would just come right back at you, jaw sticking out inviting further rebuke. He displayed a fragile charm, a characteristic that had probably endeared him to so many women. "Look, you can stay just for a few days, but no longer."

"Oh cool, Finchie. I really appreciate it. You won't regret it." A beaming smile returned to Greg's face.

"I'm already regretting it," Finch replied.

The next few days passed fairly uneventfully. Finch was aware that Greg was making a real effort to court his favour and minimise any inconvenience. Mostly he kept a low profile, working long hours and only returning to the flat late at night, often with a takeaway meal in hand. He kept disappearing from the flat for a breath of fresh air at inexplicable times, but otherwise remained remarkably low maintenance and good company. One evening, following the consumption of a particularly pungent prawn bhuna, Finch finally plucked up the courage to pick Greg's mind over his latest project.

"Greg, does the name Iona Dunwoody mean anything to you?"

"Yes, sure, isn't she the daughter of Reg Dunwoody – the owner of just about every microchip in your mobile?"

"That's the one."

"Not heard much about her recently. She's normally the sort that puts herself about a bit. She in some kind of trouble?"

"I'm not sure. Look, I don't know whether I should be sharing this with you or not."

"Then don't, my dear boy, and make both of our lives a lot simpler. It's like I always say, there are very few things in life that matter and most of those don't matter much at all."

"But don't you believe that there are some things worth fighting for, worth protecting, even worth exposing?"

"Possibly. Don't really think about it most of the time."

"I guess that's the problem. We all just push those thoughts to the back of our mind."

"Makes life a lot simpler," Greg remarked with a degree of self-satisfaction.

"Yeh, but don't you ever wonder how we got here? How things have changed so much and no-one seems bothered."

"What d'you mean?"

"Well, don't you ever feel that something has been lost or overlooked or forgotten?"

"Like your car keys?"

"No, much more important than that. Do you ever feel as though you're constantly walking into an empty room and you can't remember why you entered?"

"That's your age, Finchie."

"No, it's more than that. It's like that feeling you get when you leave the house and set out on an important journey and you're sure that you've left something really important behind, but you can't remember what it is. Something you know you're going to need at some stage, but you run through all your checklists and everything seems to be there, yet you're still left with this nagging doubt."

"You really need to get laid, my old pal. How long has it been now?"

"No, it's not that. Oh, never mind."

"Perhaps you're missing your old stamping ground then. I always thought that journalism was in your blood."

"It used to be. I just don't know what's happening to me at the moment, but I've got this big freelance project that's just fallen in my lap."

"And your problem is…?"

"The problem is that it involves some surveillance and digging about."

"So, is this where Iona Dunwoody comes in?"

"Kinda."

"Well, she's pretty high profile; I'm sure you could find out plenty of stuff about her. That's what you used to do, back in the day."

"Oh yeh, sure, that's not the problem, well not entirely. I can dust off my old notebook and camera and try to remember which end to hold, but it's the manner of the assignment. It's all a bit cloak and dagger."

"Should suit you," Greg added between burps. "You used to love that sort of thing."

"Yeh, I know, but this is different. I feel that I'm being played with by forces I don't entirely trust."

"So hand it over to Special Branch. I've got a mate who works there. I can give you his details if you like."

"Yeh, great. It's just that there's a bit more to it than that."

"Look, Finchie, how long have we known each other?"

"Too long, about twenty years, I guess."

"So, here I am, bunking down in your spare bedroom. I think you can relax a bit and make a few assumptions about my being discreet. All I need to know is – does this involve anything illegal?" Greg cast Finch a knowing look, lowering one of his eyebrows in playful manner, suggesting that he already knew the answer to his question.

"No. Absolutely not. At least not that I'm aware of."

"So, what's the problem?" Greg asked as he cracked open another can of lager.

"The problem is that they – the people who've given me this commission – they don't want the police involved. Worried about leaks and negative publicity and all that."

"Fair enough, strictly a private investigation. I can live with that. So, what do you want me to do for you?"

"Was it quite that obvious that I was leading up to something?"

"Like I said, how long have we known each other?" Greg took a sip of lager and threw Finch one of his charming, puppy dog looks.

"Can you arrange a data dump for me?"

"WHAT?" Greg exploded.

"A data dump."

"Yes, I heard you. I just wished I hadn't. Do you know what you're asking?"

"Well, yes, sort of."

"So you know just how difficult it is to pull off a data dump and how illegal it is without the correct authorisation? I thought you said there was nothing illegal involved?"

"Well, if we got the proper authorisation, then it wouldn't be illegal, would it?

Now it was Greg's turn to occupy the moral high ground and express his exasperation. He sensed he was in the presence of an old school operative working in a new environment he barely understood. "Exactly whose data are we talking about here?"

"The Van Hegel Corporation."

"Oh great, it just gets better and better."

"Well, maybe not the whole corporation."

"Oh good."

"Just a subsidiary of the corporation."

"So why exactly do you want to do a data dump of a major multinational like Van Hegel?"

"It's this Dunwoody feature. All the leads are running cold. I just keep hitting a wall. I thought that I was just losing my touch or out of step with modern ways of getting the story, but the more and more I look into the information I was given, I just get the feeling that this is where I am meant to look. It's like I am being led towards Van Hegel for a reason. Everything else is as tight as a drum."

"So it's nothing to do with the scene of the explosion? No unfinished business or personal agenda?"

"Oh, yes, it is everything to do with the scene of the explosion. I would be lying if I told you that I didn't want to know exactly why that building was targeted."

"But why a data dump? It's a sledgehammer to crack a nut."

"Yes, I know it's a bit clumsy, but all other avenues have been closed off to me. They use data dumps in police surveillance, don't they?"

"Oh I really wouldn't know about such things." Greg indulged in self-mocking, slipping in a roguish, knowing smile.

"But they do, don't they?"

"Look, you're never going to get Special Branch or anyone else in the security services to do you a friendly data dump on a major multinational as some sort of personal favour. It really doesn't work like that. There are protocols and procedures these days. Everything is monitored."

"But you do know how to arrange such a thing, don't you?" Finch knew that Greg owed him and his tone suggested that this was payback time.

"I might do. That's all I can say at this stage." Greg looked thoughtful and brooding. Somewhere deep within the recesses of his imagination the kernel of an idea was taking shape. He massaged his chin in pained resignation. More brooding followed. "Yeh, there might be a way."

"Great! I knew you would come good!" Finch's expression changed to one of relief. The close symbiotic relationship that the press and the police force had once enjoyed was now a distant memory. However, when he first started in journalism, the quid pro quo of bargaining and deal-making with the local constabulary had dominated his profession. You could always rely upon a friendly source among the local police to yield some information or turn a blind eye in return for some selective news leaking. This time all he had to offer was his goodwill and personal appreciation; the only pressure he could exert was one of friendship and the return of a personal favour.

"The security services aren't the only ones with access to the cloud. The servers also get serviced – you know, routine backups, virus scans, software updates and that."

"Doesn't that all go on in Mumbai somewhere?"

"Some still does, but a lot of multinationals got their fingers burnt that way. They like to keep their data a little closer to home these days and so they use regular data maintenance protocols to back up their local servers. It might be possible to hijack those maintenance procedures, but it could be risky."

"How risky?"

"Well, you could get caught by some internal firewall, or failing that, your entire hardware could get fried by an overload of unsupported data and you'd be identified by a permanent ID marker."

"Sounds like fun. You seem fairly knowledgeable about all this data storage nonsense."

"We don't do much chasing burglars over rooftops these days. A lot of organised crime now operates on-line. You have to keep up to speed with the thieving bastards."

"So, you can help?"

"Perhaps. Look, I might know a bloke. Leave it with me and I'll see what I can do."

Chapter 7

Judge Tobias McArthur was not someone known for his patience. He had already heard two cases earlier that day and both had overrun due to what he regarded as lack of foresight by counsel. Such negligence had contributed to the pressure cooker atmosphere of Croydon County Court which severely challenged any residual goodwill he might have felt for what should have been a very straightforward caseload awaiting his attention.

At least proceedings would not be delayed by the encumbrance of a public jury system. He welcomed the absence of jurors from his court. He regarded it as a much overdue reform by an enlightened government which saw the need to speed up a very expensive judicial process by eliminating the need to brief a group of ignorant lay people, hopelessly out of their depth within a professional legal process. He had seen too many amateurs get confused and make poor judgments over the years to mourn the passing of the jury system. It is always better to leave these things to the professionals. People like him had acquired years of experience to equip them to recognise the disposition of the guilty as well as the innocent within only a few minutes of their appearance before the bench. Trusting that process to his judgment made perfect sense in less serious and straightforward cases.

Today would be no exception; a simple matter of attempted assault and the vandalism of Crown property. Such a case should not delay him too long. All that separated Judge McArthur from a visit to his favourite gentleman's club was the formality of receiving a psychiatric report and dispatching another anti-capitalism protestor to a well-deserved custodial sentence. Times of accelerated social change always bring a reaction and Judge McArthur and his colleagues had seen many such protesters pass before their bench in the last few years. They all had their tales to tell and their causes to uphold. Anti-capitalism, anti-science, anti-globalism, anti-technology, anti-road building and anti-rail protestors, not to mention those who were pro-free speech, pro-countryside and pro-the right to free assembly along with the occasional frustrated republican or disappointed monarchist.

Judge McArthur regarded such people as well-meaning, but deluded. To call them terrorists would misrepresent their methodology for advancing their agenda, but the term 'T-squad' reflected the real threat they carried. Such groups provided a recruiting ground for those prepared to commit acts of violence and therefore there was a clear progression of intent, a slippery slope separating the ideological protestor from the armed activist. All that stood between the T-squads and full blown terror was the further 'error' of their ways. It therefore fell to people like him to nip such practices in the bud and send a clear message to those involved that there would be zero tolerance when it came to taking the law into their own hands.

If Dr. Catherine Stringer had known that the old gentleman wearing a wig who sat in judgment of her case held such views, then she might have felt a lot less confident of the outcome of her legal hearing.

"Miss Southam, am I to understand that the defendant wishes to enter a guilty plea?" Judge McArthur enquired.

"Yes, M'lud." A young female, barrister stood upright before him.

"And that you wish to offer this psychiatric report, which was ordered by the local magistrates, as some kind of mitigating evidence to weigh against that plea?"

"Yes, M'lud, but in conjunction with the other sworn affidavits which attest to the good character and previously clean criminal record of my client."

"I see." The judge paused for what appeared to be a painfully long time before considering his next question. "And the nature of the psychiatric report attests to a condition of delayed post-traumatic stress disorder brought on by personal family grief, which has….let me find the summary here…" The elderly judge fumbled through various papers assembled in front of him "….which has, and I quote, *'significantly diminished the defendant's ability to weigh up the consequences of her actions.'* Am I right to understand that you are therefore pleading for mitigation on the grounds of diminished responsibility?"

"We are, M'lud. The psychiatrist, Dr. O'Brien, believes that the personal loss of Mrs. Stringer's son as a result of an online suicide pack, just twelve months prior to the incident, induced a deep-seated paranoia, which rendered the defendant incapable of discerning the distinction between her own experiences and that of the wider community. She now blames that wider community for his death and therefore sought to exact retribution upon an elected representative of that community. This paranoia has subsequently diminished her ability to take full responsibility for the consequences of her actions." The young barrister drew breath, satisfied that she had represented her client's case fairly and accurately.

"I see. And you expect this court of law to take into consideration this personal bereavement when weighing up why someone who has been awarded…let me see…" Once again, the judge shuffled his case notes in order to locate the relevant biographical details. "…two doctorates as well as the King's Medal for outstanding contribution to British Exports in Design, should seek to turn up in Westminster with a bucket of paint and threaten a Minister of the Crown as well as defacing Crown property?" He made little attempt to disguise his incredulity at what he was being asked to consider.

"We are asking your Lordship to take into consideration not only the psychiatric assessment, but also the defendant's previous good character, her co-operation with the legal authorities and her significant, acknowledged contribution to the creative and economic wellbeing of UK plc." The young barrister looked pleased with her summing-up, given the limited time and space to present her case in what was a very busy court schedule.

"Yes, I see that there are some very impressive affidavits concerning her good character from some highly placed sources…some very highly placed sources." Judge McArthur raised his eyebrow and paused to consider his next course of action. Briefly he felt the weight of the full force of historical jurisprudence resting upon his shoulders. A piece of paper was passed to him from a court official. His eyes widened upon reading its contents. He looked around the courtroom, anxious expressions and hushed expectation greeted him. He knew what he had to do. "I think that, in order to weigh the balance of all these matters, the court will adjourn for thirty minutes, following which we will re-convene to await my decision."

With that the courtroom was cleared.

Chapter 8

S everal television crews had gathered outside the court building to capture sound bites and images of an incident that had attracted some public interest among the regional news agencies. Their output would provide the feed for the larger, global news networks and social media corporations. As a result, there were only very few reporters present, mostly junior ones sent out onto the streets by news editors seeking to toughen up rooky journalists, whose natural inclination was to source all their stories through the careful manipulation of mobile handsets and the interrogation of various online sources.

Catherine emerged from the court building, shielding her eyes from the low spring sunshine. Immediately the television crews were drawn towards her, like moths to the light.

One of the young interns seized upon the chance to take the initiative. "Dr. Stringer, can you give your reaction to your suspended sentence?"

"Well, I'm obviously very pleased that the judge saw fit to respect my right to protest."

"But the judge did describe you as a 'sadly deluded and obsessional individual'."

"I respect the decision of the court; even if I disagree with the language and sentiment behind the judge's decision."

"So what will you do next, Dr. Stringer?"

"I will seek to abide by the court's wishes and comply with the restraining order concerning the government minister, but I will nevertheless continue my campaign to expose the lie that sits at the heart of not only this government, but also at the heart of our national life. I will continue my campaign to discover why so many young people like my son have taken their lives because they feel cheated by their country and deceived by the corporations that lie behind so many of our nation's great institutions." With that she pushed her way past the television crews, accompanied by her young barrister.

Catherine made her way through the busy streets that surrounded the court building. Her young barrister explained that she had an important prison visit to undertake and headed off in search of an available eco-taxi, weaving her way in and out of pedestrians and cyclists who thronged the walkways. In the distance sirens could be heard, along with the ever-present throb of drones hovering overhead. Two police constables pushed past her on bicycles, concentrating on their head-up displays to find the quickest route to the location of some unfolding incident. Catherine felt drained of emotional energy. She wanted to get far away from the court building as quickly as she could, just in case they changed their minds concerning her sentence. She knew that she had been fortunate to get off. Her counsel had said as much, admitting that they hadn't been confident in bringing their case for extenuating circumstances.

She felt a hand on her shoulder. Her heart sank, fearing that the police or an over-zealous court official might have returned to implement some undisclosed statute of the judicial process. Instead, a young, dark-haired woman in a baseball cap and dark glasses was standing behind her in the street. "Dr. Stringer?"

"You're not another TV reporter, are you?" Catherine addressed the stranger in a somewhat curt and matronly manner.

"No, just a friend and supporter." The young lady appeared on edge and ill at ease. Her gaze constantly flickered from side to side as she surveyed the landscape. She took out a small flyer from the pocket of her combat trousers. Catherine recognised it immediately as part of her campaign literature. "I've been following your campaign."

"So have the police and the security services, my dear."

"Look, can we go somewhere more private. I saw you in court. I thought that you were amazing, or at least your counsel was. I'd like to help you."

"Help me? I very much doubt there is any way that you can help me, apart from supporting my campaign group."

"But I want to help you personally – help you to find out what happened to your son." The dark-haired stranger was shouting above the roar of traffic, as a wailing white police van passed by, it's siren harmonizing with others out of sight.

Ten minutes later they were sitting down in a franchised coffee bar, surrounded by TV monitors, leather upholstery and people leaning over tables, working on their tablets and handsets. Across the room several customers were engrossed in manipulating the three dimensional holographic displays that were a feature of the latest versions of their computer tablets. Such functions were still largely in their infancy and notoriously unreliable, yet that didn't stop an array of techno-geeks and those who liked to pose in designer viewing glasses, from gathering in public places to wave away pixels in mid-air that were only visible to themselves. They tried to hide their frustration as their attempts to interface with their holographic pixels proved an increasingly hit and miss operation, given the constraints of a public access Wi-Fi. Nevertheless, their efforts provided the landscape of a frantic t'ai chi class, complete with strange balletic contortions which non-participants tried to ignore.

Catherine settled herself into a comfortable high back leather-covered chair in a discreet corner of the café, well away from virtual t'ai chi class.

"Let me get these." The dark-haired girl took charge of the situation.

"That's very kind of you." Catherine happily accepted two large skinny lattes. "But I still don't understand what you want from me" Catherine stared into the eyes of the young lady sitting opposite her. She had removed her hat and glasses and appeared more relaxed, exuding a sense of quiet confidence and familiarity. "Tell me, have we met before?"

"No, I don't think so, but I've been following your case for some time."

"You're not one of those online journalists who wants to post my story all over the social media, are you?"

"No, not at all. Just the opposite. I'm not looking for a story or pitching for your image rights. Let me introduce myself. People call me 'Skyshadow', but that's not my real name. My real name is…is not important at the moment. What matters is what I am part of, and I think it is what you are part of as well, Dr. Stringer."

"Call me Catherine, please, just Catherine."

"Catherine, I think that you and I are seeking after the same things." Skyshadow seemed to exude increasing authority the more she spoke. The way that she flicked her hair over her shoulders and put Catherine at the centre of her attention suggested that she was used to giving explanations of her actions. "You are seeking for a truth that most people are blind to. I see you as someone who is gripped by that quest and will not give up on the prize until she has laid hold of it for herself."

"What I am seeking, young lady, is the truth about my son.

Nothing more, nothing less. Everything else is the result of what I have stumbled upon in the process."

"I appreciate that, but what I am trying to say is that you're not alone. You've stumbled upon something because you want answers about your son, but others have also made the same connections for different reasons and from different paths. We're all travellers on the same journey."

"Skyshadow, if I can call you that."

"Just call me Sky, that would be fine."

"Sky, all I am really concerned about is why Joshua took his life. Did you know that there has been a 15% increase in suicides in the last five years?"

"No, I didn't know that," Sky replied whilst taking a sip of coffee.

"No, not many people do, and even fewer seem concerned about it. So, all I did was a little digging, a little research, and I found that the Department of Health has prevented information from coming out in the public sphere. Coroners' courts and police forces up and down the country have been instructed to err on the side of caution when investigating suicides and to enter accidental death or open verdicts under very spurious criteria, in order to under-record this phenomenon. Don't you think that's somewhat strange?"

"So what do you think is happening?"

"Well, it's obvious, isn't it? The official line is that the shared national grief of recent years has brought about some kind of hysteria or chain reaction of emotional turmoil which has disturbed young and impressionable minds. You've seen the graffiti everywhere, 'WW2L4E' – it's not a web address, it's a political statement."

"Your son was part of the protest movement?"

"Not that I'm aware of. The protest movement is a symptom, not the cause of what's happening. I think the 'Great

Advance,' not the *'Garden Party Bombings',* has something to do with it. It's knocked everyone off balance."

"Ah, the *'Great Advance'.*" Sky seemed to light up at the very mention of the event, as if some great touchstone or secret password had been revealed. "Like I said, we are travellers on the same journey."

"Yes, it's blindingly obvious that if you finally discover the elusive cure or at least permanent remission for 70% of known cancers, then that's going to bring great blessings but it can also unhinge many people's expectations and securities. Some people are just pleased that they can now smoke at work again, but others see the bigger picture. They think they're immortal – like Greek gods, but they're all still going to die of something one day, just something else instead. They think they have discovered the elixir of everlasting life, but they haven't. Managing expectations arising from such a breakthrough was always going to be a nightmare, but no-one thought it through. When the Grim Reaper appears to have been tamed or at least reined in, then most people are relieved or even jubilant, but not everyone."

"Not your son?"

"I don't know. All I know is that there are a lot of people who are trying to explore the uncertainties that were removed. When you make something safe, you just shift the risks elsewhere. Why do you think there are so many people taking up extreme sports and exposing themselves to danger? They're exploring their limits, pushing boundaries, seeking new horizons to replace the ones they've surrendered. They're trying to take back control. What greater control is there than the control over life and death? Who would want to live forever?"

"Was that what you were trying to expose at the Department of Health?"

"Not entirely. You'll never get a government department to

engage with ideas like that. They just don't like anyone poking around into the medical research associated with the *'Great Advance'*. It's like you're committing heresy for questioning what's really going on. They call you destabilising and treat you like a criminal and I don't appreciate being treated like a criminal."

"Do you think that your son took his life because he wanted to make some kind of statement about what was going on?"

"I don't know. He wasn't very political. He was just young and idealistic. He didn't like being pushed around and told what to do and what to think."

"I can see where he got that from."

"I beg your pardon?"

"Uh, nothing." Sky swallowed her words, trying not to give offence. "Look, Catherine, I think you've stumbled upon something really important here. We know that the *'Great Advance'* effected important changes in our nation, but we hadn't made the connection with the government wanting to manage expectations and suppress access to information about the negative aspects of the medical breakthrough."

"Let me stop you there, dear." Catherine placed her hand on Sky's forearm. "Who is this 'we' that you talk about? So far I've told you what I am doing here, but I know nothing about what your interests are and who you represent." Catherine slowly realised that she had spoken quite openly with this young lady. Her time under arrest and under the authority of the courts had been somewhat stifling and the elation of her court release had provided something of an adrenalin surge that caused her to be less guarded than usual. Now meeting a friendly face and a willing listener who wasn't compiling a court report about her mental frailties had caused her to lower her guard and yet there was something inherently kind and comforting about Sky's presence that made her feel safe.

"I represent some of the people that you have been campaigning on behalf of." Sky was looking around the room, checking out the reaction of the other customers.

"But, as I explained, I haven't been campaigning on behalf of anything. All I've been doing is trying to understand what happened to Josh. Everything I've done has been in his name, rather than for any political cause or on behalf of a silent minority."

"Sure, I appreciate that. It's just that I don't think you realise what you have been caught up in. Your struggle is just part of a much wider struggle. We are all living such fragmented lives and operating out of silos so that no-one sees the whole picture – what they are feeling and discovering is shared by countless others."

"But we live in times of great information sharing. You can't put a lid on ideas anymore – everything is out there."

"'Man is born free, but everywhere he is in chains.'" Sky cast Catherine a knowing look, hoping that she would recognise her reference.

"I see that you are familiar with French political philosophy, my dear."

"Absolutely. We think we're free, but actually we've surrendered our freedom for what we regard as the bigger gain."

"I see," but Catherine still wasn't sure where this was leading.

"This isn't just about trading off our access to a cancer vaccine in favour of personal self-determination. There have been other vaccines in history before. No-one complained when smallpox was eradicated or HIV eliminated. No-one wants to die slowly and painfully from the illnesses our parents suffered from. Yet this latest breakthrough has been achieved at a great cost. We know so little about its suppliers and the power they wield. Freedoms have been surrendered along the way. We might have advanced, but something has been traded in the process."

"Certainly freedom of information has." Catherine was starting to understand the world view that Sky claimed she shared. "I've come across a culture of secrecy at the heart of many government departments."

"Not just there. It's across the whole information superhighway."

"But we can access everything online."

"Yes, but who controls that information?"

"We do. That's the beauty of the internet. We can do pretty much as we please. Online censorship is very hard to enforce."

"It is, but very easy to apply informally when you control the access points, the search engines, the megaservers and the virtual clouds. It's censorship by the back door. Not controlled by governments, but by large, corporate gatekeepers."

"My girl, you really are being rather fanciful now. I can ask my search engine anything I want."

"Yes, you can, but the question you ask is controlled by the information you hold. If that information is itself controlled, then you will only ask certain types of question." Sky realised that Catherine was unconvinced. She reached into her rucksack and took out a small, old-fashioned, hand-held computer tablet which she opened up by retinal recognition. She then scribbled a few words down on the back of Catherine's campaign leaflet. "Are you familiar with these words?"

"Well, yes, as an academic of course I am familiar with them. They're not matters that I claim any great expertise in. You don't come across them very much these days."

"Precisely. Then do me the kindness of typing them into this search engine."

"This isn't that old joke about the publishers taking the word 'gullible' out of the dictionary, is it?"

100

"No, but it's worryingly close." Sky looked thoughtful, yet confident, like a cat about to get the cream.

Catherine typed each word consecutively into her tablets search engine. As each word was entered her expression of incredulity appeared to grow. She looked shocked and kept repeating the exercise, whilst visually checking out Sky who just sat opposite her, arms folded and smiling.

"That can't be right. How can that happen?"

"Because we are not truly free to ask any question, when we don't know all the questions to ask."

"But there are thousands of books on these subjects."

"Ah, books, yes." Sky rolled her eyes as if remembering a long-lost friend. "And where do books live?"

"In libraries."

"So why d'you think there's been such a rush to digitalize so much information? Most public libraries have either been closed or radically downsized, whilst most academic institutions have developed more cost effective, online learning centres instead. Bookshops have disappeared from the high street. Everything has either gone over to e-books or is hosted online. Most physical books have either been archived or just get passed around charity shops and jumble sales."

"But they can't have just made these subjects disappear?"

"We don't have physical bonfires for burning unwelcome literature anymore, but the effect is similar. The information and ideas are still out there; some people are finding ways to preserve those ideas and safeguard the written word, but for most people their exposure is strictly controlled. Language is key. You don't know you're poor if you don't have a word for poverty."

Catherine felt strangely uneasy at discovering more about the hidden world she had come to believe in. It was reassuring to find further evidence that reality had indeed been skewed in a particular direction. However, what had begun as a personal quest to discover the seismic social changes that had so unsettled Josh and many others was turning into something far more disconcerting. She had drawn comfort from the idea that many people regarded her as deluded, paranoid or just plain unhinged. It provided her with a certain exotic sophistication, a cloak under which she could continue to delve into the secret world that intrigued her, without ever being taken seriously as a threat. However, discovering that she might be onto something put her on her guard. "Just who are you, Sky, or whatever your name is?"

"Like I said, I'm a friend, a fellow traveller. I've just travelled a little further with a few more companions."

Catherine looked at Sky from an angle. After her initial warmth, she was starting to feel uneasy in her company, despite her personal charm.

Sky sensed Catherine's unease. "Look, Catherine, I know that this might all appear a bit strange to you."

"Just a little."

"Yeh, that's cool. I get that. But what if I was to tell you that the posters you see on the LRT and buses, the news features, the government statements about the soft and hard threats – you know the connection between terrorism and 'T-squad' protesters – are just part of a strategy to eliminate dissent and silence opposition."

"Well, that's quite obvious to most thinking people, my dear."

"Well, I represent some of those people in the 'T-squad', but we're not terrorists, we really aren't." Sky looked around the room, as if she were expecting a reaction. "That bullshit about the T-squad being a training ground for terrorists is just a ruse to blacken the name of those who rail against the system. We're a very diverse group of people, a whole series of cells. Some of us are in touch with other cells; some just operate on their own and do their own thing. We're all coming from different positions and for different reasons, but we're united in our aim of exposing what's really going on and getting people to take action for themselves."

Sky tapped on her tablet and then scrolled down several menus using the retinal recognition cursor to reveal a grainy black and white portrait. "D'you recognise this person?"

Catherine peered at the image, shielding the screen from the glare of the sun's rays. "Yes, it looks a bit like you, my dear."

"Yeh, not the best shot in my portfolio." Sky expanded the page to reveal her portrait pasted in line with a number of other similarly ill-defined photos. Above the gallery of portraits were pasted the words, 'Most Wanted'.

"MOST WANTED!"

"Shh…, but yeh." Sky paused to compose herself. She looked around the room, but once again there was little need to be cautious; no-one glanced in their direction, the virtual t'ai chi class continued in the corner of the room, providing an absorbing distraction. Sky swiped the image to reveal the host site. Catherine recognised the familiar motif and distinctive colours of the Security Services public access website. "But it's not like you think. We're not all alike. Most of us are just peaceful protesters and campaigners, but we all get lumped together. It suits them to do that."

"But what about the name?" Catherine reached across and started tapping on Sky's tablet. "This name – Sherry Gilchrist. Is that your real name?"

"No, like I said, just call me Sky. There are reasons why they don't publish my real name, but don't worry about that. What's important is that we are both part of a movement seeking to claim back what has been taken from us. We're sisters in arms, we can help each other. We have people embedded everywhere."

"Everywhere?" Catherine raised her right eyebrow somewhat incredulously.

"Yes, everywhere. This thing is so huge that we need the broadest of alliances to expose it all. We're even embedded in the various institutions and organisations we are seeking to undermine."

"My dear, are you really asking me to buy into some kind of enormous conspiracy theory? Because I really don't believe in such things." Catherine's tone was somewhat patronising and dismissive, but she had to let Sky know that she was not that suggestible and that she had been around for long enough to have heard all kinds of conspiracy theories before.

"For what it's worth, neither do I. Look." Sky drew nearer to Catherine across the table to beckon her into her confidence. "I've shown you the security files, you must believe me that this is a serious business and you're dealing with serious people here, not a bunch of flat earthers or moon landing deniers."

"I believe that the threat is serious and that there really is something not quite right about the official version of events we often hear about. Something is missing, but that doesn't mean that there is a huge conspiracy operating to blind us all to the truth."

"But powerful forces are at work here," Sky insisted.

"Yes, but a conspiracy theory takes a huge amount of effort, co-ordination and resources to implement. Do you know just how leaky government departments are and how competitive and under-resourced? Most of them are utterly incapable of any systematic, coordinated action, malign or otherwise."

"No, it's not like that. I don't believe in official political conspiracies, but I do believe in economic ones."

"Meaning?"

"Meaning that Whitehall or the Security Services can't even organise a piss-up in a brewery most of the time. But if a version of the truth appears to be self-evident, if enough people tell you that there is no alternative and this is the way that things really work, then most people fall in line. Look at how panic sets in with food scares or GM or power lines causing birth defects. People quickly lose their faith in science and happily believe in all sorts of versions of the truth. We all follow the line of least resistance. If we see a bandwagon coming, we like to jump onto it."

"But this is not the same, surely?"

Sky looked a little taken aback and hurt by Catherine's scepticism. "Let me ask you a question for a change. Why are you sitting here right now?"

"What? Drinking lattes with a complete stranger. My girl, I am starting to ask myself the same question."

"No, what I mean is, why are you sitting here in a café with me right now and not undergoing a strip search in some Victorian penal institution?"

"Well, I think that's obvious. The wise and learned judge clearly understood the nature of my quest; he saw my good character and regarded my methods for seeking out the truth as symptoms of some kind of post-traumatic stress disorder arising from Josh's death."

"And you think I'm delusional! If you had any idea of the character of that judge you appeared before, then you would know just how remarkable it is that you're sat here at all."

"What d'you mean?"

"Look, there are people getting pulled off the street just for wearing the wrong kind of hoodie at the moment. There are spies in the sky, stop and search powers like we have never seen before, and you appear before one of the most formidable 'hang them high' judges in the land and get a suspended sentence. Wake up, Catherine and smell the coffee; nothing happens by chance. We took a big risk to get you out of there this morning."

"You mean…?"

"Yes."

"You…"

"Yes, we are very embedded. We have people everywhere. Influence can be brought to bear," Sky announced, her piercing eyes seemed to want to drill recognition of the truth into Catherine.

"But…but how?"

"Let's just say that I called in a few favours. A few highly placed character references."

Catherine appeared genuinely surprised. She was starting to understand that the journey she had embarked upon was a great deal more significant and complex than she had initially believed. Josh really had grasped the enormity of what was going on around him. She was not a free agent after all. She too was being played with and manipulated.

"So who can I trust?" Catherine asked.

Sky smiled, as if she had already anticipated Catherine's reaction. She surveyed the room once more and then lowered her voice a little, as she started to tap and slide her fingers quickly over her tablet. "This might not work here, you really need a more sophisticated interface, but let me see if I can show you something else."

"Not more search engine sleight of hand."

"No, not this time." Once again Sky checked the room before returning to her tablet. "You see that young man sitting on his own by the pot plant?"

"The one with the goatee beard and the shaved head?"

"Yeh, that's the one. Do you see the old-fashioned laptop he is using?"

"Yes."

"Anything strike you as unusual about it?"

"Apart from the fact that most people don't use laptops anymore?"

"No, especially people his age. Let me see if I can intercept the signal. Yes, here it is. One of our techies showed me how to do this." Sky swivelled her tablet around so that Catherine could see an image of the room in which they were sitting displayed on the screen. "This is a live feed," Sky explained in a hushed tone as she manipulated the image. Catherine could see that she and Sky featured on the moving image above a poor quality audio profile graph. "They usually don't get much in the way of quality recording by these methods – old technology mostly, but still quite popular with P.I. agencies and freelancers."

"So WE are under surveillance!"

"Yes, keep your voice down. Like I said, they often don't get any decent sound recordings at this distance. But he's using a rear-facing webcam to observe us. Oldest trick in the book. A bit like cutting a hole in a newspaper and poking a camera through it." Sky smiled and cast another glance over her shoulder. "I just happen to know how to hack into the frequencies they use."

"So he's a government spy?" Catherine whispered.

"No, not really. More like a private investigator doing a bit of speculative research in the hope that he can persuade someone to buy his findings or engage him as a freelance contractor. He probably followed you from the Law Court. It's mostly private firms these days. It's a competitive market and what they're trading is information."

"But it's still the government behind it all?"

"Not just them. Information gets traded pretty widely. We might live in a surveillance society, but when it comes to government, things are done on a very tight budget. Some of it is done directly by the security services, but when their paymasters are committed to the idea that the private sector is always a better option, you end up with someone like our friend over there trying his hand at a bit of private enterprise. It gets fairly chaotic."

"Are we in danger then?"

"No more than usual. The real danger is from those

corporations who have most to gain. They can afford to employ the best people and they have the widest reach. Best not to get on the wrong side of them." Sky could see the unease growing across Catherine's face. "Look, don't worry about that young man; he's just a hapless amateur, a speculative privateer."

"Yes, but I don't like the idea of being spied upon, no matter who's doing it."

"We're always being observed. CCTV, police drones, it's everywhere. You get used to it." Sky put down her empty coffee cup, closed down her tablet with a flick of her eye and tidied her belongings into her rucksack. She fixed Catherine with a kind and warm smile. "Look, there's someone I want you to meet, someone who might start to answer some of your questions."

"Not another spy or soft threat terrorist?"

"Neither. In fact, it's someone I think you already know."

Chapter 9

It was difficult to say when Eleanor first noticed Jez. He had probably been attending her gym for some time before he came onto her radar. There were always plenty of fit, young men hanging around, pumping iron and posing in front of the mirrors. Several had put themselves within Eleanor's personal space on a number of occasions. Some had even made the mistake of trying to impress her by inadvertently competing on the treadmill or the rowing machine. All such attempts were ultimately doomed to failure. Eleanor could always go longer and faster than most men of her own age, but it still provided much personal amusement to see prospective male suitors try to subtly take her on, only to fail in embarrassing, cardio-vascular breakdown.

Jez was different though. He wasn't the usual muscle-bound, grunting alpha male that tried to catch her eye. He appeared distant and remote, caught up in his own thoughts and routines. He didn't follow a particularly strenuous exercise routine, just a moderate work-out to give him a warm glow. He had long, auburn hair that hung in dreadlocks over his pale, freckled shoulders, a goatee beard and magnificent blue, piercing eyes. He was tall, thin, gangly and somewhat awkward. Eleanor couldn't help but notice his right arm which had a large red mark running down it, presumably the scar from a burn or else a birthmark. He looked strangely out of place in the gym environment; he resembled a little boy lost or someone who had wandered in by mistake. Every evening gym session she wondered whether he would be there. She even started to play a little game in which she would award herself points in terms of his attendance and what would take place between them. When he wasn't there, the day received just one point; when he was there but appeared not to notice her, it would be a two-point day; when he caught her eye and nodded in her direction, three points and so on.

Friday evening came at the end of a promising succession of mostly three point days and offered a first ever five-point moment of personal conversation over the water cooler. Eleanor was quenching her thirst whilst stretching in front of the fountain, when Jez came up behind her. She suddenly felt strangely nervous and self-conscious in his presence. He was hanging around and it seemed like an ideal situation to take their conversation further. She longed for him to make an approach just so she could appear cool and disinterested. Perhaps she had already crossed his radar and he had recognised her from the photograph posted on the gym's 'Wall of Achievement' display board. Surely he would be able to connect her with the smiling figure all wrapped up in climbing gear, standing at the summit of Everest, ice axe in hand.

She smiled at him in a silly, giggly, schoolgirl manner. He remained somewhat distant, appearing quite shy and uncertain of himself.

"I like your hair." Eleanor blurted out the first thing that came into her mind, then immediately regretted it. Why couldn't she have waited for him to speak or at least have said something more sophisticated by way of an introduction?

"Yeh, thanks…I don't do a lot with it. Just low maintenance

mostly." Fortunately, Jez didn't appear too concerned by Eleanor's frankness.

Eleanor knew that she couldn't leave the conversation there. "How do you get it into those dreadlocks then?" She couldn't believe that she was having a conversation about hair care with a bloke!

"Oh, just a lot of plaiting and a bit of gel." Jez was now looking a lot more uneasy. "My name's Jez, by the way, short for Jeremy. What's yours?"

"Oh, Ellie, short for Eleanor." Eleanor never introduced herself as Ellie to men. She usually reserved that name for her long-standing girlfriends.

"Hi, Ellie. Together we could make 'Jelly', couldn't we?" Jez forced a pun to break the tension. Eleanor smiled, but more out of politeness than recognition. It was increasingly obvious that he too was struggling with the social conventions surrounding getting to know a stranger. "I mean, Jez and Ellie. You know, our names, 'Jelly'. Not that we would er… you know…just a joke." Jez was rambling incoherently and turning an even deeper shade of crimson than the usual hue he took on when exercising.

"What happened to your arm, if you don't mind me asking?" Eleanor recognised he needed rescuing from his own rambling and therefore took the initiative.

"Oh, you noticed."

"Sorry, couldn't help it."

"Yeh, a birthmark. It doesn't bother me or anything, but I guess it's a bit striking."

"Maybe having something like that just makes you a bit different. Something special."

"Yeh, I hadn't really thought about it like that, but yeh, maybe you've got a point."

"You're not the only one."

"I'm sorry?"

"You're not the only one dealing with stuff like that," Eleanor explained while reaching down to reveal her prosthetic foot beneath her leggings. "Hasn't held me back much over the years," she added, tapping her foot to demonstrate its carbon fibre composition and still hoping he would connect her with the girl in the mountaineering photo over his shoulder.

"Oh, I'm sorry. I had no idea." Jez looked surprised, yet also sympathetic.

"Don't be. You get used to it," Eleanor replied with a growing sense of confidence.

"Right. Yeh." Jez appeared to diminish in her presence, unsure of how to respond. He hadn't expected Eleanor to make the running like she was doing. He looked nervously around the room, then back to Eleanor and then looked down at the floor. "Umm…I was wondering…"

"Yes," replied Eleanor emphatically.

"Yes, what?"

"Yes, I would like to meet up for a drink tonight."

"But I wasn't going to…umm…ask…yes, oh gosh…why not? Do you know the Irish pub at the corner of Hamilton Street?"

"No, but I can find it. How about 9.00pm?"

"Uh…yep, should be fine.…er…see you later." Jez turned to leave, not really sure who had asked whom on the date. As he made his way into the male changing room, he cast a final glance back at Eleanor who was still stretching and lunging besides the water cooler. He had managed to fix a date with the hottest girl at the gym without even trying.

Later that evening Eleanor located Mulligan's Bar on the corner of Hamilton Street, having deliberately arrived ten minutes late in order to make her appear a little less desperate than she really was. She pushed her way through a crowd of football shirted fans engrossed in some important match. Jez was sitting in a remote corner, looking slightly anxious and playing with a beer mat. She longed for him to be wearing a smart business suit over which his cascading auburn locks would be hanging casually while he played with a set of Ferrari keys – such a perfect combination, suggesting power and responsibility, yet with a frivolous disregard for social conventions. However, he was just wearing a slightly scruffy jumper, baggy jeans and a beanie hat, under which he had hidden his long dreadlocks. He was difficult to place in a tribe and he wasn't displaying any particularly recognisable brands to help locate him. Maybe he had something of the eco-warrior chic about him, although he didn't appear to be someone who was particularly concerned about identifying his brands or declaring his tribe.

Eleanor sidled over to him, initially unobserved. He appeared genuinely pleased to see her, although a little apprehensive. They exchanged awkward greetings, not knowing whether to shake hands, kiss on the cheek or kiss on both cheeks. In the end, they did neither and ended up bowing to each other and banging foreheads before sitting down.

Eleanor was used to the company of strong and competitive men, but there was something about Jez that appeared otherworldly and dreamy which she found appealing. He was also gentle and well-mannered, which was in contrast to the aggressive and often foul-mouthed men she usually dated. There was something mysterious and distant about him. He kept saying, 'Yeh, cool' in response to everything she asked him, but more in a knowing way rather than in seeking to make a good impression.

"So, how long have you been going to the gym then?" Jez asked after returning from the bar with a large white wine for Eleanor.

Eleanor thought that Jez might just be making conversation. She usually got noticed in the gym, if not for aesthetic reasons than for sporting ones. After all, she had conquered Everest and K2. Not many women had done that and her picture was posted on the 'Wall of Achievement' above the water cooler. However, she realised that Jez was entirely genuine and hadn't apparently noticed her as much as she had noticed him. "Quite some time. When I'm in the UK, I usually come down fairly regularly."

"So, d'you travel much with your work?"

"Not so much recently. I'm fortunate that I don't have to work too much. Dad's got a trust fund that supports me. I just help out in the family business when I can."

"What sort of business is that then?" Jez enquired.

"Property management. We've got quite a large portfolio, hence the trust fund. I help out with some site management work, mostly care and maintenance."

"So what takes you abroad? Holidays?"

"Kinda, more sport and recreation."

"What like netball or hockey?"

"No, a bit more extreme than that"

"Don't tell me you're a rugby player. You look too slight for that."

"No, I mean I do extreme sports. I used to do climbing and mountaineering, along with a bit of modelling and some sponsored corporate blogging."

"Modelling?"

"Yeh, you know, mostly sportswear. They like it when you're hanging off a cliff in their brand of trainers, especially when one of their trainers is strapped onto a carbon fibre prosthetic."

"Yeh. Cool. So, what extreme sports d'you do?"

"Mostly base jumping and wing suit flying."

"So that's a competitive sport these days?"

"Not exactly. To be honest, most of it is pretty illegal and subversive. We like to find increasingly bizarre locations: iconic buildings, bridges, places you're not meant to get access to. Then we film ourselves jumping off and upload the clips to popular sites, which people then circulate. If we manage to pull off something spectacular, then we get a lot of hits and end up making some money from it."

"Oh, well, keeps you off the streets, I suppose."

Jez was clearly someone who was going to be difficult to impress. He would be a far more challenging conquest for Eleanor than any of the peaks she had scaled or buildings she had launched herself off. "You might have seen the one we did in Sydney?"

"Sorry." Jez shook his head.

"That went viral. Didn't you see the group of people who jumped off the Harbour Bridge and managed to circle the Opera House before landing?"

"No. Should I? Was that you then?"

"One of them was."

"Did you get into trouble for it?"

"Not really, we usually do it in the middle of the night when there aren't too many police around. Sometimes you get caught, but mostly it's just a caution or a night in a cell and then they let you go. Once we did a set-up for some sportswear company. A sort of promotional, viral video – everyone was in on it, even the police, although it looked kinda subversive."

"Yeh, cool."

As the evening wore on, it became increasingly apparent that Eleanor and Jez occupied very different worlds. The distance between those two worlds seemed to shrink as their conversation continued. Eleanor ended up talking a lot about her childhood and living with her disability. The more she came to know Jez, the less she felt the need to explain her past triumphs and challenges, and the more she noticed how he responded to her with no trace of judgment or jealousy. He spoke very little about himself, other than the fact that he was brought up in Newcastle, was the only child of a single mother and that he worked with challenging young people.

Finally, Jez turned the focus of conversation upon Eleanor's personal motivation. "So, Ellie, I hope you don't mind me asking, but why do you put yourself in such dangerous situations? Life can be fairly dangerous as it stands, without wanting to load the dice even more."

"Well, you know how it is. I just like to push the envelope… challenge myself…experience something new."

"But you could do that painting in water colours. Why throw yourself off tall buildings?"

"Maybe I want to prove something to the people around me."

"Which people?"

"Blokes mostly, but the able-bodied generally, I suppose." She had never really reflected upon her own motivation in such a way before, but now, for some reason, in the company of this relative stranger she found herself strangely compelled to speak the truth.

"Have you ever felt…you know, really scared?"

"No, not really."

"Not even in the death zone on Everest?"

"Well, maybe there, but the only time I felt utterly beyond my comfort zone, I didn't feel afraid at all."

"When was that?"

Eleanor then proceeded to explain to Jez her recent experience in Norway, including what she had seen and felt while she was unconscious. Jez just listened, asking the occasional incisive question. His attitude was in sharp contrast to many of her girlfriends. He didn't seem surprised at anything she told him and kept saying things like, 'awesome', 'that must have been so cool' and 'what a privilege'. He appeared neither surprised nor dismissive and, in contrast to Nicola, he didn't have a ready prepared set of explanations. She even told him about Nicola and her visit to the Assembly Building with all its merchandising on offer.

"Yes, I've been to some of those places. So sad what's become of them," Jez observed.

"I'm starting to have doubts about lots of things."

"Yes, I saw your T-shirt. Quite controversial."

Eleanor proudly pushed out her chest to make sure that Jez could read the 'Say No to brands' logo on her sports shirt. Even if he didn't approve, then at least he would be forced to examine her breasts. "Yeh, probably a step too far, but I just like to wind up my sponsors by posting a few selfies on my blog. Creates a bit more traffic. It all trickles back on my side."

"Doesn't that get you in trouble with the sponsors?"

"Yes, with some of them. A couple have withdrawn their support and there's been a few threats, but it's all a game. They're just ticking boxes – the extreme sports market is too valuable for them to cut off their noses to spite their faces."

Just then Jez's mobile rang and he immersed himself deep in conversation in a language she didn't recognise and asked to be excused as he wandered off across the bar seeking a quieter location. While Jez was away, a bar steward approached the tables offering oxygen. Eleanor decided to indulge herself. She was just starting to enjoy the oxygen hit and feel energized and alert once again when Jez returned.

"I didn't know you took O2."

"Only occasionally. It came in useful at altitude and now they have these portable bottles on offer in bars, I like to take a bit when I can. It perks me up no end. Do you want some?"

"Uh, no thanks. Some of the kids we see at work use it." Jez spoke in such a way that suggested that this was therefore not something he would want to copy. "They tend to mix it with other things though. We've had a few problems."

"OK. Please yourself." Eleanor felt a little put down

117

morally by Jez's comment. It was only oxygen after all. We all need oxygen. She didn't see any danger in taking a little supplement now and then.

Jez looked at her apologetically with sadness in his eyes. "Look, this has been really cool, but I'm afraid that I've got to go. Maybe we can do this again some time?"

Disappointment engulfed Eleanor. She felt as though she had been led up the garden path, only to have the door slammed in her face. She was not accustomed to men who weren't in a hurry to go the whole way with her. "Oh, okay then. I thought...I thought that..."

"Thought what?"

"I thought that you might want to come back for coffee or something. I live quite nearby."

"Oh that's really kind, but I don't drink coffee."

"Well no, I don't much at this time of night. It was a euphemism. Look." Eleanor paused and looked around the bar. She didn't want other people to see what might appear to be the desperate act of a frustrated woman. "Do I have to spell this out for you?"

"Spell what out?"

"Coffee...my place...the whole routine."

"Yes, but I explained, I don't drink coffee."

"Look, have you ever been with someone before?"

"Been with? Yes, lots of people."

"No, I mean, physically been with." Eleanor was feeling increasingly embarrassed and not a little frustrated. What planet did this bloke live on and why did he not respond to her signals?

"Oh, you mean sex?"

"Yes."

"But we've only just met and I..."

"So what? It's what happens all the time. Look, you're not gay, are you?"

"Gay? No, I shouldn't think that I am, although I know lots of people who are."

"So have I misread what's happening here? Do you like me or not? Are we getting it together or just wasting each other's time?"

"I think…I think…." Jez seemed to be knocked off balance by Eleanor's direct approach. "I think you're wonderful, remarkable and gorgeous, but more than that I think that you are a very special person who's been given a special gift. But… sex, well that's something different. That's serious. Do you want to have sex in order to be friends or can we try a different approach?"

"Well, yes, making love is always a good place to start."

"But it's not the only place to start."

Eleanor was aware that this conversation was reflecting very badly on her. She was usually the one fighting off men or else finding new locations and ways to explore the labyrinth of sexual ecstasy with a series of willing lovers. She had never felt the need to justify such behaviour before, and she certainly wasn't prepared to beg for sexual favours, no matter how she felt about him.

"Look, if that's what you want out of our relationship, then you've probably misread me. I'm not that sort of bloke. And sex? Well, I have a particular position in regard to such things. But I think that you are pretty amazing. So, if you want to get in touch again, then this is my number." Jez slid a calling card towards Eleanor. She hadn't seen a calling card for years. It contained his contact details, along with a quirky, pencil-drawn cartoon portrait.

Despite her best efforts, Eleanor was sounding somewhat desperate and although she was not proud of the fact, neither was she prepared to be brushed off without a fuller explanation. "What d'you mean about having a 'particular position in regard to such things'? I thought you said you weren't gay?"

"I'm not. Look, you need to know that I've left a lot of things behind me in order to make certain commitments. Let's just leave it at that. But do call me." Eleanor's disappointment was plain to see. "Promise?"

"Yeh, yeh, I promise." Eleanor realised that she wasn't going to get the result she had hoped for with Jez. Not this time certainly. She had finally been outmanoeuvred by a bloke and her pride as well as her dignity was fractured.

The next week passed awkwardly for Eleanor. Her attention was still focused upon Jez. He was increasingly enigmatic and intriguing to her. She wanted to hate him and tell him where to get off with all his high-minded principles and *'I don't do that sort of thing'* put-down. After all, who did he think he was? This was the twenty twenties, not the nineteen twenties. She could have any man she chose and was certainly capable of showing him a trick or two in the bedroom department. He was just a boy really, someone who should be flattered by her attention and grateful for her consideration. And yet, as much as she wanted to hate him, dismiss him and rid him from her life, she just couldn't. He constantly occupied her waking thoughts and her dreamy moments.

In an attempt to move on, or at least to restore her wounded pride and self-confidence, she found herself flirting with a complete stranger she met in a local bar. She knew that one-night stands could be dangerous, but before she knew it he was inviting her back to his riverside apartment. Thankfully he turned out to be a fairly harmless guy and quite an accomplished lover. He also turned out to be married, not that that was a new experience for Eleanor. It just felt exciting to receive male attention once more and the night of passion that passed between them reassured her that she had not lost her allure. Although Jez would not have been aware of her liaison, she felt that she had stuck a secret blow against him whilst proving to herself that she was in charge of her love life and not the exclusive property of any one individual.

Despite her impetuous one-night stand Eleanor still felt incomplete, as if she was yearning for something she couldn't have. She realised just how much Jez was coming to mean to her, or rather how much what he represented was coming to mean to her. He still remained something of a blank canvas, albeit one that was frustratingly unavailable, and yet she couldn't help but feel a grudging respect for him for turning down her advances. She shared some of the details of the episode with a couple of her girlfriends in a secure video chatroom.

"Ellie, are you telling me that you got turned down by a young carrot top?" Gill was virtually shrieking in dismay over the video link.

"No, he's not a proper ginger and it wasn't quite like that."

"He must be gay. Must be," Gill insisted.

"No, he isn't. He really isn't. He's just different. Very different."

"What's his tribe then? He sounds really out there."

"I don't know his tribe or his brands. I don't think he does either. He doesn't seem bothered by such things," Eleanor explained.

"You'd better watch that one, love. You know what they say: 'What's the difference between a ginger boy and a house brick? At least a house brick gets laid.'"

Gill could be very cruel. However, this time her note of caution didn't ring true with Eleanor. Jez had a mysterious quality about him, and she was learning to embrace the mysterious side of her life. Furthermore, he seemed to take her experiences seriously and such confidants were hard to find. Rather than feeling threatened by him, she just felt utterly secure in his company.

Eleanor still saw Jez at the gym, mostly for two or three

point days. They exchanged polite nods of recognition across the treadmills and cross-trainers, but avoided long conversations. Eleanor kept his calling card and would often roll it between her fingers on an evening at home as she deliberated whether to call him or not. One night she was leaving the gym a bit later than normal. She made her way into the underground car park where her eco-car was re-charging. As she rounded the corner of a line of parked cars, the silence of the basement was broken by a screech of tyres as a bright arc of headlights advanced towards her. In a startled response, she dropped her car keys, after retrieving them she looked up to see a large black car bearing down on her. Suddenly she felt a hand on her shoulder pulling her back to safety between two parked cars. As she fell to the floor, she gazed directly into the face of Jez, who was now holding her down firmly.

"Keep down. They're probably just trying to scare you."

"They've succeeded," Eleanor replied while trying to catch her breath. "Look, I can handle myself, thank you."

"I'm sure you can. But I reckon you can also use some help." Jez's voice was calm but firmer than previously, displaying an authority and assurance beyond his years. She had never seen him like this before.

"D'you want to tell me what on earth is going on here?"

"I'm not entirely sure, but take it from me, you need to take care. You're on a gold surveillance list."

"A gold what?"

"Surveillance list. It relates to levels of threat and permission to advance action. Bronze is mostly interceptions and monitoring. Silver is shadowing and, if necessary, preventative action. Gold is shadowing, evaluation of threat and permission to be proactive."

"Just who the hell are you and how d'you know all this stuff?" Eleanor was suddenly seeing Jez in a whole new light. His tone was different. It was colder, modulated and authoritative. He was starting to scare her

"I'm just a guardian. I've been shadowing you for a few months now, ever since we discovered that you were under gold surveillance."

Eleanor pushed Jez away and rose defiantly to her feet. A million thoughts rushed through her mind as she struggled to form a coherent line of questioning, yet an overwhelming realisation crystallized in her mind. "You have been stalking me all this time?"

"No, not stalking you, more maintaining a watching brief. Your blogging has caused quite a stir, you know. I don't think your sponsors are as cool about your 'no brands' campaign as you think. You've opened up a whole can of worms that certain people would rather not be opened. You're not quite the valuable asset you think you are. You're more of a target."

"Target? What the hell is going on here and whose side are you on?"

"I'm on your side. I'm with the good guys."

"But just who are you?"

"Like I said," Jez paused to survey the car park for any further threats, "I'm just a guardian who's trying to keep you safe."

"Safe? Safe from what?"

"From things like this."

"Look, I can take care of myself. I don't need any guardian or protector." Eleanor was now turning her anger away from the car and its driver and towards Jez.

"I don't think you realise just how much danger you are in," Jez replied firmly.

"Well, sorry for not noticing," Eleanor announced ironically. "Maybe I didn't notice because I was just too much in l... too smitten by your charm and boyish good looks... Aaagghh..." Eleanor stormed off, pacing out angrily towards where she had left her eco-car. Immediately she froze at the sight of her vehicle. The words "WW2L4E – ARRANGEMENTS CAN BE MADE" were written across the windscreen and, where the charging nozzle was attached to the car, red drops of blood had been spray-painted dripping down the body of the car. Eleanor just stood there, rooted to the spot, mouth open in shock.

"Look. When are you going to get it?" Jez was standing beside her.

"You knew about this?"

"No, but it doesn't surprise me. This is serious, Eleanor. You need protecting."

"Oh, I get it. I get it all right. Now I understand why you didn't want to sleep with me. I'm your assignment. You don't mind a little socialising and gentle flirting, but you mustn't touch the goods because I am some kind of target who needs protecting. Well, let me tell you something, this target doesn't need you or whoever you work for to chaperone me. I've done scarier things than dodging speeding cars and this new paint job doesn't intimidate me. I don't need your help, not now… or ever!"

"OK. OK. But at least use this app. It will prevent your position being revealed every time your mobile is roaming." Jez offered Eleanor one of his business cards. On the back was a web address that Eleanor didn't recognise.

"I don't need your gadgets to protect me." Eleanor screwed up the card and threw it on the floor.

"I'm sorry, Ellie. I didn't mean to deceive you. But just understand that everything I did was because I thought you were so special. I still think that you are one amazing lady, but if you really want to know why I've been keeping an eye on you and why there are people out there trying to rub you out, then come with me now, Ellie." Jez held Eleanor's hands in his and looked deeply into her eyes. "Come with me because

I don't doubt that you can look after yourself, but you are part of something much bigger than yourself."

"You know what?" Eleanor replied furiously, "I'd rather take my chances with that speeding car and the graffiti artist. I've managed perfectly well in the past and I'll manage again. In fact, Jez, I don't need you or anyone else in my life. So, you can take your surveillance lists, your guardian role and your moral high ground and shove it up your arse."

With that Eleanor snatched away her hand.

Jez lowered his gaze. Like a punctured ball, he appeared to deflate in front of her. He turned and slowly, reluctantly walked away without casting a backward glance.

Chapter 10

A large crowd had gathered in Oxford Street, spilling out onto the road and blocking trams and buses as they intersected shoppers drawn by the gravitational pull of one of the country's few remaining high street retail centres. The enthusiasm of the crowd was undiminished by the driving rain, wind and hail associated with a sudden, summer storm. Underfoot, cardboard boxes laid crumpled and discarded sleeping bags wrapped around the legs of participants oblivious to their presence and significance. All faces were turned towards a brightly lit, glazed atrium, illuminated by flashing lights, neon signs, crisscrossing lasers and iridescent visual display units. The lighting displays emanating from the building were in sharp contrast to the greyness of the surrounding street scene, as it succumbed to the full fury of a summer storm. The gathering crowd seemed to attract more and more interest from passers-by as the light display grew in intensity and synchronized with a thumping musical backing track. A growing sense of expectancy gripped the assembled rain-soaked crowd in what resembled the build-up to an impromptu open air rock concert.

Visual displays started to flicker into life. Large laser

configured numbers appeared in mid-air over the pavement, falling sequentially in a countdown towards a future euphoric hiatus. The company logo was elevated from street level to a prominent position above the entrance to the building, accompanied by huge cheers and whoops of acclamation. At the same time, fluorescent company logos were illuminated on the clothing of randomly dispersed company employees secreted amongst the gathering crowd. Immediately each employee's illuminated clothing started to pulsate in time to the music and the synchronized countdown. Clouds of dry ice billowed out from the building entrance, framing the coloured lights and contorting the illuminated shapes formed by the lasers. An unseen detached voice erupted onto the public address system:

"London, are you ready?"

The crowd murmured in approval.

"I said, London, ARE...YOU...READYYYYYY?"

"YES." The crowd suddenly found its shared voice and common identity.

Finch had never seen a product launch like this before. He joined the perimeter of a throng of damp, expectant people, many of whom appeared oblivious to the pouring rain. He craned his head above the crowd to try and locate the faceless announcer in order to discover what was about to happen.

"We know it's raining, but it won't be long until you're inside and you can witness this amazing event. Just twenty seconds to go now.... Let's hear you make some noise."

The crowd responded with collective instinct to the invocation, releasing whoops of joy and squeals of excitement.

"It's getting close now.... Let me hear you." The announcer clearly had a hearing impediment. "All together now. TEN, NINE..." The crowd cheerfully joined in with him. "FIVE, FOUR, THREE, TWO, O...N...E..." At that point fireworks exploded from the roof of the building, more dry ice was released amidst coloured spotlights and strobe lighting. "Come on now. It's finally here. Who is our brand?"

The crowd replied in unison, "GOBLE! GOBLE!"

"Who connects us to the world?"

"GOBLE! GOBLE!"

"Who shapes our future?"

"GOBLE! GOBLE!"

"Whose tribe do we belong to?"

"GOBLE! GOBLE!"

"Who makes us the people we are?" The announcer was clearly overplaying his part, yet no-one seemed to notice or to mind.

"GOBLE! GOBLE!"

"London! Are you ready for GOBLE Six?"

"YES." The crowd's patience and excitement apparently undimmed.

"I said, are you ready for GOBLE Six?" The announcer's hearing had apparently not improved.

"Y....... E.......S!!"

"Then enter and experience GOBLE's amazing new connectivity range....The future..." – the announcer paused for dramatic effect – "starts... here."

At that signal the glass doors were thrown open to what was clearly a technology store. Somewhere inside a trumpet fanfare was sounded by two incongruously located buglers in full ceremonial military uniform, but their shrill notes were soon drowned out by the cheers of the crowd and the noise generated by a surge of wet bodies anxious to gain access to the building and get inside out of the pouring rain. Staff manning the doors were inelegantly brushed aside in what became an energetic stampede of humans obsessed by one goal. Others inside attempted to 'high five' those arriving in the store, but soon became overwhelmed by the sheer volume of animated shoppers.

Finch held back, not wishing to be crushed in the surge of euphoria. He was not there in order to avail himself of the latest smartphone technology; his reasons for attendance were far more subversive. Once inside, he walked the gauntlet of uniformed attendants, eager to 'high five' him on every step of his journey. A glossy leaflet was thrust into his hands. *'Embrace the future. GOBLE Six is going to change your life!'* he was reassuringly informed by a young female attendant with various face piercings.

"Only if it's got an app for influencing a casino wheel," he replied ironically.

Finch desperately wanted to change his life. He realised that something was missing. Perhaps that was why he was drawn into the solitary world of online gaming. He was looking for something bigger than himself to change his life, something to enlarge his imagination and reinvigorate his sense of purpose. In the past he had been energised by the thrill of the pursuit, the idea that he was contributing towards some greater public good and making a difference by exposing corruption, highlighting injustice or holding the powerful to account. He had never replaced the buzz that a well-researched story brought him. Many of those he confronted in his investigations were risk takers at heart, taking a chance with the fortunes of others, yet now he was the risk taker, chancing his own fortune in order to reproduce that glow of recognition and achievement. No electronic gadget or technological breakthrough could provide such an adrenalin hit. He needed this assignment more than he needed a big pay out from any gaming website. He wanted to feel significant again, to feel needed and to have something less self-destructive to hope for.

The pounding of dance music intensified as he scanned the technology store, looking for his contact. He could just about make out individual voices raised above the thumping musical soundtrack, sharing testimonials about the amazing new features and cleaner design. Everywhere energised young adults and teenagers were pushing their way towards payment points and delivery zones, armed either with plastic or clutching their 'GOBLE Five' mobiles in order to swipe payment for the latest model upgrade to GOBLE Six.

Finch managed to isolate one of the uniformed attendants who appeared to be more senior than his 'high fiving' colleagues and enquired about the whereabouts of his contact. He was directed towards a spiral staircase that led onto a VIP lounge apparently reserved for special guests and celebrity users. Once upstairs he passed through glass doors into the comparative calm and quiet of the hospitality centre. Waitresses in short skirts with fixed smiles were circulating with canapés and pink champagne. He declined the former, but accepted the latter.

"Do you know where Buzz is?" he enquired of one of the fixed smiles, but she just gazed blankly in his vague direction. It was clear that English was not one of her preferred languages. She looked so young, yet distant, almost controlled and unable to engage or reflect any humanity. He suspected that she might be from one of the hidden communities of migrant workers, lured to London by the promise of a rewarding career in hospitality. She probably had a PhD in Bio-Engineering from the University of Budapest, but here she was just another intern hospitality worker, another victim of economic migration.

Finally, Finch was able to find a member of staff who knew where Buzz hung out. He was then led through the VIP lounge along an anonymous-looking corridor and shown into a workshop of benches and cubicles. At one desk sat a rather large man of indeterminate Asian origin, hunched over a partly-assembled server board. Bluey-grey swirls of cigarette smoke hung over his frame, refusing to disperse. Finch tried unsuccessfully to attract his attention until he realised that the man was wearing headphones and conducting a Skyped conversation to an unseen contact in a foreign language. Finch attracted his attention by tapping on his rather sweaty shoulder. He turned around slowly and waved an acknowledgement, flicking cigarette ash over the desk in the process. He was clearly not given to effusive greetings.

Once his Skype call had finished, the man turned around, extinguished a miserable-looking roll-up and removed his headset.

"Are you the server salesman?" he asked.

"No, I'm the reporter," Finch replied, forcing a smile. "And you must be…Buzz?" Finch's expression betrayed his puzzlement.

"Yeh, I know it's a strange name. Don't blame me, blame my parents and that whole Toy Story thing that was going on at the time."

Having offered a not entirely unnecessary explanation of his name, Buzz looked around the room, examining its various partitions for evidence that they were alone. "We need to get somewhere we can talk more freely, if you know what I mean." There was no need. It seemed that the rest of the technical support department was caught up in the product launch, but Finch was happy to be directed back along the corridor to a small, acoustically sealed room.

"This should be safe," Buzz explained. "It's not just busybodies listening in, you also have to think about electronic surveillance. They've got software that can use any piece of hardware as a listening device."

"Does that happen a lot?" Finch enquired.

"Often enough. Usually for commercial advantage in this place, but…you know, you can't be too careful."

"It sounds as though you are the man I need to see."

"Maybe, but look, let's get one thing straight. I'm not political. I don't do protest. I'm just here because Greg went to college with my Dad and is a decent sort of bloke. It's out of my respect for him. I don't care what your agenda is and I don't want to know."

"Consider it done." Finch was happy to reassure Buzz. Having a straightforward business arrangement with a source was always preferable to one tainted by a political cause or personal interest. In truth, he did not understand his own motivation and why he was being drawn into a world of commercial data warfare. At one time the adrenalin of a big scoop would get him out of bed in the mornings. Yet since he had drifted away from investigative journalism, his passion had dimmed. Perhaps that was why he gambled? Both offered ways to beat the system, to put one over the big guy. However, he was no longer the same driven moral crusader, just someone trying to deliver a contract and keep his paymasters happy.

Buzz picked up a pen from the desk and started twirling it between his fingers in the manner of a marching band majorette. "So I gather you want to attempt a data dump?"

"Yeh, if that is possible."

"Everything is possible. Not everything is doable."

It wasn't the first time that Finch has found himself at the mercy of a gatekeeper to a mysterious technological universe. People like Buzz reminded him of the technical whizz kids who had started to inhabit his former profession. In their presence he always felt like an ignorant schoolboy on his first day at a new school, when everyone else already knew the rules and the world appeared a strange and unsettling place.

"So how do you want to play this then?" Buzz enquired, reminding Finch that he was here to perform a task.

"What d'you mean?"

"Well, doing a data dump has a number of risks attached."

"Such as?"

"Well, let me show you something." Buzz switched on a large VDU sitting on the desk in front of him and immediately starting to tap and swipe at the screen of his mobile. Eventually the large flat screen flickered into life. "Data is currency. It is valuable and can be traded. So people like to protect it, right?"

"Yeh, sure. Isn't that why we all use virtual clouds these days?" Finch didn't want to display the extent of his ignorance too soon in their conversation. Giving an impression of some familiarity was always preferable to handing over the entire narrative to a technical expert.

"It is, but don't be fooled. This is one of the least secure ways of storing data that's been used since a Roman librarian thought it would be a good idea to put all their ancient parchments in one library whilst the Barbarians were camped at the city gates."

"So what's the problem with the cloud then?"

"Plenty. It sounds secure to store data offsite on some anonymous virtual server, but in truth all things have to exist somewhere in space and in time. In the case of the Van Hegel Corporation that means here." At this point Buzz tapped his mobile and a street map appeared on screen. He immediately converted the map into a real-time satellite image and zoomed in on a large, secure warehouse situated on what appeared to be an urban trading estate.

"And here is…?"

"Here is an industrial estate on the outskirts of Slough. Looks pretty ordinary, right?"

"*Come friendly bombs and fall on Slough! It isn't fit for humans now.*" Finch found himself narrating one of his favourite poems.

"Sorry?" Buzz was clearly none the wiser.

"Slough, you know, *'Come friendly bombs'*. The Betjeman poem? Yes?"

"Na." Buzz dismissed Finch's comments with the disdain reserved for swatting away an irritant fly. He was clearly more familiar with ancient history than literary references and was far more focused on continuing his technical lecture. "In this one building is located one of the main servers that holds the data not only for the Van Hegel Corporation, but also for a large number of other pharmaceuticals, bio-engineering companies, telemarketing businesses and a few less well-regarded universities."

"Not any of the banks then?"

"Oh no, they outsourced to China and the Far East years ago. They don't like western governments knowing too much about where they have hidden all the debris from their misadventures."

"But aren't these places really secure and well protected?"

"It depends on what you mean by secure."

"Well, free from people gaining access to all your personal data."

"There's personal data and there's personal data."

"I'm sorry?" Finch tried to hide his frustration with the oblique explanations that Buzz was offering. "Isn't the cloud meant to be more secure than everybody keeping their personal data on their own hard drives?"

"No, of course not. The cloud is just a way to free up storage space, so that your devices can handle more increasingly data hungry applications. They aren't secure, just convenient."

"I see."

"I don't think you do." Buzz was now talking down to Finch in the slightly condescending tone that children reserve for their parents when they have to explain something they are unable to grasp. "The cloud is just a device for the convenience of providers, not users. It frees up space so that they can sell you even more complicated digital toys you didn't know you wanted and it also allows the large software providers to sell commercial information to all sorts of interested third parties, multi-national corporations, governments, third sector providers, even what remains of the National Health Service."

The look of puzzlement upon Finch's face betrayed his

continued state of ignorance. "Do you mean our spending patterns and online preferences?"

"Precisely. Every computer has a unique, dedicated code number and these show up every time we go online to download an app, view pornography or order our groceries. We leave a digital audit trail which is very easy for software packages to recognise and use to build purchasing and lifestyle profiles. Keeping everything on a cloud makes such information a lot easier to gather."

"But isn't that illegal?"

"Not as such. Why d'you think governments aren't keen to regulate digital information?"

"But it is unethical."

"Suppose so, if you believe in such things."

"So how do they get away with it?"

"That's easy. They've found a cunning way of managing the problem."

"What's that then?"

"They don't tell anyone." Buzz cracked a smile, the sort that makes you question whether you have been played for a fool or offered some important insight.

"So hacking into one of these clouds should be quite easy then?"

"Not as such. The people who operate these large servers still like to keep out the wrong sort of prying eyes."

"So how do we get in?"

"By accessing the data at the weakest point of its protection."

"And that is?"

Buzz cast Finch a weary look as if he was growing tired of providing explanations. "When someone is coming around with the equivalent of a digital mop and bucket to carry out routine maintenance." Buzz's tone indicated the self-evident nature of what he was describing.

"That's when we can carry out the data dump?"

"Yep, but data dumping is by nature very imprecise. Getting hold of data must take place at a regular IT service interval; yet organising, sifting and searching that data to remove all the crap that will overload and burn out your data receivers – well, that's where the clever stuff happens."

"Define "clever stuff." Finch realised that he was way out of his league in relation to understanding virtual data access. He had assumed that it would be possible to remotely gain access to the data archive and just go looking for the relevant material.

"We need a sophisticated data extraction tool that can hide within a virus scan programme. That's not usually a problem, but you will also need software that can handle that volume of data without setting off any internal firewall alarms and then return the data to where you extracted it without leaving a digital fingerprint. Then you'll need some fairly advanced search engine to sift through that data and someone who can define the parameters for the search in real time so that the whole process doesn't take all night."

"Hmmm. I see what you mean."

"That's not all. We will also need someone who can provide the access codes to the database as well as providing a cover for someone to get into this server warehouse and start all the electronic mop and bucket stuff."

"And the good news is…?"

"The good news is that this warehouse is operated by one of our clients and I know a bloke who owns a mop and bucket company. All the other stuff is doable, but it doesn't come cheap."

"My client has some fairly deep pockets. I'm sure that money won't be a problem." By now Finch was winging it; half of the money provided by the mysterious art-loving stranger had already been frittered away on sundry expenses and gaming debts. He just hoped that there was enough remaining to secure the technical services of Buzz and his friends.

"Yeh, but the real problem is working with the weakest point in such a project."

"And what would be that weakest point?"

"I'm looking at it right now." Buzz had fixed Finch was a steely, suspicious stare. "You are, or rather you and me. It's easy to make mistakes in this process and leave behind a fingerprint that others can detect. That's why you need my genius. But I also need someone to handle the data search in real time and that means knowing your brief and not panicking if we start to run out of access time. D'you think you can handle that pressure?"

"Don't worry," Finch reassured him, "I'm your man."

Chapter 11

The enormity of the task facing him had started to dawn on Finch. He was working in a world he barely understood, trying to use twentieth century journalistic tools to unlock twenty-first century secrets. He longed for the days when he could interrogate accounts at Company House or in the House of Commons library or doorstep conniving public officials or reluctant politicians with evidence that demanded their response. He was standing on the edge of something highly toxic with secrets buried so deep that even the questions to unlock them had become secrets themselves. Perhaps some sleeping dogs are better left to lie. Any truth that required an act of industrial espionage to expose it and a bonded warehouse to contain its extent, clearly didn't want to be found.

Buzz drove the electric utility vehicle up to a steel fence. It was 2am and the site was deserted, apart from a rather bored-looking security guard who swiped the security passes that Buzz had secured from an internal source.

"Usual routine again?" the guard enquired.

"Yeh, same old things. You know how they love their system sweeps."

"Yeh. Doesn't seem long since the last one," the guard added as the steel gate slowly slid to one side, accompanied by orange flashing lights.

"Long enough," Buzz replied, exchanging a knowing look with Finch.

Five minutes later they were inside an ordinary-looking warehouse. Large cooling mechanisms and fans throbbed overhead, keeping the servers in top condition. Featureless racks of black, reflective polycarbonate encased row after row of silicon circuitry. Sections of lighting burst into life as they walked between the racks of servers, only to dim behind them as they exited each section. The building felt strangely cold as air-conditioned blasts of air descended upon them. They arrived at a computer terminal nestled within a small, acoustically isolated cabin. Buzz broke out his toolkit and produced a rather battered-looking laptop along with a mobile phone, various hard drives, cables and different-sized black boxes.

"Is that it?" Finch enquired.

"What did you expect?"

"I don't know. Something a bit more…high tech? Especially given what I've been paying you."

"This is all we need from here on. This is the really clever stuff." Buzz was waving a small data stick. "This contains some basic virus scanning software." He then proceeded to plug the data stick into the computer console. "It's coupled to this decoder and scrubbing device, so that no prying eyes will notice what we're doing." He then connected the device to his mobile and the laptop along with an external hard drive. "We then data dump everything into here. Hope it doesn't burn out the motherboard or set off too many alarms before sending it to…" – he then produced a tablet computer – "…this search engine, where you get to ask all the relevant questions in real time before returning the data, hopefully unnoticed, to the main server."

"You make it sound very straightforward. Have you done many of these procedures before?" Finch enquired.

"No, this is my first time," replied Buzz, "but I've downloaded a very detailed protocol manual."

Despite Buzz's inexperience, the protocol seemed to proceed smoothly. At one point the download froze the laptop, locking it into an irritating, pulsating display. Buzz explained that he had anticipated such a problem which was why he was using such an ancient laptop. The huge amount of downloaded data had overwhelmed the motherboard, but he had a back-up system in place with an external hard drive so that all the data could be successfully recovered.

Finally, Buzz turned to Finch. "This is where the clever stuff happens."

"Define 'clever.'"

"Getting out without them knowing we got in. Oh shit! Shit, shit, shit!" Buzz was staring wide-eyed at his display screen. The words 'Protocol integrity breach' were flashing discreetly in the bottom, right-hand corner."

"What does 'integrity breach' mean?" Finch enquired, although he really didn't want to hear the answer.

"It means we really need to leave…right now," Buzz snapped as he quickly disconnected all his hardware before hurriedly throwing it into his rucksack. "Come on. Go! We need to go. We've triggered an alarm."

"I don't hear anything,"

"No, but the people who don't want us here have." Buzz appeared bright red in the face, his arteries were standing proud on his neck. "Hopefully they'll think we just messed up, but let's get out of here just in case."

"But we haven't finished."

"Yes, we have. You'll have to run with what we've already got. Now, move or you'll be on your own."

Finch didn't need to be told twice. He had fled from places

he wasn't meant to be before, but that was when he was a young reporter and when a NUJ card and press pass provided a sense of moral certainty that he was on the side of justice and free speech.

Rather than return by the route they had entered, Finch led Buzz down the rows of darkened servers, setting off lighting sensors as he went. A fire door appeared before them. Buzz went to open it.

"No, it could be alarmed," Finch reminded him.

"Too late to be worried about such things," said Buzz as he threw his considerable frame against the door.

Instead of emerging outside, the two of them fell into a dimly lit corridor.

"Quick, this way." Finch barked out the directions with great authority, but in truth he didn't have a clue what he was doing or where he was going, he just felt that, as the senior partner, it was his role to take a lead. A series of doors appeared on the left-hand side of the corridor. They tried each one in turn, until one yielded in reluctant submission. It led into a brightly lit room with a table, kitchen area and pool table. Coffee cups and cigarette stubs lay on the table, evidence that this room had been recently vacated by night staff alerted to investigate the security breach. A row of grey, steel cabinets covered one wall. Finch grabbed a uniform from inside one of the cabinets and threw it at Buzz. "Here, try this on."

"You are joking," Buzz replied as he examined the uniform and held it up against his over-sized body.

Finch quickly examined the other steel lockers until he found an extra-large uniform.

"Time to go even deeper undercover," Finch announced.

"Did you ever do this sort of thing when you were working as a reporter?" Buzz enquired.

"No, but I did when I was trying to escape from a Whitehall

department after a romantic liaison with a minister's special advisor."

"Nothing wrong with that."

"There was when he was still married to her at the time."

Soon both were dressed and slipped out of the staffroom into the corridor outside. By now iridescent orange light was bouncing around the corridor and in the distance raised voices and slamming doors could be heard. A figure with a torch appeared around the corner.

"Check out the staffroom. They haven't left the site," he barked out towards Finch and Buzz, before returning in the direction he had come from. Finch held up his hand in acknowledgment and headed off back down the corridor towards the staffroom.

Further down the corridor another open door led them into a darkened room, illuminated by a series of display screens. Under the screens sat a large desk populated by a number of hand-held computers and tablets.

"Jackpot!" Buzz exclaimed, "a chance to cover our tracks." Soon he was manipulating the computers and bringing up different images, whilst Finch stood guarding the doorway.

"Look, shouldn't we be leaving? We've been riding our luck so far."

"Yeh, just as soon as we can remove our digital footprints from the database." Buzz tapped one of the nearby tablet screens. "Just…like…that," he added as he struck the screen with gleeful exultation. "Right. Now we can go," he exclaimed.

Finch opened the door of the CCTV room only to discover voices and movement outside. "Not a good time," he whispered, closing the door and jamming a galvanized porter's trolley under the door handle. He motioned to Buzz to keep quiet.

Outside the voices grew louder and more distinct. Suddenly they were directly outside the door.

The door handle twitched and rattled in its mounting, then it turned more vigorously. Finch hung onto the trolley and tried to immobilize the handle as much as he could while Buzz leaned his considerable weight against the trolley. "Did you lock the control room, Yuri?" a voice from outside enquired.

"Uh, don't know. Perhaps I did," an eastern European accent replied.

"Idiot."

With that the voices gradually faded into the distance, exchanging insults and profanities as they melted into the background noise.

Finch waited a few moments before cautiously opening the door once again. This time the coast was clear. He motioned for Buzz to follow. They followed the fading voices down the corridor, desperately seeking an exit. Turning the corner, they were confronted with another identical corridor and no clue how to make good their escape.

"Have you any idea where you're going?" Buzz hissed at Finch.

"No, have you?"

"No."

"Right, only one thing for it." Finch located a wall-mounted panel for the fire alarm. Jabbing his elbow into the panel, the glass shattered and total mayhem ensued as carbon dioxide warning lights suddenly burst into life, accompanied by a different sounding alarm.

"CO_2 for the server room," Buzz explained, "standard precaution," as he and Finch quickly made their way down the corridor following the fire exit. Suddenly they reached what appeared to be an external fire door which yielded to deposit them outside in the cold night air. The night sky was lit up by orange flashing lights and the muffled sound of a whooping fire alarm.

A burly-looking man in a high visibility jacket approached them. Before he had time to question them, Finch took the initiative.

"Some idiot's set off the fire alarm. Do you know where the fire assembly point is?"

"Yeh, main car park."

"Someone needs to take charge. They're running around like headless chickens in there."

"Bloody foreigners," the high visibility jacket replied, "haven't got a clue. Should be picking potatoes, not guarding computers." With that, he set off towards the building with a renewed sense of self-righteousness purpose. Finch and Buzz made their way through the car park and up to a now unmanned security barrier. Buzz located the release mechanism and slowly the steel gate slid open only to be greeted by two rattling fire engines, their blue lights flashing as the rather bored-looking occupants sought access, only to be waved through by Finch and Buzz with quiet efficiency. At last they were free to make good their escape, deciding to split up and make their separate ways back home.

The next week was spent poring over the details of what the aborted data dump had revealed. The more Finch delved into this secret world, the stranger and more disturbing that world became and the more he realised how naive he had been in exposing himself and Buzz to the risks of such high stakes commercial espionage. As if to underline his fears, he received a frightened phone call from Buzz late one night.

"I know I said I didn't want to know what you were up to, but d'you have any idea what a can of worms you have opened?" He sounded haunted and fearful, his voice trembling and his youthful self-confidence long since departed.

"No, what's happened?" Finch was starting to feel foolish for attempting to uncover something he barely understood the significance of.

"Let's just say that I've been warned off. My passwords and user identities have been wiped from a number of protocols that I use regularly. It's as if they are onto me and have marked my card."

"Sorry to hear that, Buzz. Is there anything I can do?"

"No, but I'm going to ground for a few weeks. Don't get in touch. I don't want any more association with this. I received a visit at work today that made me feel very uncomfortable."

"You mean you were threatened?"

"Not physically. These types never work that way. They don't need to, but they can wipe you out in other ways. Simply make you disappear. Take you out of the game and bury you so deep that even your own mother can't find your digital identity. You just cease to exist in all official records. Bank accounts, national insurance, identity cards, driving licence, passport, you name it."

"Did someone threaten to do that?"

"No, they just put themselves into my field of view. Let me know that they were around and what they were capable of. It was all very veiled and cryptic, but the message was clear."

"Shit. I'm sorry to hear that." Finch could hear the fear cracking up Buzz's voice.

"Yeh, well so far it hasn't happened, but I'm not prepared to hang around in case it does. I've safeguarded what I can and I'm going to lay low until all this blows over."

"I'll do whatever I can to protect your identity."

"It's already too late for that."

"But…"

"Just leave me alone. You never knew me, we never met. Okay?"

"Plausible deniability all round. I don't even know your real name and I never reveal my sources. Take it from me, I will protect your identity."

"Whatever." Buzz was clearly not in the mood to be

reassured. "Just destroy all your evidence of contact with me and I'll do likewise. If you try to contact me again, you'll find all my numbers have been cancelled. Goodbye, Finch. I'd like to say that it's been fun meeting you, but that would probably be a lie." The phone fell silent and no further contact with Buzz followed.

Buzz's decision to go to ground underlined what was at stake in the investigation. Finch had put himself in danger before; he had adopted false identities and even told lies in order to win the confidence of those he sought to expose or extract information from. Previously, however, the lines of engagement were drawn more clearly; he had known his enemy and the nature of his quest. The prize and the public interest of his story far outweighed any attendant risks to himself or those drawn into his investigations. Now all those lines were blurred. He didn't even know whether he was working for himself, the government or some other, more sinister interest. He wasn't even sure whether he was serving the great public interest or just his own more personal agenda to discover the reason for the bomb blast. The assignment felt deeply flawed and compromised. All he could be certain of was that he had now crossed the Rubicon. He had stepped over into dangerous territory and there was no going back. His professional pride and personal investment prevented him from doing so. Whatever he was looking at, he had to see it through and to expose its reach and significance.

He sensed a connection between his investigation and his personal struggle to understand the broader changes taking place around him. The unsettling sense of absence, the feeling that something had been surrendered or obscured from view that would provide insight into his own restlessness – all contributed towards an awareness that sinister forces were playing out around him. Friends and colleagues occasionally discussed such innate feelings; yet most put them down to the fallout from some kind of shared national grief. However, a shared national grief could not completely account for this nagging strangeness. The *'Garden Party Bombings'* had taken place many years ago, but what emerged from that time was a national consciousness tainted by a culture of fear and secrecy. If truth is the first casualty of war, then a silent war was raging all around, yet hidden from view. It was like staring into an empty bird cage and not knowing where the occupant was or what kind of species it had been.

As Finch further examined the documents produced by the data dump, a picture gradually started to coalesce before him. This picture not only involved the Van Hegel Corporation and its various subsidiaries, but also public research bodies and government ministries. Public safety was clearly at issue, with evidence suggesting a huge cover-up to suppress the details of the side effects of the national vaccination programme that had been at the heart of the *'Great Advance.'* The Van Hegel Corporation had enjoyed a very cosy relationship with various private research bodies and government departments and these relationships begged further investigation.

The following days passed quickly. Finch was starting to come back to life. Once again he was a man on a mission, energised as his prey had started to come into view. His investigation became all-consuming. The more he discovered, the more questions it raised and the more emboldened he felt in his pursuit of the truth. He also reflected upon Buzz's words about data security and realised that he needed to take measures to protect the content of his own research. He had seen how exposed online data storage could be, so he forsook electronic methods of data storage in favour of rather old-fashioned and low-tech methods such as hiding sensitive information under floorboards or in biscuit tins or else mailing it to secure post-boxes. He longed to share his findings with Greg, who was now sharing his flat on a semipermanent basis, but didn't want to expose him to the same risks Buzz had faced. Furthermore, it was apparent that what he was investigating depended upon the co-operation of many agencies and interests, the police included. There were very few secure places for this information and very few people he felt he could trust.

His suspicions were reinforced whilst out buying some beer and milk one day. As he crossed the road to take his usual shortcut through the park, a grey Mercedes Benz pulled up alongside him. The rear window rolled down and, thinking that this was another lost tourist or foreign diplomat asking for an explanation of the congestion charge, he casually leaned in only to be greeted by a rather large, olive-skinned man with a beard and wearing a business suit and a very serious expression.

"Mr. Leroy Finch?"

"I'm sorry, but do I know you?" Finch enquired before immediately stepping back.

"No, but my employer would love you to join him for lunch." The comment took Finch by surprise.

"That's very kind, but my Mum told me not to accept offers from strange men."

"But my employer insists, Mr. Finch," the bearded man replied, this time with a little more menace in his voice. At this point Finch became aware that an even larger man also in a suit and wearing an earpiece and sunglasses was standing behind him, blocking his retreat. "He really does insist and I'm sure that you wouldn't want to…" – the bearded man struggled to locate the right words – "…disappoint him, would you?" At this point the other, larger man reached across to open the car door in a manner that suggested he had little choice other than to get in.

Finch was then escorted politely but firmly into the rear of the Mercedes, which then sped off with great purpose.

He attempted to engage the bearded man and the driver in conversation. He remembered his fieldwork training from many years ago when he had briefly served overseas in some dangerous and politically unstable countries. The kidnapping training, he had received impressed upon him the need to engage his captors in conversation in order to develop a sympathetic relationship with them. He wasn't sure if he was facing such a situation now, but it was advisable to suspect the worst, especially given the nature of the world he was now investigating.

"You know I'm just a jobbing journalist, don't you?"

No reaction.

"Thought so. Who is this employer of yours then?"

Still no reaction.

"Are we going somewhere nice for lunch?"

The silence continued.

"Are you aware that I'm a vegetarian and lactose intolerant?"

"Everything has been taken care of." At last the bearded man was provoked into a response.

"Oh good, I was hoping for a nice lunch. I don't get out much these days."

Finch's strategy was proving ineffective. The cold silence remained as the car swept into a Mayfair apartment block and dipped down into a secure basement car park before coming to a sudden halt with a squeal of brakes. Finch was then escorted from the car to a service lift and taken up to the top floor. Once inside the lift, he discreetly felt inside his jacket pocket and activated the record button of an ancient Dictaphone. Old journalistic habits die hard and obsolete technology can have its advantages: it doesn't register with the security scanners and whatever was about to take place, he wanted a record of the event.

The lift glided to a halt and the mirrored doors slid open with a reassuringly benign swoosh and ping. The sight that greeted him took him somewhat by surprise. The interior of the penthouse apartment was decked out in period furniture in a design reminiscent of a Swiss mountain lodge. Pine panelling covered the walls, apparently supported by exposed wooden beams. A large stone fireplace sat in the middle of the room whilst brightly coloured hangings decorated the walls and occasional rugs adorned the polished marble floor. Beside the fireplace sat a handsome-looking man in a crisp white shirt and navy trousers. He wore rimless spectacles beneath a mop of thick, blond hair and sat cross-legged, reclining whilst reading from a computer tablet. He immediately removed his reading glasses in order to rise and greet Finch.

"Good afternoon, Mr. Finch. I'm so glad that you were able to come along." The man's voice betrayed a slight Germanic accent, although his English, like everything about him, was sharp and impeccable.

"I didn't think I had much choice," Finch replied through clenched teeth, reminding his host that his attendance had not been entirely voluntary.

"Ah, yes. I'm sorry about the nature of your arrival. But I really don't have a great deal of time in London and this was one of a very few windows in my diary. It would have been so sad to have missed this opportunity."

"And the gorillas who brought me here, do they share your sadness?"

"Oh, they like to play their little games, but they can take their responsibilities a bit too seriously at times." He immediately ushered the two hired hands to the other side of the room where they stood, motionless and impassive, overseeing the proceedings.

"Apology accepted."

"Oh, I never apologise, Mr. Finch. I never feel the need."

"Somehow that doesn't surprise me."

"Come, come. I fear that we are getting off on what you

English call the wrong foot, yes? Please join me at my table. I have arranged some lunch by one of your city's finest chefs."

Finch was directed towards a large, black marble table which was beautifully laid out with white linen and silver cutlery. Two blond-haired waitresses attired all in black appeared silently and started to serve at the table, whilst avoiding all direct eye contact with Finch and his host.

Finch decided to seize the initiative. "First things first. I don't like to eat with strangers. So just who am I sharing this meal with?"

"Sorry. I should have explained." The host settled himself in his chair and cleared his throat. "You can call me Friedrich, but that isn't my real name. I am essentially a proxy. I have been engaged to make contact with you on behalf of people who are not able to meet with you directly."

"So who do you represent?"

"I represent the people you have stolen information from, Mr. Finch." His words appeared to hang in the air, accompanied by the mild suggestion of menace. "Please do start before your potage goes cold." Friedrich gestured towards the dish placed in front of them. "Those people," he continued, "do not feel any sense of moral obligation to meet with you personally, so they have engaged me, as a long-time friend or colleague, to represent them on this occasion."

"So let's cut to the chase. You represent Van Hegel."

"Oh come, come. I thought better of you than that. This really isn't quite so simple. I thought that you of all people might have realised that by now."

"Okay. I get it. You represent a matrix of shared interests, but at the centre of that matrix lies the dominating presence of the Van Hegel Corporation. You can't hide buildings as big as this one. It'll be possible to find out just who's renting it."

"That is why they have engaged a proxy, Mr. Finch. Nothing will show up on any leasing agreement. Smoke and mirrors, Mr. Finch. You are playing with the big boys now." Friedrich appeared irritated by the direction of the conversation. "Look, can we not just enjoy this meal and see if we can reach some shared understanding concerning where we are coming from?"

Friedrich's offer appeared attractive, so Finch decided to probe no further at that point and to let his host make the next move.

"So I am honoured to be sharing this lunch with the great Leroy Finch."

"Hardly 'great,'" Finch replied in self-deprecation.

"On the contrary. Your reputation precedes you and your legacy remains, even today. Leroy Finch, the 'Rottweiler of Wapping'. Your career at The Economist, The Times, Financial Times and as foreign correspondent for both the Daily Telegraph and The Independent, that's quite a CV. It reads like a history of British journalism."

"I think that you overrate the significance of my career."

"Oh, I think not. Are you not the man who brought down the Chancellor of the Exchequer?"

"Maybe I played a part. A small part."

"So, how the mighty have fallen." Friedrich sat back in his chair, caressing his wine glass. His tone suddenly changed. "Mr. Finch, are you aware of the penalties for commercial espionage in this country?"

"Yes, I am." Finally, the gloves were off. "Are you aware of the penalties for failing to register the results of crucial clinical trials on vaccines that have been given to over fifty million people in this country and the resultant litigation, not to mention criminal charges, resulting from suppressing the evidence of dangerous side effects relating to licensed medicines. Do you know what happened to makers of thalidomide?" Finch allowed himself a smug smile; he had not felt this way since his early door stepping days in journalism.

"You really do not understand what you are looking at, do you, Mr. Finch? Perhaps that is to your advantage. Perhaps it is not." Friedrich kept staring into mid space as if he wasn't entirely concentrating upon their meeting. His glazed, fixed stare became increasingly unsettling.

"What is to my advantage is that I have evidence that Van Hegel has applied pressure to influence the outcome of field research on its anti-cancer vaccine. The very same vaccine that provides millions of people with the false hope that they are now suddenly protected from the viruses that trigger malignant tumours in 70% of the population."

"So you think that Van Hegel has been producing unsafe vaccines with dangerous side effects?" Friedrich asked calmly.

"Yes, I do."

"And you have evidence to that effect?"

"Well, not exactly, but I have evidence that Van Hegel has suppressed the results of clinical research into the side effects of those vaccines. Research that reveals the presence of a certain protein found in all the samples that could potentially be the trigger for a whole range of unpleasant side effects." Once again Finch paused in self-satisfaction. "Looks like a smoking gun to me."

"Tell me, Mr. Finch, have you ever suffered from appendicitis?"

"Strange question, but no. Have you?"

"As a matter of fact I have and very painful and dangerous it can be, if not discovered and dealt with promptly."

"And your point is?"

"My point is that a grumbling appendix is a dangerous irritant, but once it is removed, you never miss it. Life carries on very much as it always has done, because an appendix causes us pain when it is inflamed but otherwise we can simply live without it and suffer no ill effects."

"What does this have to do with unexpected side effects from a mass vaccination programme?"

"Very little. That is my exact point. Correlation does not mean causation. Just because there might be side effects doesn't mean that those side effects are critical or life-threatening or even measurable. They are just unexpected outcomes. A harmless protein. A distraction. An irrelevant sideshow whilst the main event carries on spectacularly and safely. Puff, there goes the appendix, the organ I never knew I had and I will certainly never miss."

At this point Finch noticed Friedrich leaning his head to one side and touching his ear. Someone, somewhere was listening in, prompting and directing.

"So you're saying that those side effects are benign. They don't harm people or cause any significant problems."

"Precisely. Every action has a reaction. All drugs produce some side effects, but that doesn't mean that those consequences are harmful. They might even enhance or improve the quality of life. Make it better, rather than worse. Not all secrets are harmful secrets, Mr. Finch."

"So why do they still remain secret? Why not publish and be dammed? Let the whole medical and scientific world know that the only unforeseen outcome was a harmless side effect." Finch felt emboldened by the realisation that his words were being heard and scrutinized by a wider audience.

"Well, let's just say that not everyone shares that opinion. Public opinion can be quite suspicious and somewhat volatile. You will remember back in the noughties there was a medical scare brought about by just one rogue doctor and some highly questionable research into the MMR vaccine and the onset of autism. Despite overwhelming evidence to support the safety of the vaccine, many parents decided to decline vaccination and many years later measles outbreaks became common in England and elsewhere. Nobody wants such a scare to arise again. It was thought better to…," – Friedrich struggled to find the right phrase – "…to manage such information in the interests of greater public safety. The greater public good overrides the public interest of this information."

"So you are just serving the greater good, protecting the public from misinformed, potentially harmful speculation?"

"Now, finally, you are seeing the bigger picture, Mr. Finch. So you see, there really is no story here, no smoking gun or at least not the story you hoped to find."

"Okay, one final question." Finch finished his lunch and pushed his plate away. "If all that is true, then why I am sat here eating this Michelin star cuisine, with a proxy representative of a large multinational who are too afraid to put in a personal appearance and why was I brought here under duress by two gorillas?"

"Oh, please forgive the…," – once again Friedrich paused to search for the right words – "the theatricality of our little liaison. I'm afraid that the people I represent don't take kindly to commercial data being accessed by someone with such a reputation for loose talk and campaigning journalism. Maybe a little overreaction; perhaps we can both learn from our mistakes and come to some kind of mutual understanding that will avoid such mistakes in the future?"

Friedrich smiled, his words as smooth as butter. He was good. He had clearly been appointed to his role for his presentational skills. He exuded an air of calm authority, displaying an unhurried manner that could defuse even the most intense of threats. Finch realised that he was the subject of a high-level public relations exercise. A thoroughly professional job had been done on him, but there was little point in arguing the toss with Friedrich. He was just a front man, put up to protect those with real power and influence. Nevertheless, he had discovered enough about those involved not to be deceived by the polished public relations act he had just witnessed. The fact that so much attention had been lavished upon this diversionary meeting reinforced his resolve to delve further and deeper into his investigation. In a strange way this choreographed meeting had strengthened his resolve. Friedrich had inadvertently reminded him of his back catalogue of investigative journalism and how that had helped to bring about real change. He would deliver on this commission, if it was the last thing he did. He would find out the truth that had been hidden from him. It was time for the 'Rottweiler of Wapping' to bare his teeth.

Chapter 12

It was a warm and sunny day in Cheltenham. Catherine cupped her hand to shield her eyes as she stepped out of an eco-taxi in the town centre. She hadn't visited Cheltenham for a number of years, not since she had been invited to speak at the Literature Festival when she had a book to promote. Now she was back amidst the Regency charm of this Cotswold town during the festival week again. Uniformed security contractors endeavoured to mingle surreptitiously among the Georgian architecture; their mirrored shades, stab vests, baseball caps and earpieces in sharp contrast to the relaxed casual dress of the impeccably well-behaved festival goers. Some of the security contractors carried automatic weapons in front of their chests, their demeanour not entirely appropriate for the cerebral profile of the event.

Apart from the raised security threat, little had changed since Catherine's previous visit. The creamy limestone architecture appeared as timeless as ever, exuding period confidence and solidity. Sweeping crescents of elegant Regency townhouses punctuated by tall Ionic columns gave way to the whitewashed domes of former municipal buildings, many of which acted as venues for the festival. Marquees and

157

tents adorned the town parkland spaces providing additional venues, whilst young volunteers in promotional tee-shirts circulated in the streets, swiping the mobiles of visitors with discounted special offers and details of forthcoming events. Everywhere quietly subversive statements adorned the pillars of large buildings declaring: *'Books are Back; Books are Best; Books are Brilliant',* fluttering defiantly in the breeze. It was an incongruous setting to stage a quiet revolution.

For Catherine, it was good to leave the bustle of London for the gentle thoughtfulness of a town dedicated to hosting festivals which informed the mind. Unfortunately, any pleasure derived from returning to Cheltenham was overshadowed by the serious intention that had brought her to one of her favourite towns on a delightful sunny day. Sky had organised a meeting with an old friend who was giving a lecture at the Festival and promoting his latest book. They had arranged to meet outside a small tent pitched on the edge of a town centre park. Sky was wearing a pink wig, a suede waistcoat and a long, floral skirt over army boots. Not the subtlest of disguises, yet clearly a necessary precaution in view of the notoriety her profile still attracted among the various security services. She was smiling and holding a water bottle as if her life depended upon it, but otherwise she looked relaxed and clearly at home within her new persona, mingling with festival goers who were totally unaware of her security status among the nation's most wanted.

Upon seeing Catherine, she slid back her sunglasses onto her pink hairline.

"Catherine, so glad that you could make it."

"Glad to be here." The two of them embraced and air-kissed, their appearance resembling that of an austere aunt and wayward niece, greeting one another after an enforced separation. "I didn't recognise you at first," Catherine added.

"Yes, it pays to keep people guessing when it comes to being out in public." Her explanation didn't entirely add up. Her appearance attracted more attention than it deflected. She was clearly in need of wise counsel when it came to knowing how to blend in. The more ordinary she tried to appear, the more extraordinary an impression she made. "There's less CCTV here, but as you can see, plenty of eyes on the ground." Sky rolled her eyes towards one of the armed security contractors. He remained impassive in response, a paramilitary statue imprisoned behind his mirrored sunglasses.

Catherine's fascination concerning Sky's true identity had been heightened by an encounter a few days previously. She had been working at her office in college when she received news that a representative from the Design Council was waiting for her in reception. Her curiosity pricked, she invited the representative into her office only to discover more pseudonyms and false identities.

What followed involved a rather officious young lady, who simply referred to herself as 'Valentine', revealing that she was not a member of the Design Council, but rather someone representing the security of the realm. The young lady then proceeded to probe her for information concerning Sky, reminding Catherine that she was still bound by the conditions of her court order and any failure to co-operate would involve very serious consequences for her future liberty.

Catherine managed to avoid disclosing the true extent of her association with Sky, but the tone of Valentine's questioning and the level of veiled threat she put across in their meeting left her in no doubt that Sky remained of great interest to the security services. Eventually she managed to convince Valentine that she was just a naïve academic, obsessed with her own deluded beliefs and not a new T-squad recruit or in any way connected with political dissent.

Valentine's visit had sufficiently disturbed Catherine's equilibrium to provoke her to research Sky's identity with greater vigour. She undertook the usual online searches which threw up a bewildering amount of gossip, rumour and promotional material. There were several blogs dedicated to the activities of the T-squads and Sky's name came up on a number of occasions. Some sites were critical of her activities and offered various speculative explanations of her true identity and motivation; others were more sympathetic, casting her as someone who was prepared to make a stand against the incursion of surveillance upon ordinary people and the way in which multi-national corporations had benefited from the 'The Great Advance'. Other sites were so effusive in their praise and adulation of Sky that she had clearly become rather iconic, representing the voice of repressed feminists, the urban poor and disillusioned intellectuals. There were no photographs of her other than the one posted on the official Security Services most wanted gallery. Her description on that site merely referred to her promotion of acts of civil disobedience and spreading seditious propaganda. The lack of hard evidence had created a powerful mythology around Sky, with some people even suggesting she had undergone radical cosmetic surgery in order to change her appearance, while others claimed that she was either a movie star researching a role or a protest singer operating under a false identity. One online newspaper was even running a campaign to expose her as a fraudster and product of a migrant family living on benefits.

Wherever Catherine looked, it proved impossible to find a comprehensive and coherent picture of Sky. Her online presence suggested her influence was as much symbolic as real. She seemed to represent an idea, a cause and subversive attitude, with scant evidence to connect her with particular acts of terrorism or civil disobedience. Catherine even tried to use her university's database and digital archive to find additional information about Sky, but all it threw up was a few research topics and dissertations about her role as a feminist and post-modern political icon.

Sky's mystique merely added to her sparkling appeal in Catherine's eyes. Their growing friendship made her feel apprehensive, but also excited and full of hope that the nearer she stayed to Sky, the closer she would move towards understanding the forces that caused Joshua to take his own life.

"So what is it with this place?" Catherine asked. "Last time I was here it was like an English tea party; now it resembles more of an arms convention."

"Well, let's just say that people have finally cottoned on to what events like this represent. This is one of the few occasions when ideas are freely discussed and books celebrated. You can't control hard copy in the same way as online text, especially when so many authors like to show up to promote their work and where the public get to meet their literary heroes"

"I see what you mean."

"Come on." Sky took Catherine by the hand. "There's someone I'd like you to meet."

Catherine hadn't seen Liam Redcar since he contacted her ten years ago to help research a documentary he was making about Charles Rennie Mackintosh and the Art Nouveau movement. She had known Liam at university before his big break into stand-up comedy. As his career rocketed to new heights of fame and influence she had lost touch, although she remained something of a fan and admirer. She saw him appear in a Samuel Beckett play in the West End, but otherwise the documentary provided her most meaningful recent connection and had proved to be mutually beneficial to their respective careers. Comedians often want to be taken more seriously and the documentary clearly helped Liam to gain credibility as a social historian and cultural commentator, whilst the public exposure had furthered Catherine's own career to a lesser extent whilst briefly providing her university with a celebrity namecheck in their prospectus.

A large poster of Liam wearing a comedy hat and a startled look greeted them on arrival in the Town Hall foyer. Copies of the latest edition of his autobiography were piled high on one table, along with smartcards giving access to recordings of his latest Radio Four comedy quiz. However, pride of place was given over to multiple copies of Liam's retrospective on the life of evolutionary biologist and radical secularist, Sir Clifford Latimer, which he was promoting at the festival with a short lecture and a number of interviews.

Catherine and Sky filtered into the auditorium and discreetly found their place towards the back of the room. Liam appeared on the stage, accompanied by raucous applause and appreciative yelps of admiration. He immediately launched into a short, illustrated lecture, featuring a number of clips from a TV documentary that accompanied his book. Liam was clearly in his element, charting the career and controversies that surrounded the life of Latimer. He couldn't avoid various comic asides and satirical sideswipes at Latimer opponents, although he did not hold back from exposing a number of contradictions arising from the eminent scientist's own methodology and beliefs. A short interview followed, retracing much of the ground of his lecture, whilst allowing room for Liam to reflect upon his many other interests and projects, drawn from his career on stage, film and TV. Questions from the floor mostly related to the subject of his book and provided opportunities to reinforce the shared veneration of Latimer that remained even now, so many years since his death.

As the lecture finished, Liam was whisked off to the foyer to sign copies of his book and to press the flesh of his many fans and admirers. Catherine and Sky found a quiet corner for personal reflection upon what they had witnessed.

"So, just how do you know Liam Redcar?" Catherine asked

Sky, anxious to penetrate the secrecy of her world and curious that someone so powerfully identified with mainstream culture should be associated with her political radicalism.

"Oh, Liam has been a mover and shaker for some time. It's just he hasn't been quite sure until recently which side he was batting for," Sky explained, throwing Catherine a knowing look from beneath her pink fringe. Catherine was puzzled by her response but decided not to push her further.

Eventually the queue of excited book buyers abated and Liam looked up into the eyes of Catherine. He immediately recognised her and greeted her warmly with an embrace. A look was exchanged between them, the significance of which was known only to themselves.

"Oh, what might have been, Catherine!" Liam exclaimed. "You're still a fine-looking woman."

"And you," replied Catherine, giving Liam a huge, big sisterly squeeze, "are still a hopeless flirt."

Liam theatrically rolled his eyes, blew a kiss and winked. "Takes one to know one, my dear." He immediately looked across to Sky. "And who is this gorgeous young lady?"

"Stop fooling around, Liam, you know who I am," Sky replied, rather firmly putting him in his place. She was clearly well-versed in the art of rebuffing amorous advances.

"Ah yes, I didn't recognise you under all that circus gear. It's good to see you as well. Just what are you calling yourself these days?"

"Sky, you know it's Sky."

"Oh yes, Sky," Liam replied with a nod of recognition.

Being in the company of Sky reminded Catherine of her idealistic youth spent with Liam and other lovers, debating Nietzsche and Derrida late into the night in some dope-fuelled, heady, intellectual atmosphere lubricated by quantities of vodka and coke. Sky shared the same unbridled self-belief of her younger self, along with the ability to give the impression that everything was corresponding to some great, predetermined plan. However, unlike Catherine, Sky's self-confidence appeared to be anchored in the security of a privileged background rather than academic rigour. She displayed a kind of knowing detachment, evident in the way she spoke and her body language. Here was someone who was going to change the world; all she was waiting for was the right opportunity and the right cause to follow.

"Let me take you to lunch," Liam insisted. "I'm staying at a half-decent hotel up the road. They'll find us a table."

Half an hour later the three companions were sitting down to enjoy lunch in the slightly faded glory of a large, Regency hotel restaurant, surrounded by indoor plants, crystal chandeliers and crisp, white linen. In the corner of the room a string quartet gently swayed and coaxed mellow chamber music from their instruments. Ladies in hats and gentlemen wearing blazers and chinos mingled with each other, served by a small army of waitresses in black dresses and starched aprons.

"I love this place, even for Cheltenham it's so retro. Most of the furniture and fittings were brought in from China, but you could never tell, could you? It's like being back on a film set. I don't know what tribe lives here, but there's probably a *My World* community of followers somewhere."

Catherine and Sky had to agree with Liam's assessment of the hotel's surroundings. It felt strangely out of kilter with a world chasing after modernity – a bubble of nostalgia extruded into a technological age to remind people of gentler times.

"So," Liam clapped his hands together, "what can I do for you lovely ladies?"

As Catherine explained what had taken place over the last few months, Liam appeared genuinely troubled and concerned for her.

"I'm so sorry to hear about your son, Catherine. I really

had no idea. It's been so long. Is there anything I can do to help in any way?"

"Come on, Liam," Sky adopted a firm tone. She was clearly not someone intimidated by his reputation. "With your connections you're one of the very few people who know where all the bodies lie."

"Oh that it was that simple, darling. You think because of the world I inhabit that it's just a matter of consulting a little black book, making a few calls and instantly you have all the answers. It just doesn't work like that. No-one is in charge anymore. It's all got completely out of control. Anyway, I'm just a marginal figure, a player in a sideshow whilst the main event plays out elsewhere. The real stuff is happening outside of the official channels."

"Yes, but you of all people still sit in the middle of those networks that do know what's going on."

"Do not mistake public profile and a few friends in government for real power. The people who make all the important decisions are well hidden from public view. Everything's outsourced, decentralised and dispersed – way beyond public accountability or media spotlight."

"Look, Liam," Catherine stepped into the conversation, "the reason I'm here is quite simple. I'm here because I want to understand why my son took his life and why other mothers and fathers have buried their children in similar circumstances. I'm not here to save the world or bring down the government. I'm just here because of Joshua." Catherine's voice started to falter. It was the first time since Joshua's funeral that she had felt so moved. "I don't expect you to understand how I feel, but that's why I took my stand and that's why I accepted Sky's invitation to meet with you today."

Liam touched Catherine's arm, then leaned back in his chair and offered Catherine a serviette to dry her eyes. "Actually I understand a lot better than you realise." With that he reached into his jacket pocket and unfolded a piece of paper. It was a printout of an email. "I've been carrying this around for the last six months or so. It helps me to gain a sense of perspective." He flattened the paper out and passed it to Catherine. It was a report from a Harley Street consultant neurologist, outlining the results of various neurological tests that had been carried out over a number of weeks.

"I'm sorry, I don't understand what this means."

"Just look at the last paragraph," Liam directed her.

"What does this Huntington's pathology mean?" Catherine enquired, fearing that she already knew the answer.

"It's not good. It's in my system. Not everything can be cured by a simple vaccination these days. The disease is a genetic disorder and progressive in its effects. At the moment, I feel mostly fine, a few tingling sensations and a slight loss of co-ordination, but then most people assume that I'm just fooling around. However, it will only get worse and ultimately it will lead to loss of mental capacity, dementia and an early death. So, you see, you're not the only one carrying a burden."

"Is that why you abandoned the dark side and have been so helpful to us?" Sky had obviously been unaware of Liam's medical condition.

"Let's just say that it wasn't the only reason for my change of heart, but it was a contributory factor. I don't want to be remembered as someone who helped to close down civil liberties and freedoms. I'd prefer to be regarded as someone who sought to uphold them."

Shocked looks were exchanged across the table. All of a sudden words seemed inappropriate and an awkward, solemn stillness descended upon the gathering and was only dispelled by the arrival of food.

"Right, let's get down to some serious business." The arrival of lunch seemed to reanimate Liam. As he tucked into his beef wellington, he reached into his shoulder bag and took out a small, black disk with an aerial attached, which he placed on a nearby empty chair. "Despite the appearance of our surroundings, these places can have lots of unwelcome ears. This little box of tricks should allow us the freedom to speak more openly." A pulsing blue light appeared on the black disk and this seemed to reassure Liam that it was safe to speak openly. He beamed a self-satisfied smile. "Cathy, how long have we known each other?"

"Oh, off and on, I would say about thirty years."

"Thirty years?" The realisation of the passage of time seemed momentarily to lie heavily upon Liam. "And we shared some sweet moments together, especially in those early student days. Yeh?"

"Yes, I guess so…I wouldn't have wanted it any other way." Catherine reached across to touch Liam's hand.

"In those days we all believed in a brave new world. Remember how the Berlin Wall had come down, the new millennium was upon us, the internet was unlocking huge creative possibilities. No planes had flown into any twin towers; no financial systems had collapsed, plunging the world into economic meltdown; and no energy crisis had forced us to go cap in the hand to the Russians. What did we used to say was our worst enemy?"

"Ignorance itself," Catherine proudly announced.

"Quite right. Ignorance itself. And what we saw as the friends of ignorance were intolerance, superstition and tradition. If we needed any confirmation, it came in 9/11."

"I guess so."

"So we used to bang the drum for a new liberal order based upon reason. A new enlightenment. A secular future in which the ignorance of the past would be banished."

"I think that I departed from you at that point. For me it was just about making creative statements, painting with a much wider palette, drawing from every available source. I didn't want to deconstruct anything."

"You found your way in the academic world; I found mine in the performing arts. Stand-up was the new rock and roll. Comedians were packing out arenas and I wanted some of the action. I knew it would never last, but I wanted to surf the wave while I could."

"So how did you get into the whole secular campaigning thing?"

"From stand-up. It started to get harder to find new angles and new material. The whole PC agenda became quite restricting, but if you appeared on stage and said you were an atheist, then you could immediately win an audience over. It was easy and I guess many of us got lazy. Writers had been portraying people of faith in unflattering terms for years in drama; we just picked up the ball and ran with it. You could build a whole routine on taking the piss out of creationists or sinister priests or lampooning obscure parts of the Bible. You couldn't be racist or sexist, but it was totally legitimate to mock organised religion and its ideas."

"But why religion?" Catherine asked.

"I have to admit that the *'Garden Party Bombings'* were something of a game-changing moment. The power of religionists to influence minds and wills in the name of intolerance and violence brought about a considerable cultural backlash. We hit back with the only tools we had available to us – those of persuasion, satire and ridicule."

"But didn't you turn those tools on the wrong targets?"

"Perhaps, but we were artists, comedians and actors; we were looking to have a bit of fun, not to start a war. So we took on those who we regarded as religious extremists."

"But why organised religion? The churches and faith communities were not exactly hot beds of international terrorism. They weren't blowing people up."

"It was a bit like being hit by the playground bully. When you eventually get back on your feet, you hit the nearest person standing by in order to recover your wounded pride."

"But why pick on churches?"

"They were one of the last remaining symbols of absolute moral authority. I guess we just needed some kind of big picture to rail against."

"But weren't other faiths a more obvious target?"

"Oh yes, but we couldn't do that for obvious reasons." Liam made eye contact in a knowing way. They both knew what he meant. "So we chose softer targets."

"So how did you get from there to becoming the self-appointed thought police?" Catherine's question cut through the air with an icy penetration.

"Whooh, that's not fair. The war against religious extremism was waged mostly online, not on the stage. The real thought police live in those shadows. We just surfed the wave."

"Okay then, where did the wave take you?"

"It was just a bit of fun most of the time. But then I started to read more widely and share platforms with well-known secularists."

"Like Latimer?"

"Yes, and others. I looked around the world and wherever I turned my gaze, religion seemed to be standing in the way of progress. Holding back contraception in Africa, condoning homophobia, restricting important genetic research, preventing assisted suicides, recruiting suicide bombers, oppressing women, teaching people that evolution was a theory and a seven-day creation was a fact. Not to mention the abuse of power, paedophile priests, political leaders getting together to pray on the eve of a war. These things became not just the subject of my comic routines but the landscape for my political awakening. I thought that the only way to get ourselves out of the economic and moral mire was education and at the heart of education should sit reason and science, not faith and superstition."

"Not all religion is bad. You're an educated man; you shouldn't compare the worst practice of religion with the best of reason and science."

"No, you're quite correct, but it wasn't about trying to convince everyone to see things from the same place. That's where I depart from Latimer and others. They use far too broad a brush. You can't base your whole thesis on the sort of half-baked opinion you hear down the pub that religion causes all the world's problems."

"You always were a bit of an academic snob," Catherine commented.

"Perhaps. But the more I read, the more I came to believe that we could all live more moral, less ignorant lives if religion were removed from the public realm. It wasn't the cause of all the problems, but it certainly was a contributory factor. If only religion could be taken out of our national institutions and educational structures, then we could be free to determine our future based upon reason and a shared commitment to tolerance and self-determination."

"So what went wrong?" Sky asked ironically.

"Nothing went wrong. Just the opposite, but no-one was planning any great coup or takeover. Like I keep saying, we were just surfing the wave. And the wave that came to town was the *'Garden Party Bombings'*."

"So you seized the opportunity created by the actions of a few religious extremists?

"Well, yes, or no, not really. It wasn't like that. We just found a more sympathetic ear after the *'Garden Party Bombings'*. Many of us had been campaigning for constitutional and educational reform, but suddenly we were pushing at an open door. Organised religion came to be seen as the enemy of civilisation

– it was guilt by association. As a result, everything got voted through on the nod with no real objections raised, not even from the faith communities. The bishops had pretty much lost heart and seemed ready to withdraw from the House of Lords. Mind you, all the money they got from the sale of land and property to the heritage lobby seemed to buy a lot of their goodwill and co-operation. Likewise, the other faith leaders. By the time that legislation was passed, they were a spent force. They had a few concerns about their pension funds, but in the end a willing procession of grey-haired faith leaders meekly walked off into the sunset to their nursing homes or else just faded back into their own little communities."

"I don't remember any great protests at the time, but surely there must have been some resistance?"

"Not really. It was a bloodless coup. After the *'Garden Party Bombings'* there was little sympathy for faith communities, especially ones that made a fuss. The tide just turned against them. Any protests were regarded as illiberal or, worse still, treasonable, so the whole thing was subject to a news blackout – total reporting restrictions were applied."

"I wondered why it never appeared in the news media."

"You don't want to be seen to be implementing a crackdown on religion when there are still so many people wanting to wage war against you in the name of religion. The global consequences would be horrendous."

"So better to just airbrush them out of the cultural landscape?"

"Not totally, just deny them a platform," Liam replied while taking a sip of wine. "As Spike Milligan once said, 'The best cure for sea sickness, is to sit under a tree.'"

"So you saw yourself as ridding society of a great sickness?" Catherine asked.

"More of an unnecessary distraction. A way of thinking that had outgrown its usefulness."

"But how could such people just disappear?"

"Simple. You just deny them the oxygen of publicity. Information is power, and following the '*Garden Party Bombings*' the mood of concern around national security created something of a consensus among the information gatekeepers to move unpopular people and unpopular causes further towards the margins of society. Eventually one day no-one even notices or cares that they have quietly slipped away from view."

Catherine looked shocked to discover that the person she had shared such common cause with in the past could now approve of the kind of repression she thought they both abhorred. She had thought better of Liam, especially given his reputation as a free-thinking libertarian.

"Look, I'm not proud of my part in all this, even if I was more of a cheerleader than a prime mover. But it was an extraordinary time and such times call for extraordinary measures. Anyhow, the reporting restrictions were rarely used. Eventually it all just quietened down and people kinda forgot all about it and got on with their lives. It was yesterday's news and there were more important things on people's minds, I guess."

"So why didn't you just settle for the gains you had made during that time?" Disapproval was starting to show in Catherine's tone of voice.

"It did feel like a hollow victory. A bit like being four-nil up at half-time and then in the second half the opposition fails to come out onto the pitch."

"So why push on?" Catherine asked. "It all seems so mean-spirited."

"We didn't push on. We had achieved all we wanted. We had a secular state and nobody was complaining. We were dismantling the apparatus of our campaign, but then something else hit."

"The *'Great Advance'*?" Catherine suggested.

"Precisely. The *'Great Advance'*.

"That's what I still don't fully understand," asked Sky. "I know that something shifted following the *'Great Advance'*; the public mood changed, but what I don't know is why and how. Presumably the result of some kind of unforeseen consequences?"

"That's one way of putting it." Liam shifted in his seat, like he was exploring the edge of his comfort zone or rehearsing for a new play with an unfamiliar cast. "It was like it sealed the deal."

"So presumably the *'Great Advance'* just made people feel more self-reliant and secure, like they didn't need a God anymore?"

"That's what most people thought at first. That's why many of us didn't question it. It just seemed that we'd all outgrown our dependence upon pre-scientific thinking. Science had scaled the ultimate summit; finally, the cure for suffering and disease was within our grasp. There was no limit to what science could achieve and no need to look elsewhere. Faith and religion were redundant – banished to a footnote in history. We had grown up and embraced empiricism as the provider of all the answers." Liam took another sip of wine. "Made perfect sense as far as I was concerned."

Catherine was feeling a growing sense of indignation. The more she discovered about what had been removed from public life, the more she mourned its passing and the angrier she became. She had never held any strong religious convictions or even spiritual beliefs, but this felt like cultural vandalism. In the field of the arts it was impossible to make sense of cultural history without an understanding of basic religious narratives and ideas. Whatever she felt or understood personally, there were issues of justice and authority at stake.

Could Joshua have been haunted by such a sense of cultural realignment?

"But that doesn't account for the loss of religious vocabulary and practice or that sense of emptiness that people keep talking about. The kind of emptiness and hopelessness that caused my Joshua and countless others to give up on life."

"No it doesn't," Liam admitted. He appeared forlorn and regretful, as if mourning for former times. "What slowly became apparent was not that something had been lost in our national life, but rather something had been stolen, taken away without consent or mandate. That's why I want to put something back, while I still can."

"So is that why you're now helping out Sky and her friends?"

"Kinda, although I'm somewhat outside of the circle of trust these days. But it just rankles with my sense of fair play. It's as if the collective spiritual consciousness of the nation had been mugged and we had been sold a pup in its place."

"And the pup is?"

"Look around you. What is happening in all the former cathedrals and churches?"

"Shopping mostly."

"And what has shopping become?"

"Some might say a pseudo-religious experience." Catherine was starting to make sense of her landscape.

"Yes, and no longer a means to an end, but an end in itself. The cult of retail therapy. Look at the triumph of branding and the tribal identification people are encouraged to develop with those brands. It's not just a marketing strategy, it's a faith. One faith merely replaces another. Science hasn't really triumphed, market economics has."

Just then their conversation was interrupted by a text message reminding Liam of another engagement. He hastily cleared away his surveillance protection device before a small entourage of minders arrived to escort him to his next personal appearance.

"How did you know I was here?" he asked a small, Chinese girl in a festival tee-shirt who appeared to be in charge.

"We track all speakers by their mobile's GPS," she informed him, "just in case they forget where they are going."

Liam rolled his eyes. It seemed that there was little point in trying to avoid surveillance. "Good to know that someone's looking out for me," he added ironically, and with that he and Catherine exchanged a somewhat awkward and brief farewell, neither wishing to dwell on the significance of the moment and the likelihood of their meeting again. Liam turned to leave and then, catching Catherine's eye once again with a look that spanned the years of their friendship and bridged the chasm that separated their two worlds, he blew Catherine a tearful kiss and disappeared from sight.

Suddenly Sky grabbed Catherine's arm. "What time is it?"

"Nearly two o'clock, I think," Catherine replied.

"Oh good, we might still be in time. There's something going down that you really must see." With that, Sky directed Catherine out of the hotel and towards the town centre, hurriedly pushing their way past festival goers and shoppers at a rather undignified pace.

"Quick, we really need to hurry. You don't want to miss this," Sky explained.

Eventually they reached their destination – a paved precinct area surrounded by shops, offices and an old-style department store. There were a few performance artists dressed as golden statues as well as some jugglers and a number of people handing out free samples of food and alcohol in order to coax shoppers into one of the adjacent tapas bars.

Sky caught Catherine by the arm again.

"Just wait here a moment and see what unfolds."

A few moments later a young man in sports gear wandered

into the middle of the precinct, carrying a folding chair and violin case. He then sat down and took out his violin, while in an adjacent doorway a young African lady put together a brass trumpet with meticulous care. Nearby a man with a shaved head save for a long, plaited ponytail produced a magnificent-looking double bass from a carrying case. Beside him a group of two older ladies and three gentlemen gathered together, apparently engrossed in deep conversation.

"What's happening?" Catherine asked.

"Just wait and see."

A short distance away two young ladies in hoodies stood motionless in the middle of the tidal flow of shoppers, apparently frozen to the spot. One of them took out what appeared to be a mobile phone and held it at arm's length in front of her mouth. By this time the violinist had started to play a couple of bars of a familiar prelude, prompting the young lady to throw out her chest and sing.

"Hal-le-lu-jah, Hal-le-lu-jah, Hallelujah, Hal-lel-ujah."

Immediately one of the golden statues echoed an operatic reply.

"Hal-le-lu-jah, Hal-le-lu-jah, Hallelujah, Hal-lel-ujah."

Two more young people produced stringed instruments from their rucksacks and immediately formed a string section around the seated violinist and double bass player. Nearby the doors to the pavement tapas bar were thrown open to reveal a pianist leading the accompaniment whilst other shoppers suddenly appeared with various brass instruments and began to join in. By now a group of older men and women had started to provide a counterpointing response to the soloists whilst those handing out free samples had started to erect folding crates to stand on, whilst lifting their voices to join the chorus. One of the jugglers bellowed out a powerful baritone refrain.

"The Kingdom of this world is become…"

The sense of bewilderment among the other shoppers and passers-by was heightened as a group of young people started to form a human pyramid. Soon acrobats began climbing onto the assembled pyramid, suspending each other in various implausible positions, their hands outstretched to the heavens. Two young girls and a street cleaner began to mime to the music and then balletically interpret the triumphant themes through the medium of dance, apparently captivated by the melodies. Everywhere people were transfixed by what was unfolding before them, and so an audience formed around the performers, their hands outstretched, capturing the event on their mobile phones.

"King of Kings… Hallelujah, Hallelujah

And Lord of Lords… Hallelujah, Hallelujah." The music ascended to heights.

"King of Kings… Hallelujah, Hallelujah

And Lord of Lords…"

At that point fire-eaters appeared, punctuating each phrase of the chorus with an explosion of flames. Windows above the surrounding shops were flung open to reveal even more members of the choir joining in from various vantage points. Everywhere people stopped or else moved towards the centre of the forming crowd, their mobile phones held high in the air to record the proceedings. The acrobats started to perform backflips and somersaults, coordinating their routine with that of the dancers, lifting the smaller performers onto their shoulders and high above their heads, their faces beaming with delight.

The music and movement reached a triumphant climax. Spontaneous applause and cheers filled the shopping precinct, followed by flashes of light from various mobile phones. A private security contractor repeatedly pressed his earpiece to his head, straining to hear the replies of his supervisor. A police officer stood transfixed, and then joined in with the applause.

Toddlers danced around their parents and clapped their hands with glee. High fives and embraces were exchanged among all the performers and then seamlessly and efficiently the musicians, singers and dancers melted back into the crowd, secreting their musical instruments into cases and rucksacks and covering their costumes with sombre clothing. Complete strangers were seen to spontaneously embrace whilst others wiped away unexpected tears. A woman stood frozen to the spot, lost in her private thoughts as people manoeuvered around her. A man knelt on the ground as if trying to reconnect with a distant memory, tears streaming down his face. Doors and windows to the surrounding shops and wine bars were then quietly closed as the performers returned to their previous routines or continued with their shopping. Bewilderment and curiosity spilt over into a number of pavement conversations. Everywhere there was a sense of wonder and transcendence, although many people appeared confused about what it had all meant and who the people were. After a while private security contractors appeared from a nearby department store and encouraged the crowd to disperse, curtailing any further spontaneous reactions.

Sky turned to Catherine. "Now d'you see why I didn't want to miss this!" she exclaimed, beaming from ear to ear and wiping her eyes.

"Yes, it's been a while since I witnessed a flash mob event."

"Still technically illegal after the *'Garden Party Bombings'*, but nobody seems to enforce the ban anymore," Sky explained. "Hopefully not too much CCTV footage as some of the performers are still on various surveillance lists."

"Are all these people colleagues of yours?" Catherine enquired.

"No, not all. Some just like the music. I know one or two, but they come from different networks and cells. We might all share a common concern, but we don't often get to meet up."

"So you don't do this sort of thing regularly?"

"Only when it's fairly safe and there might be a sympathetic audience. There's lots of ways to register your dissent. Some turn up in Westminster with a bucket of whitewash, while others choose to sing and perform."

"Well, whoever was responsible, they have produced something really amazing," Catherine concluded. "Look, I still don't know what you are all up to, but if what I've heard and seen today is anything to go by, then I want in."

"Don't worry, Catherine," Sky remarked, "you have been for some time."

Chapter 13

The sun rose the following day, heralding new possibilities for Catherine. After a healthy continental breakfast in a franchised city break hotel, she and Sky stepped out into the street, eager to embrace the opportunities of a new day. Catherine gazed around the Regency façade of the town centre. It had an ageless quality, exuding confidence and solidity. It was a strange location to host a counter-cultural event. A town of contradictions. A place where people originally came to see and be seen, to take the spa waters and walk among its period colonnades and terraces. Since becoming the location of the government secret listening post, it had become associated with the very security services given the task of protecting the nation from political and military threats, yet now it was mischievously taking a gentle sideswipe at the political status quo. A resort town, thumbing its nose to modernity, celebrating the sheer joy that ideas and freedom of thought bring, right under the gaze of those who wanted to limit the public's access to such freedoms.

If Cheltenham could change, then so could she. Deep inside her something had shifted. She had let go many of the fears she had carried for so long. She still bore the pain of

Joshua's loss. Nothing would ever fill the chasm exposed by his tortured soul being rent from her. Yet strangely, there in the sunshine of a Cotswold town, surrounded by a celebration of all that expanded the imagination and embraced the future with hope, she started to believe that one day all might be well again. The human spirit remained unbowed; she too could flourish once more. She could be part of something, a connected being, made whole and completed by others. Sixty years after a British Prime Minister claimed there was no such thing as society, Catherine finally knew that she wanted to belong; she wanted to find her place within a bigger picture. She was not just an isolated, meandering individual, bumping up against other individuals, but rather a dependent, vulnerable creature who needed other people and became complete through her connection with them.

Sky, however, remained something of a closed book to Catherine. After the revelations and insights of the previous day, she had retired to bed early without disclosing much more about herself or her real intentions for their visit to the Literature Festival. She looked uncomfortable in her pink wig and charity shop outfit, like an exquisite bouquet of flowers shoved into a beer glass. Yet she had an inner radiance and poise that shone through her disguise and refused to be extinguished. Catherine knew that, despite her mystery, she had somehow connected with her on a deep level. They not only shared a common quest, but increasingly a mutual identity.

Sky once again assumed control over the business of the day. She had tickets for a special festival event and wanted to make the most of the opportunity to hear the speaker. Together they boarded a specially chartered eco-bus that took them directly to the racecourse on the edge of the town. Upon entering the site, they were directed to a large conference arena, where they managed to clear the considerable security, thanks to a couple of VIP passes that Sky had somehow managed to source. From there they were escorted past long queues of patient festival goers and piles of books bearing the image of the speaker, up to a balcony where a cacophony of raucous applause and cheering voices signalled the start of the event.

They had arrived just in time to see Lord Geoffrey Deacon, world-renowned biochemist and father of the *'Great Advance'*, welcomed onto the stage, accompanied by flashing lights and a thumping, triumphant soundtrack. Eventually the whoops and screams of adulation died down and Lord Geoffrey was able to address the crowd, promoting his remarkable memoirs. He spoke about his childhood, his education and career in medical research and how ordinary it had all been until he had met up with another remarkable scientist, whose studies seemed to complement and reinvigorate his own research. Through their shared endeavours and unique partnership, they had been able to identify and profile the molecular structure of a whole family of viruses that acted as triggers to the processes which caused the cell mutations associated with many common cancers. As he recalled those historic events, the enormity of what he was describing impacted his audience. Often he would have to pause to allow yelps of appreciation and acclamation to be expressed by the audience. It was hard to imagine if there had ever been one man to whom so much was owed by so many.

Once Lord Geoffrey had completed his lecture, there were a number of pre-arranged questions from the audience. Many of these related to future projects or speculation about the total eradication of the main diseases associated with ageing and the effect this would have upon an increasingly elderly population. Other questions merely reflected thanks and appreciation for helping to lift the great shadow of cancer that had hovered over so many lives. Among the warmth and appreciation was one spiky question raised by a faceless questioner.

"Lord Geoffrey," the questioner enquired, "are you aware of any significant side effects as a result of the vaccination programme that arose from your research?"

"Well, I am not responsible for the public health programme that used my research," Lord Geoffrey replied, "but as far as I am aware, the clinical trials were thoroughly audited and trialled and there have been no serious medical side effects as a result of the vaccination programme, neither here nor in the other countries where it's been rolled out."

"But what about the non-medical side effects?" the questioner continued. "Are you aware of the sociological and psychological impacts arising from the widespread take-up of the vaccine?"

"I'm not quite sure I understand your question, but I must repeat that this vaccine has been thoroughly tested and there is absolutely no evidence of any harmful medical effects arising from its use."

"So you're quite happy to recommend the vaccine?"

"Yes, absolutely. I have been vaccinated myself. So have all my family."

With that comment the session was quickly brought to a conclusion.

Catherine leaned across to Sky. "I think that's some kind of record for me."

"What is?" Sky asked.

"Being in the presence of greatness twice in two days."

Sky returned a knowing look. It was impossible not to be in awe of Lord Geoffrey and the significance of what his research had achieved. This quiet academic had acquired huge public affection since he was revealed as the creative genius behind the research which led to the *"Great Advance."* Despite his shyness and diffidence, it was impossible not to be inspired by the significance of what he had achieved.

As Sky and Catherine made their way back into the centre

of town, weaving in and out of various groups of tourists and promoters handing out publicity materials for forthcoming lectures and new publications, the sound of raised voices could be heard from a marquee set up in a city centre park.

Sky turned to Catherine and said, "Oh no, it looks like Gerald is winding people up again."

"Who's Gerald?" Catherine hissed through clenched teeth, trying not to display her ignorance or draw attention to herself.

"The speaker. He's part of one of our cells, but not very good at making friends on occasions like these." Sky paused. "Always entertaining though," she added with a mischievous look.

Catherine and Sky tentatively opened a panel at the rear of the marquee and slipped into the back of the assembled audience.

"… I am not alleging brainwashing, but rather distraction therapy," Gerald explained. "Pacifying the masses with the promise of shiny, new things. Distracting people's attention away from what is happening by creating a boom in consumer spending, whilst at the same time deploying the thought police to control what is published and how we think."

"That's bollocks. Total crap," a heckler shouted.

"Rubbish! Get off." Raised voices erupted from the audience.

"D'you expect us to believe that? You're the one whose mind is being controlled," another inquisitor shouted.

"Let him speak. Let him speak." Other faceless voices joined in support from the auditorium whilst a vocal part of the audience aired their hostility, booing and telling him to 'get off'.

"Thank you, thank you." Gerald tried to quieten the audience, raising his hands in passive submission to dampen the hostile reaction. "Ladies and gentlemen, this is actually what my book sets out to explain. Powerful interests are at work among us. Not just governments, but large corporations working in conjunction with the scientific community to create a hegemony of passive acquiescence. A conspiracy of deception. Winston Churchill said, *'A lie gets halfway around the world before the truth has a chance to get its pants on.'*

"Boooo."

"Idiot."

"Get off."

An angry objector grabbed a roving microphone. "You're just anti-science, anti-capitalism and anti-progress. You're a Luddite, a flat earther."

At this point the hecklers and opposing voices started to become more organised as a section of the audience started chanting.

"FLAT EARTH. FLAT EARTH."

Some people started stamping their feet, whilst others turned on those who were objecting. Fierce arguments broke out with lots of raised voices and finger pointing.

"Is this typical of the level of debate at the Literature Festival these days?" Catherine asked Sky.

"Only when Gerald's in full flow," Sky replied.

Meanwhile the chanting of 'flat earth' continued to grow in volume and resonated around the venue. By now a number of uniformed security contractors had appeared in the marquee. One of them tried to escort Gerald from the platform, but he refused, standing firm instead.

"You see, this is exactly what I am trying to say. They won't let you speak openly..." Gerald's voice trailed off as he was unceremoniously hauled away from the platform. In the meantime, flower displays were knocked over and chairs upturned. More security arrived. Police with dogs entered the tent as pushing broke out in the audience and several punches were thrown.

"Can you all please clear the tent." An announcement was made from the platform. "Clear the tent."

Catherine and Sky fought their way out through the agitated, dispersing crowd. Sky was knocked to the floor by a group of young men who tried to rush the platform. Catherine dragged her to her feet, but her pink wig fell to the ground, exposing her dark hair beneath. Catherine realised that this was the first time she had ever seen Sky without some kind of head covering.

"You okay?"

"Yes, fine," Sky reassured her.

"Academic debate was never like this in my day," Catherine commented ironically.

More private security contractors and police started to converge on the marquee. Soon the unmistakable sound of a police drone could be heard overhead amidst the shouting and barking of police dogs.

"Let's get out of here," Sky shouted. "This could turn ugly."

They made their way through the developing melee into the park outside. By now the area was awash with security; some in uniform, some wearing plain clothes, but all distinguished by their earpieces and their serious intent.

"Where did all these security people come from?" Catherine asked no-one in particular.

"This isn't good," Sky explained. "They've been looking for an excuse to close this festival down for years. This is playing right into their hands."

As they threaded their way through the tented village, the crowds and noise thinned out but Sky was still walking briskly and purposefully.

"What's the hurry? Remember my legs aren't as young as yours," Catherine called out after her.

"We need to keep walking. Just walk." Sky was carrying her wig, her gaze was fixed straight ahead, trying to avoid eye contact with anyone passing by. She took Catherine's arm and marched her quickly away from the area.

By now Catherine was aware that they were being followed. A large Mediterranean-looking gentleman with a beard had crossed over the road and was matching them step for step as they strode out along the pavement. He stood out from the crowd by the suit he was wearing and by his menacing manner.

"Who's he?" Catherine asked Sky.

"I don't know, but he's moving in the wrong direction to be part of festival security." Immediately Sky tugged Catherine's arm and they both turned sharply to enter a narrow passageway. Sky pushed Catherine into a doorway and then flattened her own body against the wall. The man in the suit walked past, apparently unaware of their detour. Sky breathed a deep sigh of relief. Catherine's heart was pumping furiously; she was not used to such exertion. "Let's get out of here," she said anxiously.

The two of them slipped down the passageway and onto a residential street that carried on towards an assembly building, only to see the same man in a suit now coming towards them. They turned into the entrance of the assembly building, hoping to find sanctuary inside, but the door was locked. The man in the suit was bearing down on them. He reached into his jacket pocket and removed a pistol from its holster. He smiled in a cold manner as he advanced towards them and flicked his head to one side, indicating the direction he wanted them to move in. Catherine looked across to Sky, hoping that somehow she would instinctively know what to do in such circumstances. Sky's look of terror revealed just how out of her depth she was feeling; her usual calm efficiency having deserted her. Catherine's heart was pounding inside her chest as she found herself paralysed by indecision.

Suddenly there was a popping sound and a buzzing

followed by a crackling noise. The man in the suit froze, his eyes bulging and mouth open, then slowly he slumped to his knees and then onto his face. He twitched and writhed as he lay on the hard ground. Wires could be seen coming from the back of his neck and leading back to two strangers standing behind him. One of them was holding a Taser gun out in front of him.

"Good shot, Greg," the unarmed man announced.

"This really is my last favour. Don't ask for my help again," the man with the Taser replied.

"If you value your lives, then you'd better come with me now," the unarmed man commented. "When this one recovers, he's gonna be one unhappy bunny."

With that Catherine and Sky stepped over the man in a suit as he lay twitching inelegantly on the ground. The two men led them around the corner and into a sea of festival goers. They kept looking back, but the man in the suit failed to surface. Eventually the two men led them into an underground car park. The man who had used the Taser then high-fived the other man and headed off in another direction.

"You're with me from now on," the other man explained and opened the door to his car.

"Yes, but…?"

"Look, I know you're frightened," he said. "If the truth be known, then I've been bricking it for the last twenty minutes. I don't normally do this sort of thing, but these aren't normal times. You can either take your chances with our friend with a sore head back there, or you can come with me and I'll try to explain as much as I can."

In view of the circumstances, Catherine and Sky concluded that they really didn't have much choice. Five minutes later they were in the backseat of the stranger's car, forcing their way through traffic, trying to leave the town centre behind.

"My name," announced the stranger, "is Leroy Finch. I'm

not a policeman or security contractor. I'm a journalist, or at least that's what I used to be."

"Your voice is familiar," Catherine noted. "You haven't been on TV or something, have you?"

"No, not me. Strictly hard copy and low profile," Finch replied.

"I know why you're familiar. It was you asking Sir Geoffrey those awkward questions earlier"

"Just looking for answers and you, young lady," Finch cast a glance in Sky's direction, "are someone I have been hoping to meet for some considerable time."

Sky remained silent as she tried to scrape her hair back and tie it with an elastic band. She looked crumpled and dejected, like a cornered animal, resigned to her fate, her confidence all but eroded.

"Can anyone tell me just what's happening here?" Catherine felt the need to remind the others of her presence.

"I'm not sure I can," replied Finch, "but I think that your companion probably has more of an idea than both of us."

Sky remained impassive.

The car made its way through the outskirts of Cheltenham before taking a side road that eventually led to a small airfield surrounded by industrial buildings. The car swung into an unmarked opening which led up to a manned security barrier. A brief exchange followed between Finch and the two members of security staff, ending up with them being invited to look into the rear of the car. Apparently reassured by what they saw, the car was waved through and onto the tarmac.

"Right, we're here," Finch announced as the car came to a halt.

"Yes, but why are we here?" Catherine asked.

"Perhaps your friend can explain. After all she owns all of this!"

Chapter 14

Weeks had passed since Eleanor had last spoken with Jez. She had deliberately avoided the gym, not wanting to meet him at the water cooler again. The very idea of him stalking or watching over her was highly disturbing. One minute there was this fit young man with a dreamy expression and faraway disposition whose eyes kept meeting hers across the treadmills and cross-trainers; then the more she found out about him, the weirder he became. He didn't take oxygen, didn't do sex, he didn't even work out all that seriously, yet he saw himself as some kind of self-appointed guardian and protector. It seemed that rather than him being the object of her weird fantasies, she might just be the object of his.

"You were right, Gill," Eleanor announced, as she handed Gill and Nicola a bottle of chilled Pinot Grigio and pulled up a chair to join them at one of their girl's Friday night out at a local tapas bar.

"Right about what?" Gill replied

"Right about Jez – the bloke I've been trying to date from the gym."

"Oh, the carrot-topped Geordie boy."

"He's not ginger, he's auburn, but he's also not so innocent after all."

"Tell me more." Gill put down her mobile and made eye contact with Eleanor, suddenly gripped by renewed interest in her love life. "Has he been showing you a few tricks in the bedroom after all?"

"No, nothing like that. Seems delusional. Sees himself as some kind protector or guardian assigned to look after me."

"There you go. What did I tell you about guardian angels?" Nicola sat back in her chair, a smug look upon her face, finally vindicated in her own eyes.

"One delusion doesn't prove another delusion. I thought that he was mysterious, a bit different. Like he had hidden depths, but now I realise that he is just a bit odd and slightly sad."

"So what prompted this new assessment? Has he been stalking you?" Nicola asked.

"Not really; well, sort of, I suppose, but not in a sinister way."

Eleanor then described the incident in the car park. Nicola appeared somewhat dismissive of the idea of her life being threatened but urged her to take a break from what she regarded as an obsessive infatuation with Jez.

"Look, Ellie," Nicola insisted, "you need to let go of all these new friends and new ideas. They won't bring you any joy."

"And I suppose you know what will bring me joy then?"

"Possibly. Possibly not. All I know is that you've been through a lot and you need a break. You need to get a little fun back into your life."

"Any suggestions?" Eleanor asked, not really wanting to hear the response.

"Funnily enough I do." Nicola explained, "We're having a girly weekend away at my parents' holiday home. Gill and the others are all coming. Why don't you join us?"

"It will be a man-free zone. Time to reconnect with your feminine side," Gill added.

"Chance to consume large amounts of wine and chocolate as we lounge around in our pyjamas whilst giving each other makeovers and watching old movies. How does that sound to you?"

The proposition of such a weekend carried very little appeal for Eleanor; it was the sort of activity she usually shied away from. However, it did promise to be a man-free zone and would provide any ideal way to take her mind completely off Jez.

A week later she found herself at the wheel of her small electric eco-car, heading into the unknown as the car bravely struggled to cope with the stormy conditions arising from a sudden summer downpour. It was a rather ancient eco-car and not blessed with either great power or prolonged battery life. Battling against the weather was draining her battery as her lights and wipers worked overtime to penetrate the darkness and driving rain. As her car laboured along flooded country roads at 25 mph, she became aware of the bright lights of a large 4x4 vehicle following her. She envied the power and durability of such a car in comparison with her own flimsy town car which struggled in such extreme conditions.

The four by four followed her for some distance and as she slowed on the hills she became aware that it was following rather uncomfortably close behind her. She slowed almost to a halt and ventured to lower her window in order to wave the car on. However, the 4x4 displayed no intention to overtake, but rather continued to follow at rather unnervingly, close proximity. As she approached a small humpback bridge, the glare of the other car's headlights in her rear-view mirror became intolerable. She decided to stop and take issue with the driver, but as she did so, her car was shunted from behind. She tried to apply the brakes, but her vehicle was no match for the solidity of the overbearing four-by-four. Then with one almighty shove her small eco-car was rammed once more and pushed off the road and through the supporting wall of the humpback bridge.

Fortunately, the car landed the right way up in the swollen river a short distance below. Brown bubbling waters cascaded over the bonnet and swirled around the cabin. Eleanor decided to get out as quickly as possible. She was vaguely aware of the other vehicle driving off, but most of her attention was taken up with trying to get out of a car that was now filling rapidly with foaming water. It proved impossible to force the driver's door open against the raging torrent outside, just then the car's electrics failed, plunging her into near total darkness and preventing her from opening any of the windows.

Eleanor decided the only way to get out was through the car's rear door. She fought and fumbled her way over the seats of the partially submerged car which was now listing forward into the oncoming flow. She had climbed Everest, run a marathon in Death Valley and base jumped from some of the world's highest buildings, but this was not how she intended to die. She had experienced one close shave with death; she was not going to let this river take her.

Summoning all her strength, she managed to force the rear door to yield, helped by the fact that it was now partially clear of the water as the car began to sink nose down into the river. Lowering herself into the cold, swirling waters, she realised that she would have a better chance of survival by staying close to the vehicle. All around was darkness and stillness save for the gushing torrent. Desperately she clung on to the rear of the vehicle, convinced that another car would soon pass by and see her predicament, yet none came. After what was probably fifteen minutes hanging onto the rear of the car in the hope of rescue, she was feeling increasingly cold and weak. She remembered all her survival training and how hypothermia could slowly creep up on victims almost unnoticed, causing them to lose consciousness and quietly slip away. She started to count out loud to keep up her concentration. She was not going to fall asleep and slip under the flood waters. She kept telling herself that she could do this and not to give up. She could barely feel her legs, but took the decision to try and swim to safety whilst she still had the strength and core temperature.

The river bank was only about fifteen feet away but the swollen waters picked her up like a cork and spun her around relentlessly. Ferocious torrents of water threatened to overwhelm her as she was carried further downstream, bobbing around like driftwood, struggling for breath in the fast flowing water. She could see the vague outline of her stricken vehicle disappearing into the distance as she managed to catch hold of the branch of an overhanging tree. She hung onto the branch for her very life, catching her breath and recovering her strength. Every now and then branches and submerged debris would collide with her, but somehow she managed to hold her body against the raging force of the river, breathing deeply and trying not to hyperventilate. She pulled herself partially out of the water, swinging her legs over the branch in order to secure her position and was then able to pull herself along the branch before dropping into shallower, calmer water. From there she finally succeeded in dragging herself up onto the river bank.

As she lay on the partially flooded river bank, she sensed that something was very wrong. She looked down to see that her prosthetic foot was no longer attached and her leg stump had cut a channel through the mud alongside her good leg. Her whole body felt numb and unresponsive and she couldn't remember if her false foot had become detached in the car or later on in the river.

Having lain on the river bank for some considerable time, she succeeded in hobbling along beside the raging river to locate a partially submerged branch which she was able to retrieve from the river and improvise into a crutch to assist her general movement. Once in place, she was then able to use the branch to lever he tired body back up to the small humpback bridge where her car had previously entered the water.

As Eleanor limped and stumbled her way back along the country lane, she knew she was in trouble. Even though she had escaped the flooded river, her core body temperature remained very low. She had seen climbers get into trouble when hypothermia had set in, but, unlike them, she had no access to shelter or warm clothing, whilst the loss of her prosthetic foot meant that she was unable to warm herself up through physical exercise. Her only option was to continue to shuffle along wearily in the hope that someone would find her. It suddenly dawned on Eleanor just how isolated and vulnerable she was. At least a climber experiencing difficulties had colleagues and fellow climbers to call upon, but she was quite alone and possibly still under threat, unsure where to go for help or who she could trust. For the very first time Eleanor felt afraid. This was not the same kind of fear that people experience standing on the edge of tall buildings or pushing themselves to the very limits of their personal endurance. She had experienced and conquered such feelings many times; this was a different kind of fear, the fear that comes from feeling totally lost and alone. It was a solitary fear associated with the total surrender of self-control. She needed help and she needed it quickly.

After a few hundred yards of trying to retrace her journey back along the country lane, the night sky lit up with the distinctive outline of vehicle headlights. The heavy rain has ceased by now and the night sky took on a semi-luminous hue which at least provided some light to guide her. Nevertheless, she remained supremely cold and dangerously weak, continually gasping for breath and shaking uncontrollably.

Momentarily her spirits rallied at the sight of the approaching car. She immediately started shouting and waving her arms, summoning up strength from untapped reserves, only to check her actions as she realised that this could be the same four-by-four returning to check that she really had been taken by the swollen river. Curtailing her enthusiasm, she collapsed into a nearby hedge and waited to see the outline of the approaching car. Fortunately, the reassuring appearance of a commercial hybrid van came into view and through the judicious use of the improvised crutch she managed to place herself in front of its path, forcing the van to a sudden halt.

A burly man in a reflective jacket slid open the door and was about to give her a mouthful of abuse, only to be stopped in his tracks at the sight that greeted him.

"Bloody hell, luv. What's happened to you?" Eleanor must have presented quite a shocking sight. Plastered in mud, covered in cuts and bruises, she was leaning on her improvised crutch in order to re-balance her body and wheezing from the cold night, barely able to speak. Never had she been so pleased to see an Electricity Company engineer before. Her trembling body fell into his cabin in an untidy, soggy heap, pausing only to ramble incoherently about her car going into the river. By now she was shaking so violently from the cold that she struggled to offer any clear explanation of what had happened to her. She sensed his shocked reaction to her missing foot and tried to explain, but numbness froze her jaw and rendered any explanation even more incoherent.

The engineer wrapped her up in his coat and a blanket and set off towards the nearest hospital, stopping only to report the incident to the local police. She didn't provide all the details of the incident to the police, thinking it best to report it as an accident. She was still unsure of the identity of her attacker and uncertain exactly who she could trust and thought it best to play the role of the idiot city dweller hopelessly lost in rural

Oxfordshire, who had recklessly lost control of a lightweight eco-car on a narrow country road. The police appeared persuaded by her story, but insisted she report to the local hospital in order to check her out for any symptoms of hypothermia. Eleanor was reluctant to do so and used what remained of her innate feminine charms on the white van man to drop her off at the cottage Nicola has booked for the weekend instead. Arriving at the cottage four hours late and resembling a drowned rat, draped in a car blanket, Eleanor summoned up enough energy to blurt out a vague explanation of her ordeal to her girlfriends. Two hot showers and a hot bath later, she was able to raise her body temperature enough to stop shaking before she fell into an exhausted, troubled sleep.

The following morning, she awoke in crisp, clean sheets and a warm bed.

"This is becoming a bit of a habit." Nicola was standing over her, wearing a worried expression. "How many times are you going to dice with death? You even manage to turn a girly weekend away into a white water rapids ride."

"It wasn't my idea, take it from me," Eleanor replied. She then filled Nicola in with a fuller explanation of what had happened to her, leaving out the details about the four by four ramming into her. "I guess I must have skidded on the crest of the bridge and lost control."

"You look like shit." Nicola's assessment was quite accurate. Eleanor had been battered and bruised by her ordeal, the combination of collisions with driftwood and hiding in a hedgerow.

"Thanks a million. Not my best look, I guess."

Nicola quickly changed the subject, not wishing to distress Eleanor further. "Look, d'you want the good news or the bad news?" she asked cheerily in a change of mood.

"Oh, hit me with the bad news first. I've had plenty recently."

"The police have recovered your car from the river."

"That's the bad news?"

"No, the bad news is that it's a total wreck."

"Oh, don't worry, it always was. And the good news?"

"The good news is…" Nicola paused for dramatic effect and reached down under Eleanor's bed. "Guess what they found in there?" She proudly held Eleanor's prosthetic foot aloft which was adorned by a bright yellow bow and a bunch of flowers. "We've even cleaned it up for you, although in fairness, it still smells of the river."

"Don't worry. My leg goes into it, not my nose," Eleanor replied with a sense of elation. "Thanks, Nicola, you're good friend." The two of them embraced and kissed.

"Don't do that to me again, Ellie. Promise me. Gill and I and all your friends couldn't stand it. We don't want to lose you. It's time to start taking fewer risks and looking after yourself more."

"I know."

"Whatever you're getting into, it's time to get out."

"I promise. I promise." In that short moment Eleanor had an epiphany and realised just how vulnerable she was. She wasn't superwoman; she didn't have to carry all her burdens on her own. She could have very easily drowned and no-one would have known and no-one would have come to her help. It was time to seek the protection of others.

Fifty miles away Jez was feeling miserable. He had been asked to do something and had failed in his task. What was more, this wasn't just some simple task or errand; it actually involved someone he had come to care very much about. He had made a decision some time ago to dedicate his life to the service of others. Such a promise came at a cost. He knew that his pledge would be costly – not just financially, but emotionally and socially. However, he had never quite realised what paying that cost would mean.

He wanted to give himself to serving the greater good, but what greater good would be served if he just felt miserable and lonely? Eleanor had got under his skin. She was there every time he closed his eyes. He saw reminders of her among the broken people he worked with. He caught himself recognising her in a crowd, only to be disappointed when he got closer and saw that it was just someone who looked similar. He wrote her letters and drafted emails that he never sent. He even found himself doodling little caricatures and cartoons of her during boring business meetings.

She felt like unfinished business. He had let her down when she was at her most vulnerable. He had failed, not only in terms of the task he had been appointed to undertake, but also as a friend and fellow human being. He realised that she valued her independence and self-reliance, yet he should have made it easier for her to receive his help and protection. What was the point in dedicating his life to caring for other people if he wasn't able to help the person he cared about the most?

Suddenly his mobile lit up and burst into life:

'Ok i give in. when can we meet? Ellie.'

His heart leapt within his chest. He immediately sent back a reply:

'r.u ok? Has anything happened? J'

He waited for what seemed like an eternity, wondering why she hadn't replied immediately. Finally, the answer came:

'i've decided that if i cant stop running, then at least i need 2 find a running partner. come & get me. orchard cottage, balham lane Ox. rg96tx. Ellie'

The following day Jez located the remote cottage, knocked on the door and was shown into the living room by Nicola, only to see Eleanor surrounded by homemade cards, flowers and helium-filled balloons. Jez parted the balloons to see her swollen, lacerated face. All his protective instincts welled up within him. He just wanted to sweep her into his arms, but

199

realised that this was neither the time nor the place for such public shows of affection.

Eleanor let out a little yelp of delight. "Jez!"

"I would ask what happened to you, but I guess this is just another day at the office for a thrill-seeker like you."

"Not quite. I just fancied taking a midnight dip in a raging river."

Eleanor's comments were disarming and dismissive, but Jez could see a clear change within her. There was real fear in her eyes and a fragility he had never seen before. As he approached her, she caught his arm and pulled him towards her.

"You win, Jez," she whispered.

He could see that it took a lot of courage for her to speak this way. She waited until Nicola had left the room and then deliberately lowered her voice, speaking softly and slowly.

"This is getting serious. I want to know what's going on. I want to know what you're up to. I can't face this on my own."

"What really happened?"

"I don't know, but I was followed and then shoved off the road." Her voice broke and faded. "I was left to die out there, Jez. Does this gold surveillance you spoke about involve assassination?"

"No, it shouldn't do. Something's wrong."

"Then who are these people and why am I their target?"

"I don't know, but from now on you need to trust other people, Ellie. Leave things with me and I'll get you out of here."

Chapter 15

The next couple of days passed uneventfully.

Eleanor stayed on at the cottage with Nicola, who had decided to take a few days off work to look after her. Eleanor's parents arrived to visit her and passed an awkward couple of hours in her company, mostly making tutting noises and shaking their heads in disbelief at what they assumed was another example of her reckless, risk-taking behaviour. Not wishing to alarm them, Eleanor managed to keep the true nature of her ordeal secret, along with the real cause of the accident.

Eventually, when she felt stronger, Eleanor persuaded Nicola to provide her with a lift to a nearby garage, explaining that she needed to sort out some paperwork for her wrecked car. She would then return home by her own means later.

Eleanor walked past the garage reception and showroom in order to seek out the customer car park at the rear of the site. She located an ancient-looking Land Rover Discovery and slipped into the rear foot well of the vehicle, covering herself with a large blanket and waited motionless for the driver to return. Five minutes later a tall mechanic returned to the vehicle and drove it around to the reception area at the front of the site where a customer was waiting nervously. Papers were exchanged and then the customer retrieved his vehicle and drove off, pausing only briefly to acknowledge the mechanic and to thank him for all the care shown to his classic four by four.

"Are you all right in the back, Ellie?" Jez asked as he cleared the garage forecourt and entered the main dual carriageway that led back towards the big city.

"Of course I'm all right. I'm used to hiding in the back of filthy Land Rovers," Eleanor replied as she revealed herself from under the car blanket.

"Did anyone see you arrive?"

"No, just Nicola, but she thinks that I've come to inspect my car and sort out the insurance."

"Good. Sorry about all this cloak and dagger stuff," Jez apologised, "but this really is necessary from now on."

"Even out here?"

"Yes. They found you once, they can find you again, especially with the latest facial recognition cameras. So stay low until we get nearer to home."

The rather uncomfortable journey that followed took Eleanor back into the throbbing heart of the city and through some of the poor and neglected parts she was unfamiliar with.

"Is this where you live?"

"Yeh, isn't it great? I wouldn't want to live anywhere else," Jez explained with obvious pride. Their car was suddenly lit up by the penetrating beam of an overhead searchlight. Bathed in quivering light, the car felt almost translucent. "Don't worry. It's just a drone looking for dealers. They never use a battered wreck like this." Sure enough the searchlight quickly moved on to alight upon other nearby vehicle before disappearing over an old warehouse building.

Shortly afterwards Jez turned the rattling Land Rover into a street of terraced houses. Many of the properties were daubed with graffiti and political slogans. Homemade banners hung from a number of windows, each declaring their defiance and identifying their territory through their association with various local community groups. Jez drove a little further to an adjacent street where some of the houses were boarded up. He parked outside a large terrace house that stood between two apparently derelict and empty houses. The building rose majestically into the night sky, displaying the fading grandeur of former years. "We're here," he declared cheerfully.

Eleanor examined the façade of the building and forced a smile. There were few apparent signs of life. Some diffused light escaped from an upstairs window and there was a muted sound of music coming from somewhere inside. "Is this some kind of squat?" she enquired, hoping that it wasn't.

"No. It just looks that way. We like to think of it as an urban monastery," replied Jez proudly.

Eleanor was still trying to unpack what Jez had said about a monastery, whilst he led her into the building which was illuminated with candles and gas lamps. "Have you been cut off?"

"No, we like to generate our own energy where we can, but unfortunately solar power is a bit unreliable. We have an agreement with the utility company, but we have to make a few savings at the moment until we get back into credit with them." Jez's manner was very matter of fact, as if it was normal to live by gaslight in the middle of twenty-first century London.

Upstairs they entered a large communal kitchen where Jez introduced Eleanor to one of the other residents. She noticed his hands first; they were unscrubbed, weathered hands; hands that had struggled, hands that were cracked from hard work, but strong. The hands greeted Eleanor with a vice-like grip that conveyed solidity. They belonged to a bald headed, tattooed man in his mid-forties.

"This is Brillo."

Eleanor looked puzzled.

"Yeh, not his real name. It's just he can get a bit abrasive," Jez explained.

The man rolled his eyes, as if he had heard this explanation a thousand times before. "And I thought it was because I was useful to have around and made other people shine," Brillo replied ironically, his gaze fixed firmly on Eleanor.

Jez then introduced her to the other residents. "This is Lucinda and this is Faith." Two young ladies, one European and one Chinese, looked up from food preparation duties and nodded in Eleanor's direction. "This is Sanjeev. He's our techie." A young Asian man in a smart suit greeted Eleanor with one hand whilst texting with the other. "There are a couple of other people who live here, but I guess they're not around at the moment." Jez scoured the room and checked the body language of the other residents for confirmation. "There's someone special I'd like you to meet."

"Aren't we all special, Jez?" Lucinda corrected Jez whilst peeling vegetables.

"Of course you all are," Jez replied and then went over to give Lucinda a warm hug and a little squeeze. "But I want Ellie to meet the boss. Is Sister Bernadette in?"

"She's upstairs. With a client. Should be finished soon," Faith added.

Eleanor drew close to Jez and held onto his arm. She was feeling completely out of her comfort zone and in need of some physical reassurance. She pulled him towards her, whispering through clenched teeth, "What's going on here? What's this monastery and Sister crap?"

"Well, that's what we are. Maybe not a perfect description, but it'll do. We're a community of believers living under a rule of life. Part of that rule involves how we are led and directed. That's where Sister Bernadette comes in."

"Woah…let's back up here a little." Eleanor let go of Jez, clearly trying to process a whole series of new ideas and experiences.

"Don't worry. It's all cool." Jez's words trailed off as he went upstairs to locate Sister Bernadette whilst a large mug of coffee was placed into her hands by Brillo. He gave her a knowing look, a nod and a smile that suggested she was not the first visitor they had entertained who had brought a whole series of questions.

"Here y'are, luv. Wrap y'self round that. Don't worry, we haven't all got two heads, you know." Brillo's tone was reassuring.

"Are you all…" Eleanor hesitated "…believers here then?"

"Oh aye, luv," Brillo replied. "We all believe. Everyone believes in something; you just need to discover what that something is and then live by it. What d'you believe in?"

"I don't really know. A friends of mine tried to persuade me to believe in angels."

"Oh, all that mythical crap. More like shopping by stealth than a faith to live by. You don't want to be bothered by that bullshit, luv. Just an opiate to pacify the masses."

"Yeh, I kinda reached the same conclusion myself." Eleanor looked around the room, her eyes flickering with information overload. Uncertain whether she was in a safe place or in greater danger than before.

"You look like a rabbit caught in the headlights."

"Yeh, I guess I'm just trying to work out why I'm here and what here is."

"We get a few visitors with the same look in their eyes," Brillo reassured her.

"What about those two men who came last month?" Faith asked in faltering English. "Something strange about them."

"Oh aye. The posh ginger bloke in a flat cap and his minder. Now, if you want to see a fish out of water, they were a classic case." Brillo took out a small leather tobacco pouch and started to form a roll-up. "Something not quite right about those two. You could spot it a mile off."

"They ask many, many questions," Faith explained.

"Oh aye, a bit of an agenda with them," Brillo added.

"Do you think they were spying on you?" asked Eleanor.

"Oh aye. They were spies all right, but not the usual types." Brillo looked thoughtful and distant as if he was recalling some unsettling memory.

"What d'you mean?"

"Something didn't quite add up. More concerned about us recognising them, if anything. They got a clean bill of health, cleared our usual vetting checks, but you can tell when someone is ex-military. They both had that air about them and the younger one was keeping an eye on the posh bloke as if his life depended on it." Brillo explained, while taking a deep drag from his roll-up. "And he was carrying."

"You mean, he had a weapon?"

"Oh aye." Brillo sensed Eleanor's unease. "Anyhow, always assuming that you haven't come to spy on us, let me see if I can guess your story." Brillo pulled up a chair next to him and invited Eleanor to sit down. He studied her carefully as if she were an unusual work of art, whilst pulling strange, inquisitive expressions, intended to make her laugh. He leaned back in his chair, extinguished his roll-up, scratched his chin and then pointed at Eleanor whilst holding his coffee cup in his other hand. "All I know from Jez is that you're here because you're under surveillance, but my guess is that you were educated privately and raised in some leafy part of Surry. Daddy subsidised your lifestyle, but you managed to escape his grip and now you have a career of your own. How am I doing so far?"

"Not bad, do continue." Eleanor was starting to enjoy Brillo's directness and found his manner rather entertaining.

Her gaze once again was drawn to his hands. He had great hands. They looked as though they had been honed from solid marble. They were powerful hands. Rough and chapped, the sort that never appear properly clean. Hands that had worked hard in an age when fewer people had to use their physical strength as a way of earning their living. Hands that could be relied upon.

"You probably had a quite a sheltered life," Brillo continued, "but recently I would guess that something extraordinary has happened to open your eyes to a totally new perspective on life. You don't know what to do about this experience and so you're looking in all sorts of places for answers. Now, judging by all those cuts and bruises, you've probably started to ask too many questions and put yourself in line for some unwelcome attention. Hence Jez had to bring you in." Brillo leaned back on his chair with a smug look on his face. "How did I do?"

"About seven out of ten."

"Only seven! What did I miss out?"

"Plenty. This for starters." Eleanor immediately put her leg on the table and took off her prosthetic foot.

"Bloody hell." Brillo appeared quite taken aback and suddenly Eleanor was aware that all eyes in the room were now turned upon her. "A few of my old mates have got prosthetics, but I didn't see that one coming, luv."

"Most people don't," Eleanor replied whilst reattaching her prosthetic foot, "and that bit about a sheltered life… think again."

Just then Jez arrived. "Sister Bernadette is free now. Come upstairs, you two need to chat."

With that she was shown into an attic room which was being used as a study where a large lady sat tapping away at an ancient typewriter. She rose to meet Eleanor. She was wearing an array of flowing colours – purple, pink, brown and green. It was difficult to work out where her clothes began and ended; there appeared to be yards of different coloured materials wrapped around her in various ways. If this lady was a nun, then clearly she was not conventionally dressed. She was adorned in a modest amount of make-up and large earrings and had a wild mop of somewhat unkempt black hair with blue streaks, whilst around her neck spectacles hung from a cord. Despite her somewhat chaotic appearance, there was something about her that exuded calmness and understanding. She was like a kindly long-lost relative that you were immediately able to connect with, knowing that she would instinctively understand and accept you for who you were.

"Hello, Eleanor. We've been waiting to meet you. Jeremy has been very concerned." With that Bernadette embraced her and beckoned her to sit down on a slightly saggy sofa. Bernadette then sat opposite her in a brown faded armchair, she tucked her legs under her and sat quite still, studying her. "Please relax. We're quite informal here."

Momentarily Eleanor was lost for words. "Are you… are you a…a.."

"A nun?" Bernadette interjected.

"Yeh, it's just all this Sister crap. Oh, pardon my language." Eleanor found herself apologising nervously and showing a deference towards Bernadette that even surprised herself.

"Well, I would never call myself by that title. But in terms of how we seek to live here, then you could say that I'm a nun."

"But…"

"I know I don't look like Julie Andrews or Sister Act, do I?" Bernadette seemed to anticipate Eleanor's reaction.

"No." Eleanor realised that she had no cultural reference point for such an encounter. She felt as if she had fallen down the rabbit hole and landed in Wonderland. "So what is this place all about then and what do you and Jez represent?"

"We try not to represent anything. We try just to live authentically and by that, I mean that we try to locate our lives in the same place as our words."

"So, is this a…a monastery?" Eleanor struggled to even form the word in her mouth, it felt so ludicrous and alien to her.

"We seek to be a community of people serving our local community. We live in a modern way with modern challenges, but draw upon some of the wisdom of the past to be our guide."

"It all sounds a bit hippy to me. You're not into any weird beliefs or free love or growing your own dope, are you?"

"No, none of those things, although loving our neighbour is something we take seriously."

"Yeh, but who is your neighbour?" Eleanor asked rather irreverently.

"Someone else was once asked that question." Bernadette smiled knowingly. "Eleanor, have you any idea what's going on in terms of a big picture here?"

"What I do know is that nine months ago I hit the ground very hard in Norway and ended up looking down on myself as people tried to resuscitate me. What happened next, I still can't make any sense of, but I know it felt as real as you and me sitting here. In fact, it felt more real. It felt right and purposeful, as if this was how things were meant to be. It felt like returning – to my true home." Eleanor looked around the room. "Did you all have something like that happen to you as well?"

Bernadette just nodded. "No, not really, my dear. You truly have received a very special blessing. We all see things from a particular perspective, but each of us has arrived here by different paths. Some of us had special experiences to open our eyes such as the birth of child or a loss of loved one; others read the sacred texts and discovered the stories of faith for themselves; still others found that they didn't quite fit in and rejected the pressure to conform, join a tribe or adopt a brand or even get vaccinated. Some of us have always believed and saw no reason to change, no matter what had taken place."

"So what I saw was real?"

"What you saw was a sign, a tap on the shoulder, a reminder that there is something beyond our material world."

"But why me?"

"We can never know the answer to that question, my dear. Think of it as a personal wake-up call. So many people have forgotten how to believe; it's like something has been switched off inside, but what you have woken up to is something really important and most precious."

"But ever since my accident, whenever I've tried to explain to people the impact of this experience, they either disbelieve me, want me to get friendly with my guardian angel or else apparently they want to kill me just because I've broken some mysterious taboo in speaking about it. And now, with the greatest respect," Eleanor paused to regain her composure, "I discover that a group of vegetarian, eco-warrior monks have been stalking me for my own protection."

Bernadette smiled, "Oh, we're not all vegetarians, I can assure you. Some of my best friends eat meat. Which reminds me, before we talk we need to eat. Food is always a good way to get to know each other and I think it's time for us to share hospitality." Bernadette's suggestion appeared rather obtuse, but Eleanor was learning that whatever was going on, she was at least safe now. Explanations would follow in due course.

The evening meal took place around a large wooden refectory table. It had been such a long time since Eleanor had eaten with other people in such a way, probably not since boarding school. Normally she ate off a tray in front of her smart TV or grabbed some street food or else ate out at a restaurant with friends, but this felt very retro with Bernadette sitting at the head of the table clearly operating as the mistress of ceremonies. Each person present at the meal seemed to have their duties to perform and contributed in different ways.

Eleanor was intrigued by the priority they gave to eating together. "It's been a while since I actually sat down and shared a meal together like this."

"We're a community built on hospitality and so eating together is important to us. It's not just a way of forming community, but also a sign of what being part of a community means," Bernadette explained.

Eleanor didn't have a clue what Bernadette meant, but smiled politely and nodded as if in agreement.

"Oh aye," said Brillo, "we do a lot of eating here and sometimes we manage to fit in work between courses."

A brief word of thanks and gratitude was offered before the meal. Then they all ate together. Despite Eleanor's expectations, the meal was neither vegetarian nor entirely solemn. Indeed, copious amounts of homemade beer and wine flowed throughout, which quite shocked Eleanor as she assumed that they would all be teetotal and prudish.

As conversation ensued and those present relaxed into laughter and gentle self-parody, Eleanor started to enjoy herself. They were a diverse group of characters and much less uptight and image-conscious than her girlfriends. They were quirky, occasionally breaking out into foreign languages when they wanted to clarify certain points in their conversations, yet constantly forthright and highly motivated, challenging each other without appearing threatened or competitive. Eleanor started to warm to them; they felt more like a family than a gathering of friends or housemates.

"So, Eleanor," said Bernadette as she reached out to touch Eleanor's outstretched hand. The others seemed to recognise a hidden signal and started to gradually clear the table. "You want to know why Jez brought you here and why your safety is under threat?"

"Yes, I think I'm owed that much at least."

"Well, as you have no doubt realised by now, we are a community of believers, living in a time when belief has been largely discredited and pushed to the margins of mainstream life."

"I'm not sure I understand."

"Some people might think that we are nostalgic for some kind of former era or a primitive world view that has been eclipsed by more progressive ideas."

"Is that why you were using a typewriter earlier this evening?"

"I hadn't thought of it like that, but using a typewriter is a lot more secure than any firewall and a very useful way of keeping sensitive information away from prying eyes. We like to utilise ancient approaches to modern problems, but we don't see our role as guardians of the past, rather as bearers of hope for the future."

"Now you've lost me completely."

"Your experience up in Norway was an insight. A jolt to attract your attention. A peek into a reality that has been closed off to many people."

"So was it real?"

"Maybe, maybe not. I don't know. It's just one of the mysteries of life. But what I do know is that we all experience such moments. For you it was your accident in Norway. These things come to us from outside to suggest another world, another reality, another perspective. They are signposts to other ways of thinking and other ways of living."

"Is that why I'm here? Is that why people are trying to intimidate me or even rub me out?"

"Possibly. Have you shared what happened to you in Norway with many people?"

"No, not really. Just with a handful of friends and then posted a few things on my blog and Twitter feed."

"Oh, I see. And if you don't mind me asking, just how many followers do you have on Twitter?"

"Only about a couple of hundred thousand, but it's come down a bit recently."

"TWO HUNDRED THOUSAND!" For the first time since she had met her, Bernadette appeared taken aback and surprised. "Are you some kind of public figure or do you just have a lot of friends?"

"No, I just do crazy stunts and like to post the videos online. It brings in a lot of followers as well as some income. You should try it…or no, I guess you wouldn't." Eleanor corrected herself.

"Anything else?"

"A bit of modelling. Some commercial endorsements, mostly for sportswear and outdoor pursuits gear, but less than I used to. I've posted a few selfies about branding recently and it's lost me quite a bit of work."

"That explains it," Sanjeev muttered and immediately stood up, gripped by a sense of purpose and quickly made his way out of the room.

Bernadette gave a deep sigh. "What happened to you in Norway is not exactly empirical evidence, but publicly sharing experiences like that would make people stop and think, particularly when those experiences change your behaviour and you start disassociating yourself from the values that other people hold dear. If that starts to erode the consensus that has been constructed, then you could be perceived as a threat to that consensus. And that would certainly put you in danger as a result."

"Enough danger to want to have me killed?"

"That still doesn't quite make sense. We're all a little puzzled that your story has produced such an extreme reaction," Bernadette explained.

At that point Sanjeev re-entered the room, computer tablet in hand and a look of vindication on his face. "Gold surveillance," he announced. "Gold surveillance. It still doesn't explain why you are on a gold surveillance list."

"What is gold surveillance then?"

"It's one of the highest security threats. It's normally reserved for proven activists, rather than ideological threats." Sanjeev tapped the screen of his tablet to reveal a live satellite image of Greater London populated by a series of yellow spots. "These are all the active surveillance targets in this area."

Eleanor peered over his shoulder to see a number of flashing numbers recorded over a grid of the city.

"These numbers represent people who are currently under surveillance. The different colours relate to the perceived security risk."

"How did you get access this information?"

"Best not to know." Sanjeev appeared slightly embarrassed and Eleanor was aware of disapproving looks aimed in his direction from around the room. "After the 'Garden Party Bombings' all CCTV images have to be archived for at least a year for security reasons. Most operators simply don't have that sort of storage capacity so they upload them onto a cloud on a virtual server. These servers are not exactly secure and all you need is an interface with some facial recognition software and, lo and behold, all the cameras that have been recording car number plates and looking for shoplifters become part of a national surveillance network. It's Big Brother by the back door."

"Is that legal?"

"No, not at all, so when people find a way to hack into this network those who operate it can hardly make a fuss."

"So how come they know where I am? I've been using that app that Jez gave me and my mobile is turned off most of the time."

"Yes, that app of mine is OK up to a point, but you can still be followed by other means."

The look of incredulity upon Eleanor's face displayed her deep unease with the thought that she was being constantly monitored without her knowledge.

"If you really want to know, then it's quite simple." Sanjeev explained, "All that sportswear and designer clothing you like to wear is connected to online devices. You probably wear a heart monitor in your sports bra and pedometer in your waistband?"

"Yeh, so what?"

"Well, they all upload data and so they'll give away your location to various servers."

"Still doesn't explain why I'm being monitored and followed."

"No, but my guess would be more to do with a cock-up than a conspiracy. If you had a number of high-risk surveillance targets following you online or downloading your videos, then you soon get cross-referenced on someone's watch list. The next thing you know, your name is out there as a threat or subversive influence. Once you're on a watch list, then that information has a value and can be traded just like any other commodity. It might be that your number simply attracted some speculative attention which resulted in it becoming overvalued and falling into the hands of some private operator trying to make a name for themselves."

"But doesn't anyone check out to see what I'm actually saying and doing?"

"Look, no-one's in charge, it's a jungle out there. Since security was scaled up, the costs soared, so it was outsourced to save money and the anarchy of the market took over. You can't have such widespread coverage as well as complete control and accountability." Just then Sanjeev's eyes lit up. "Whooh, this is what I was looking for." Turning his tablet around so that Eleanor and Bernadette could see more clearly, he started to explain what the images meant. "This is a network surveillance feed from yesterday. This yellow number 276 is a unique surveillance identity. Look, you can follow a track of their movements."

Eleanor peered into the computer screen, not really sure she wanted to see what Sanjeev was talking about.

"This could be you. Is this where you met Jez yesterday?"

"Yes, I think so, more or less." Eleanor traced the various occurrences of a yellow number 276 over the display with her finger, trying to recall the journey she had taken with Jez. "Yes, that's the garage when I met Jez, but look, it runs out just here." Eleanor pointed to the bottom of the display where several other yellow numbers were located.

"Hmm. Just as I thought," said Sanjeev, catching Bernadette's concerned expression, "they know you're here."

Suddenly some of the calmness that had enveloped Eleanor since she arrived in the community abandoned her. Once again she felt under threat, confused and angry, as if she was the victim of some huge misunderstanding. She looked towards Bernadette for reassurance.

"What have they got to fear about me and my little adventures? Are they worried that too many people will start visiting their local assembly buildings again?"

"Oh, my dear, have you visited one of those recently?" Bernadette enquired.

"Yes, not long ago."

"And what did you think of it?"

"I think that it was all about manipulation and marketing. But there was still something about the place, something that suggested there was a larger story being played out, yet one which was hidden from view."

"Did you look at the stained glass?" By now Jez had returned to the table, three large mugs of herbal tea in hand.

"Yes, I did."

"Did they give you any clues?"

"Not really. A lot of people with tea plates behind their heads." Jez and Bernadette smiled at each other. "Nicola said that they were all connected with various angels. There was this really fit-looking bloke in the centre of things though. He had this massive plus sign behind him. I found that a bit confusing."

At that point a familiar look crept across Bernadette's face. She smiled, rose from the table and removed a black leather-bound book from a drawer in a cabinet. "Have you ever seen this book before?"

"No, is it a recipe book?"

"More of a guide book," Bernadette explained. Then for the next hour she and Jez slowly took Eleanor through some of the most important stories from the book and explained that the really fit-looking bloke with the plus sign was actually a historical character that millions of people over the centuries had come to believe in and follow. The plus sign was a drawing of a wooden cross, the means of his execution and a symbol of his death.

"He is the reason we are here," Bernadette explained. "Everything we work for, everything we believe, the way we try to live our lives. It all comes from our desire to serve and follow him."

"So why have I never heard about this sacred book before and this carpenter who changed so many people's lives? How come these stories have been forgotten?"

"We know that change has been happening slowly for many years, but in this country, the pace of change accelerated dramatically in recent times. The ground shifted after the 'Garden Party Bombings'. Laws were passed, institutions reformed and projects mothballed, but then something deeper and more personal took hold. A sort of falling out of love. First of all, we thought that it was just national grief – a hysterical public reaction to something people couldn't accommodate rationally. But that didn't explain the suddenness or severity of the loss of spiritual roots and vocabulary. Next thing we knew, all the churches were empty."

"Churches?" The word seemed to hang in a vacant space before Eleanor, inviting further exploration. It carried an air of familiarity, yet without recognition, like the answer given at a quiz the split second after you were searching in your mind to remember it. "I know I should know what they are, but can you remind me?"

"They are just groups or communities of believers. They used to meet in those strange gothic assembly buildings."

A sense of recognition and understanding gradually began to dawn upon Eleanor. She had instinctively known that such places were important, but hadn't known why.

Bernadette continued, "All of a sudden everything went into meltdown. A kind of collective, national amnesia. Many of the faith leaders took early retirement or else became dispirited and gave up. Some got into all that angelic merchandising nonsense, whilst others came to form communities of resistance and faith, like, well, like this one. Isn't that true, Jez?" Bernadette looked across to Jez for confirmation.

"You are some kind of faith leader then? What did they used to call them? Priests?" Eleanor was starting to make sense of the landscape she inhabited. Words were suddenly forming in her mind from the deep recesses of long forgotten or overlooked memories.

"Well, I would have been if I had finished my training," Jez replied somewhat awkwardly. "But I still took solemn vows. I made a commitment – to worship God, to serve others and to give up certain things that get in the way."

"Oh, that explains the sex thing then." Jez's demeanour and moral values were now starting to make sense.

Bernadette cast a quizzical glance in Jez's direction and raised an eyebrow.

"We've all taken vows here. Vows of poverty, obedience and chastity, but they are very provisional. They get reviewed each year. We can decide to marry and have families and that, but often we find that pairing up in a community like this can make things a bit…" Jez looked to Bernadette for approval of his explanation, to see her nodding gently, "…a bit complicated. So, most of us decide to make that sacrifice, at least in the short term."

The following morning Eleanor started to learn more about how the community operated. Each member had an area of work that they were responsible for. Their work formed part of the agreement or vow they had taken when they signed up for membership of the community. Brillo worked in mental health, running a support group for those suffering with depressive illnesses, Lucinda helped out at a local mother and toddler group and Faith helped to run a workshop teaching people how to grow their own vegetables and cook nutritious food on a budget. Sanjeev helped Jez, working among local unemployed young people, whilst Sister Bernadette provided a kind of drop-in service for people from the local community, offering a range of services from legal advice to mediation, guidance with benefit claims and help with various practical needs. Two other community members apparently ran a multi-media studio and were working with some of the young people making music and online movies.

Eleanor realised that much of her life had been orientated towards meeting her own challenges and satisfying her personal needs. She realised that what had happened to her in Norway was some kind of revelation, indicating there was a bigger world out there than the one she had constructed around herself. She had told herself that her achievements were intended to inspire other people who faced similar obstacles, yet now she realised that her drive to achieve was largely about proving to herself that she was worth something. Such considerations appeared superfluous in the community where she now found herself. Their motivation appeared to be orientated externally towards serving others for a higher purpose, rather than towards proving themselves.

"It's amazing what you all do, but aren't the government meant to be doing these things?" she asked Jez as they set off on a short familiarisation tour around the various projects where the community members worked.

"They are, but they don't," Jez explained. "Successive governments have run down their social care programmes in places like this ever since the big crash in 2008. These communities never really recovered from the age of austerity. The people who never caused all the problems ended up paying the greatest price. Charities and community organisations have been picking up the pieces ever since. If we weren't doing all this stuff, then nobody else would."

"How can you hold it all together?"

"What d'you mean?" Jez asked as they entered a dilapidated former Victorian library building that provided the base for the youth centre that he worked out of.

"Well, how can you and your friends prop up places like this?"

"We can't. It's a struggle. Fortunately, we are not the only community group working around here. There are lots of others. Some faith based, others not. But financially we can't do it alone. We all have paid jobs or other means of supporting ourselves financially. Some make a bigger contribution than others."

"Sanjeev?"

"Yeh, well, Sanjeev is a bit of a star in lots of ways, but everyone plays their part. Mind you, if it wasn't for Sanjeev and his techie pals, then we would never have discovered the threat you were under in the first place."

As they moved through the youth centre building, they encountered two youths in a small side room, playing pool.

"Yow… Jez, my main man," one of the youths exclaimed as he high-fived Jez like a long-lost friend. "Where you been?"

"Oh, I've been around."

"Who's your bitch then?"

"Look, CJ, you know my rules. She ain't my bitch and what did I say about showing strangers respect?"

"Yeh, man. I know's them rules." CJ started to study Eleanor in greater detail, looking her up and down, whilst leaning his head to one side.

"Hi. I'm Elean…"

"I knows who you is, my girl. You is the girl that does them scary stunts. You are one crazy bitch. Total respect, my girl. You have real balls."

Jez looked shocked. "You recognise her?"

"Sure, I've seen her videos. She's all over YouTube."

"Are you sure it's her?"

"Let me see." With that CJ walked over towards Eleanor, pool cue in hand, and tapped her leg, which made a hollow, synthetic noise. "I'd say she was that chick, man. Unless they made two."

"Thanks, CJ. That's really helpful information."

"No probs, my man. See you around."

Jez took Eleanor by the hand and turned her around. "I think we're all starting to get the picture here." With that he took Eleanor through the shell of the youth centre building into the street outside.

"Am I in danger here?"

"Strangely enough, on these streets you're probably OK. We don't attract too much attention from the security industry. Mostly they recognise the kind of work we do. Besides, there are too many other problems for the authorities to deal with around here than those whose out-of-body experiences challenge the secular hegemony. But…"

"But what?"

"We need to make you a bit less recognisable. Tone down your celebrity status so that you blend in a bit more."

"How are we going to do that?"

"I don't know. But there's someone around here who might just be able to help."

Chapter 16

The seatbelt sign faded to off and Finch wearily lifted himself out of his seat and placed a shoulder bag on the cabin table in front of his companions. Carefully removing the contents, he spread out a number of papers and files and two data sticks on the table surface. He examined the blank looks that greeted him, searching for any signs of recognition. None were forthcoming.

"You know what troubled me for so long wasn't the bomb explosion. It wasn't the circumstances in which I lost my job. It wasn't even the fact that I was approached by the security services – I've crossed swords with them before. It was why was I being approached to find a lost heiress? Surely they had their own people to do such things? What was the story here?" Finch looked across to Sky, not really expecting an answer. "Someone decides to drop out of high society and go native with a bunch of anti-capitalism protestors. It's an interesting subject for a documentary or even a Sunday Review article in the old days, but why were the security forces so interested in the errant daughter of a multinational dynasty?" Finch paused, inviting a response. "Care to offer any answers?"

Catherine looked across to Sky. She remained expressionless and impassive.

"Then I got to look at all the leads I was given. Doesn't it strike you as a bit strange that I am supplied with all the evidence and then invited to fill in the missing pieces? Why me? There are plenty of other hacks who could have looked into this. I wasn't the obvious choice. Out of the game for too long, you see – very old school. But then one day I get caught up in an explosion at the Van Hegel Building and the only reason I'm here talking to you now is because this woman…" Finch moved the grainy CCTV photo of the woman at the scene of the bombing towards Sky, "…pushed me to the floor seconds before and probably saved my life."

"Nothing to do with me." Sky dismissed the photo and diverted her gaze away from Finch.

"You know what?" Finch replied with a degree of self-satisfaction, "I actually believe you. You see, you are sitting here now feeling rather awkward about the circumstances of our meeting and the fact that we are enjoying the hospitality of an airline in which you're the major shareholder. You're probably weighing up all sorts of contradictory thoughts at the moment, wondering what to say and whether you can trust me or not. But you know what, my dear? You and I might just have a great deal in common. Not this photo – this is a red herring – but the fact that we've both been set up, haven't we?"

"I don't know what you mean," Sky replied.

"Maybe you don't. But you'll recognise these photos." Finch spun his computer tablet around to face Sky and Catherine and then proceeded to display a gallery of photos of Sky. She was wearing a whole range of designer dresses and photographed in various exotic locations and with a number of A-grade celebrities on her arm as well as sharing the company of many well-known European and US politicians. "You really get around, don't you?"

Finch kept scrolling the photos in front of Sky, trying to provoke a reaction but she just looked away, not wanting to acknowledge that the woman in the designer dress was her. Catherine looked aghast.

"Are these photos genuine?" she asked Sky, but she already knew the answer. The fact that they had secured access to a private jet merely on the basis of Sky's personal appearance at the airfield persuaded her that Finch was exposing a hidden truth, but a truth she really didn't want to confront.

"You work it out."

"I don't think I can. When we first met, I asked you who you were and you said 'just a friend and fellow traveller.'"

"Well, has anything happened to make you doubt that? All I've shown you, all that's happened today – has any of it been false? Have I misled you in any way?"

"Yes, you have."

"But everything I've told you has been true, Catherine, it really has. My own identity, or rather who I used to be, is really not that important. What's important is the journey we now share."

"Yes, but everything I've discovered since Josh's death has revealed that we are living in two separate realities: the official version and the true version. We live in a culture of deception. That's what disturbed Josh. We've all got so used to living with falsehood that we can't recognise the truth anymore. And you're part of that culture of deception."

"I haven't deceived you, Catherine. You must believe me."

"I don't know what to believe. I'm sharing a journey in your family's private jet, surrounded by photos of you mixing with the icons of power and influence, people who represent the very forces that I thought you were committed to bringing to account."

"I am," Sky insisted, her voice faltering.

"So whose side are you on?"

"Your side! The right side. You can trust me, Catherine, you really can. I would never do anything to hurt or mislead you. I really wouldn't."

"Look," Finch interrupted, "I don't know what's going on between you, but what I do know is that we've both been set up. Look at this photo again." Finch once more called up a copy of the grainy CCTV photo on his tablet and immediately enhanced it to reveal the partially hidden face. "I was misdirected to make the comparison between this photo and this one." Finch swiped a glamorous photo of Sky onto his tablet display screen.

"Looks like the same person to me," Catherine commented.

"That's what you're supposed to think," Finch explained. "But look at how the shadow of the chin falls in a different direction to that of the clothing. Pretty crude Photoshop, and take it from me, I know a bit about photo manipulation."

"So the woman in the photo isn't Sky after all."

"No."

"Then who is it?"

"I really don't know, but I think Sky does."

All eyes were once again directed upon Sky. "Look, it doesn't really matter. I wasn't there. I wasn't even involved with the covert operation." There was a significant pause as both Finch and Catherine awaited further information from Sky.

"The young woman is called 'Amanda'," Sky revealed with a weary sigh, "she's part of a splinter group committed to direct action, but I don't share their aims or methodology. Anyhow she was arrested last month and there's been no contact since then."

"So I was set up to take a personal interest in finding you."

"Congratulations, you succeeded." Sky had sat back in her seat, resting her chin on her splayed hand, inviting further probing.

"But the girl in the photos. The rich heiress. Why give it

all up?" Catherine was intrigued by the juxtaposition of the glamorous, celebrity lifestyle and the passionate, thoughtful person she had grown so close to.

"Are you going to tell her?" Finch invited Sky to disclose further information, but Sky just waved away the invitation with a dismissive waft of her hand.

"You seem to have all the answers."

"The answer to your question about what happened to the celebrity heiress, promoting her family's brand all around the world, is absolutely nothing. She's sitting right here. Nothing has changed apart from the clothes and the hairstyle. This young woman, who likes to call herself Skyshadow or Sky or Sherry Gilchrist or Tabitha O'Reilly or whatever, is still Iona Dunwoody, heiress to the Dunwoody fortune and guardian of Dunwoody's global interests."

"What?"

"No, it's not like that."

"YOU BITCH." Something snapped within Catherine and she picked up the nearest thing to hand, which happened to be a bunch of papers and a photo, and threw them at Sky. "You were spying on us all the time!"

Sky had succeeded in igniting something powerful within Catherine – her capacity to believe again. She had opened her eyes to the possibilities of a better future, but now that belief had been snatched away. She had made her believe in her quiet revolution, only to discover that the revolution had been betrayed by its leader.

"How dare you play with my emotions and lead me on! Pretending to be a friend, when all along you were betraying the very principles and people you claim to champion." By now Catherine was standing over Sky and hitting her over the head with a rolled-up bunch of papers. It was a pathetic, almost comedic gesture, but the only way she could express her disappointment and anger.

"But I haven't. I haven't." Sky was grimacing and cowering in her seat. A male attendant suddenly appeared and started to restrain Catherine, but Sky just waved him away. "Look, it really isn't that simple. I haven't betrayed anyone or any cause. I'm not a spy, neither am I a liar."

By now Sky was sobbing and demonstrating a vulnerability that Catherine had never seen in her before.

"OK, ladies, let's all just take a chill pill here," Finch interrupted, feeling the need to defuse a situation he had done much to create. "Perhaps Sky can offer us some explanation. I would certainly be interested to hear one."

Sky decided to relieve the tension by ordering drinks from the attendant. They arrived promptly and with calm efficiency. "First of all, Mr....uh... Mr...?"

"Finch. Just call me Finch. Like the bird."

"Look, Finch, you come rushing to our aid, like some great urban superhero and then start throwing all sorts of accusations and half-baked theories around. We're both really grateful for your help and protection, but just where are you coming from and how d'you know all this stuff?"

"I told you, I was recruited. I'm just a journo who got caught up in the latest T-squad crap and so my personal interest was activated to do some off the record digging behind the scenes."

"So you're not Special Branch or a spook?"

"No, I'm just someone who used to do this sort of investigative journalism for a living and who received certain information from people who clearly want to get to you, but not for the reason they told me."

"So what did they tell you?"

"They told me that your family wanted you back, but that they wanted me to find you because that would be more discreet and attract less public attention."

"That's bollocks. My family have known where I was all along."

"Like I said, we've both been set up." Finch looked vindicated. No longer the informed inquisitor, but a fellow victim.

"So how did you find out?" Asked Catherine her curiosity and self-control now apparently restored.

"I managed to get hold of various financial records relating to the Dunwoody Corporation. It was all a bit confusing. Smoke and mirrors. Various payments channelled through off-shore intermediaries, capital payments made to look like revenue, revenue made to look like capital. You know how it is. But what they couldn't completely hide was a series of payments from a family trust fund made to Iona and payments drawn down on that account that continue right up to the present day. It was as if Iona or Sky or whoever, was still on the payroll and working for the family firm."

"Banged to rights." Sky was now chuckling to herself and holding out her hands to Finch as if to invite a pair of handcuffs to be clamped to them.

"So, you admit that you've been working for Dunwoody all along?" Catherine was still trying to make sense of where Sky's loyalties lay.

"YES. I admit it. I'm still supported in that sense, although I'm not exactly regarded as employee of the month at the moment. What neither of you seem to understand is that my continuing family interests are not incompatible with my involvement with the insurgency and trying to expose what's really going on. I'm in the most wanted gallery because of what I have achieved and what I know, not because of who my family is. You saw how that hit man tracked us down. That was real, not staged. D'you think that would have happened if I wasn't regarded as a genuine threat?"

"It would make a convincing cover story," Catherine remarked.

"It would, but it doesn't. I'm really not that good an actor.

You've seen my attempt to get into another character. All these crimes against fashion." Sky pulled at her skirt as if to indicate that this wasn't her preferred manner of dress.

"So what's your true motive then?" Finch still had so much he wanted to ask her.

"I guess I became bored with the whole red carpet lifestyle. The ball gowns, the sucking up to politicians, the paparazzi constantly following you around. I wanted out. I wanted to be ordinary, but do something worthwhile, something that really made a difference. So, I just disappeared one day and adopted a different persona. Eventually the family found out where I was, so I did a deal with them. They agreed to finance me and leave me alone, and in return I agreed to find out what I could about some of their competitors and feedback any information. It was all fairly straightforward."

"Except it wasn't, was it?" Finch was growing tired of all the games being played out in front of him.

"I'm sorry?"

"I've given you plenty of opportunity, but you just can't help yourself, can you? I can tell when you're lying because your lips move."

"I'm telling the truth," Sky insisted.

"Yes, but not the whole truth. You're just as dishonest as those you are seeking to expose."

"That's unfair. Everything I do is for a reason. I've never set out to deceive anyone."

"What about me, Sky?" Catherine asked. "Don't I deserve the truth, the whole truth? The truth is meant to set you free. You cannot set others free if you're not free yourself. Just tell me the truth."

"Okay, okay. It's pretty much like I said, but the only thing I left out was the truth of my own change of mind, my own conversion to the cause, if you like. The more embedded I became, the more committed I felt. Eventually I didn't have to pretend anymore. Like I said, I'm really not that good an actor. I was won over. I wanted to find out why so much had changed and why no-one appeared to have noticed or was bothered as a result. The more I looked into those issues, the more concerned I became about my own family's involvement in what had taken place. The more it appeared that Dunwoody's were complicit with Van Hegel and others in a web of information management, the less proud I became of my family's name. The brand was tainted. The more I became Skyshadow and the less I wanted to be Iona Dunwoody."

"But you still took the money."

"Sure I did. Money can't solve all the problems in the world, but denying yourself the resources to wage a campaign, well, that's just reckless. I could either expose Dunwoody's by bringing the whole rotten edifice down around my head, or I could use my position to bring about real change and reform. I want to redeem the family business, to lift the slur on its integrity. This is our family business. I'm a third-generation board member. One day I'll take full ownership of the business; I want to inherit something I can be proud of, not something I want to disown."

"So you are basically trying to bring about change from within – to extricate your family interests from the unsavoury side of business practice." Catherine wanted to find it in her heart to forgive Sky and believe in her again. She wanted to believe. She needed to believe.

"Yes, and we're making progress. Why else do you think people are getting so uptight and wanting to intimidate us? With my resources and connections, I can speak power unto power. I can start to unpick the fabric of lies that has been constructed to shield people from the truth."

At that moment, the seatbelt sign pinged into life and an attendant came along the aisle to collect empty wine glasses and direct the passengers to prepare for landing.

Finch reached across to touch Sky on the arm. "One final question."

"Okay."

"The Smiling Cat. Is it you by any chance?"

"No, not anymore."

"So, it was your mouthpiece at one time?"

"Yeh, I did a couple of stints. There's a sort of rotating editorial. It's safer that way. But I haven't blogged under that avatar for some time." Sky paused, sensing some personal investment. "Any special interest to you?"

"Just curious," Finch replied casually.

Upon arriving back in London, Sky suggested that they spend a couple of nights at one of Dunwoody's apartments in Chelsea. She explained that it was usually empty and she could use it whenever she wanted. Finch wanted to return to his own place, but Sky managed to persuade him to spend a few days lying low. He finally agreed as it occurred to him that he had already been targeted by the same hit man in London and it was likely that his flat would now be under surveillance awaiting his return. Greg could pick up a few personal items and rendezvous with him when it was safe to do so.

Catherine was still nursing profound disappointment towards Sky, feeling that she had been let down and misled. She had known Sky for barely a few weeks and yet she felt protective towards her, like she had become the daughter she never had. However, as they relaxed in the executive apartment, feasting on Thai food and Indian beer, care of an online delivery service, the atmosphere slowly began to thaw somewhat between the companions.

Sky maintained a discreet distance from Catherine and busied herself with catching up on various emails and texts. Every now and then she would look over to Catherine, catching her glance in the hope of receiving a sign of acknowledgement or a look that might indicate approval or forgiveness. Yet a physical and emotional distance remained between them, reinforced by the separation of their years and a shared stubbornness that refused to back down and concede an apology to the other party.

Catherine decided to make the first step towards restoring their enigmatic friendship.

"Those photos that Mr. Finch showed us."

"Finch, just Finch." A detached, muffled voice from the adjacent kitchen corrected her.

"Those shots that Finch had of all those events you attended and those special people you met. I never saw you with anyone else in those photos."

"I'm sorry?" Sky appeared confused by Catherine's line of questioning.

"You know. A family member perhaps or a boyfriend? A chaperone?"

"Hello, Wilma. When does Fred get home? What part of the Stone Age do you come from, Catherine? No-one takes their boyfriend to those events. Chaperone, really?"

"Have you seen the news feed?" Finch called out from the kitchen, clearly absorbed by the multiplatform access to various news media afforded by the apartment. "The disturbance at the Literature Festival is all over it. Loads of mobile phone footage. It's all over the Twittersphere. Your mate Gerald Forsythe clearly made a big impression."

"But you must have had boyfriends."

"It's FOSDYKE. Gerald Fosdyke and he's not my mate," Sky called out to Finch. "Why must I have a boyfriend?" Sky asked, directing her question back to Catherine. "Perhaps I wasn't interested."

"So, no boyfriend then?"

"No! Look, I don't need a bloke to protect me or guide me. I make the decisions about my life. Sometimes I would go home with a bloke after such events, sometimes with a woman. Most of the time I would go to bed early with a bottle of Bolly and a good novel."

"They're talking about banning it." Finch's commentary from the kitchen cut across their conversation. "Some kind of monitoring of festival speakers in the future."

"And your parents. I didn't see them in any of the photos."

"No. Well, there's a good reason for that."

"And that reason is?"

"Because I chose not to be photographed with them. It was bad enough having to do all those corporate events over the years. Paraded at every charity ball from here to Beijing and back, knowing that you are just some kind of trophy to bring the company respectability and kudos. I didn't want to become an appendage to their entourage, so I tended to avoid all the 'happy family' photos they wanted to syndicate around the world."

"This cannot be for real." Finch's commentary from the kitchen continued. "Who do they think they are? Everyone's a potential terrorist and security risk these days."

"So, you don't get on with your parents then?"

"Well, let's just say that they have their own lives and I have mine. If we can minimise the frequency with which our two orbits collide, then we're all a lot happier. I was taught well. I learnt that any happy family moments were more about business than about genuine affection. So now we connect more as business partners than as parents and daughter."

"I'm sorry to hear that."

"Don't be. It's just the way it is. Always has been. Always will." It was obvious that Catherine had struck a sensitive chord with Sky, so she decided to drop the subject and enquire no further.

"Idiots, complete idiots." Finch entered the room, mid-rant. "Have they never heard of free speech?" The distant looks that greeted him indicated a total lack of recognition and

234

thinly veiled contempt for his intrusion. "The...um...news... you know; the festival bust-up is all over it."

"Just piss off, Finch." Catherine directed Finch back to the kitchen. She was reminded just how little she had missed the company of men over the years. They could be great for sex or putting up shelves, but when it came to possessing the sensitivity required to navigate complex emotional landscapes, they were hapless amateurs, incapable of reading the signs or responding appropriately. Why couldn't Finch see that Sky was just a young woman caught up in a complex nexus of powerful interests? She was just as much a victim as either of them. They had all lost something. The events that followed the *'Garden Party Bombings'* had robbed the whole nation of its innocence and hope, and they all shared in the resulting deficit. At least Sky was trying to recapture something that had been surrendered; perhaps that was the only shared experience that genuinely united the three of them.

The following day passed awkwardly. It was apparent that Sky felt uncomfortable back in the company apartment. Not only did she appear ill at ease with the apartment's lavish surroundings, she was also unwilling to be seen entering or leaving the building. She clearly didn't want to give the impression that she was back on the block or in any way associated with the corporate world of her family. She busied herself with messages and correspondence, acting more like a lodger who had organised a sleepover and was nervously awaiting the owners' return, than a legitimate tenant.

Finch and Catherine did their best to tiptoe around each other, maintaining a discreet distance and keeping contact to a minimum. This proved difficult, given their proximity and shared predicament. Catherine knew that she should feel gratitude towards Finch. After all he had rescued her from a possible abduction, but she still couldn't come to place her trust in someone who was a member of a tainted profession, who by his own admission had been commissioned by the security services to track Sky down and bring her in. Whilst she was inclined to give Sky's motives the benefit of the doubt, she remained suspicious that Finch was driven by the prospect of landing a good story rather than any altruistic motives.

Meanwhile Finch was still very much researching the field in order to develop the scope of his investigation. Old journalists never die; they just learn new tricks. He opened up his tablet to examine his case notes. Sky and Catherine had large files against their names. Each contained a personal profile containing his own psychometric evaluations based upon their online presence and any further information he had been able to acquire through what remained of his personal network of journalistic sources. Each profile also contained his own comments about their likely motivation and his probability rating for their anticipated response based upon an old analytical formula of field and form acquired from horse racing. There were multiple entries for both Sky and Catherine, but far more for Sky. She remained the greatest enigma and the most speculative outside bet. If she were a horse running in the 'National', she might represent an interesting each way bet, but if she were an opponent sat opposite him at a poker table, she would be impossible to read. She had woven too many false identities and invented too many cover stories to be taken at face value again.

He saved his notes and put away his mobile. In the light of so many uncertainties being played out before him, Catherine and Sky would remain primary sources of information, rather than trusted colleagues and friends at this stage.

Time stretched out before the three companions, gnawing away at the energies of each of them as they longed to return to their shared quest to find out more about the web of secrecy that had robbed each of them of so much. News from the outside world barely penetrated their hermetically sealed confinement and when it did, it came with a brutal, cold reality.

A chorus of bleeps and digital alerts directed each of the flat mates towards important breaking news as texts sequentially appeared on each of their mobiles, pointing them towards catastrophic events unfolding many miles away. Finch immediately accessed the satellite news channel to discover the extent of a catastrophic tsunami that had engulfed the Canary Islands at the height of the holiday season. Horrific mobile phone footage appeared of huge tidal surges overwhelming coastal communities and devastating shops, nightclubs and restaurants as people struggled to escape. Some of the images were too horrific to believe and appeared more like the computer-generated special effects of a disaster movie. However, these images were real and their consequences were on a scale too terrible to comprehend.

As the news story played out, Finch grew increasingly impatient. The old, story-chasing instinct, recently rekindled within him, once again came to the fore. He longed to find out more, to travel to the affected area and get the real story behind the mounting death toll, but he knew that those days were long gone. He would once again have to become a reluctant voyeur of the unfolding tragedy. He paced around the flat like a caged animal. Muttering and cursing to himself and occasionally lashing out to hit a wall or punch a scatter cushion, in frustration.

Spending time in a confined space amidst great uncertainty was becoming quite stressful for Finch's companions as well. Sky acted like a grounded teenager, resentfully pacing around the apartment, barely controlling her pent-up energies, whilst networking with various contacts and researching online sources of information. Catherine, on the other hand, appreciated the peace and lack of activity more than her companions. She enjoyed solitary activities, such as reading long and demanding novels, yet she too had unfinished business and it was she who first broke cover by reconnecting with the outside world.

"Sky, can I use the landline to make a phone call?"

Sky and Finch exchanged concerned looks.

"I think so. First let me ensure that we can connect through a secure line." Sky immediately picked up the landline, punched in several numbers and spoke to an operator to ask for a secure line code. Once received, she tapped in the code and handed Catherine the retro 1970's style trim phone handset. "Okay, go ahead."

"Hang on, hang on." Finch intervened. "Before you call anyone – just who are you going to ring and what are you going to arrange?"

"Look, I have to call the court officer on a weekly basis. Just to let her know that I haven't skipped the country and that I haven't broken my court injunction order. It's all pretty straightforward."

"Yes, but you are ringing a legal institution on the landline from a corporate property. Isn't that going to look strange? We can't be too careful."

"The secure line isn't traceable, not even by the security industry, and they wouldn't be looking for Catherine anyhow," Sky explained. "It's me they are after, remember?"

"Very well," Finch said, but remained unconvinced. He didn't mind putting himself at risk in an investigation. That had often happened in the past, but now he was associated rather too closely with those he had been appointed to investigate. It all felt rather messy, as though boundaries had become blurred and he didn't quite know where his responsibilities lay.

Catherine completed her call and managed to satisfy the court clerk that everything was fine and normal.

"I heard about your court appearance." Finch tried to make conversation with Catherine, following her call. "That was a pretty spectacular act of public protest you were planning. Kinda wish you had carried through with it."

"Yes, so do I sometimes. Although it would have put me in an awful lot of hot water."

"I guess so. You were pretty fortunate to get off so lightly."

"I know. People keep telling me that. I think that I have someone to thank for that." Catherine glanced in the direction of Sky, who was engrossed in her mobile wristband.

"Oh, I see." Finch wondered whether he had Catherine all wrong. Maybe her connection with Sky was less about her own need and more about a common cause. "Look, Catherine, I feel as if we have rather got off on the wrong foot. I'm sorry about your son. I guess it must be appalling to lose someone in such circumstances. I've never lost anyone that close, except for my wife, but that's not the same."

"Your wife died?"

"No, she left. I suppose I drove her away, although I didn't see it like that at the time." This was probably the first time that Finch had spoken so candidly about Hannah's absence and his own culpability in precipitating her departure. Gradually Finch and Catherine discovered a shared vocabulary of loss that guided their subsequent conversation and over the next two hours. They both spoke openly about their lives, their careers, families, lovers, shared interests and old friends.

"You teach History of Art then?" Finch enquired of Catherine.

"Not just the History of Art, but also Design and Commercial Art."

"This is going to sound really dumb."

"No change there then."

"But I don't suppose you have any contacts in the science faculties at the University?"

"No, not really. We don't have a science faculty where I teach," Catherine explained in a slightly dismissive tone. She thought that Finch would have realised the narrow range of specialist academic subjects that a modern university teaches.

"No contacts in the scientific community then?"

"None, although a really good friend of mine is related to some sort of top behavioural zoologist, but…"

"But what?"

"But he has a certain reputation."

"Reputation for what? He doesn't like to date undergrads, does he?"

"No, nothing like that. He's just a bit…you know…out there."

"So he looks like Einstein and has halitosis."

"Oh, you've met him."

"No, just a guess."

"Well, let's just say that he is lacking a few social skills, but he's very well regarded in the academic world. Written loads of stuff about animal welfare and behaviour. What exactly are you looking for then?"

"Don't know. It's just that I've got all this data from the field studies and clinical trials of the vaccination programme and I don't really know how to make sense of it. Back in the day we had science editors I could speak with or else I'd go and pick the brains of one of our regular science contributors, but now it's a lot harder to access such advice, especially with us being locked down in this apartment."

"Sure, I understand."

"I don't think that we need particularly high level input here, just a bit of background knowledge really. Any chance he could help me out? "

"Well, he might be your man. I'll have a word with Sky about getting out under the wire and see what I can arrange with my contact."

Chapter 17

C atherine emerged from the Phoenix LRT station and headed off into the city streets. She made her way along Cromwell Road past crowds of excited school children queuing up outside the grand gothic architecture of the Natural History Museum and proceeded past the grand frontage of the Victoria and Albert Museum which was promoting an exhibition of late twentieth century Brit Pop memorabilia. Shortly after the towering splendour of Imperial College rose into view, its red brick façade emboldened by the pedestrianisation of the surrounding roads and a recent Lottery funded facelift. The august surroundings of such an ancient seat of learning contrasted sharply with the casual, modernism of her place of work. This felt like grown-up school, a place of serious learning and she couldn't help but feel a little apprehensive about the meeting she had set up only a few days previously.

Her feelings of apprehension were heightened by thoughts of joining Finch later that day for a meeting with his handler at the Cresta Coffee National Gallery. Her familiarity with the visual arts being called upon to support Finch although Sky was concerned about her becoming embroiled with affairs of national security. Both meetings felt like a step into the unknown, but at least the world of academia provided a familiar landscape in which to further research the field study findings that Finch had acquired.

After making a few enquiries she was directed down a tiled corridor, past various recently extinct exhibits in glass cases overlooked by a large marble statue of Lord David Attenborough frozen in time doing a piece to camera. As she descended into the bowels of the basement she was immediately confronted with an assault on the senses arising from the screech of various animals and the smell of damp fur and urine. A short security check, involving the customary X-ray and electro-thermal body scan followed. Having endured the ritualistic humiliation of strangers examining her unclothed body image, she then passed through the scanning machine and was re-united with various metallic personal items before being met by a member of staff who escorted her down a dimly lit subterranean corridor to an anonymous looking security door. A quick swipe of a security badge and the door yielded with a re-assuring hiss of solid dependability.

Once inside, she was greeted by the sight of an older man with thinning hair and huge, untidy side burns which swept around his entire chin. He was wearing a badly stained white coat and was carrying a rather large ginger cat under his arm, the same colour as his spectacular side burns. Inside the laboratory were two or three other cats as well as a rabbit that was lolloping around on top of a desk and who appeared thoroughly at home in the surroundings. The man seemed to be lost in thought as if looking for something he had misplaced.

"Dr. Underwood?"

"Yes, hello, who are you?" The man looked up as if irritated by the interruption.

"Catherine. Dr. Catherine Stringer. Deborah, the Dean of Faculty at Croydon University mentioned…"

"Dean of Faculty? Never heard of her?"

"Deborah Underwood? Dame Deborah, your cousin. She gave me your name, I just…"

"Oh that Deborah, yes, yes, interfering old busy body. Thinks she's some kind of academic, just because she teaches media studies to a bunch of high school drop outs."

"Well, I think…" at this point Catherine wanted to take issue with her old school academic colleague and enlighten him about the importance of acquiring multi-platform communications skills in a knowledge based global economy. However, she realised that she had not come to defend the academic credibility of her colleagues or profession and so decided to let the comment pass. "Deborah said that you would be willing to answer a few questions for me." Catherine realised she was speaking slowly and loudly in the manner reserved by the English for addressing those of foreign tongue, hearing impairment, advanced years or low education attainment.

"Who are you then?"

"My name is Catherine Stringer, like I already said."

"Yes, I know, I know what you said. Tell me, do you like animals?"

"Yes, I suppose so, some of them at least."

"Oh good, then hold Horatio Hornblower will you." With that the man handed the overweight ginger cat to Catherine. "Yes, yes, I think, I recall something about it." The man started to dig under various papers arranged on his desk in search of some kind of documentation.

"You're not from the police, are you?"

"No."

"Security services?"

"No, I'm an academic and mother…"

"An academic, are you?"

"Yes, I'm Dr. Catherine…"

"I know. I know. I heard you earlier. What are you researching into?"

"Well, I'm not actively researching at the moment, I've here more out of a personal interest, trying to build up a background picture with a journalist friend of…"

"A journalist? I didn't know they still had foot soldiers. I used to talk a lot to journalists at one time. I even appeared regularly on TV. I don't suppose Deborah told you that?"

"Well, yes, she did actually. I gather it was some time ago…"

"She's a pain in the arse and a frightful snob, that's what Deborah is. If you ever met her, you'd agree as well. Yes, you would."

"She's exactly a very good friend of mine as well as a colleague and I wouldn't…"

"So what does Deborah want?"

"Deborah doesn't want anything. She just thought that you might…."

"So you're not working for Deborah then?"

"No, I'm not."

"Well, that's just as well then, because it's all about animal behaviour down here. If you've come here for some Media Studies project, then I can't help you. It's years since I did any TV. Did I tell you that I used to be on TV?"

"Yes, you did."

"They used to be loads of work when all the Discovery Channels were producing documentaries and films. Falling over themselves to out commission each other they were. They'd often ask me to do pieces to camera. I was considered interesting and rather striking in those days. Then, they started to chase another demographic and it all got a bit slick and interactive. They wanted eye candy for a younger audience. What did they call it? Hotspur! Do you know about hotspur?"

"No, but I know about Tottenham Hotspur."

"Oh very good. I see you made a joke there." Suddenly Dr. Underwood's expression changed, "Why are you holding Horatio Hornblower?"

"You gave him to me."

"Did I? Then put him down for goodness sake. You're not some sort of undercover operative from Health and Safety are you, sent to check up on Horatio and his friends, they don't like us having animals wandering around down here. I don't suppose you would tell me if you were undercover, wouldn't be much of an undercover operative if you did, would you?"

Dr. Underwood appeared to be arguing with himself and was still not entirely certain why Catherine had arranged to meet him. He continued to dig among the pile of papers strewn around a nearby desk.

"No, I'm not undercover, I'm a…"

"Yes, you're an academic. I know, I know. What sort of academic are you?"

"Art and design. Commercial art mostly."

"Well I'm not sure if I can help you much. You probably need the Royal College of Art next door."

"No, it's you I've come to see. I have some SCIENTIFIC DATA that I was hoping you could help me with." Once again Catherine found herself in default mode, spelling out certain words phonetically.

"Okay, I'm not deaf, you don't need to shout. I'm Dr. Robert Underwood by the way." Dr. Underwood offered his hand in formal greeting.

"Yes, I know." Catherine responded but by now she was starting to question why she had arranged this appointment and how helpful it would prove to be.

"Sorry it's all a bit chaotic around here." Dr. Underwood removed a Perspex rabbit cage from a stool and invited Catherine to take a seat.

Catherine eventually found herself coming within the orbit of Dr. Underwood's planet with a reasonable chance of affecting a safe landing. "I wonder if you can take a look at some data that I received."

"Yes, yes, surely." The doctor finally began to focus. "What sort of data is it?"

"It is mostly clinical data from a series of drugs trials and field studies arising from a vaccination programme."

"Well, my dear girl, then you don't need me. You need a medical doctor or a pharmacologist. I just study animal behaviour and pathogens."

"But, it's just some basic data. Deborah thought that you might be able to apply your general knowledge to this field."

"Oh I see. Deborah is now some sort of expert on medical research is she?"

"Not really. It's just a long shot. I didn't know where to start. Look, I know this might all seem a bit crazy, but we've stumbled upon something we think is really important. We're not scientists, you're all we've got. So maybe you could just have a little look. I know it's not really your area of research, but Deborah trusts your judgment and thought that you might be a,...a sort of safe pair of hands." Catherine's voiced trailed off into a kind of hopeless, desperate attempt to plead for help.

"That's all right my dear. It's not your fault." Dr. Underwood looked sympathetically towards Catherine for the first time. "Just because that old fool teaches media studies, she thinks she's an authority on scientific research. I mean, what's the point in media studies? If the whole world is going to rack and ruin, the last thing you need is another costume drama or cookery programme."

"Yes, but can you help?" Once again, Catherine tried to drag Dr. Underwood back toward her subject of enquiry.

"I don't know. I doubt it. I'm more a zoologist – cats and dogs mostly. Fascinating creatures, you know. We've lived with them for thousands of years, they share our daily lives but we know virtually nothing about how they think. My major breakthrough research was into comparative intelligence in the animal community. You know the way that cats look at you with that knowing, mysterious look, whilst dogs just look pleased to see you. Well, you'll never guess what I discovered."

"What?"

"Cats are really, really stupid, virtually nothing going on upstairs. Whereas dogs…"

"Look, Dr. Underwood," by now Catherine was growing increasingly impatient with the wondering mind of her expert witness, "that all sounds fascinating, but I really would appreciate it if you could just take a look at the data we've come by."

"Just what exactly do you want me to look at?"

Catherine reached into her bag and took out her tablet and then proceeded to display some of the key findings from the various research papers that Finch had been studying. She tried to explain the source of the data, remembering some of the background information that Finch had provided. The more results she displayed on the screen, the more Dr. Underwood became quiet and focused in steely concentration. "Do you recognise these peaks that keep occurring on the graphs?"

"Yes, it's a very simple chromatogram. Those peaks are various proteins that occur in these samples." The doctor continued to study the graphs and eventually took over control of the tablet as he began to flick to and fro in the various reports that Catherine had opened. "These are blood samples from patients in clinical trials and field studies I assume?"

"Yes, I think so. All I know is that this data was hidden away very securely and that lots of people don't want anyone else to know about it."

"Yes, I can understand." Once again, the doctor appeared lost in thought and self-contained.

After a period of about twenty minutes in which Catherine became acquainted with all the various feline members of the laboratory team along with discovering the name of the rabbit and the fact that he didn't like to be handled, she finally challenged the doctor to give his reaction to the research findings. "So, what is this data telling you?"

"First of all, let me remind you what I said earlier. I am not a medical doctor or a pharmacologist. I know a little biochemistry but that is of a very general nature."

"So what is your very general understanding telling you?"

"Well, the protein that shows up in these samples is part of a group of proteins that I'm familiar with. The existence of such a protein is not intrinsically dangerous to human or animal health. It is more like a messenger. The blood samples from the vaccine trials show the presence of particular genes that have been switched on to produce this protein. This is what the peaks in the graphs show."

"So all is well then?"

"Medically, as far as my untrained, eye can see, yes these proteins will not affect human health in any of the usual, recognised ways."

"But?"

"But?"

"Yes, I thought you were going to raise a qualification to your statement."

"I was going to say that this group of proteins does have a role in inhibiting key receptors in the neural cortex. That's the brain, my dear."

"Yes, I know."

"Well, our genetic profile or make up is not fixed, it can be altered. The body's genetic programme organises the division of labour within our body, it can make a single gene accessible or inaccessible to the whole cellular apparatus in the brain."

"So could this vaccine cause brain damage?"

"No, not brain damage. Nothing as serious as that. These proteins are usually associated with self-awareness, rather than cognitive skills or motor abilities."

"I'm sorry, you've lost me."

Doctor Underwood stood upright and walked across to a large flat screen in the corner of the laboratory. He touched the screen, typed in some digits and immediately a molecular hologram was projected onto the table top and started rotating before him. He put on a pair of 3D spectacles and studied the image intensely. Several minutes passed whilst he scrutinized the protein's structure. "I explained that my field of study is to do with animal behaviour. That's why I used to do all those wildlife programmes on the television. Did I tell you that I used to be on TV?"

"Yes, about a dozen times."

"I might be reading too much into these studies in my initial assessment, but I'm studying the genetic and behavioural differences between humans and animals. You probably know that we share 99% of the same genes with the higher primates, but did you know that we also share 70% of our genes with a halibut and 30% with a cabbage. We are very alike, but I am concerned with what makes us different and unique – what makes human's human and animals animal."

"Isn't it something to do with opposable thumbs?"

"A lot more than that my dear girl. I am looking into consciousness, self-awareness, not problem solving. The genetic makeup of our very psyche or soul." The doctor paused to manipulate the hologram before him. "I could be making a rather speculative jump here, but the group of proteins identified in those samples belongs to the family of proteins that relate to human consciousness in the cerebral cortex. They are the bearers of the human soul, a network of cerebral processors that determine our self-awareness and how we process that awareness in relation to the wider world. These parts of the brain are highly responsive to external stimuli, both cognitive and experiential. They can become highly developed or else passive and unresponsive – what stimulates or suppresses such development is still largely a mystery to us."

A wry smile came over Dr. Underwood's face. "They are building blocks of what we now understand as consciousness. Some of us even call them the 'God particles'!"

"Isn't that something to do with quantum physics?"

"Yes, it is, but we scientists like to have a little joke with each other, now and then. We don't get out much you know, especially those poor sods stuck in a hole in the ground at Cern." The doctor chuckled to himself and looked across to Catherine with a mischievous glint in his eye.

Finally, some humanity began to show itself in his demeanour. "We call them 'God particles' because they are part of a mysterious range of higher level brain activities that seem to set us apart from our animal relatives. They are associated with higher or even, metaphysical awareness. Some people call it spirituality or a higher purpose. Our capacity to find identity and meaning beyond ourselves in art, music or the wonder of the universe. It's more than our ability to fashion tools that sets us apart from the primates you know. We are only at the very edge of understanding these issues, but it is the isolation of such proteins that is leading us into this area of research."

"Do we all have these particles or proteins?"

"Yes, absolutely, they are genetically determined, it's just that in some people they are more developed, whereas in others less so. They can also be affected not just by our own thoughts and feelings but also by external intervention."

"Such as by a vaccine?"

"Yes, in theory, it is possible that they could effectively be switched off and on. Just like a light bulb."

Chapter 18

Gentle birdsong filled the air as Catherine stepped out into the warm embrace of a bright new day. She had decided to dispense with her usual commute on the Light Rapid Transit system in favour of a purposeful walk along familiar streets. The morning air lifted her spirit and put a spring in her step. It was one of those days imbued with rich, invigorating sunshine that puts a smile on the face of strangers and always made her appreciate what was good about being alive. She remembered earlier, more innocent times, days spent with friends and lovers, gentle summer mornings and long, lazy afternoons discussing art and politics. She also remembered Joshua, but differently now. His boyish good looks, his wicked sense of humour, his laconic smile and his dreamy imagination. Whatever had taken place with Joshua in the past, and whatever was taking place in the world around her, it was time for her to move on, to embrace the future with hope and seek a new beginning. She was sure something good was about to happen.

As she made her way along Cromwell Road and through Belgravia, where she saw a large crowd gathered outside a whitewashed Georgian building. Above the portico hung a forlorn-looking orange and yellow flag, fluttering at half-mast in the warm summer breeze and suddenly Catherine realised the connection between the news story from a few days previously and the embassy building in front of her. Garlands of flowers had been placed on the pavement outside the embassy or else tied to railings. Makeshift memorials adorned the adjacent gardens and messages in Spanish, reflecting people's heartfelt sorrow and sympathy for the people who had lost their lives in the Canary Islands, were placed against the railings. Some people were just standing and weeping silently; others appeared restless, as if looking for somewhere to direct their anger. An atmosphere of emptiness hung in the air, as if there was something important to be done, but no place or no occasion for it to happen.

Catherine quickly moved on through the streets of Victoria, only to discover another gathering outside a large travel agency superstore where an impromptu shrine had been constructed to honour those who had lost their lives in the Canary Islands tsunami.

Catherine decided to stay and to share the moment.

"Have you lost someone as well?" A young man with a shaved head, carrying an unlit candle and a can of lager, had stepped out from the crowd to address her.

"Yes, I suppose I have, my dear, but not in this latest disaster." Catherine's words hung in the air, as if her loss was in some way in competition with the loss being expressed by those who had gathered on the pavement.

"So much pain, I guess. Hard to know what to make of it all and what we're meant to do. Anyhow, there's going to be a few moments for reflection in a while. We've managed to persuade the CEO of one the travel firms to say a few words."

"Oh, I see."

"Yeh, he'll be leading a few minutes' silence to remember

those who have died, just as soon as a TV crew arrive to film it all."

Catherine decided to stay a while in order to show her support for those gathered outside the superstore. Eventually a television crew arrived and a nervous-looking, well-groomed man in a suit was ushered forward to lead the time of silent reflection. However, as silence eventually descended, Catherine's nerve failed her. She saw the cameras scanning the crowd and picking up the reactions of distraught relatives and people holding lager bottles aloft in order to remember all the night clubbers who had perished. Suddenly Catherine remembered that she was meant to be maintaining a low media profile, so she decided to slip out of the crowd and make her solitary way to her planned rendezvous with Finch.

A short distance away another crowd had gathered for different reasons. Trafalgar Square was packed with tourists and visitors. The newly landscaped piazza was populated with couples happily holding hands and taking photos in front of the Gallery. Some playfully acted the fool in front of camera phones, whilst others splashed in the fountains, trying to gain some respite from the heat of the day. Among the crowd Finch stood observing the frivolity with a mixture of sadness and nostalgia. As he looked around the crowds in the square, it became apparent that the smiles and laughter were reserved for friends and lovers. Couples gazed at each other, drawing strength and inspiration from each other's company. He longed to recapture such moments, to be young, innocent and in love once again. To feel Hannah's warm breath upon his neck, to put his hand around her waist and once again make plans for a shared future. Such times were now a distant memory and he knew he could never experience again the sense of hopefulness and expectancy that they once shared.

Elsewhere in the piazza groups swapped information between themselves and shared mobile phone images. Everywhere people clung to their technology, constantly checking their mobile phones for text messages or twitter updates, locked in and self-sufficient. The scene could have been played out in the queues for Disneyland Paris or in a shopping mall or travelling to work. Culture was being consumed, hollowed out and sucked dry by information-hungry technology. There was no shared sense of appreciation or gratitude, no rejoicing in the freedom to experience the moment and wonder. No-one lifted their gaze to the sky or replenished their spirit by drawing inspiration from their surroundings. No-one looked up or looked around; each of them plugged in, yet set apart; a community of solitude disconnected by the connections they sought to make.

Eventually the outline figure of Catherine came into view.

As she approached, Finch began to look upon her in a new way. She was quite a few years older than him, yet she had retained her figure, along with a certain energetic vigour and spark. She could appear a little formidable at times, and although she was very different to Hannah, she displayed vulnerability beneath the surface along with a generous spirit that was rather appealing to him. His mind started to wonder whether she might just be a good outside bet for a bit of mutual companionship and maybe even some meaningless casual sex. As she approached, he quickly put the idea out of his mind, choosing to concentrate on the task in hand instead.

He greeted Catherine, but she appeared troubled and distant, explaining that she needed some time to process her thoughts and emotions, having encountered a memorial event for the victims of the tsunami, and immediately made for a distant corner of the gallery away from the greatest concentration of visitors. She reassured Finch that being among so much beauty and the work of the great masters would help her to re-focus and besides that she had important news to share from her meeting with Dr. Underwood. They agreed to meet in half an hour in the bar.

Inside the gallery stern and purposeful faces focused on learning and education. Official guides overloaded groups of tourists with historical and technical data, whilst individuals trailed in their wake, plugged into their mobiles, scrutinizing the exhibits with the thoroughness of a shopper searching for bargains. Blank looks covered the faces of those who struggled to make connections between what they saw and what lay beyond and behind the exhibits. Visitors devoured brochures and consumed commentaries; only a few just sat and stared.

Finch's liaison had been arranged in a small chamber, just off one of the larger, more popular galleries. Across the room a man in a white linen jacket and a panama hat stood admiring one the paintings. As Finch approached, the man tipped his hat in recognition.

"Good afternoon, Mr. Finch. Isn't it just a lovely day?"

"Uh, yes, I suppose it is, although all the news is bad."

"So I hear, so I hear." The art-loving handler remained impassive and still absorbed by the sight of the painting. "I also hear that you have been making news of your own."

"Oh, yes, kinda. You heard then?"

"You know that the private use of Tasers is strictly illegal, so too the unauthorised obtaining of data."

"Yes, as you put all that information my way, what did you expect?"

"Don't worry, Mr. Finch. You have nothing to fear from us in that regard. We live in difficult times. Such times call for… unorthodox methods." The handler turned around to look at Finch, "Anyhow, if we had wanted to bring you in, then we had plenty of opportunity."

"Then, why didn't you?"

"Oh, it's a lot more entertaining this way." The handler allowed himself a smile and a muted chuckle. "You really have been playing games with the big boys, haven't you?"

"Look, can we just cut to the chase? I've got some pretty heavy shit that I want to put to you. Not least of which involved me being taken uptown by a bunch of corporate thugs."

"How very unfortunate."

"Unfortunate! Is that all you can say? You set me up and now you owe me some kind of explanation."

"All in due time, Mr. Finch. All in due time. First of all, tell me what you see in this picture." The handler drew his attention to a small, dark oil painting in front of them. "It really is most magnificent; don't you agree?"

Finch was irritated by his handler's reluctance to account for his treatment. He wanted explanations, not art lessons. "If you're going to be doing all this art appreciation bollocks again, then I've got my own expert on standby outside."

"Yes, I'm sure. Look again, Mr. Finch, look again. What do you see?"

"Bloke in a loin cloth carrying a lump of wood, telling some scared-looking old bloke which way to go."

The handler massaged his sweating brow in disappointment, removing his panama in the process, which he then used to waft in front of his face to provide some relief from the heat of the day. "Sometimes I despair of the journalistic profession. You really don't know anything about the characters in this picture?"

"Not really."

"So it would appear." The handler looked genuinely disappointed. "Why d'you think anyone would choose a path that would inevitably lead to their own death when they had the option of escape and following an alternative path?"

"I don't know. Some kind of suicide wish? There's a lot of that going on today."

"So there is, but no, that's not what I mean. Look at the painting again. It's called *Quo Vadis?* by Annibale Carracci. Quo Vadis is Latin for *'Whither goest thou?'* or *'Where are you going?'* It is the words of the disciple and fisherman Peter to the raised

Christ. Peter has been imprisoned for being a follower of Christ, but has been given an opportunity to escape Rome where he was due to be executed as a criminal, in the same way as Christ was executed or crucified in Jerusalem many years before."

"Look, I didn't study classics. I don't know about these ancient myths."

"Oh, this isn't about some academic subject of inquiry; that lump of wood you refer to is a cross, a particularly nasty method the Romans reserved for killing their political enemies."

"Yes, I see those around quite a lot. *'Be positive'* signs most people call them. I thought that they had some historical or religious meaning. You seem to know a lot about these things."

"Don't you read books anymore, Mr. Finch?"

"Occasionally, but mostly e-books or online learning resources. I know paper copies are coming back into fashion, just like vinyl records did. People like to go retro. "

"Hmm, so I hear." The handler remained singularly unimpressed with Finch's lack of knowledge and appreciation, and returned to the subject of the painting. "Look, here on the road out of Rome Peter meets his Lord and master and asks, 'Where are you going with that cross?', to which he replies, 'I am going back to Rome to be crucified all over again'. Peter is struck by conscience and realises that he must return to Rome and face his fate. Don't you find that's wonderfully descriptive of where we find ourselves today, Mr. Finch, especially when you realise what Peter represents, or rather what he used to represent, to so many people?"

"Uh…kinda, I think. Not sure really." Once again Finch felt out of his depth and comfort zone. Where had Catherine gone? She could make a real difference and provide some much needed professional advice.

"Why would anyone freely choose pain, suffering and death? A delightful conundrum."

257

"Yes, I guess so. 'Cancel cancer: get vaccinated today'. Isn't that what the vaccination campaigns were all about?

"Oh, it's a lot bigger choice than just vaccination programmes. Here is represented the eternal choice. The offer of life or death, security or vulnerability. The choice to receive or to give. To preserve self or to offer yourself. Losing in order to gain."

"Still not quite sure what that has to do with anything." Finch was getting increasingly irritated with his handler. He had the innate ability to unsettle him and put him off balance. In his company he always felt as though he was struggling to make up lost ground – always behind the curve of the ball.

"I don't know whether your ignorance is charming or just confounding the problem."

"Look, I've not come here to speculate upon the hidden meaning of some old painting. I've got some information for you as well as some questions. So are we going to do this or not?"

"Of course we are, Mr. Finch, all in good time."

"Well, let's go and find the bar. I don't know about you, but I'm parched."

Finch then led his handler through a number of chambers, down some stairs, past a party of Chinese tourists and into a subterranean bar. Finch desperately needed a drink, but he also wanted to take the initiative once again and put his handler at more of a disadvantage than when he was quizzing him about art. Finally, his handler sat before him, hat removed, but retaining his jacket along with his impeccable demeanour.

"D'you mind if I smoke?" he asked.

"Actually I do mind. You've loaded me with all this crap. You've told me lies and set me up. I'm not going to play your nice, cosy games any more. I want some answers."

"We all want answers, Mr. Finch, but I'm paying you to

provide me with answers, not for me to furnish you with them."

"Well, at least do me the kindness of telling me your name. Just who am I dealing with here?"

"His name is Leander Hamilton, I know him as Leonard, and he's the father of my son." A voice came from an adjacent table where Catherine was quietly sitting on her own.

The handler's eyes nearly popped out of his head, his mouth dropped open in shocked surprise. "I...I...I've never seen this woman before," he blurted out.

Catherine swivelled around to look directly at Finch's handler. "Oh, don't give me that old crap, Lenny. You haven't changed over the years." She must have been observing them for some time. There was no semblance of doubt in her voice as she pinned him to his chair with an icy look of veiled contempt.

"Leander...well, well, well. You're Catherine's old man. Who would have thought?" Finch was starting to enjoy the handler's awkward position. "How long have you known that he was my handler?"

"About ten minutes. I knew Leonard worked for the Foreign Office, but we haven't exactly been close over the years. Ever since he left me to bring Josh up ON MY OWN!" Catherine spat out the final words through clenched teeth.

"What d'you mean, I left you? You didn't want me. You pushed me out. You had everything you needed." Leonard was becoming human. A real man with a real back story. No longer the remote, art-loving automaton, calling all the shots.

"You had your career. Nothing got in the way of that. I always suspected that you did something secret; you used that mystery as a way of holding me at arm's length and dictating the terms of our relationship." By now Leonard was putty in Catherine's hands. Finch had hoped that she might be able to lend him some moral support and balance out his cultural

259

knowledge deficit; he had never anticipated developments taking such a personal turn. "What you couldn't live with was the fact that I had a mind as well and a career, and I wasn't prepared to sacrifice either of them in order to become the nice, sweet stay-at-home partner you wanted, especially one who didn't ask too many questions when you disappeared abroad for a few months."

"But, but you knew that I had to travel. My work often took me away for periods of time."

"Working away is one thing, abandonment is something else. You just left, without explanation and it was impossible to contact you. You just disappeared."

Catherine's tirade was finally interrupted by the bar manager, who intervened to ask them to quieten down and remember the needs of other customers. Leonard and Catherine looked suitably chastened, but sat there staring intensely at each other, nearly thirty years of pent-up emotion, questions and recrimination waiting to be discharged.

"I'm enjoying this," Finch remarked.

"Piss off, Finch. You know nothing about this man."

"You're right, I don't, but I'm enjoying finding out."

"You put her up to this, didn't you?" Leonard turned his anger towards Finch. "You set me up. How did you find out about us?"

"Well, first of all, I didn't set you up. This is just one of those happy coincidences that occasionally play out before your eyes. However, if I had somehow managed to find out your identity, along with your relationship with Catherine – whom I met for the first time only a couple of days ago – then not only would I be some sort of genius, but I would also be wonderfully compensated for having been played for a patsy all along!"

"But how did…why have…? Oh, shit. Look, Catherine, I just wanted to say that all these years…I've been such a fool…I mean, it's really good to see you again and it's…oh, shit. I just wanted to say I'm sorry."

"Sorry?"

"Yes, I'm sorry."

"Is that all?"

"I had hoped that we might meet up again one day. I had such a lovely speech planned. I even hoped to take you to the Royal Academy; I know how much you love that place. I just never expected us to meet up again in such circumstances."

"Oh, you are so full of crap at times. You work in government security."

"Shh." Leonard grabbed Catherine's leg and gripped it tightly. This was another side to his handler that Finch had never seen before – a cold, steely determination to protect his anonymity whatever the cost. "Do I need to remind you of the importance of discretion? Whatever your personal feelings are towards me, there are important matters at stake here. Important for you as well as for me."

"Precisely," Catherine hissed through clenched teeth. "You have access to all sorts of information. You must have known where I was living all these years, my work, my family circumstances. You of all people cannot claim to be ignorant of my situation…our situation over the years." Catherine's eyes were blazing in anger as years of hurt and unresolved bitterness boiled over.

"Well, yes, I was aware, but there really was no need to consider you a threat or even think about getting back in touch."

"What about my boy? What about Joshua? Did you not think that he might need to know who his father was?"

"I really had no idea. I knew that you had a child, but I didn't know that he was my son. How would I know?"

"Work it out, think about it. Can't you remember when we were together?"

261

"Yes, but I wasn't sure of his birthday and there was a lot going on at that time. You had a lot of admirers. We had a fairly…a fairly open sort of relationship." Recognition began to dawn upon Leonard. Memories flashed uncomfortably before him, draining the colour from his face. "Oh, now I remember. Was it Geneva?"

"Yes, it was Geneva, you prick. Don't you even remember that?"

"Yes, I do, but I was…"

"You were working, weren't you? Ah, now it all makes sense. I thought you were even more remote and self-obsessed than usual in Geneva, but you didn't really take me on a romantic short break, did you? YOU WERE WORKING!" Once again anger erupted from within Catherine as fellow drinkers looked on, partly amused and partly shocked to see the argument continue.

"Oh, Catherine, I'm so, so sorry." Leonard held his head in his hands, contrition poured out of him. "What can I say? I've been such a fool all these years." He was beating his head with his fists in frustration and self-chastisement, castigating himself for the errors of his past. All of a sudden the legacy of divided loyalties, false identities and the secret lives of those intervening years weighed physically upon him, presenting an unbearable burden. Words failed, excuses departed, only regret remained.

"Okay, Len. Okay." Catherine softened her demeanour and touched Leonard on the arm in a reassuring manner. "It was a long time ago."

Leonard looked up, a drowning man about to grab hold of a serpent. "And your boy, Joshua, how is he keeping?"

"Oh, fuck you, Len." Catherine rose and stormed off in tears, knocking over a chair in the process.

Leonard made to go after her, but Finch stopped him. "Just let it go, mate. Let it go." He was starting to feel a degree of sympathy towards Leonard, even though he had been enjoying his discomfort.

"What did I say?"

"More than you realised," Finch replied. "When you previously worked for the Foreign Office, it wasn't in the diplomatic service by any chance?"

"No, it was just a cover for... Oh, I see what you're saying."

"For someone working in the intelligence industry, you really aren't that well informed."

"I'm sorry, but I had no reason to keep abreast of his situation. What happened to Joshua?"

Finch swallowed hard and summoned up all his emotional courage. "You know all those young people who keep taking their own lives. All those jumpers..."

"No!" An awful recognition suddenly dawned on Leonard.

"Yes, I'm afraid he was one of them. Drove a classic Aston DB9 off Beachy Head by all accounts."

"Oh, poor boy, my poor boy." Leonard choked up.

"Yes, I'm afraid so, very James Bond. I guess like father, like..." As soon as the words left his mouth, Finch immediately regretted it.

"Don't you dare..." Leonard caught Finch with a withering stare, as fierce as any physical punch, both chastising him for his comment, but also begging him to show compassion.

Finch realised he had overstepped the mark. He sensed the ground giving way beneath him; opening up an emotional chasm he was incapable of traversing. Whoever Leonard was and whatever he represented, he was after all just a man, flesh and blood, someone with a past, someone with feelings and connections to people. He deserved to have been told in a more compassionate manner.

"Look, I'm sorry, Leander."

"Leonard, if you must use my name."

"I'm sorry, Leonard. It must be hard to learn that you

have a son and then to discover that he's been taken from you."

There was no reply from Leonard. None was required.

Finally, Leonard straightened himself up and strengthened his resolve. "This is all rather difficult for me. I hadn't expected our meeting to unfold in this manner, but now that it has, then this must be our very last meeting. I'm sure that you understand why. All I ask is that you lay aside your tabloid instincts to take professional pleasure in my misfortune."

"Agreed." Finch was grateful for an exit strategy. He was feeling somewhat culpable and uneasy being present at such a personal moment for both Catherine and her former lover. At that point Catherine returned to the table, her emotional equilibrium restored. She was trying very hard to remain dignified and calm and hold herself straight and tall whilst remaining silent. It was obvious that she had been crying and had made a poor attempt at restoring her make-up in the nearby toilets. Each party silently acknowledged the other and there was a collective release of breath, as if to confirm that a line had been drawn under recent revelations and recriminations. It was time to move on.

"I would be grateful if you could furnish me with the documentation you have come by in your investigations." Leonard endeavoured to return to his previous disposition with what remained of his dignity.

Finch handed over a large file, along with a data stick. "I don't know why you want all this. I suspect that you already have most of this information."

"It is helpful to confirm what we know. We often have to outsource parts of our operations these days. It's all part of the new political reality we live under," Leonard explained.

Leonard briefly flicked through the files that Finch had provided, displaying neither a glimmer of recognition nor any surprise to indicate the true value of what had been so hard to come by.

"I still don't buy it."

"Buy it? Buy what?"

"I don't buy the line you spun me about wanting to find Iona Dunwoody and her family wanting her back."

"I am assuming that you haven't found her then?"

"To be honest, I stopped looking."

"Then you have defaulted on our agreement, Mr. Finch. That is a very serious matter."

"The reason I stopped looking was that I realised that you already knew where she was and what she was doing there."

"What makes you think that?"

"Oh, just a few little clues. The badly photo-shopped image. The suggestion that I might owe her a debt of gratitude for saving me from the full force of the bomb blast. But more importantly, the trail of breadcrumbs that led conveniently towards the real issue here, namely the role of Van Hegel and others in the vaccination cover-up."

Leonard shuffled awkwardly in his chair, as if once again a truth had been exposed. "I didn't think that image would convince you. I can remember the times when we had experts to do things like that. Now we give those sorts of jobs to fresh-faced graduates."

"What I'm intrigued to know is why you really wanted to find Iona Dunwoody. Are you just trying to subvert the movement that she's clearly a willing part of?"

"No. You really don't know what you are investigating, do you?"

"Enlighten me, Mr. Leander Hamilton from the Foreign Office, former lover of my colleague here." Finch slowly and deliberately described what he had recently discovered about Leonard in order to remind him of the advantage he still believed he held over him.

"Are you trying to threaten me, Mr. Finch? Because if you decide to play that game, then I should remind you of your own sad past and the people who wish to learn more about YOU so that they can recover certain outstanding debts."

"OK, so we've both got something on each other. Can we therefore reach some kind of mutually beneficial understanding?"

Suddenly Leonard froze in his seat, his eyes fixed straight ahead, as if he was straining to hear something. He touched his ear several times before abruptly standing to gather all his papers. "This conversation will have to continue elsewhere at another time. The perimeter has been breached. We all need to leave…right now!"

Catherine looked aghast. "Is this just one of your old stunts again, Len? Because if it is, then I…"

"For goodness sake, Catherine, trust me on this one. We've had an alert from the facial recognition cameras around the gallery. It appears our little spat earlier has attracted some unwanted attention. If you value your safety, then come with me NOW." The authority and urgency of his tone left Catherine and Finch in no doubt that he was serious. They quickly rose and followed him out of the bar.

Leonard grabbed his briefcase and was soon making his way upstairs, looking over his shoulder as he fled. He was puffing and blowing and clearly not accustomed to making an exit in such haste. Catherine and Finch followed close behind, anxious not only to secure their own escape, but also to keep close to Leonard, who remained their best hope of finding the answers that they both so desperately sought.

"But you're the government. Just who on earth are you running from?"

"I'm running from the same people you've been running from," Leonard explained, "the enemy within."

Minutes later they were making haste down Haymarket towards the West End, weaving in and out of bemused pedestrians, anxiously checking over their shoulders for signs of a pursuit. Finch thought he saw a couple of figures following them at pace, but he couldn't be sure. Leonard and Catherine were both blowing their cheeks vigorously and struggling to keep up with Finch. Leonard was repeatedly talking into his jacket lapel with increasing urgency. Eventually they reached a quiet side road and Finch pulled them into the rear doorway of an Indian restaurant.

"OK then, where are the bad guys or is this just another ruse to avoid answering my questions?"

"Like I said, you really don't know what you're looking at, do you? I've called for back-up, so if they can find us, the chances are that the people we are running from can also find us," Leonard explained in breathless tones.

"But just who are we running from?"

"The same people that took you uptown and tried to abduct you in Cheltenham."

"What? Van Hegel?"

"No, not just them, they're merely the paymasters. There's a whole industry dedicated to maintaining the deception. Large corporations like Van Hegel and KPR."

"Who?"

"You won't know anything about KPR. Just another multinational that has commercial interests invested in the *'Great Advance'*. They've grown so fat on the proceeds that they've become virtually untouchable. Like modern day kingmakers, even governments fear their power and influence. Then there are corporations like Dunwoody and others who are the owners of capital; those who control everything, but make nothing. All they're interested in is keeping people buying the kind of toys that so many have turned to for comfort since the *'Garden Party Bombings'*. Then there's another layer of interests. Those who seek to gain by maintaining an atmosphere of fear, the ones who've made money out of the war against terrorism."

"Are they the ones with the guns?"

Leonard nodded breathlessly.

"The problem is that surveillance has gone down-market. Cheap, easily available equipment combined with political ideology have let in a whole series of private operators. Former mercenaries and ex-squaddies returning from deployment overseas find work in private security companies licensed by the Home Office. A whole cottage industry has grown up. It's totally out of control and completely unaccountable."

"So that's your angle. You're trying to wrestle back control of the security industry into the public sector," Catherine interjected.

"It's all changed, Cathy. It's not like the old days."

Just then a shadow fell across the three companions as two large men in tee-shirts, jeans and baseball caps loomed up in front of them. One of them was the olive-skinned man with a beard that had cornered them in Cheltenham.

"It certainly is a new world these days," said the man with a beard as he reached inside his jacket to produce a pistol and silencer. "So sad therefore that you won't be seeing much more of it."

The three of them cowered breathlessly in the doorway. Catherine started beating the door of the restaurant in order to attract attention. Finch tried to reason with the men, but it was clear that they were not in the mood for conversation.

The second man touched his ear. "Target identified," he whispered into the collar of his jacket. "Requesting authority to serve notice." There was a short pause, then a look of recognition spread across his face. The two men lifted their hand guns and released the safety catches.

A popping sound crackled around the doorway. The second man looked disbelievingly into his jacket to see a crimson rose of blood blossom. The bearded man suddenly took aim.

"NO!" Leonard cried, throwing himself in front of

Catherine as more popping noises crackled and reverberated around the restaurant doorway.

The bearded man fell sideways, a small, blackened hole in the side of his head. The other man gradually slumped to the floor. Two more shots were heard and then he moved no more.

Behind them two armed policemen were crouched with automatic pistols pointing towards the fallen men. They rushed forward and pressed the downed assailants to the ground in order to neutralise any remaining threat. The bearded man let out a grunt and a sigh, then sighed no more. The other man lay twitching on the floor, injured yet still alive.

By now Catherine was screaming. "Len, Lenny. Speak to me, Len. LEN!" She cradled Leonard's fallen frame in her arms, supported by Finch. Leonard's eyes were rolling and blood was seeping from his mouth.

"I'm so sorry, Cathy." Leonard gasped. "So very sorry for the pain I caused. You deserved so much better than me."

"It's okay. It's okay. You didn't cause me any pain. It was just meant to be me and Josh. We coped. We did all right."

"Did he ever…ever ask about me?" Leonard voice was fading as more blood erupted from his mouth.

"Of course. He was a bit like you in so many ways. Obstinate, single-mined, lost in his own little world."

A thin smile crossed Leonard's face. "Thank you." He looked towards Catherine and then across to Finch. "Quo vadis? Mr. Finch. Quo vadis? Then he fell silent.

Chapter 19

Morning mist hung over the cemetery as the casket was lowered into the earth.

The funeral itself had been a modest and restrained affair, devoid of the colour and imagery so precious to its subject, not even a union flag draped over the coffin to indicate the years of dedicated service rendered on behalf of the country he loved. An understated funeral to befit the life of someone who lived in the shadows and kept so many secrets. Nothing to indicate the nature of Leander Joshua Hamilton's commitment to the security of others, not even a mention of his posthumous Distinguished Service Medal in the heavily edited eulogy and official records. Only those who had witnessed his untimely death along with very close family members knew of its significance. The official report attributed his killing to collateral damage arising from a gangland turf war on the streets of central London. Never had such a description been so apposite and yet so misleading, much like the man himself. He had certainly died trying to defend the organisation he had proudly served from the threat of outsiders invading their territory.

As the casket was sprinkled with earth and single red

roses cast into the grave by family members, Catherine and Finch looked on, each considering the contradictions that surrounded Leonard's life. Hero or villain, saviour or conspirator, lover of art or controller of information, Leonard had spent so many years slipping out of the light and into the dark that he remained an enigma right to the bitter end. Whatever they thought of him, his courage and conviction had ultimately shone through when it was needed most.

A small crowd had assembled around the graveside. Several men in dark suits hung around in the background, hiding amongst the canopy of trees and trying not to be too conspicuous, yet clearly moved by what was taking place. Towards the front stood a woman in a dark suit and veiled hat, accompanied by what were clearly her grown up children, one of whom was holding a small child in her arms.

As the service concluded, the woman in the veiled hat thanked the attendant and was comforted by her family. Catherine hadn't attended a funeral since the death of Joshua. There was much that reminded her of that sad occasion. The minimal use of ritual, the absence of prayers, the use of silent reflection, story-telling and sharing of memories by family and friends of the deceased. The event resembled more of a celebration of someone's life for the benefit of the living, than an occasion to consider their passing and to find hope in the idea of a continued future. References to the past skilfully avoided the details of Leonard's profession. It felt comforting, affirming and life enhancing yet also functional and contractual, a bit like the closing of a chapter or signing off on a deal.

As the crowds of mourners gradually began to disperse, Catherine approached the woman in the veiled hat. She suspected that Leonard had a family and immediately identified with the sacrifices they must have made over the years. Finch warned Catherine that speaking to the family could

271

be provocative, yet she disregarded his advice. She needed closure, both for herself and for Leonard's family and even though it would be difficult, she knew this was something she had to do.

"Hello, Mrs. Hamilton. I'm Catherine Stringer. I'm terribly sorry about your loss."

"Thank you my dear, it's lovely to see you. I'm so glad that you were able to come." The woman was clearly imbued with innate goodness or else she had a hide of sheer leather.

"I...I was...with Leonard towards the end." Catherine tentatively offered an explanation to her identity.

"Yes, I know who you are dear. It's all been explained to me. The important thing is that you were someone who Leonard cared about and that's all that matters."

Catherine melted in the presence of this stranger and just stood there with her mouth open, offering no words.

"Don't you know who this is Mum?" The younger woman with the small child tried to cajole her mother away from offering Catherine any sympathetic reception. "If it wasn't for her, then Dad would still be here." She added indignantly.

"Your father made his own choices Melanie. He always did with us and he continued that way right up to the end. We never understood those choices and we never will, but he believed that what he was doing would save lives, and so it was. That's all we need to know."

Catherine struggled to know how to respond. "He...He was a good man. I know that and I think we all know that as well."

"He certainly believed in the power of ideas to bring out the good in people." The lady smiled and then looked directly into Catherine's eyes, "What do you believe in my dear?"

Catherine was taken aback by the directness of her question, especially given the emotional turmoil that she must have been navigating. "I'm not sure what I believe in, but I think that I want to believe."

"Then your tribute to Leonard can only be to follow your desires. Look for the higher purpose and accomplish the work that he died to advance."

Catherine departed from the graveside strangely uplifted. Her act of altruism to comfort the grieving family had actually rebounded upon her as she was enveloped in the love and grace of Leonard's widow. She would never know the influence that she would have exerted upon Leonard over the years, nor the pain, disappointment and lies that she would have had to bear, but her compassion overwhelmed and inspired her. She had surely encountered great goodness.

As Catherine walked away, she looked back towards Leonard's family who were by now assembled in a group around his widow. The two women exchanged knowing looks as Catherine departed the graveside, connecting across the vast landscape of time and opportunity, sharing an unspoken connection with someone who had shaped their lives and broken their hearts. Finch comforted her with a firm arm around her shoulder. There was nothing more to be said.

"Mr. Finch. Miss Stringer. May I have a word with you?" One of the men in a dark suit was addressing them. Puzzled, yet still in a state of quiet reflection, they followed him up to a large, dark people carrier with blacked out windows that was parked at the edge of the cemetery. "Please, if you are able." The man gestured towards the door of the car which duly slid open with quiet efficiency.

"Hang on a minute." Finch protested. "Just who are you?"

"We represent His Majesty's Government. You are quite safe with us, Mr. Finch." The man in the dark suit replied.

"Just like Leander Hamilton was safe." Finch muttered under his breath as he and Catherine stepped inside the vehicle. In the rear seat sat a woman in a trouser suit with grey hair scooped back into a bun. She looked up from her computer tablet and removed her glasses. "Please, Mr. Finch,

Dr. Hamilton, sit down. Would you care to join me for a cup of tea?" She gestured towards a china tea set laid out before them on a small fold down table.

"Tea? You're offering us tea?" Finch appeared genuinely taken aback.

"It's such a lovely way for strangers to discuss their differences. Don't you agree?"

The pair nodded in compliant acquiescence. The lady then reverted to hostess role, dutifully preparing a pot of tea which she then poured out accompanied by convivial conversation and biscuits. She pressed a button on a console in front of her. A glass screen slid down separating the driver from the rest of the cabin. "Can you ask Mr. Falshaw to step inside for a moment please?"

Finch looked puzzled, but also somewhat relieved, as if scales had fallen from his troubled eyes. At that moment, the door slid open and Greg stepped into the back of the car to join the grey haired lady.

"I've asked Mr. Falshaw to join us. I hope that you don't mind. I thought that you might have a few things you would like to ask him."

"One or two." Finch replied.

"You've probably realised by now, that Mr. Falshaw has been on secondment from Special Branch. Mr. Hamilton regarded your safety as paramount and wanted to ensure that someone was watching your back as it were…and so it proved."

"So, you haven't been doing me any personal favours then, Greg, you've just been on assignment all along."

"Well someone had to mind your backside." Greg replied.

"And the domestic crisis? Was that all part of the cover story?"

"Not entirely. You know what I'm like." Greg and Finch exchanged knowing looks. "I might have laid on the emotional devastation a bit thick, but I had been kicked out, I just wasn't in quite so desperate a need for accommodation as I made out."

"I see." Finch replied with a sigh, just another instance of Greg's misdemeanours that had been laid at his door over the years, only this time, there was a more kindly intent. "So when Leonard said that he would be keeping an eye on me that was…"

"Yep, you're looking at him." Greg replied. "Last person you'd suspect would be the one right under your nose."

"The sly old dog." Finch felt like he had been outwitted in a card game by the convincing poker face and bluffing strategy of another player. He now realised why he was such an unsuccessful gambler. Despite all his years of hardnosed journalism, he still naively took people at face value. "Is there anyone left who has actually played it straight with me?" Finch asked in desperation.

"Sometimes, not knowing the whole truth is the best way to stay alive, Mr. Finch. In Mr. Hamilton's case, he actually told you very plainly what he was trying to achieve."

"Something about cleaning up the department and getting rid of all the private security contractors getting under your feet?"

"That's one way of putting it. Yet even freelancers have their uses."

"Keep your friends close to you and your enemies even closer."

"Quite." The grey haired lady took a sip of tea. "I think that it might also be fair to say that Mr. Hamilton did overstep his brief at times and mixed his personal agenda with that of his official duties somewhat." She peered over her glasses to indicate mild disapproval. "But that's all in the past now."

"Overstepped his brief! You really are a supercilious bastard." Catherine intervened, "This man has just laid down

275

his life for his country and that's the way you talk about him."
She was red in the face, the veins in her neck sitting proud and
registering disgust.

"Quite so." The grey haired lady replied as if she was
wafting away an irritating wasp, "and you can take it from me,
that his country is most grateful."

"Grateful! Grateful?" Catherine was still incandescent
with moral rage.

"Yes. More tea?"

"No, I don't want any more of your bloody tea."

The grey haired lady seemed utterly cold and removed,
dismissing Catherine's obvious indignation. She poured
another cup and then straightened up. "Unfortunately what
Mr. Hamilton was unable to tell you before he died, was that
he was also charged with a higher task."

"Such as?" Finch enquired, whilst Catherine continued
muttering profanities in the corner.

For the first time the grey haired lady looked uncomfortable
and shuffled uneasily in her seat. "Let's just say that he was
charged with establishing a counter intelligence initiative
against the second front in the war against terror."

"Second front? Which second front?" Finch could hardly
believe what he was hearing. He had received off the record
briefings from members of the security services before, but
rarely had they delivered any decisive information. More
often than not they had merely confirmed the authority of his
sources, rather than offering any fresh intelligence.

"Well the enemy within, of course. I'm sure Mr. Leander
must have explained his brief to you."

"Not entirely. Our conversation was kinda cut short."

"Oh, how unfortunate."

"Yes cut short by his UNTIMELY, VIOLENT DEATH."
Now it was Finch's turn to give vent to his anger.

"Well anyhow," the grey haired lady continued. "A line has

now been crossed in the internal feud that has been raging for the soul of our nation's security. It's time for decisive action."

By now both Finch and Catherine were boring holes in the grey haired lady with their combined icy stare, demanding an emotional reaction or at least a sign of some humanity. None came.

"A line has been crossed? You mean a man has died. A good man. I've had about enough of this bullshit." An exasperated Catherine rose from her seat to slide open the car door, only to be greeted by the cold, blank expression and huge frame of one of the men in the dark suits that had greeted her earlier. His impassive response blocking her exit was sufficient inducement to re-direct her back inside of the car.

"Hear her out, luv, just hear her out." Greg tried to reassure Catherine before looking across to Finch. "You've gotta trust them on this one, Finchie. Take it from me, you haven't got much choice."

"Thank you, Mr. Falshaw." The grey haired lady gestured to Catherine to re-occupy her seat in the car. "Mr. Finch, Dr. Stringer, I feel you might have misjudged Mr. Hamilton and the approach he made."

"I just want someone to tell us the truth!" Finch spat out the words in exasperation. "The story about wanting to find Iona Dunwoody was just part of a web of lies. You've been playing me for a fool right from the beginning."

"On the contrary, Mr. Finch. What Mr. Hamilton told you about her was totally true. She is of great interest to us. We remain very anxious to discover her whereabouts."

"Cut the crap. You know exactly where she is. Otherwise we wouldn't be sitting here with you, now." Catherine added.

"Oh yes, but sadly, I fear that she has once again gone to ground." At that point the grey haired lady reached into a handbag beside her feet and took out a small folded note. "We found this in the apartment you have been sharing."

Catherine looked shocked. The wind taken out of her sails, just as she was about to let rip once again. She slowly opened the note to see a few words of Sky's beautiful copper plate writing: '*Sorry. Must go. Keep the faith! Sky.*' "When did you come across this? There was no message when we returned to the apartment."

"I know. The apartment had already been swept clean by one of our teams."

Finch examined the note, flipping it over, as if looking for hidden clues. "Typical," he said, "Dunwoody stationary. You can take the girl out of corporate life, but you can never take corporate life out of the girl."

Catherine and the grey haired lady exchanged looks, for the moment Catherine's fury at the dismissive attitude of Leonard's employer replaced once again by curiosity and intrigue in relation to Sky.

"I'm afraid that we have no idea where she is. So, if you…"

"Yes, yes, Dr. Stringer we know that you aren't hiding anything in relation to Miss Dunwoody. That's why you're drinking tea with me and not wearing an orange boiler suit on some remote island." For once, a note of real menace entered their conversation. The grey haired lady stiffened her posture as if to underline the veiled threat. She then put down her china tea cup, furrowed her brow and looked at them both over the top of her expensive, designer spectacles in the manner of a disapproving school teacher.

"You see you have been told more of the truth than you realised. People like Iona Dunwoody or Sky or whatever she now calls herself, are actually fundamental to our mutual interests. In fact, you might even say, fundamental to our national interests."

"And those interests are?" Catherine piped up.

"Security, community stability, social cohesion. The heightened state of fear and suspicion benefits no-one. If we have a stable society, able to express itself freely and in tolerance of all, then we don't need all the extra apparatus of security and surveillance."

"And all those hopeless amateurs cluttering things up for the professionals?" Finch enquired.

"Well, let's just say that everything returns to its default position."

"And that default involves, leaving the state to look after our security?"

"There are some areas of government that really should be a no-go zone for out-sourcing experiments."

Finch sat back in his seat with a look of self-satisfaction and vindication, as if finally re-assured of an unspoken thought. "So what's in it for us, then?" He enquired coolly.

"If you deliver, Iona Dunwoody, you get your big story and you my dear," the grey haired lady turned to address Catherine, "gain some sort of closure for why your son took his life."

"And you get to play with your old toys again."

"It's a win, win situation." The grey haired lady concluded, allowing herself a brief, half smug smile.

"Win, win for whom?" Finch asked.

"For everyone."

"Including your political masters? I can't see them being happy to hand back the keys to the toy cupboard to you overnight."

"For them as well. They want an exit strategy out of the current impasse."

"Really?"

"Oh yes, social cohesion is very high on their agenda. Criminalizing a whole section of the volunteer culture is in nobody's interests. You can't build a fair and supportive society based on mutual fear and conspicuous consumption. You need social capital. Strong communities rooted in social enterprise, philanthropy and shared values. Take away the nation's soul and it's not just the nation's health that suffers, it's also the economy – and the economy is something that gets everyone's attention."

"So you want us to bring in Iona, I mean Sky, from the cold for a nice cosy chat with those who've placed her photo on the most wanted list."

"Let's just say that she's a good starting point and her amnesty will be guaranteed."

"And why would she be willing to do that?" Catherine asked.

"Because for some reason, she seems to trust you, more than anyone else."

"So you want me to betray her?"

"Not betray, rather enlighten her as to where her best interests lie. Like I said, we will guarantee her immunity from any prosecution."

"You obviously don't know Sky very well." Finch added. "She is not naturally given to trusting people."

"Even those who have protected her?"

"It won't be easy." Catherine added. "Why should she trust you anyhow? What can you do to show some good faith?"

The grey haired lady stared thoughtfully out of the car window. The morning mist had lifted by now and watery sunshine bathed the cemetery. The silence was interrupted by a bleeping noise. She touched a hidden earpiece and listened intently to the caller. A look of intense concentration and seriousness stole her attention away from the occupants of the car.

"I'm afraid that this meeting is over. Look, leave that with me. They might be something we can do. In the meantime, Mr. Falshaw will be your new liaison officer. I will contact you again when I have some more information. Good day, Mr. Finch, Dr. Stringer."

With that the door glided open again and the two figures emerged into the sunlight to consider their next move.

Chapter 20

It was a hot, sultry night and Eleanor lay drenched in sweat. A warm, blanket of humid oppressive air hung over her prostrate body and refused to be lifted. Outside the silence of the night was broken by the rumble of thunder and rain drumming against windows and cascading down broken guttering. The storm had woken Eleanor from a vivid, sensuous dream and she remained in a state of arousal. She and Jez has been entwined in a passionate, warm embrace, her fingers tracing the contours of his long, sinewy torso as he caressed her naked breasts. She couldn't remember what had brought them together, only how evocative and real it had felt. She longed to return to the narrative of her fantasy, but realised that just as in real life, such dreams were impossible to recreate.

She struggled out of bed in order to persuade a reluctant sash window to yield to the night air in the hope of gleaming a breadth of cooler, refreshing air. By now the rain had abated, yet the atmosphere remained warm and heavy. She stood framed in the window, her bedclothes clinging to her damp body. She smoothed the contours of her breasts beneath her vest, longing to re-create Jez's passionate touch and the cascading brush of his long, auburn hair.

In the distance the throbbing rotor blades of a surveillances drone punctuated the stillness of the night. As the rumble of the drone gradually melted into the background other night sounds slowly grew to fill her room. The screech and rattle of the first LTR train of the day, the rumble of long distance flights stacking up to land at Heathrow and then imperceptibly, the ever louder distinctive chirrup and tweet of a solitary blackbird as the neighbouring songbird community cleared their collective throats in order to join in with the daily dawn chorus. Eleanor loved living in the city, nowhere else could the approach of a new day be greeted with quite the same eclectic symphony of sounds and sensations.

As she lay on top of her bedding, trying to cool down, the stillness of the breaking dawn was disturbed by the noise of an approaching car. Slowly it drew to a shuddering halt as doors were slammed and people spoke in excited tones. Eleanor initially tried to ignore the noises in order to return to the comforting images of her dream, yet her curiosity finally drew her towards the open window where she peered through the half-light of dawn to see a large, dark Range Rover waiting in the street below, its doors open wide and headlights piercing the melting dawn. Two women stood on the pavement besides the car. One had her head bowed, whilst the other stood over her holding her firmly by the shoulders in an act of re-assurance. Suddenly there were sounds of movement across the street followed by a door opening as the two women continued in conversation, they briefly embraced before being joined on the pavement by a third figure who passed a suitcase to the woman being comforted.

After a while, the two women reluctantly parted, as they did so, the face and outline of the woman offering comfort came into view beneath the street light, it was Sister Bernadette. Bernadette returned to the car and passed a small object to the other woman before returning to the Range Rover which then swept off purposely down the road. The two remaining figures stood facing each other for several moments before shaking hands and then parted as the woman hastily crossed over the street and disappeared from view, followed by the sound of a house door closing below her and footsteps gradually fading from earshot.

Eleanor returned to her bed, puzzled, yet still lost in thought. The sights outside seemed as surreal as her fantasy world. It seemed that all around her thinly veiled secrets entwined with deceptive roles hidden from view. Even her new life had become an exercise in misdirection. For three weeks, she had been a resident at the Anastasis Centre which ran a series of therapeutic programmes for people living under the shadow of substance abuse and addictive lifestyles. Her day job conferred upon her a whole new identity as well as the challenge of learning a new skill set. As far as her public profile was concerned she remained Eleanor Dupree, extreme sports junkie and occasional sportswear model, but in reality, she spent most of her time at the Centre, teaching fitness, sport and healthy living to a group of needy residents. Her on-line presence continued uninterrupted and she still interacted with people through various blogs and social networks as Eleanor, however, off-line she lived quietly, away from the public sphere as part of a small residential community in Peckham under the pseudonym of project worker Charlotte Lister. The re-invention seemed to be working well. She had not been bothered by any further signs of surveillance for weeks, whilst everyone at the Centre, save for the Manager, knew her only as Charlotte. Her new identify even allowed her to see Jez during days off and at the weekend.

As Eleanor lay on her bed, wrestling with the images of the night, she tried unsuccessfully to return to the comfort of her dream. Her girlfriends had often shared such stories, often after several glasses of pinot grigio. She suspected that half of such stories were made up on the spot in order to impress or shock an inquisitive audience. Sexual competitiveness remained a feature of their social interaction although she preferred not to speak of her own liaisons, either the real ones or the fantasy versions. Instead she chose to compete and prove herself in other ways. When it came to sexual conquests she had little to prove, she knew she could have any man she wanted, but she had little appetite to parade such trophies for the entertainment of others.

Jez was different though. He was unfinished business and he had connected with her in a way that no former sexual liaison ever could. He was under her skin, part of her, completing her. Every ounce of her being pulsated with longing for him, not in an adolescent obsessive manner, but rather, intuitively, deep within her, each fibre of her humanity demanded that they should be together. They belonged; they were one spirit, one essence, one being. They shared an intense understanding, as if they could anticipate each other's thoughts, moods or decisions. She longed for his physical presence, to be swept up off the ground in his overwhelming embrace, to lose herself to him and to surrender to his gentle passion. Most of all, she longed for him in a way that she had never longed for another living person. She didn't just desire him, she wanted to be part of his world, to breathe the air he breathed, to share his hopes and dreams. Her greatest wish was to please him as well as to be pleased by him, she craved for the self-giving of his very soul, not just wanting to be desired, but to be loved.

While the city gradually stirred into life around her, she considered what made Jez so special. He was one of the very few men she had actually pursued, so why had he caught her eye so much amidst those pumping iron in the gym? Perhaps it was his tall, gangly awkwardness, his slight frame, his long auburn dreadlocks and pale, freckled skin in such contrast to the pumped up, steroid enhanced, alpha males she normally hooked up with? Perhaps it was his innate shyness, the fact that he appeared reticent and unsure of himself. Whichever way she looked at it, Jez, just didn't make any sense. He was untypical of her peer group, an outsider in many ways. Perhaps that was his attraction? He was different, illusive and difficult to fathom, displaying an inner depth and sensitivity whilst others showed only power and bravado. Most of all, he was tantalizingly unavailable to her. He was just out of reach. He was the forbidden fruit, the ultimate conquest, the final challenge for her, a distant country awaiting exploration.

Despite the vivid details of her dream, Jez's appeal wasn't simply about sex, neither was it about conquering the ultimate challenge of a man beyond her reach. This was no idle adolescent infatuation or obsession, she was genuinely knocked over and awe struck by the presence of another human soul. She had run up against something she had never encountered before. It made no sense, it couldn't be explained or compared or quantified, it was totally unreasonable and disproportionate, and yet it remained the most wonderful, remarkable, humanity defining emotion that she had ever encountered. It drove her mad, but also filled her with hope whilst threatening to overwhelm her. Her desire for him exposed her emotionally in a way that could pierce her very being with pain and loss. She was hopelessly vulnerable before him. She longed for his presence as someone longs for cool, refreshing water in the heat of the night. It was the only explanation to the way she felt, she was smitten, she was in love.

Eventually her thoughts were interrupted by the sound of her radio alarm dragging her back into the reality of her daily routine. There was much to do at the centre today and her official duties demanded that she maintain the false persona and relationships of Charlotte Lister. Her dual identity was starting to present a number of challenging issues, in particular how to explain her non-attendance at various social events to her increasingly curious girlfriends. By now her range of excuses by way of minor illness or previous engagements were wearing a bit thin. Nicola and the other girls were becoming more persistent in their questioning and curious as to where she was spending her time. She was living in two worlds, her previous life of adrenaline-seeking excess and alcohol fuelled socializing sat awkwardly alongside that of her new life of quiet, sobriety, early nights, regular routine and public service among needy people. Her two names helped her to live with the polarities of her identity, whilst her modelling portfolio still subsidised her new, more modest lifestyle. Despite the contradictions of her dual identity, her new persona afforded her both a degree of protection and also the freedom to explore the love and significance she was seeking.

Today promised to be a challenging day. The news about the tsunami had hit her local community hard. A number of the residents had friends or relatives holidaying in the Canaries at the time the wave struck and frantic efforts had taken place to find information about those missing as well as those who had sadly lost their lives. Eleanor had been drawn into these efforts on behalf of one resident in particular. Kimberley was one of the more demanding residents at Anastasis. She was a long term heroine user who had been admitted to the community on a number of occasions in the past. She was one of their longest standing residents, with apparently intractable needs and had asked Eleanor to help her locate her missing boyfriend who was working in Lanzarote. Kimberley's attachment to him appeared more than just personal and she suspected that he was also one of her regular dealers. Whatever the relationship, she had learnt that his name was included among those missing presumed dead, although at present, no body had been found. Eleanor had promised to take Kimberley to a vigil that Jez was organising at a local Food Bank. Such an occasion would also provide her with an ideal opportunity to meet with Jez once again.

By the time the minibus arrived at the Anastasis Centre, most of the residents had decided they wanted to attend the vigil at the Food Bank. It proved to be quite a feat of organisation to squeeze in all the residents into the minibus, along with sufficient project workers for their supervision, but the judicious use of back up transport resulted in the entire group arriving safely at a former pub now being used as a Food Bank. As they arrived outside the faded Victorian charm of this former drinking establishment, the leaded glass windows were already steaming up suggesting a large crowd gathering within.

The group from the Anastasis Centre barged their way into the building displaying an enthusiasm rarely witnessed in the building since its original use. Once inside, however, they were greeted by a strange, unfamiliar stillness, punctuated by a gentle, ethereal music. People were standing shoulder to shoulder, some using electric fans to try and cool down in the absence of modern air conditioning. A sign greeted them just inside the door. *'Turn off all mobiles as you enter – do not disturb the stillness of this place'*.

Further inside the room figures crouched, kneeling on the floor gazing up at metal racks of candles flickering in the natural light. On the bar sat a large two handled wok from which sweet smelling fumes of incense gradually filled the room. Behind the bar were placed various signs relating to the distribution of food parcels and the need to provide appropriate vouchers for their collection. Around the room, display screens were running a series of silent news images from the scene of the tsunami showing flattened buildings along with the reactions of loved ones and survivors.

Standing in front of the bar was the figure of Jez, wearing a white, hooded robe. Eleanor's heart leapt within her before she chastised herself for considering her own selfish needs at such a solemn and sad occasion. She had always held a fascination for men in uniform, but seeing Jez for the first time apparently representing something official and mysterious, made her swoon once again.

After an extended period of silence, Jez finally spoke. His words were soft, thoughtful and slow paced. He spoke about how an experience of loss was part of what made us human and how such an occasion was an important moment for those present to take time out in order to consider how loss had affected their own lives. He explained that some might feel undirected anger, not knowing who or what to blame, others might feel powerless and vulnerable because they had little or no experience of having lost a loved one. Still others might feel bewildered because they had nowhere to take such thoughts and feelings. He therefore assured them that this occasion provided both the time and place to express those thoughts and feelings.

As Jez, spoke Eleanor connected with what he was saying, but also found herself connecting more with the person of Jez. She just felt enormous pride in what he was trying to do and drew confidence from his presence and quiet authority. As she was listening to Jez, she became aware of the shaking figure of Kimberley besides her. She looked to see her crying uncontrollably. She put an arm around her to re-assure her, even though she had been told not to physically touch any of the residents for fear of how such an act could be interpreted. Nevertheless, it felt like the most caring and human thing to do and Kimberley responded by falling to the floor in a crumpled heap and then just resting with her head in her hands.

While Eleanor knelt beside Kimberley, Jez spoke further telling stories from the Bible about how Jesus felt when a friend of his died and what he did in response. He then invited everybody to write down their honest feelings on pieces of paper which were then collected up by a number of stewards. Once people had done this, they were encouraged to light candles as a way of saying a prayer and then place the candle in front on a large cross shape made from chicken wire which had been secured to one of the green tiled walls that lined the former public bar. At this point the stewards began pushing the pieces of paper containing people's feelings into the chicken wire cross. The vigil concluded with some reflective popular music and a collective prayer which some people knew the words for, whilst others required a prompt from the various display screens.

As the vigil finished, Eleanor spotted the distinctive outline of Sister Bernadette standing by the fire exit and made her way towards her through the crowd. After suggesting that they retire to the comparative privacy of a former games room, now used for storing non-perishable food, Eleanor decided to tackle Sister Bernadette about the events of the previous day.

"Can you tell me just what's going on around here?"

"I'm sorry."

"I saw you."

"You saw me."

"Yes, I saw you last night, outside the centre."

"The centre? When?"

"About five, this morning."

"Aahhh. I see." Bernadette looked thoughtful.

"Is there something you need to tell me?" Eleanor felt slightly guilty trying to put Bernadette on the spot, yet she felt that she was owed an explanation.

"Please, let's sit down for a moment." Bernadette made herself comfortable on top of a large sack of rice and invited Eleanor to join her atop a pile of tomato soup cans. She looked tired and slightly troubled and appeared to be nursing a sore back. Eleanor had never seen her look quite so ill at ease. "I guess that it was a rather public place to choose. I should have known that."

"So just what were you up to?"

"Can I first ask you a question my dear?"

"Sure, go ahead."

"How have you been treated since you came to stay with us in community?"

"I would say by and large, very well."

"Have you felt that you have been taken advantage of in any way?"

"Well, you are getting me to do a lot of exercise classes at a reduced rate, but apart from that, then no, not really."

"And how would you say your life has changed since you came here."

"It's changed totally."

"In what way?"

"In every way. You've looked after me, protected me, shared your meals and your lives with me. You've given me a new sense of purpose along with a new name."

"Anything else?"

"Well yes, I think that I've found a place where I feel I belong."

"That's good to hear, so, if you don't mind me asking you a direct question as well, then, why are we having this conversation?"

"Why?"

"Yes, why?"

Eleanor felt as though she had been outwitted by Bernadette. "Because all of that means nothing, if it's been predicated upon a lie."

"So you feel that you've been lied to?"

"I don't know. I just want to understand."

"Do you have to understand in order to love people or do you love people as a way of understanding them?"

"Oh, I don't know. You're playing your word games on me. All I want to know is whether I can really trust you?"

"If your life has truly been touched by the people you have met in community, then you have answered you own question, my dear."

"So that's it then?"

"For the moment, yes." Bernadette replied calmly.

"You're not going to tell me. I've just got to trust you?" Eleanor just stared at Bernadette in exasperation, hoping that she would yield, but she just smiled and softly held her hand.

"If you know that you are loved, then you will also know that you can trust those who love you."

"But don't I deserve some kind of explanation?"

"Deserve? Oh, that's a very strange notion to carry around in relation to oneself." Bernadette then looked deeply into Eleanor's eyes and saw her troubled spirit and frustration. She could see her inner torment – wanting to believe, but struggling to do so. "Do you want to tell me what's really bothering you Ellie?"

Eleanor realised that Bernadette could read her as well as any book and there was little point in pretending any more. "I don't know. I guess it's just with this thing between me and Jez. I can't really make any sense of it and I don't know what to do."

"Oh, I see." Bernadette sat back on her sack of rice as if she had half anticipated Eleanor's response.

"It's like I've lost control of something. I just don't know what to think or feel any more."

"And your problem is…?"

"My problem is, what do I do next?"

"Look Ellie, I can't speak for Jeremy or for anyone else really. We all have to be accountable for our own thoughts and actions under the rule of life that we have committed ourselves to. But I do know that he cares very deeply for you."

"I know he does, but that's not good enough for me. It's like this rule of life thing is getting in the way, suffocating me, robbing me of the happiness I could enjoy with Jez."

"Oh my dear, you couldn't be more wrong. The rule of life brings freedom, not confinement. The first thing that the rule tells us is that 'it's so not about us.' We are to look outside, rather than inside in order to find meaning and purpose. We do that through serving others, through prayer and following the pattern of the one who came to serve others. I have dedicated my life to such an understanding and so has Jez, although it will mean something different to each member of the community."

Eleanor stood up and started to pace around the store room, angrily kicking at pallets of food with her prosthetic foot and muttering obscenities.

"Please, sit down Ellie." Bernadette begged her, "I know it won't be hurting you, but this food is intended for other people in greater need than both of us. Look when Jez first made the connection between the girl he saw at the gym and the name and face that appeared on the gold surveillance list, he was genuinely moved by compassion for you."

"Compassion maybe, but I don't want to be an object of care and compassion. I don't need compassion. I can look after myself." Eleanor snapped back angrily.

"Perhaps you can, but Jez thought that you needed a protector, a guardian and in the light of what subsequently happened to you, he was proved quite correct. You are free to come and go as you please, but Jez is still concerned for you and he feels that your staying here with us and living as Charlotte Leicester…"

"Lister."

"Sorry, Charlotte Lister, is still the best way to help you."

"I guess so." Eleanor sighed and collapsed onto a large pile of toilet rolls. "It's just that I've never felt like this before. I just can't get him out of my head. He's there as I fall asleep and in my waking thoughts. I just know that we are meant to be together. There's something special between us, more than just chemistry or sex, it's like it's something deeper, something truly…" She hesitated, seeking the right words, "well spiritual, is the only word for it. Does that make any sense to you?"

"Oh yes, a lot more than you would ever think. You're not the first person to ever fall in love." Bernadette admitted with a degree of familiarity.

With that the two of them stood up and embraced before walking back together into the bar of the former pub. As Bernadette left, Eleanor stayed behind in the bar. She was strangely drawn to the flickering light around the chicken wire cross. As she approached to examine the cross in more detail she caught the sight of Jez emerging from the store room, carrying his white robe. He must have been in there for some time, getting changed out of his clerical clothes. Eleanor felt hugely embarrassed. She tried to catch his eye, but he just walked passed, distracted by an older woman who was still deeply troubled and being comforted by two friends. Once again, Eleanor wanted to talk with him, but he was pre-occupied by the needs of the older woman and her friends, so she decided to return to the cross and examine the messages that people had folded up and pushed into the wire structure.

Many of the messages were obscured or else impossible to read. Some had drawn pictures or sad faces; others had just written angry words or obscenities or questions about who was to blame. Others messages were clearer, but truncated:

…you are loved

Why did they take you away from…?

…I'm so very sorry…

My beautiful child.

… so fucking unfair

Hope is gone.

…now at peace…

If only we could have…

…now that you are in a much better place.

I will always love you.

I'm sorry I couldn't…

…I wish it had been me instead.

Reading the messages pressed into the shape of a cross describing how people felt, finally started to make sense to Eleanor. Somewhere deep within her a door opened, she stopped fighting and started to receive.

Chapter 21

Eleanor had never seen Jez looking so excited. He burst into her aerobics studio full of purpose, his face flushed with anticipation. Once her lesson had finished and the half a dozen rather overweight young mums had slipped outside for a smoke, Jez was finally able to greet her with uncharacteristic enthusiasm. She had hoped that the news he was pregnant with related to her in some way, so it came as something of a disappointment to discover that his urgent announcement related to a forthcoming meeting.

"The ground is shifting Ellie. All the cells are gathering together. This could be a game changing moment that affects all our futures. There's going to be a Synod!"

Eleanor was none the wiser, so Jez explained to her that this was a kind of clan gathering of various groups to decide upon a future course of action. It didn't sound particularly exciting to her, yet Jez explained that such a gathering was highly unusual and would be taking place at an annual *'Hark in the Park'* festival meeting at the Sandown *Bet Today* racecourse.

Summer festivals had become rather passé. Eleanor had attended several over the years although their popularity had reached something of a hiatus in the early twenties when they provided the only way that musicians could make money following the free to download revolution. Jez explained that attending 'Hark in the Park' was more of a networking occasion and less of a musical festival and this year's event provided the ideal opportunity to convene the Synod meeting.

The idea of a change of routine coupled with the possibility of escaping the security lock down she had been living under for the last six weeks held some appeal for Eleanor. She was also intrigued to discover more about the significance of the gathering taking place at the festival.

A week later she and Jez along with Bernadette and Brillo crammed into Jez's old Land Rover to slowly push their way along congested roads out of inner city London and towards the gated communities and leafy suburbs where the racecourse was situated. The roads were awash with late summer rain provoking the group to recall stories from previous years of camping amidst fields of mud whilst rain soaked tented villages were blown away by tempestuous gales. The rain had eased slightly by the time Jez swung the rattling frame of his ancient four-by-four onto the large, exposed parkland in the middle of the racecourse which provided the location for their campsite. Pitching a tent in the gently, penetrating drizzle presented something of a challenge to Jez and Bernadette as they wrestled with guy ropes, wet flapping canvas and inflatable mattresses. The experience of bivouacking in a snow storm in the death zone of the Himalayas meant that Eleanor took the challenge completely in her stride whilst Brillo effortlessly prepared their evening meal, regaling them with stories of having completed the same task under incoming fire in Helmand province.

By the time Brillo had served their supper, the rain had stopped and late evening sunshine bathed the campsite. By now the field was starting to take on the appearance of a tented village as inappropriately dressed town dwellers arrived to erect their glamping tents and occupy mobile homes alongside weather beaten eco-warriors and anti-capitalism protesters who unfurled tepees and improvised shelters whilst building open fires and erecting flag poles to display various slogans and tribal symbols.

It felt good to be outside of the city and the camping environment provided Eleanor with opportunities to entertain her hosts with stories of exciting expeditions around the Alps and Himalayas. The camp site provided one of the very few environments where Eleanor felt comfortable within her own skin. Here was a place where she could finally display the sort of leadership and practical skills that Jez and Bernadette were so clearly lacking.

The following day the festival began to fully kick into life. By now a large tented village occupied the grassland common that formed the inside of the race track, whilst further afield white marquees and tepees peppered the morning skyline, accompanied by coloured banners, flags and wind chimes whose panels and pipes fluttered in the morning breeze. Throughout the village improvised wind turbines buzzed and rattled, providing a rhythmic backing track to the events of the day.

Overnight Bernadette had explained that the festival was a broad based gathering comprising people from various faith communities around the country as well as those they worked alongside or who shared their values. However, despite the atmosphere of free association, there remained certain constraints upon what could take place on site. The local council were not prepared to license an overtly faith based festival, so the organising committee had marketed the festival as a cultural event celebrating innovation in the arts and social enterprise. This meant that the event still retained a slightly subversive feeling, as if people couldn't quite believe what they were able to get away with.

All around the site a mood of celebration ensued. It was as if people were emerging from their rabbit holes following a summer storm and munching on the fresh grass of freedom of expression. For many disparate groups the festival provided a sort of collective bubble extruded into a hostile culture where like-minded people could finally associate freely without fear or threat. Everywhere festival goers were re-uniting with old friends and renewing associations. Bernadette could hardly walk more than a few yards without being recognised or greeted by friends or colleagues, whilst Brillo and Jez hugged and high-fived various acquaintances drawn to the event from other parts of the country. Eleanor recognised some of the project workers from her neighbourhood, but mostly she was surrounded by a sea of unfamiliar faces. That was until the morning air was punctuated by a familiar laugh that drew her attention to the distinctive presence of an old friend.

"Hello Nicola." Eleanor addressed a young woman in front of her wearing designer wellies, a tweed jacket and matching trilby.

"Ellie! Wow, really cool to see you." Nicola immediately flung her arms around her and kissed her on the cheek.

"Yeh, arrived last night. Didn't see you as a festivalgoer."

"No, first time. Hope to get into some really 'out there' tribes and brands while I'm here." An awkward pause fell between them as they both eyed each other up, wondering where to begin their conversation. "So where have you been, all this time. You haven't returned my calls. It's been ages since we shared a bottle or two."

Since moving into the urban community, Eleanor had been keeping a low profile with her former girlfriends and keeping them at arm's length with a number of lame excuses for not getting in touch. She realised this was a necessary diversion yet she still felt a degree of guilt over how she had been treating Nicola and the other girls. Some kind of apology seemed necessary. "Sorry I haven't been in touch. Life gets busy and things move on. You know how it is."

"So are you camping?"

"Oh course. Aren't you?"

"Certainly, we're at the far end of the racecourse with all the other Mongolian yurts."

"Glamping it up then, I assume."

"You could say that. Where are you camping?"

"Just behind those poplar trees, near the Celtic knot flag. I'm with Jez and some friends."

They continued in conversation for some time. Nicola appeared genuinely interested in Jez and had a number of questions about the community that he was part of. Her questioning continued, becoming increasingly probing, as if she was still suspicious of his motives and intentions. Eventually, the conversation started to reveal the gulf of understanding that still prevailed between Eleanor and Nicola. Despite all her interest in angels and guiding spirits, she still appeared too remote and calculating. They parted, still on parallel paths in life, agreeing to meet up for a coffee soon, but fearing that his might never happen.

As they parted, Eleanor suddenly realised that she had been talking openly with an old friend as Eleanor Dupree and not as Charlotte Lister. Jez explained that she was among friends at the festival and that she could leave Charlotte Lister back at the Anastasis Centre. The festival was certainly devoid of surveillance cameras and security guards. At any other event of that size, there would have been a strong security presence, yet there were no security checks, no body scanners and no drones hovering overhead to disturb the atmosphere of free association. It felt truly liberating.

As Jez and Eleanor moved around the site, low morning sunlight gradually diffused the overnight, lingering clouds until the whole site was bathed in warm, golden sunshine.

Everywhere people of different tribes, races and ages rubbed up against each other. Scruffy eco-warriors and anti-capitalism protesters mingled with suburban, silver haired ladies carrying baskets of homemade organic jam and artisan breads. Privately educated city workers in designer wellies and waxed jackets mixed with former crack-heads in hoodies, swapping music via their mobile interfaces; whilst groups of young people with special needs, accompanied by their support workers, helped each other pick their way around pools of standing water.

Eleanor was intrigued to see large numbers of Chinese young people flocking together in excitable groups, many of them partaking in impromptu communal singing, although she couldn't recognise any of the tunes. There were people from India in brightly coloured saris and samba dancers from Brazil intent on treating the rain soaked ground like the practice park for street carnival in downtown Rio. Russian acrobats and gymnasts performed for the crowd whilst a group of African drummers, veterans from the recent mineral wars raging on the continent, just seemed happy to be there and to offer a lament for their troubled land.

Among the crowd, Eleanor bumped into a former climbing colleague, an American man mountain called Chuck Harvey whom she hadn't seen since her adventures on K2. Chuck had been known as 'Chuck Wagon' among the climbing community due to his ferocious appetite, now many years later and having given up such strenuous activities he had grown into his nickname. He remained however, the same old, instantly recognisable Chuck to her. They exchanged greetings and swapped news, filling in the gaps since their last meeting. He explained that he was now a student pastor at a US University and loved his new role on the campus.

Walking among the tents and stalls surrounded by so many people who were obviously delighted to also be among friends, the positivity of the occasion started to rub off on Eleanor.

She started to feel more at home among this group of like-minded misfits, yet most of all, she felt totally secure with Jez, she knew that in his company she would always feel totally safe. She reached out to touch his hand, sensing the need for physical contact and the further reassurance of his touch. Much to her surprise, he immediately received her hand as if it was the most natural and consequential thing to do. It was almost as if he had been waiting for such an invitation.

"Okay then, this is nice." Eleanor responded, stating the obvious. She had shared physical intimacy with many lovers, yet this innocent, almost child-like gesture of intimacy seemed imbued with more significance than any sweaty night of passionate sexual activity. "So what does this mean then?"

"It means, whatever you want it to mean." Jez replied calmly. "I just don't want to let you go."

"You mean; you're worried you might lose me in this crowd?"

Jez stopped and looked directly at Eleanor, his deep blue eyes penetrating into her very core. "No, I mean, I just don't want to let you go…ever." His words seemed to root Eleanor to the spot and sap her of her bravado. She desperately wanted to examine their significance but the moment was stolen away from her by two young girls emerging from the crowd, arms outstretched in exuberant greeting towards Jez, yet totally oblivious to Eleanor's emotional connection. Jez finally emerged from beneath their over effusive hugs, red in the face and bearing an embarrassed explanation.

"Don't worry, Ellie. Just a couple of my former charges. Meet Rhonda and Jules."

Greetings were exchanged but Eleanor could barely contain her irritation and repeatedly stabbed Rhonda and Jules with visual daggers demanding they back off from her newly acquired boyfriend. Despite her contemptuous looks, the two girls remained unaware of Eleanor's feelings and persisted in passing on greetings and news from various friends many of whom appeared to be young and female. While Eleanor quietly simmered on one side, she checked out the girls to assess their level of threat. They were at least ten years younger than Jez and would probably have known him from his various youth work activities. Eventually after much gossip was exchanged they drifted away and merged back into the crowd from which they had come. As they left there was something about their appearance that pricked Eleanor's curiosity.

"Sorry about that." Jez apologised once again.

"That's Ok. I understand," Eleanor lied. "But what's with the designer dirt?"

"Sorry?"

"I couldn't help but notice their muddy knees. Looks like they're wearing the field as some kind of trophy."

"Oh, they've been praying." Jez explained. "A lot of that goes on here. Some of the venues can get quite boggy. Sometimes people go at it all night long."

"I thought this was a networking and cultural event. You know, trendy art and radical politics shared over frothy coffee."

"It is, but it's also one of the few venues where we can practice our faith openly and unapologetically."

"What d'you mean?"

"World music provides the ocean on which we can all sing and praise openly, sailing our boats in different styles. The visual arts are a great way to encounter meditation. Workplace time management programmes provide a platform for a number of spiritual disciplines and lifestyle stress relief is a wonderful entrance point into experiencing prayer and mindfulness. We have to market it that way in order to get a license from the council, but we're free to interpret the themes quite creatively."

"You crafty buggers."

"Well you need to be creative when you're forced into the

shadows" Jez replied with a mischievous smile. "Anyhow we find that people are so switched off to many of the traditions we hold dear, that the only way to reach them is through a living encounter. Just talking about such things is no way to bring about change; people are impervious to words and ideas until they see them in action. So here, is a place where we can literally get hands on doing stuff."

"Hence the muddy, praying knees."

"Yep. The mud is optional, but prayer gets to the heart of transformed communities."

Eleanor and Jez continued to walk hand-in-hand towards the racecourse building. Eleanor hoped Jez would add to what he had said earlier about never wanting to let her go, but he just seemed absorbed by his own thoughts and was treating Eleanor as if they had always been a couple. A sense of nostalgic, romantic longing stirred within her. She desperately wanted some kind of recognition of their new status. Perhaps a written declaration of undying love, an expensive gift or better still, Jez going down on one knee and producing a ring to the accompaniment of a full symphony orchestra playing the theme from Dr. Zhivago, silhouetted against the backdrop of a crimson setting sun. Jez however, remained thoughtful and quiet, not feeling the need to add to his earlier words, yet deep inside she knew that something had changed, privately, almost imperceptivity, tectonic plates had shifted, just as powerful as those that released the giant tsunami in the Atlantic. She knew deep down that nothing would ever be the same again. A life shaping rubicon had been crossed, a Copernican revolution had taken place, she and Jez were now an item, they were a couple. She made a mental note to update her *My World* status.

Outside the main exhibition hall, a large sign declared '*Athenian Marketplace*'.

"So where are all the mugs and tee-shirts then?" Eleanor

asked, fearing the marketplace might be similar to what she had experienced in the Assembly building.

"Still in their boxes, I guess. This is a market place for ideas, not merchandise."

Inside, the hall was buzzing with noise and energy. All around the room white sheets hung at various stations beneath which people gathered in small groups to listen to speaker panels or else debate among themselves. Various titles were projected onto the white sheets in order to form discussion groups. Such titles as: *'Migration policy', 'Reconfiguring the global flow of venture capital', 'Cooking on a tight budget', 'Life after trafficking', 'A God of colour in a black and white world', 'Bringing back the Beat box', 'Sculpture in public places,' 'Life on the margins', 'Coping with loss', 'Teaching your kids at home', 'Living with global warming' and 'Re-discovering silence'.*

Eleanor noticed more people taking off muddy boots and shoes and sitting down on large, woven mats around each debating station. Despite being dressed for the camping, they too displayed most mud in the region of their knees. "More pray-ers?" Eleanor asked, but she had already answered her own question.

She looked around the building, it was buzzing with noise, expectation and activity. She was surprised to discover that the exchange of ideas could be so exhilarating and decided to check out the group re-discovering silence, reasoning that this would prove to be an interesting challenge in such a noisy venue. Fortunately, upon entering a partitioned section of the marketplace, she was issued with a wraparound headset which enabled her to screen out all the distractions. Once settled, she laid down on a mat and listened to soft music, birdsong and the sounds of waves crashing on the shore, accompanied by holographic images from the natural world and stories from some of the sacred texts that Bernadette had shared with her. After a while she began to really enjoy the experience and found

305

herself drifting off into a very pleasant, relaxing sleep. When she awoke, she found Jez sitting beside her, smiling broadly.

"Did you find that illuminating?" He asked ironically.

"Yes, until I fell asleep and dreamt I was swimming in a pool of liquid chocolate."

"Sounds as though, it's time to eat. Do you know how long you have been asleep?"

"About twenty minutes, I guess."

"More like nearly two hours. I've been to two seminars whilst you've been exploring silence."

By the time they arrived at the 'cake and bake' café, the marquee was already full of hungry diners and there appeared to be no free spaces.

Eleanor scanned the room, anxious to find a table now that her dream about chocolate had stimulated her appetite for something sweet and calorific. Someone was waving to Jez from across the marquee. Jez took her by the hand with a thinly veiled sense of purpose.

Beside a table draped in a red gingham table cloth, sat a smiling middle aged lady. Next to her sat a hunched, brooding figure furiously tapping away on his tablet computer. Their collective body language conveyed friction and distance, yet the lady looked eager to become acquainted.

"Hello Jeremy, I thought I recognised you from the seminar earlier. Come and have a seat next to us."

"Yes, you're the lady who lost her son." Jez appeared to know the woman. "I'm sorry; I've forgotten your name."

"It's Catherine, my dear."

Jez turned towards Eleanor clearly in need of some kind of explanation. "We met in a seminar about coping with loss. Seemed like quite a cathartic moment."

"I'm finally getting used to the idea that it's good to talk about such things." Catherine announced and then turned her attention to Eleanor. "And who are you, my dear?"

Jez paused trying to assess the degree of trust he should offer this stranger. "This is Charlotte."

"Lovely to meet you." Catherine paused, then reluctantly turned towards the hunched figure beside her. "And this is Leroy, Leroy Finch."

"Finch, just Finch." He barked back, barely lifting his gaze from the computer screen and clearly still dealing with repressed emotions.

"Finch?" Jez enquired.

"Yes, like the bird." Finch growled.

"Have we met?" Jez's curiosity was momentarily re-awakened.

"I doubt it. Not unless you've lived in the Westminster bubble or the world of investment derivatives which…" Finch briefly looked up from his computer to run a contemptuous eye over Jez, "…I suspect you haven't."

"Don't worry about him." Catherine explained. "He's just doing his grumpy old man impersonation."

Eleanor tried to seize the initiative and wrestle a response out of the impassive Finch by offering a firm handshake. "Hi, I'm Ell… I mean, Charlotte," she immediately winced in regret for her bravado and unintentional slip.

"Someone else who doesn't know who they are." Finch added caustically. He then looked up and appeared to come alive in front of them, as if suddenly gripped by a sense of purpose. "On the other hand. You do look familiar, my dear. Let me see." Finch inspected Eleanor with all the rigor of a mechanic running a critical eye over a malfunctioning ancient combustion engine. His eyes fixed upon her muddy footwear. "Do you buy those boots in pairs or just as singles?"

"Sounds like you've been found out," Jez added.

"I've been doing a lot of trending recently," Finch explained, "and some people attract a lot of attention on social media, especially when they start denouncing all the brands that used to sponsor them."

"It appears as though I've been banged to rights." Eleanor felt unnerved by Finch's familiarity with her former lifestyle. "I guess you know my real name." She turned towards Catherine, "It's Eleanor, Eleanor Dupree, but most people just call me, Ellie."

Just then a waitress wearing a red and white gingham dress and large white belt arrived at the table. She had long, golden, wavy hair, striking red lipstick and icing sugar brushed over her face. She was carrying a note pad and a forced smile. She avoided eye contact and nervously took their order for more tea and cakes before clumsily shuffling off to the kitchen, tripping over an adjacent table in the process.

"So, what's your story, Jez?" asked Finch.

Jez bristled at the question. There was something slightly unsettling about Finch, as if he was trying to lead him somewhere he didn't want to go. "Just the usual. Hanging around, looking up a few old friends and taking in the atmosphere."

"And you, Ellie. This is hardly the place for extreme sports."

"Jez, brought me here." Eleanor explained. "Not quite my scene but I'm trying to keep an open mind."

"There must be something in the air."

"I'm sorry?"

"No, carry on, love."

"Well, I guess that I've been on a different path recently."

"Is that why you've been tweeting against your former sponsors."

"Kinda. It's not just that but there's been all sorts of stuff happening that's caught my attention and taken me places I've never been before." Eleanor stopped herself, sensing unease that Finch was coaxing information from her. "Look, I don't really know who you are."

308

"I'm really a writer, a journalist by profession, but don't worry I'm not here to expose you. I'm here because of the rumours of something big breaking."

"Oh, you mean the Synod?"

Jez kicked Eleanor's prosthetic foot under the table trying to prevent her from blurting out any other sensitive information.

At that point the waitress returned to the table bringing more tea and cakes. Finch turned to greet her only to see her freeze in disbelief and drop the laden tray.

"Oh shit. Shit." She spat out the words in a state of panic. Turning as red as her gingham dress she struggled to pick up tea cups and Victoria sponges, assisted by Catherine and a concerned Finch.

"I didn't mean to scare you, love." Finch tried to re-assure.

"He can have the effect on people." Catherine tried to lighten the mood.

The waitress quickly scuttled off in the direction of the kitchen, before returning with a dustpan and brush and an even redder expression. She busily swept up the debris, and apologised profusely whilst trying not to make any further eye contact with those present.

In the meantime, Finch was like a dog with a bone, scouring his tablet for images, before eventually finding what he was looking for. By the time the waitress returned to the table with a fresh tray of tea and cakes, he was sitting there beaming at her, arms folded with a look of smug self-satisfaction.

"I really am, most terribly sorry." The waitress explained.

"On the contrary, this is turning into a very good day. I think that I'm the one who is in your debt." Finch announced.

"I'm sorry, sir." The waitress replied.

"Why don't you introduce yourself properly? After all, the last time we met, there was little time for formality."

The waitress appeared deflated and once again avoided all eye contact. "I don't know what you mean, sir."

"Let's just say that it's a long way from bomb making to cake baking."

"Look! I'm no terrorist. Active resistance doesn't mean resorting to violence. I didn't sign up to bomb and kill. I just…" Her words trailed off, realising that she had inadvertently outed herself.

"I'm sure you didn't. That's why you tried to get me out of the way didn't you."

The waitress wearily lowered herself onto a nearby chair. "What d'you want? Have you come to hand me in, because that's been tried already."

"No, it's like I said. I want to thank you. You probably saved my life."

"You mean this is the girl in the photo. The one used to expose Skyshadow."

"Skyshadow? You know, Skyshadow." Jez asked excitedly.

"Yes, I do, but not as well as Catherine does." Finch explained whilst casting a knowing look in Catherine's direction.

"Wow. That's amazing. Truly awesome."

"Is anyone going to let me in on all this?" Eleanor enquired.

"Skyshadow is a bit of a legend. She's a great benefactor, but more than that, she's a..a.."

"Traitor, is the word you are looking for." Finch interjected.

"That's not fair, you know that's not fair. She's just a bit of an enigma and often she is misunderstood, but she's trying to do the right thing."

"Is that why she did a runner?" Finch asked.

"You don't know her like I do." Catherine replied.

"I know that she has run away from her responsibilities and from the promises she made to you and to others."

"Well, I believe in her, and her intentions. You might

be considering that offer from Lenny's boss, but I'm not." Catherine fixed Finch with one of most disapproving stares.

Eleanor and Jez looked on incredulously as the bickering between Catherine and Finch resumed. They felt like guests' gate crashing a private family dispute. Finally, Finch turned away, raising his hands in a mock gesture of submission. "Look, we're never going to agree on this one, but as far as I'm concerned, the only person that Skyshadow or Iona Dunwoody or whoever she is calling herself this week, really cares about is herself and her family empire. She's corporate right through to the soles of her designer shoes."

"That's not true." By now the waitress had composed herself. "You don't know her. You don't know what she's done for people like me."

"So now, you're...sorry I still don't know your name, love."

"Amanda, my name is Amanda."

"So, now you're an expert on Skyshadow as well as direct political action."

"Look, I don't know why you're at this festival, but the reason I'm here is that I believe in something. Something that's worth fighting for."

"Worth, bombing and killing for?"

"No, nothing is worth that. Things just got a bit crazy. Some of us saw the power that people like Van Hegel wield and just wanted to strike a blow in return."

"So the ends justify the means."

"No, but democracy is flawed. No-one votes anymore. All the politicians have become clones of each other whilst the multinationals have their balls in a vice most of the time. Their friends in the security industry are just playing everyone for a sucker. They don't mess around, so neither did we."

"Is that why you took such direct action?" Jez asked.

"Someone had to. We used to say that when you're

311

confronting evil, 'It's not sufficient just to bandage the wounds of the victims beneath the wheels of injustice. Sometimes you have to be prepared to drive a spoke into the wheel itself.'"

"Does that include waging a war of terror?"

"Look, we didn't choose the terms, we just acted in a way that would expose the real criminals and terrorists. We never sought to kill anyone. It was just collateral damage."

"So the ends justify the means." Jez added.

"Look, I admit it, we over-stepped the mark, but do you realise the power of these multinationals. They operate an effective cartel on those magic bullets they've manufactured to keep everyone believing they'll live forever. A twenty-year patent they've got on those drugs. They've effectively blocked the development of cheaper generic alternatives so that they control the whole market, not just here, but globally. Do you realise what leverage that gives them? No government could ever oppose them, even if they wanted to. Think about what that does for the democratic process we're all meant to believe in. We were freedom fighters – true democrats. People should be grateful for what we did. Anyway," Suddenly, Amanda stopped herself as if realising that she was wearing a waitress's uniform, not military battle dress, "that was then, and this is now."

Just then Finch's phone started to vibrate. He quickly swiped the screen to identify the caller. The result filled him with a mixture of nervous excitement and perilous dread. This was a call he had been anticipating. He arose and quickly sought the solace of a quiet corner of the room.

Eleanor tried to ignore the interruption. "So now you're terrorizing people with your baking?" She added with a smile.

"This wasn't exactly a career choice, more like work experience after I was sent back over the wall."

"You mean, they let you out of prison?"

"Let's just say that a deal was done. The release of political prisoners creates a lot of good will."

"Hang on a sec." A moment of epiphany suddenly gripped Eleanor. "This release of political prisoners. It didn't involve someone called Sister Bernadette, did it?"

"Don't know about any sister, but there was a rather sweet lady by the name of Bernie who came to see me and got me out of that detention centre. She was the one who set me up with all this girly gear." Amanda replied whilst trying to brush icing sugar off her dress.

Eleanor and Jez exchanged knowing looks with each other.

"Anyhow," Amanda continued, "there's talk about some kind of Synod happening. Rumours that the war is over now – turning swords into ploughshares."

"War. What war?" Eleanor looked at Jez and then to Sky. "I didn't know we were at war."

"What about your car ending up in a river?" Jez reminded Eleanor. "Seems like rules of engagement to me."

"Well, whatever is happening," Amanda added, "the tide is turning and I for one think that's no bad thing." With that Amanda got up to return to her duties, before looking back to add, "Oh, and enjoy your cake. You can never have too much cake."

Chapter 22

A beam of bright light arced across Eleanor's semi-conscious face. Outside her tent there were footsteps and uneasy movements. Somewhere in the distance the distinctive rumble of rotor blades threatened menacingly. A shadowy figure appeared outside and then the whole tent shook as the figure beat vigorously on the stretched canvas.

"Out now. Get up please." An unfamiliar staccato voice violated the night air.

"It's OK, Ellie, but you need to get up." The more familiar voice of Jez added reassurance to the stranger's command.

Eleanor nervously unzipped the tent and poked her head out into the damp, night air. It was raining steadily as she peered into a beam of several flash lights trying to make out the identity of silhouetted figures standing over outside the entrance. She then caught sight of the distinctive head cameras and body armour of two members of the security services, armed with Tasers and clearly in no mood for polite conversation. Behind them stood Jez, hands outstretched in a gesture aimed to calm and reassure her. Alongside him stood two other much larger security guards one of whom had Brillo in an arm lock.

"Miss Dupree?" One of the security guards enquired.

"Depends on who is asking." Eleanor replied shielding her eyes against the beams of light emanating from several head cameras.

"You need to come with us, now." His reply gave the impression that this was not the time for questions and negotiation.

Eleanor quickly pulled on what clothes she could find to hand. Her heart was pounding deep within her chest as a million thoughts and feelings raced through her mind. As she emerged from the tent, more lights converged on the spot. Raised voices from neighbouring tents blended with screams and shouts of protest. Angry words were exchanged all around in an atmosphere of increased confusion as the throb of rotor blades and hovering drones combined with the sweep of arc lights and the barking of orders and call signs.

"Don't worry Ellie. It's going to be all right." Once again Jez tried to reassure Eleanor. His comforting tones were in sharp contrast to the surreal scene surrounding her. Brillo remained held in forceful restraint, blood seeping from his nose, yet it was apparent from the mood of his captors that he had not come willingly or without a struggle.

"Where is, Mr. Patel? Sanjeev Patel?" One of the men in body armour barked angrily.

"He's not here." Jez replied.

"But we know he is with you. He's one of your group."

"Look pal." Brillo growled. "When he says he's not here, it's because he's not here."

"But we have orders for him as well."

"Well, I'm sorry to spoil your day."

"You must know where he is."

"Just leave it. He's clearly not here. I didn't see the man you described." A voice came from behind where Brillo was being restrained. Eleanor could hardly believe what she was witnessing as the hooded figure of Nicola emerged from the darkness.

"Nicola!"

She looked away, trying to hide her face, yet her waxed jacket and designer wellies clearly marked her out in sharp contrast to the company she was keeping.

"Nicola. What are you doing here?" The words froze on Eleanor's lips as the terrible realisation of her question slowly dawned on her.

"I never meant for it to turn out like this, Ellie. You must believe me."

"Like what?"

"I kept trying to steer you away from what you were doing, but you just got all weird on us. I was trying to be your friend."

"Friend? Friends don't betray each other."

"It's not how it appears. They just want you to answer a few questions and give them some information."

"And the hit man in the car and running me off the road. They weren't interested in asking any friendly questions."

"It was never meant to be like that Ellie, it really wasn't. I was just passing on information. I didn't know how it would turn out."

"But why Nicola. Why?" Eleanor's voice broke with emotion.

Nicola looked increasingly awkward and embarrassed. "The old reason, Ellie. The reason why everything gets done."

"Not money. Surely not for money."

"You don't understand. You just don't get it. You never will." Nicola once again turned her face away.

"But you're loaded. You have it all."

"Not everything, Ellie. Not everything. A little freelance work buys a lot of goodwill with my creditors."

Just then a helicopter appeared directly overhead, it's down draught flattening the ground below. When Eleanor looked again Nicola had gone, disappearing into the wind and rain as unexpectedly as she had appeared.

The man in the body armour looked into his wrist mounted mobile device, scrolling down the screen several times before touching his earpiece in an expression pained with anticipation. "Gold command. Section 14 all secure. Objective completed. Repatriating three, repeat three hostiles. No eyeball or intel on fourth." He waited briefly for a reply. "OK. Come with us now." He ordered abruptly.

They were then marched through the unfolding chaos of a campsite awakening from slumber to find snatch squads of three or four security guards picking up different groups of individuals, knocking on camper doors and unzipping canvas. Throughout the campsite the hiss and crackle of Tasers being discharged could be clearly heard. Everywhere tents were being trampled underfoot and camping equipment overturned. Children cried, dogs barked, shock and incredulity prevailed.

Eleanor, Jez and Brillo threaded their way through the rain soaked field to a cordon of armed security guards encircling the entrance to the conference centre buildings. Once inside the cordon a fleet of electrically powered minibuses with blacked out windows awaited them outside the conference centre. Overhead powerful searchlights from two hovering helicopters picked out the silhouetted figures of confused campers as they crisscrossed the concourse.

Assorted groups of people were lined up and repeatedly checked off against various lists. Eleanor looked across to Jez, hoping to see his calm re-assuring presence, yet all she could see was his limp body being pushed around by over-bearing security guards. Eleanor tried to check out the other groups of detainees for signs of Sister Bernadette, somehow feeling that if she was here then somehow everything would be all right and she would be able to make sense of it all. Yet there was no sign of her and even Jez appeared powerless to protect her anymore.

Her group were then stood in line behind the cursing figure of Brillo and directed through a mobile body scanner, followed by random body searches before each detainee was labelled with a wristband which was furthered scanned by a hand held device before each detainee was then led into a waiting eco-minibus. There must have been a dozen or so minibuses in total, each of which was filled with festival goers and checked off against a head count before forming a convoy which was then escorted by blacked out four by four vehicles off the site and down through the neighbouring streets.

Half an hour later the minibus convoy came to a halt at a large double iron gate. The iron gate swung open silently and effortlessly, ushering them onto a long entrance road leading up to a large, country house. The building resembled a stately home, the type that either gets bequeathed to the National Trust or turned into an expensive hotel or conference centre. The fleet of minibuses glided smoothly around to the rear of the house before coming to a halt and depositing their contents at the back entrance to the building.

Once inside they were greeted by still more security guards, yet thankfully less confrontational. They were led through oak panelled corridors and a series of ante rooms into a large banqueting hall with high, plastered ceilings and tall windows, yet decorated in a modern style with brightly coloured wall hangings, soft furnishings, subdued coloured lighting and flat screen TV monitors.

As the room gradually filled with more people Eleanor started to recognise some of the people she had met earlier at the festival. She also recognised Amanda, the young waitress from the cake and bake although she no longer wore her uniform and instead was bearing a dark bruise over one of her eyes and was restrained roughly whilst cursing and kicking out at her captors. Among the various musicians, artists and poets asking what crimes they were being charged with, stood the unmistakable figure of Catherine, her voice raised in indignation, castigating every person she could find who appeared to carry some sort of authority and demanding due legal process should apply to their detention.

"Do you know who I am?" Catherine asked angrily of one of the more senior looking security guards. There was no reply. "What you are doing is profoundly undemocratic and completely illegal. We still have the rule of law in this country you know." Still the body armoured security guard remained implacable. In an act of desperation, Catherine resorted to the kind of veiled threat she hoped she was morally superior to. "I can call upon people in the security services who can vouch for me. We were guaranteed protection. We had a mandate to be at this festival."

It was obvious that Catherine's pleading was falling upon unreceptive ears, so she decided to strike a more conciliatory tone with the armed figures that surrounded her. "Can't you tell your bosses that this festival carries no threat to the security of the state? Surely even you can see that." The security guards just looked straight ahead, unmoved and inert, as if awaiting some word of command that would galvanize them into action. "It's just a bunch of 'weirdy beardy' people, harmless dreamers exploring alternative lifestyles. What kind of threat are they to national security?"

Once again Catherine was aware of her own vulnerability. The campaigning spirit that had spurred her on through previous entanglements with the authorities had now ebbed away. No longer secure in the knowledge of the justice of her own cause, nor able to draw strength from Sky and all her mystery and intrigue. Even Finch had abandoned her, slipping away quietly into the world of secret briefings and anonymous sources the previous evening, his non-appearance displaying a widening fault line in their relationship. She would never betray Sky to the authorities, no matter what incentives were offered or assurances given, Finch on the other hand, still retained the instincts of a journalist who wouldn't rest until he was able to deliver his story. His drive to reveal the truth had overridden the professional distance that political journalists are meant to display even in the white heat of an opportunity to get to the heart of a story. She knew he had surrendered his neutrality the day he accepted his commission from the intelligence service, just as she had crossed over a similar line the day she met Sky. She hated him for that, but also hated herself for being in a position where once again the person she cared about had been taken from her.

Gradually a mood of resignation settled over the room. People began to sit in groups on the floor to swap stories and seek explanations. Some began to sing, others raised their voices in occasional shouts of defiant protest, still others sat in quiet, thoughtful reflection as if in prayer.

Jez and Eleanor managed to re-unite and soon became re-acquainted with Catherine in order to share their experiences. Jez was more guarded than usual and cautioned against sharing any information about the community he belonged to back in the city. Finally, as the passage of time started to erode his self-restraint and ignite his latent curiosity, he turned his questioning towards Catherine.

"Where's your journalist friend?" Jez enquired. "He could have come in useful on an occasion like this."

"Yes, I know. Bloody useless. He came over all mysterious and disappeared just after we met up yesterday."

"So what did you mean by talking about the security services vouching for you?" Jez asked.

"Sorry?" Catherine appeared off balance as if uncertain what she had disclosed in an unguarded moment.

"You said that the security services could vouch for you and you had some kind of mandate to be here."

"Yes, I probably did. It's just the red mist descending. You'll say anything when the survival instinct kicks in."

"But not that specifically."

"Well, I was angry and confused. I just said the first thing that came into my head. Trying to provoke a reaction I guess."

Catherine realised that her bluffing had not convinced Jez but she was grateful that he had decided not to pursue the matter further. She settled down in a corner of the room, hoping that she might be left alone and given the benefit of the doubt in terms of how she came to be included among the group of detainees.

Time passed slowly for those held in the room. No further information or explanations were given and gradually those detained came to accept their fate. An hour or so passed uncomfortably but then an inquisitive murmur began to spread throughout those assembled as people's attention was drawn to the night sky beyond the room's large feature windows. In the distance a speck of light appeared and started to grow in size and in intensity. Soon it became apparent that the light was moving towards the building, dipping down and hovering as its outline gradually came into focus. Shadowy figures appeared outside illuminated by floodlights in the grounds. The throb of rotor blades penetrated the night air as the distinctive outline of a helicopter came into view, its searchlight sweeping a path through the night sky. The helicopter descended gently onto an adjacent tennis court followed by another helicopter, then another, until eventually four helicopters had all lined up on the hard standing outside of the house, each of them discharging indistinct figures onto the ground who then formed into small groups heading towards the house.

A few moments later the pounding of boots on wooden floors could be heard in the corridor outside. The noise grew in intensity before finally the doors burst open and a group of bedraggled figures in waterproof clothing entered the room, escorted by more security contractors. The group shuffled wearily together, peering out from beneath hoods or beanie hats as if awaiting some terrible fate. Many were elderly and bore world weariness redolent of many struggles; others were younger, angrier and more fearful. Among the uniform greyness stood the unmistakable figure of Sister Bernadette. She appeared even more serene than ever. Her presence stood out from among the group not just by virtue of her shape and scale, but also because she conveyed a benign calm and maternal solace. She gazed towards Eleanor and Jez and nodded slowly in recognition, exuding a deep preparedness as if such a meeting had long been expected. At her sight, audible sighs of relief combined with ripples of positivity among those detained. The unspoken message was quickly received by those who knew her, *'Sister Bernadette was here – she would know what to do.'*

Bernadette just smiled and looked around those gathered and then beyond them, as if transfixed by an inner stillness. She breathed deeply, her chest swelling and contracting rhythmically. All eyes were upon her, yet she seemed both distant and yet deeply engaged, gripped by a sense of latent expectancy, the kind that precedes an important announcement or the beginning of a long journey.

At that point the attention of the crowd was wrestled away from Bernadette and towards a man in a crisp white shirt, rimless glasses and a mop of blond hair who entered the room. "Good evening ladies and gentleman, and," he paused to survey the room, "my apologies for keeping you all waiting without an explanation. Please, you must be all tired. I have arranged for food and something to drink," with that he beckoned an unseen colleague and immediately tables were brought in along with bottled water, fruit and sandwiches. "I am sorry that this is all I can provide, but events have rather, you might say, overtaken our plans."

Once again, attention turned towards Sister Bernadette but she remained silent, refusing to confer any explanation whilst encouraging those present to sit and eat.

"Allow me to introduce myself." The man in the crisp white shirt addressed the crowd, this time from a small platform and microphone in the corner of the room which had been hastily assembled. "My name is Friedrich Weimar and I represent a number of philanthropic foundations entrusted with guaranteeing the flourishing of public welfare during the recent raised security threat."

A lone voice from the floor rang out. "You mean, you're a private security contractor."

"No, on the contrary, despite what I will admit does look like a rather heavy handed way of arranging this gathering, I do not directly represent the security services although we have been liaising very closely with them during this operation."

"What operation?" Somebody shouted out.

"You mean, a witch hunt by the thought police." Brillo's gruff tones could be easily identified.

"Mercenary." A raised voice cried out.

"Private army." Another raised voice added.

"Fascist state." Still others added.

"No, no." Friedrich's voice boomed out as he tried to still the various outbursts. "Allow me to explain." Eventually the room fell quiet, anticipating that some answers might finally be forthcoming. "I represent a coalition of the broader public interest. Those who seek to enhance public security by neutralizing the voices of extremism, as well as delivering pathways for the improved health and prosperity of the general public. We work with many governments and in many different countries investing in the sort of public health programmes that have raised the life expectancy of millions and given hope to countless generations."

"Not in my name." Another voice from the floor rang out.

"Who wants to live forever? WW2, L4E. WW2, L4E." Once again, the assembled group found its voice as they grew in self-confidence raising their protest chant.

"WW2, L4E. WW2, L4E. WW2, L4E."

At this point, several security guards stepped forward, their Tasers held menacingly across their chests, in order to reinforce the power dynamics of the situation facing those in the room.

"Please, please, may I remind you that you are all here, because of your association with those destabilizing forces that are seeking to destroy such a precious public health legacy. You are here because of your support, either explicit or implicit, for extremist groups that have struck at the very heart of this nation. Those subversive influences who seek to undermine the progress that has brought us all so many benefits. Some who are even trying to overturn the basis of our economic resilience, the market consensus that is guaranteeing a more prosperous retirement for future generations." Friedrich paused to survey the room. "You see, ladies and gentlemen, we are not monsters. On the contrary, we are trying to help, to build up, to make a better future for everyone." Friedrich looked around the room in self-satisfaction and smiled an icy smile.

"What if we don't want to be part of your progress and economic resilience?" Brillo, once again was emboldened to speak out.

"Why would anyone not want to be part of something that brought material benefits to so many people? Heath, wealth and security is our legacy. Who would refuse such things? Only an enemy of the state."

"So anyone who disagrees or who wants to live differently is an enemy of the state." Catherine asked.

"No, you are free to live as you please, as we all are."

"So why are we here?" Catherine once again called out.

"You are here because you represent a challenge to the rule of law, to the stability and values of civilized society. Former terrorists are now walking the streets freely; other law breakers are being invited for informal discussions with policy makers. Hard won freedoms cannot be surrendered to the kind of extremist ideas and belief systems that struck at the very core of our national life.

"So what do you want?" Catherine once again took the initiative.

"All we want is to restore the natural equilibrium. To ensure that everyone goes about their business without imposing their ideas upon everyone else. We just want to ensure stability and security and those things depend upon not returning to the anarchy of the past. Ladies and gentlemen, we are here to safeguard the greater good."

"Who decides the greater good?" A voice from the back of the room shouted.

"Well, people like me…I mean we don't." A worried expression fell across Friedrich's face. He touched his ear several times before composing himself and continuing. "Our intention is to distract people, I mean help people, from asking the really important questions…to keep them passive and keep them buying…I mean to help them flourish." Once again, Friedrich tapped his ear several times and started looking around the room, his cool, composed demeanour disintegrating visibly before everyone's eyes. "You see; I am just a puppet…I'm a what?"

At that point, one of the hooded people standing alongside Sister Bernadette, lowered her head covering to reveal long, black hair, complete with a headset and microphone. "I am just a front man." The figure announced.

"I am just a front man." Friedrich echoed. "I mean; I am not a front man."

"Sent by people like my father." The figure continued.

"Sky!" Catherine shouted and rushed forward to embrace her, only to be stopped by a member of the security services. 'Skyshadow', the word reverberated like a mighty wind throughout the room.

"Who's that?" Eleanor asked Jez.

"A friend." Jez replied. "A good friend to people like me."

What then followed appeared to happen in a series of snap shots, as if time was suddenly allowing all the normal rules of response and reaction to be paralyzed by a set of unexpected circumstances. Gradually, almost imperceptibly, the room filled with new arrivals. Some arrived silently and secretly, whilst others must have slipped off their headgear and produced weapons from beneath layers of waterproof clothing. The exact chronology of events was difficult to track. The room was plunged into a smokey darkness punctuated by thunder flashes of light creating a strobe lighting effect that revealed movements from every point of entry. Loud crashes shook the room as framed figures in combat outfits and night vision goggles moved deafly to and fro, their progress tracked by strobing bursts of light. Most of the delegates fell to the floor as the Special Forces soldiers dressed all in black beguiled and overpowered their confused opponents assuming control by stealth, rather than by overwhelming force or violence, until finally the room was secure.

When the smoke cleared all the security guards had been restrained and disarmed, although incredibly without any casualties or any weapons being discharged. Some lay twitching on the ground, others cowed before the automatic weapons wielded by the figures in black. Still others stood upright, hands held behind their heads in a submissive pose. Friedrich could be seen kneeling on the floor, crumpled under the physical presence of a uniformed soldier, his spectacles removed and his calm demeanour considerably ruffled. Elsewhere Tasers laid scattered on the ground amidst the baseball hats of the security guards whilst outside the rumble and throb of more helicopters could be heard announcing further reinforcements in order to complete the operation.

Among the debris and the thinning smoke two bright beaming, uncovered, non-military eyes could be clearly detected from the smiling face of a relieved looking Leroy Finch.

Chapter 23

Finch gazed around the room and surveyed the debris left by the Special Forces.

Empty smoke canisters and thunder flash cartridges littered the ground. Pools of water collected where the sprinklers system had been partially activated and the crumpled figures of various security contractors could be seen huddled in their body armour, their hands tied behind their backs with electrical cable grips, lay like broken flowers, bent double and humiliated by a passing storm. Finch knew he ought to feel elated or at least some semblance of pride for being part of such a timely rescue, yet in truth everything felt like a jumble sale at the end of the day where all the good items have been picked over, so that what remains is just an untidy mess for someone to sort out. His innate belief that the pen was always mightier than the sword also lay in tatters. He had crossed a line from which there was no turning back. He was no longer an observer in search of a story, he was a participant. It was never meant to have come to this. He had learned many years ago to remain neutral, to avoid taking sides, to report the news rather than affect the news. He had now stepped well beyond that point. The call he had received the day before changed all that. His Secret Service handlers had made it quite clear that they now owned him. The death of Leander had finally sealed that deal. His loyalty now lay with their cause and in ensuring that nothing stood in the way of securing the settlement that Leander had been trying to advance.

In truth, he had been a willing recruit. He had known for some time that something was wrong. The world he was presented with just didn't make any sense. His innate curiosity prevented him from accepting the version of reality that most people would have accepted. A journalist can be removed from the story but you can never take the story completely away from the journalist and so he could always spot a cover up and detect the spinning of an unpalatable truth. His antennae for spotting bullshit remained undiminished. He knew he had been set up as soon as he saw the CCTV photo of the hooded stranger. Coincidences like that don't just happen to former investigative journalists struggling under a mountain of debt. The whole scenario was just too neat to be taken at face value. Other people's lies are easy to spot – his own were much harder.

He had told himself that he just didn't care anymore. The profession he cherished had receded into a world of commentary and opinion – voyeuristically providing the subtitles to a current affairs narrative viewed through social media where everyone with a mobile device was elevated to the status of a news gatherer and expert source. At the same time, the people he cared most about had abandoned him, leaving him rootless and at the mercies of his inner demons. Yet if he no longer cared then why had he taken this commission and why was he now standing amongst the wreckage of an internal battle over national security in which he had stepped over the line of journalistic neutrality to take the side of one force over another? Old journalists don't die; they just move on to explore more demanding projects.

In the far corner of the room sat Catherine and Sky deep in conversation and sharing an intimate moment. Sky looked visibly shaken, apparently over-awed by the suddenness and efficiency of the Special Forces operation. Despite her dramatic entrance, she appeared strangely vulnerable, like a child standing on the end of a diving board for the first time. Catherine was offering her comfort and reassurance, yet the burden of self-doubt seemed to weigh heavily upon her usual self-confident demeanour. Catherine on the other hand, had clearly found what she was looking for, or at least she was nearer to discovering what she had been truly seeking.

Finch would always remain deeply connected with Catherine no matter how their paths might diverge in the future. Their common denominator was the same man who had touched their lives in different ways. Meeting Leonard Hamilton in the art gallery had probably saved his life just as much as his sacrificial act had saved the life of Catherine. The irony of such a realization was not lost on Finch, after all, Leonard was a man of multiple identities, someone who lived in the shadows and used mystery as a way of exerting control. However, despite all his deception and posturing, Leonard had revealed something very important to Finch, the capacity to look and to see something greater beyond – something worth living for, even something worth dying for. He had stepped out of the darkness and opened his eyes – he had helped him to believe again. He had gifted him the possibility of living just as powerfully as he had gifted Catherine her continued existence.

"A most satisfactory operation." A voice appeared from behind Finch, it was the grey haired woman in the car he had met at Leonard's funeral. "You should feel very proud. We might not have been able to pull this off without your help."

"Spare the praises." Finch replied disdainfully, his gaze fixed straight ahead. "It all looks like a mess to me. How do

I know that you won't turn out to be just as twisted as these guys, now it's your turn to take over the asylum again?"

"You don't, Mr. Finch. You'll just have to trust us that we know how to run things a bit better than the alternative."

"Like Leander Hamilton trusted you?"

"Leander was an idealist, more of a poet than a…"

"A spy?"

"Than a servant of the crown." she insisted, her steely voice cutting through Finch's sardonic tones. "His commitment came from a very personal place. He never completely compromised that, even right up to the end."

"Is that why he was still a field officer and not sipping tea out of china cups like you?"

"Probably, but he operated according to the highest traditions of the service, even when it meant making the supreme sacrifice."

"He was worth ten of your kind." Finch snarled.

"Possibly, but we all have our different ways of serving the best interests of our nation, Mr. Finch. You included."

"You wouldn't recognise the best interests of a nation if they hit you in the face."

"Oh, that's where you are greatly mistaken, because this particular operation today might have served our own internal affairs well, but it has also cleared the way for something I think you might be very interested in." The grey haired lady paused to move a smoke canister from under her designer footwear, "Something that is very much concerned with the best interests of everyone."

"Hello." A tall, gangly figure and a limping girl approached the pair. "You're Leroy aren't you – Mrs. Stringer's friend?" Jez said.

"The name's Finch," Finch replied, "and right at this moment, I think that Mrs. Stringer has found a better friend." He nodded in Catherine's direction, where she and Sky were still in deep conversation. As he turned around he discovered that the grey haired lady had slipped away as discreetly as she had first appeared.

"Who was that you were talking to?" Eleanor asked.

"Just someone sent here to clear up the mess."

"So how come you're leading this little invasion? I thought you were a journalist."

"I am. I'm just a civilian who hitched a ride." Jez's look of puzzlement grew, begging a further response. "I guess I'm here to help clear up the mess as well. I was given a commission some time ago and I was reminded that I had a deadline to meet to ensure a certain publication could take place. Well, I just delivered on that commission." Finch added, as much to convince himself as to convince Jez.

The following day the festival site displayed an eerie stillness. Many of the festival goers had returned home and crumpled tents littered the campsite, evidence of the incursion by the security services the previous night. Despite the thinned-out crowds, pockets of the defiant festival community remained. Revolutionary slogans were daubed on makeshift banners, whilst some had erected signs from flag poles displaying slogans of resistance. Others were repairing their flattened tents and comforting those upset by the violent campsite incursion. Elsewhere people were gathering in groups to share their undamaged possessions and discover news about friends who were still missing. Everywhere stories were being shared and people were exchanging words of encouragement and defiance, even those inclined to drift away were greeted by calls to rebuild the shattered community as an act of civil protest.

Brillo was picking his way through what remained of his tent whilst Jez stood over him, Eleanor still clinging to his side as if by letting him go she might forfeit her very life.

"Bloody savages, all of them." He muttered under his breath. "Disgrace to the uniform. If they'd seen what I'd seen, they'd realise how freedom is won. They wouldn't be so keen to trample it all under foot then."

"Have you seen Sister Bernadette?" Jez asked.

"Yes, she's over at the conference centre," Brillo replied, "something's going on and they want us to be part of it."

As Eleanor and Jez approached the racecourse conference centre buildings they could see that a sizeable crowd had assembled on the concourse outside. There seemed to be an excited buzz of expectation among those gathering, in contrast to the weary defiance of those repairing the campsite. People were pushing together, gripped by a sense of purpose to get inside. Eleanor spotted Catherine and Finch already inside the building. They were protecting Sky from the crush of the crowd, forming a human cordon around her, as they led her through the growing throng. People were trying to reach out to Sky, as if they just wanted to touch her and know that she was real and was actually among them. Sky appeared somewhat awkward, yet summoned up enough courage to high five the occasional supporter.

As Catherine, Finch and Sky disappeared from sight, Eleanor and Jez joined the crowd and were swept along inside the main auditorium at the centre of the conference suite. Inside large video screens were positioned all around the room along with table and chairs arranged in clusters. At one end of the room a small platform had been set up on which was placed a sofa and arm chairs grouped around a lectern and microphone.

As they made their way to one of the clusters of chairs, excitable conversations could be heard among those seated. The talk was all about good news.

"What are they are saying?" Eleanor asked.

"Don't know, Ellie."

"I heard someone say something about the war being over."

"The war is over?" Jez suddenly came alive. "They said that the war was over."

"Yeh, at least I think so. Sounded a bit like that."

At the point an elderly lady with kind eyes caught Jez by the arm. "That's right dear. It's our V-day. The war is finally over. It's all going to get back to normal."

"The war! Gosh, it's finally over. Don't you see what this means, Ellie?"

"So the girl from the cake and bake was right. It's swords into ploughshares time."

"Yeh, isn't that wonderful. Simply wonderful."

All around the room the assembly crowd were embracing each other, back slapping and high fiving. They all seemed to be aware of the significance of what was taking place. Some whooped and yelped. Others urged and encouraged each other with motivational chants. Still others formed huddles and quietly bowed their heads in thoughtful reflection and stillness.

Suddenly the doors of the conference centre were thrown open to loud applause and yells of support. A group of four people were escorted through the foyer entrance like minor celebrities. At the head of the group was Sister Bernadette leading three figures in dark suits. Shouts of encouragement were raised for the party as applause and appreciation rang out. At first there was an audible gasp at the sight of three, rather stern looking strangers, so overdressed for the occasion and clearly unfamiliar with their surroundings. Then a moment's silence was broken by a solitary voice.

'Go Sister, go.' Someone shouted out. The cry was immediately taken up by the crowd of well-wishers, who spontaneously started to sing the response by way of encouragement to Bernadette. 'Go Sister, go Sister, go.'

'Go Sister, go Sister, go.' The chant was taken up by more and more people, mirroring the atmosphere of a pop concert.

'Go Sister, go Sister, go. Go Sister, go Sister, go.'

"Are synods always like this?" Eleanor enquired.

"I'm not exactly sure," Jez admitted, "this is my first one."

Sister Bernadette and the three strangers made their way onto the platform where they eventually took their seats. Bernadette appeared somewhat embarrassed, yet purposeful.

Meanwhile in the auditorium talk was continuing about the war being over. Sky's name was being mentioned a great deal, yet often provoking disagreement as people took sides in relation to her role and reputation. Eventually conversations became muted and the room stilled to a hush of expectancy.

At that point, Sky entered the room and hesitantly took up occupancy of the platform. Catherine and Finch followed on behind, taking up their places at one of the tables scattered around the room.

Suddenly there was movement on the platform as all eyes fixed upon the figure of a rather portly, older gentleman in a threadbare cardigan who approached the microphone. He had kind eyes and an expression that suggested familiarity with such an occasion. A choked ripple of applause seeped out as the audience struggled to discern the appropriate conventions for such an occasion. The older gentleman held up his hand in polite recognition of the underwhelming reception and smiled kindly.

"Yes," he acknowledged, "I thought I was dead also." His opening remarks succeeded in disarming the tension of the occasion with warm laughter. "But as you can see, the rumours of all of our deaths are greatly exaggerated."

"Who's he?" Eleanor asked Jez, whilst trying not to appear too ignorant.

"Just a guy, who used to be somebody," Jez explained with a smile and a knowing look.

The older gentleman in a cardigan cleared his throat and thanked everyone for attending at such short notice. He announced the reason for the gathering, describing how the festival had brought together a range of representative groups who had been invited to form a synod together with a hastily assembled network of partner communities and organisations via various live video links. He explained how they had been drawn together by the values they shared and how they had been called upon to respond to a credible offer from some very highly placed sources in the nation's public life.

As if to reinforce his assessment, a video message from the Prime Minister was then relayed to the gathering, attracting a rather mixed reception despite her warm and conciliatory message. This was followed by a short piece to camera from the new King explaining how he had been struck by the work of the faith communities and how he had seen first-hand the difference they were making among the most deprived and marginalized communities in the land.

Eleanor gulped in recognition of the significance of the occasion she was witnessing and glanced over to Jez for reassurance.

"This must have been planned for some time."

"So it would appear." Jez replied beaming from ear to ear apparently lost in thought.

"I never knew that something so important was afoot."

"None of us did." Jez explained. "Although, I suspect that Sister Bernadette knew something. She's very good at keeping secrets."

"I can certainly vouch for that. She never let on to me."

After the video presentations, a tall, dark haired lady in a smart, pin striped suit stepped up to the microphone. She explained that she had been delegated to approach representatives of the various faith communities with an important offer. This offer would be repeated to the representatives of the other faith communities and their third sector partners at various festivals in the next few weeks, including the Fusion Food Festival in Birmingham, the World Music Fair in Neasden, and the Asian Business and Fashion Week in Manchester.

The tall, dark haired lady was followed onto the platform by a series of officials similarly overdressed for the occasion who proceeded to present animated presentations featuring tables, graphs, organisational flow charts and thought clouds of various kinds. References were made to grants and loans for capacity building and constitutional amendments to allow faith representation at various levels of local and national policy making. The presentations were phrased in management speak, a feature that did not escape the attention of those listening many of whom started playing 'management speak bingo' ticking off phrases such as 'step change', 'going forward', 'in-the-round', 'stakeholders', 'drilling down', 'blue sky thinking' and 'social capital', whenever they cropped up in the presentations.

"In the end," the dark haired lady explained, "what we are offering is a partnership. A chance to form a coalition of the willing, in order to build more cohesive and sustainable communities. A place at the policy making table underpinned by an amnesty from any outstanding prosecutions and control orders. Together we can work hand-in-hand, expressing faith in our shared future."

As the platform presentations came to an end all the contributors were thanked for their time and responses were invited from the floor of the synod. This produced an awkward silence as various people examined their footwear whilst others struggled to make sense of the offer that had been put before them. The older gentleman in a cardigan endeavoured to handle the trickle of questions that tamely followed before finally suggesting that a personal response should be received from the floor to reflect the range of views represented in the room. Once again a diffident silence fell upon the gathering, as if those present appeared either unwilling or unable to seize the moment.

At the back of the room Catherine stiffened her spine, summoned up her strength and moved purposefully towards the platform. She was not normally given to extravagant gestures of self-promotion, but there was little that appeared normal about her life at the moment. She visibly shook with fear as she ascended the platform and faced the sea of gathered delegates before her.

"I'm not very good at these sorts of things. The only reason I am standing before you now, is because of Joshua, my son. I still don't understand why his life ended so prematurely and what set him on the path he followed and yet his story has taught me that we still need unchartered territories to explore, rather than virtual, pre-programmed ones. We need to offer our children something to live for, values to believe in, rather than brands and tribes to label us. We need to give them a vision of a better world, not just a promise of shiny, new things. Most of all, we need people who can inspire and lead us, who can bring out our potential to overcome, people who embody hope in an uncertain world." Catherine, paused as if gathering her thoughts. "Several months ago I met such a person. I would like to invite Sky onto the platform to speak to us."

The room erupted with relief and approval. By now people were demanding Sky to speak, but instead she tried to wave away the attention.

"SKYSHADOW! SKYSHADOW! SKYSHADOW!" Still, Sky remained rooted to her seat.

Catherine approached her, "Come on, Sky this is your moment. Your destiny."

Sky looked up into Catherine's eyes. "But I'm not worthy of all this. I don't deserve to be put on any sort of pedestal."

"But I believe in you," Catherine insisted, "and so do these people here. Don't they deserve to hear from you?"

"SKYSHADOW! SKYSHADOW! SKYSHADOW!" the chanting continued.

Sky looked around the room trying to assimilate what was taking place. "I really can't do this." She mouthed to Catherine.

Eventually the name chanting and foot stomping reached such a crescendo that Sky was forced to approach the speaker's lectern.

"I guess that some of you know who I am."

"SKYSHADOW! SKYSHADOW! SKYSHADOW!" The chanting started once more. Sky raised her hand to still the crowd's reaction. "Yes, some of you are sisters and brothers in arms. People who have literally risked life and limb to expose the vested interests that were blinding people to the truth about themselves and the world they live in. We have only just found out how far those interests were prepared to go in order to rub out the voices of dissent from those who want to live another way."

At this point, growing in self-assurance, Sky raised her hand in a clenched fist. A number of other delegates joined her in the gesture, sensing some kind of kinship being affirmed.

"Only, I have to say sisters and brothers, real liberation comes from knowing the whole truth."

At this point a yelp of sisterly delight went up from the assembly followed by more chanting of Sky's name. Sky raised her hand in order to calm the delegate's response.

"Unfortunately most of you don't really know the whole truth about me." The mood of the crowd changed as bemused curiosity fell on the room. Sky then went on to explain how three years ago she had embedded herself among various T-squad groups and those fighting the power of multinational corporations in order to profile the competitive edge those corporations wielded and to reform one corporation in particular, the one founded by her father, Reginald Dunwoody.

There were audible gasps of astonishment in the auditorium

as Sky mentioned the name of her father. She then went on to explain her family's commercial interests and how she was planning the development of a new kind of global capitalism, where control of capital would be vested in employees and small shareholders, rather than faceless institutional investors.

At this point whistles and jeers started to break out from the delegates, especially among the anti-capitalism protesters who sensed that their revolution was being betrayed by its most influential leader. Sister Bernadette, looked impassive, as if she was hearing a penitent soul unburdening herself before her.

Someone stood up incredulous at what they were hearing, "Do you mean that all along you were really operating as some kind of fifth column, advancing a commercial strategy in the cause of globalization, rather than trying to undermine it?"

"No, I've been trying to bring about change from within."

Another delegate from the floor accused her of being more concerned with her family's reputation and her personal ambition than with any broader concern for other people.

"No, it wasn't like that." Sky tried to explain, but she had clearly lost the room. She looked across to Catherine for re-assurance. Catherine appeared bewildered, yet managed to summon a convincing thumb up, mouthing the phrase, 'Go for it', across the platform.

Sky held up her hand to acknowledge the mixed reaction her business strategy was receiving. "Sisters, brothers, I understand your reaction. I'm not proud that I deceived people or that many of you feel let down by me. To be honest I've been feeling like shit for some time, even pulling off that coup d'état earlier hasn't change the way I feel about myself, so I want to apologise for the hurt I know I have caused to people who welcomed me, trusted me, confided in me and even worked for me. I did what I did, not in order to deceive you, but because it was the only way I could see for me to justify my disappearance to those who wanted me back. But I have to tell you now, quite categorically that I am never going back." Sky held up a photograph of herself and her father with a former US President. "Iona Dunwoody is no more," with that she tore the photograph up into pieces. "She has attended her last function on behalf of the family business. From now on Skyshadow is my name and Skyshadow is my identity."

"But whose side are you on?" a heckler called out.

"That's for each of you to decide by my actions. All I can say is that I intend to cast light into the dark shadows of our nation's life by working on your behalf to use the resources and influence of business to sponsor mentoring schemes for those who fall out of education, to establish trust funds that will invest in innovation and skills development, to provide resources and infrastructure to volunteers who work with the most vulnerable in our society. In short, I will seek to be a bridge builder and philanthropist to make this new partnership work."

Sky sat down to muted applause. It had been a hard sell. A palpable sense of disappointment persisted among those present. Many in the audience remained unconvinced and sceptical not knowing whether such a high profile leader was a gamekeeper turned poacher or a poacher turned gamekeeper. Yet Catherine put a comforting hand on her shoulder and patted her on her knee, conveying approval. Sky looked into her eyes hoping to find unconditional support, yet Catherine averted her gaze, still trying to process Sky's exact intentions and motives.

"You get it, don't you?" Sky pleaded with Catherine.

"I think so," Catherine replied, "but it's going to take time. These people have placed a lot of trust in you – we all have. We just need to know that we're all in this together."

By now there was considerable disturbance within the room as various groups began arguing and debating with each other. Some people were standing and shouting, others were chanting polemic slogans, while still others seemed to be knelt in their circles in an attitude of prayer.

The older, gentleman in a cardigan approached the microphone once again. "I'm not usually given to being this directive, but I feel that we should now adjoin in order to pray. Wherever you are and whoever you normally pray to, then this would be an appropriate time and if you're not normally in the habit of prayer, then I suggest a moment of quiet, modest reflection."

The suggestion seemed to meet with the approval of the room, along with those participating via the various live links. Eleanor looked towards Jez for direction. She had only attended prayers as part of the daily rhythm of life at the Anastasis Centre or when staying with Jez, she didn't really know what to do. He held her hand and squeezed tightly. It felt good.

Finch, Sky and Catherine remained perplexed with the call to prayer but decided to follow the suggestion about an attitude of quiet reflection instead.

A reverential hush descended upon the room. The atmosphere felt heavy, yet peaceful, full of activity, despite the apparent inactivity. Some of the delegates sat in small circles and started to sing quietly, others chanted while some lay prostrate on the floor or removed their footwear. Everywhere important decisions were being wrestled with and quietly chewed over.

The next hour passed easily and solemnly as delegates considered the enormity of the change they were being asked to embrace. The silence and stillness provided a welcome space to inhabit after so many words and the frenetic upheavals of the last few days.

Eleanor had enjoyed her experience of re-discovering silence through the virtual meditation in the Athenian Marketplace the day before and was happy to explore another opportunity to be quiet and still. As she lay on the floor she discovered that she was able to meditate and allow her imagination and energy levels to reset. Once again, she found herself in a happy place as fears and uncertainties melted away and time appeared to stand still in an eternal moment of mindfulness.

Catherine used the time of quiet to investigate her own contradictory thoughts and feelings. Her mind had been in such a whirl that she hardly knew which way she was facing. The midnight raid and her detention, followed by the sudden, violent ending of her captivity and now the revelations about Sky, just when she had felt that she could trust her unconditionally – it was difficult to know what to think anymore and who she could trust. Perhaps she had invested too much hope in Sky, seeking to discover in her all the answers to questions that remained unresolved about why Joshua took his own life. Yet despite all the turmoil and confusion, she started to sense a reassuring certainty about her own life, an unmistakable sense of calm, above and beyond anything she had experienced since Joshua's death. She realised what she had been gifted was immeasurably greater than what she had lost. Somehow she sensed that all would be well in the end, even if all was not well at the moment. She wanted to tell someone how she felt, sensing that this was probably the outcome the older gentleman had in mind when he had invited them to pause for reflection. She reached out to touch Finch's arm, but Finch was no longer there.

"Ladies and gentlemen." Finch had broken the silence and was standing on the platform, tapping the microphone in order to persuade it back into life. All eyes in the room were now fastened upon him and he had absolutely no idea what he was about to say. "I…I don't really know why I am here today, other than a few months ago I met a stranger in an art gallery who asked me to look beyond what I could see, in order to

343

understand the bigger picture. I'm still not sure quite what that bigger picture is, but in these last few months I have been blown up in a bomb explosion, I've broken into a high security database, been threatened by a representative of a large multi-national and I discovered that one of my oldest friends was working undercover as a personal bodyguard. I even stumbled into rescuing two ladies from an armed assassin, got caught up in the crossfire of a fatal gunfight and helped the Special Forces conduct a covert operation." Finch looked around the room. "It hasn't been dull."

Awkward laughter rippled throughout the auditorium. "But the biggest lesson I've learnt is to look and to listen. That's rather ironic, because as a journalist, all my professional life I've been encouraged to 'observe and report' and not to rest until the real story was exposed. However, there's a big difference between reporting what is happening and understanding its significance."

Finch looked around the room. The eyes of an attentive audience were fixed upon him. "A dying man reminded me that the question 'where are you going' is the most liberating and formative question of all. It is asking us what are we prepared to die for? For that man, the question began and ended with the idea of being prepared to lay down his life for the sake of something he believed in. I think that I now understand just how powerful is that willingness to discharge the power that others expect us to wield. The ability to surrender our self determination to a hidden force, some might call it faith, others might talk about a positive mental attitude, whatever we call it, the knowledge of that way to live has been taken from us. We have been robbed of the language of faith and inoculated against the freedom to explore it. Whatever we believe in, it is the freedom to choose that is worth defending, even dying for. When we are asked, 'where are you going?' we are being forced to consider what we stand for and if necessary, what are we prepared to die for? The question before us is not about should we decide to join with those in a position of power for the greater good of all, but rather what sort of power do we want to exercise? The power of force or the power of example?"

Finch's words were greeted by warm and generous applause. Many stood to applaud and the reaction continued for what Finch found to be a rather uncomfortable length of time, before finally dying out. At that point, it was suggested that the meeting discuss the proposals from the government delegation in more detail. This suggestion met with Eleanor's approval as she wanted to indulge in some gentle stretching and to have a good scratch of her itching stump.

Small discussion groups formed in various parts of the building, pouring over the paperwork provided by the civil servants whilst various responses were received from those delegates joining the gathering by live-link. Much debate followed concerning procedural arrangements, constitutional apparatus and financial protocols. Discussion continued throughout the night with small groups sending delegations to each other in order to canvas support or discuss points of contention. As they entered the small hours, many appeared worn down by the debate and all around the auditorium energy levels started to flag as increasing numbers started to bed down for the night either by lying on the floor or using chairs to improvise their sleeping arrangements. Finally, discussions petered out and without any signal being given, the room became a dormitory for the worn-out delegates.

Eleanor eventually made herself comfortable wrapped in a blanket and lying across a number of stacking chairs and fell into a deep sleep. As she slept, she recalled her flight down the Norwegian fjord. She felt the wind upon her face and rattling through her wing suit, only this time, she didn't spiral out of control, but rather soared ever higher and higher until she found herself above the clouds and back in the place where she had glimpsed her out of body vision. The experience of being overwhelmed by an enormous sense of goodness and love enveloped once again. As she descended she felt totally secure and held within a safe embrace. The fear that had been her constant companion through so many challenges seemed to melt away in front of her. When she awoke, she knew she no longer had anything to fear.

As the room gradually came into focus around her, Eleanor felt Jez's warm breath upon her face and realised that she was wrapped in his arms. As she stirred, she realised that he was already looking deeply into her eyes.

"The answer is yes, Ellie." Jez announced.

"You mean; I've missed the vote."

"No, the result still isn't in yet. I mean, Yes, to me and you. I don't want to lose you. Not now, not ever. I'm going to review my vows to include you within them. That's, if you want me."

Eleanor reached out to Jez and kissed him deeply in a way that seemed to unite and seal what lay between them. A kiss that transported her once again to a distant place.

In the auditorium other people stirred and coughed. Bodies stretched, joints creaked and throats were cleared. Gradually the murmur of voices grew in volume as hot drinks were handed out whilst those sleeping were politely woken.

The older gentleman wearing a cardigan shuffled somewhat hesitantly onto the platform, supported by one of the young government officials in a rather crumpled business suit. He held a brown folder in his hand. Having adjusted his glasses and blown his nose several times, he addressed the gathering. A hush of expectation descended upon the room as a strange stillness enveloped the gathering. The older gentleman cleared his throat.

"Ladies and gentlemen, delegates and friends, fellow travellers. It has been a rather long night, but having spoken with all the groups now and having received their responses and reflections, we have finally reached a decision." He paused to look across to Sister Bernadette. She gently nodded her head in silent confirmation. "And what is more, I think we have a common mind over how to move forward from here."

Just then, warm milky sunlight pierced the auditorium as the first rays of a breaking dawn settled upon the room and bathed everyone in a warm, glowing light.

It was going to be a lovely day.

Epilogue

The time 7.54 am appeared over the illuminated sign of the station platform. Below the words *'Next train 3 minutes…Phoenix Enterprises for London apologise for any delay caused,'* scrolled across the display in linear repetition. No-one complained, no-one frowned, no expectations were disappointed, instead occasional glances were cast in the direction of the display board by commuters shuffling on their feet, their attention absorbed into the mobile technology held in their hands apparently unmoved by the inconvenience. Each new arrival on the platform faithfully repeating the same well-choreographed routine of checking arrival times before tapping, scrolling and swiping their way into another world apparently oblivious to the one they were occupying.

The air temperature continued to soar as hazy clouds melted into the bright glare of another sultry, summer's day. The atmosphere remained heavy, yet surprising still, save for the occasional distant rumble of circling planes queuing up to land at an ever congested Heathrow. Gone was the sound of hovering drones that had regularly inhabited the morning skies, although an occasional muffled siren could still be detected in some distant part of the city.

Video screens flickered over the heads of the commuters displaying rolling news stories interspersed with familiar brands and aspirational images of happy city workers. A solitary sombre message appeared promoting the availability of public vaccination, yet partially obscured in caveats and sub text explaining that while such programmes were entirely safe they should be undertaken as part of a considered lifestyle choice.

Further down the platform a group of Asian girls dressed in white tee shirts handed out bottles of drinking water to passengers as they assembled. Some enquired as to their reasons before politely declining their offer, but most seemed grateful to accept the act of kindness in the spirit it was given. Several puzzled commuters examined the bottle suspiciously, looking for a corporate identity that would betray the marketing strategy, yet none was immediately apparent save for a discreet feline logo at the corner of the labelling. Each of the girls just smiled kindly as people thanked them, whilst refusing any offers of payment. Elsewhere other members of the white tee-shirt group weaved in and out of commuters picking up litter with mechanical sticks before depositing the debris into bright yellow plastic sacks adorned with the same feline logo. Some commuters stopped to chat; others nodded in appreciation, yet most remained unmoved, statuesque obstacles as the litter pickers slipped silently between them, paralysed by their technology and their desire to isolate themselves from those around them.

Half way down the platform a public health poster still bore the fading graffiti: 'WW2LFE', yet someone had recently added the words: '...WHEN YOU DON'T KNOW WHAT TO LIVE FOR TODAY'.

The squeal and clatter of metal on metal announced the impending arrival of the promised train which duly disgorged its passengers onto the platform. Those assembled stepped forward, pressing themselves into the already densely occupied carriages, seeking the elusive reward of an available seat.

Once underway people settled into the familiar routine of slurping coffees, sipping bottled water and interrogating their mobile devices for ever more digital information. One man stood out from the crowd as he opened up a hardback book and noisily flicked through its pages. It could have been a spy novel, but it just might have been an illuminated history of post-romanticism, it was hard to tell and no-one seemed to care, although secretly a few envied his courage to swim against the flow and stole a discreet look over his shoulder remembering the distant pleasure of an encounter with a paper based communications platform.

Elsewhere two lovers kissed lost in a haze of mutual affection, whilst nearby someone gazed out of the window and dreamt about a different world and the idea that it might be possible.

Further down the carriage a pair of smartly dressed men started arguing about politics and freedom of expression. Their raised voices causing a number of fellow commuters to furrow their brows and roll their eyes. Some tried to ignore their discourse yet it was impossible not to be engaged by their passion. A few muttered about nothing ever changing and the futility of holding any such convictions, yet most were secretly following their every word. Eventually their argument abated and the tone of the voices became warmer and more convivial. After a brief pause in their conversation, one of them leaned forward and shared a joke. It was a rather old joke, but a good one and well told. It caused a gentle titter to radiate throughout the carriage as a warm, familiar smile returned to the faces of the morning travellers.

Sitting opposite them, an old newspaper journalist looked up and bathed his face in the morning sun. Unafraid, he smiled and considered all that lay before him with hope and gratitude before returning to read his copy of 'The History of Impressionism'.

About the Author

Mike Burke is an Anglican clergyman who lives near Bristol. He is married with two grown up children. As well as spending over 20 years in parish ministry in Sheffield and Gloucester, he has worked with various charities and mission agencies in project management, fundraising and mission consultancy. He writes out of a desire to imagine how faith might contribute more creatively towards a compassionate and more equitable post-Christian European culture.